A Dance of Moths

Dedication

This book is dedicated especially to my dear wife,
Margaret Joyce, who stood steadfast beside me
during the tumultous years it took me to write it

To the memory of my father, Goh Lian Swee

Also to my mother, Lim Siew Chee
My sisters Poh Leng, Rosalind and Irene
My children Kasan and Carmilla,
Kagan, Kajin and Kakim
And to my prospective grandchild (due in January 1996).

A Dance of Moths

Goh Poh Seng

Select Books

© 1995 Goh Poh Seng

Published by
Select Books Pte Limited
19 Tanglin Road #03-15
Tanglin Shopping Centre
Singapore 247909

Cover Design by Goh Kajin
Printed by Kairos Design

Printed in Singapore

ISBN 981-00-6866-2

*The lines of lyrics quoted in this book
are the property of their owners*

All rights reserved. No part of this publication may be reproduced, stored in a retrieval system, or transmitted, in any form or by any means, electronic, mechanical, photocopying, recording or otherwise, without the prior permission of the copyright owner.

 **Goh Poh Seng**, a medical practitioner, was born in Malaya (as it was then known) in 1936. He received his medical degree from University College, Dublin, and practiced medicine in Singapore for twenty-five years.

One of the most prolific writers of modern Singapore, Goh began as a pioneer of Singapore drama in English with three plays performed in Singapore, *The moon is less bright* (1964, 1990), *When smiles are done* (1965) and *The Elder Brother* (1967). *When smiles are done* was also performed, as *Room with Paper Flowers*, — a quotation from part of its last line — in Kuala Lumpur in 1969.

Goh's first novel, *If we dream too long* (1972) won the National Book Development Council of Singapore's Fiction Book Award in 1976. It has been translated into Russian (serialized in *Novi Mir*) and Tagalog, and has been accepted for translation into Japanese. It has been used as a text by the Department of English at the University of Malaysia, and is being used as a text in the University of Singapore and the University of the Philippines. It was followed by his second novel, *The Immolation* (1977).

His three published collections of poems are *Eyewitness* (1976), *Lines from Batu Ferringhi* (1978) and *Bird with one wing* (1982).

As a full time medical practitioner who writes only in his spare time, Poh Seng is unusually prolific. His works have appeared in numerous magazines and anthologies, including *The London Magazine*, *Poetry International*, *Commonwealth Poems of Today*, *New Voices from the Commonwealth*, *New Pacific Quarterly*, *The Sun Dancing* (Kestrel; ed. Charles Causeley), *Only Connect* (East-West Centre, Hawaii and Flinders University), *The Poetic Language: An Anthology of Great Poems of the English-Speaking World* (Macmillan; ed. G. Dutton), *USA Poetry Review*, *Canadian Literature Review*. His works have been translated into Chinese, Malay, Tagalog, Russian and German. For three years he was invited to sit on the original panel of judges for the *Asiaweek* Short Story Competition. In 1983 Goh was awarded the Singapore Cultural Medallion.

Goh Poh Seng now lives and works with his wife and family in Vancouver.

Acknowledgements

George McWhirter for many helpful suggestions,
R. Nallamma Winslow
nit-picker *par excellence*
sound and tactful editor,
Lena Lim U Wen, my publisher
for her courageous enterprise and faith

Foreword

Goh Poh Seng's versatility as a writer can be seen in his plays, novels and poems. He began as a pioneer of Singapore drama in English with three plays performed in Singapore in the 'Sixties. One of these was performed again in 1990, in the *Theatreworks Retrospective of Singapore Plays*, for a new generation of Singapore theatre goers. He has three published collections of poems, while his first novel, *If we dream too long*, (which was followed by his second novel, *The Immolation* in 1977), won the National Book Development Council of Singapore's Fiction Book Award in 1976.

An eagerly anticipated work, *A Dance of Moths* comes at the end of a long period of gestation for Goh's third novel and his most ambitious work to date. It marks a new stage in Goh's development as a writer, fulfilling the promise of his earlier works.

The main theme of the alienation of the individual from the society of which he is a part, and of searching for meaning in his life, has been treated to some extent in Goh's first novel, but the main protagonist of *Dance*, Ong Kian Teck, is not like the young clerk of Goh's first novel, with wistful, unexpressed yearnings for a fuller, richer life. When we first meet him, Ong appears to have realised the Singapore dream — in his late thirties, he is happily married with two young sons, successful in his career, has a circle of friends in the professions, a private apartment and a car.

Ong's story parallels that of the second protagonist, Chan Kok Leong, a young accounts clerk. Indeed, their stories are developed in alternate chapters, each unaware of the strands connecting them to each other until the very last chapter. Common to both stories is the sense of isolation and the lack of communication - between friends, between husband and wife, between parents and their adult children, all locked in their separate worlds. Kian Teck tells his wife the story of the dance of the moths "We too are fatally attracted towards the lights, the flames, around which we dance and dance ... finally to die, for ... we have no knowledge of, and hence no fear of death. Death also has no meaning, and we shall die without knowing why. Our fate is that we are never to find out why." There is a hint of redemption and meaning through a kind thought or deed, but perhaps this is not enough and comes too late.

The novel's gallery of recognisable and memorable Singaporean characters is associated with Ong and Chan respectively, including family members, friends, acquaintances and outsiders. There is great virtuosity in style, depth of characterisation, dialogue and description. For example in the rift between Ong and his wife, Li Lian, the silences, the hurts and misunderstandings are carefully built up until the stage is reached when Li Lian reaches the limits of her forbearance in her outburst: "... you don't really understand me. You've never *tried* to understand me. You've never really listened to me, or wanted to hear what I have to say. I do have needs, you know, ..." while his response is equally hurt and angry.

At a different social level, Goh successfully conveys the authentic ring of Kok Leong's Third aunt, as she provides comic relief in teasing him about having a girl friend. Another comic and clever scene is where Kok Leong is trying to propose to Emily while she is absorbed in speculations about her boss (Ong) whose wife she sees at the Shangri la Hotel.

Goh's richly and acutely detailed descriptions evoke the sights, sounds and smells of Singapore, and will be recognized as such by Singapore readers. There are many other vivid scenes, such as the description of a cockfight in Bali. Nor does Goh shrink from depicting the seamy side of life, from girlie bars and gang fights to the unpleasant toilet care which Kok Leong's mother and sister uncomplainingly minister to his totally helpless retarded sister, Siew Wan.

A Dance of Moths is a mature and major work which will be compelling reading for an earlier generation of Singapore readers familiar with Goh's earlier works. It will also deserve the attention of and study by a new and younger generation readers and students of Asia-Pacific literature, of which the Singapore output is a part.

Hedwig Anuar
Chair. National Book Development Council of Singapore (1980 - July 1995)
1995

"Damocles never danced better than beneath the sword."
- Nietzche

A Dance of Moths

Part One

1

Ong Kian Teck was sitting alone on a stone bench along the Esplanade. It was twilight, a time of day he found most difficult to bear, filling him with a restlessness which left him floundering. The flotilla of ships in the Singapore harbour had turned spectral with lights. A large oil tanker, elephantine, lumbered sedately out towards the open sea. As Kian Teck rose to go, a white sea swallow, *burong chamar*, flew out seawards, coming to terms with the night. He felt himself disqualified from this grace.

He had not walked very far when he came across Old Ho, the park keeper, sitting on a bench further down the Esplanade. Ho was wearing a green short-sleeved shirt with the lower buttons missing; through the gap a roll of his fat belly protruded. He wore his usual pair of creased, grey trousers and dilapidated rubber slippers. His small pudgy hands were folded primly, like a priest's, on his lap. Suddenly, he looked up and recognized Kian Teck.

"Mr. Ong!"

"Hello, Ho!"

"I didn't expect to see you here." As usual with Kian Teck, Old Ho spoke in a mixture of Singaporean English and Hokkien, the Chinese dialect used predominantly in Singapore. Saliva dripped from the corner of his thick-lipped mouth, bloated with a large tongue and bad teeth. A few black hairs grew on his upper lip, part of his general unkemptness rather than an adornment. Maybe because Kian Teck knew he was a

Part One

diabetic, he thought his breath smelt sweet and mouldy. "I've been thrown out of my room!" Ho announced in a hoarse, weary voice.

"Sorry to hear that."

"That nasty landlady I told you about? Well, she threw me out." He breathed in a slow pant, like a tired dog.

Kian Teck had met Ho a few months earlier in Kampong Java Park when he had taken up jogging, hoping that regular physical exercise would dispel his sense of listlessness, of being vaguely indisposed. He had gone for a medical check-up, and was assured by his doctor that there was nothing seriously wrong.

"Then why am I so lethargic?"

The doctor said that Kian Teck needed to tone up physically, and should exercise to build up his stamina. A body is just like a machine, he lectured, and parts will run down unless they are properly serviced and cared for.

So Kian Teck had bought a pair of Adidas running shoes, some thick socks to cushion his tender soles, shorts and towelling shirts, and then went to the park three or four times a week after work to jog.

Kampong Java Park, converted into a public park in the early 'seventies, had formerly been one of Singapore's oldest Christian cemeteries. The dead must give way to the living in this crowded city, the Government proclaimed, so labourers and bulldozers set to work.

In the past, Kian Teck sometimes drove by of an evening and saw through the window of his car, unintentionally and not for long, the weathered headstones arrayed like a tableau in a dream. Pale whitenesses amongst the tall grass, motionless against the shifting hours, almost a secret imposition into his brain, entering quietly like water, there they stood, idioms beyond his knowing.

Then the exhumation began. Plinths and plaster angels were hauled down, slabs of marble and stone with inscriptions commemorating "*Loving Mother of....*" and "*Loving Husband of....*", all were broken down and carted away by trucks. With them also went ribs, thigh bones, phalanges, pelvises, vertebrae and hollow, sightless skulls. Those with descendants who cared were taken to be re-interred in the new burial ground at Lim Chu Kang, right next to the factories sprouting up in the new Jurong Industrial Estate. The unclaimed were cremated or disposed of somehow, the responsibility of public servants.

A pond was dug and gradually filled with brown water and fish. Rushes and water lilies were planted in the ooze. Some earth was heaped into low mounds to please the eye with their swell, turfed and planted with small trees, graft-stumps and shrubs.

One would have expected the flora to explode, a profusion of green leaves and vibrantly-coloured flowers to blossom from soil so enriched by the shedding of flesh, from ruptured entrails and organs, seepage of blood and lymph. But the trees there grew slowly, inching upwards month by month.

And it was there, late one afternoon, that Kian Teck had first met Old Ho.

The day had an oppressive quality. Kian Teck was not clear what had imparted this to the afternoon, for the grass and trees were bathed in sunlight. It could have been his own tiredness.

He caught sight of a fat man, sitting so still, as though soldered to the stone seat, his large head hunched over a notebook. He looked up as Kian Teck jogged past and Kian Teck nodded at him briefly. The narrow path wound around the pond, whose circumference was about five hundred metres. The next time, the old man nodded in acknowledgment. Later, as he approached again, Kian Teck slowed down, not because he wanted to make his acquaintance, but because he was winded. By the time he reached the man, Kian Teck had already slowed down to a walk.

"Good evening, sir!" he called out, speaking in English

"Good evening," Kian Teck replied.

The old man was the very picture of shabbiness. He wore a dirty, white cotton shirt, crumpled grey trousers, and old shoes of an indeterminate colour, the left one unlaced, the lace drooping on the ground like a thin, grey, long-dead worm.

"You're very energetic."

"Not at all. My doctor advised me to exercise. That's why I'm here."

"What could be wrong with a young man like you?"

"I'm not so young. I've passed my thirty-seventh birthday."

"That's young. I'm fifty-four."

"Well, that's not old either."

"No, I'm old. I *feel* old. I'm a sick man."

"You don't look it," Kian Teck said consolingly, and felt foolish for this politeness, this commonplace lie. The fat old man laughed.

"I'm suffering from high blood pressure, and I'm also a diabetic. Here, look at this." He showed Kian Teck his notebook. The pages were ruled into columns, intersected into squares. The squares were coloured green, blue, yellow and orange.

"I test my urine for sugar each day, and then note down the colour in the chart. As you can see, my diabetes is not well controlled."

"That's too bad," Kian Teck said.

"Every month I attend a Government Outpatient Dispensary, and each time the doctors tell me off. They say that I'm overweight, that I should diet. Well, they don't really have to scold me, you know, now that inflation's here. Food is getting so expensive I can hardly afford a decent meal."

"Yes, it's bad."

"It's desperate, for the poor, like me. Perhaps for you it's different."

"Well, everyone's affected."

"What do you do, if you don't mind my asking?"

"I work in an advertising agency."

"Bet you're one of the bosses."

"Oh no, not really," Kian Teck said modestly, although he was the director of the Creative Department.

"It's become so bad, I can't carry on. I tell you, mister, this year I wish I was dead!"

Kian Teck was startled. The old man looked at him fully in the face and repeated glumly: "Yes. 1974, a year I wish I was dead!"

"You shouldn't say such things," Kian Teck said, reprovingly.

"Why not? What's there to live for?"

"What about your family?"

"My wife died many years ago."

"What about your children, then?"

"I have a daughter whom I brought up myself. Now she's grown up, she's left me. So if you ask me, mister, I'll say, what's so good about a family? Might as well not have one."

"Is your daughter married?"

"No. She's working as a steno or a secretary. I don't know where. Doesn't tell me anything. Only, now and then she hands me ten dollars. And I brought her up myself when her mother passed away; saw to her schooling and everything. Now she won't even bother to give her father the hundred bucks he needs to enjoy himself with."

Kian Teck didn't know what to say. He thought, how often one hears such tales. They're as old as humanity.

"No, my life isn't worth living any more. You know how much I have to pay for my room?"

Kian Teck shook his head.

"Seventy dollars a month! And you should *see* the place. No windows. Dark as night during the day. And nowhere to cook or wash. Just four blank walls and a light bulb overhead. Not really fit for a human being to live in. Can't call that a home. And you know something else?" he went on, breathing heavily. "One's supposed to be lucky to have such a place for that price! Nowadays, a room would cost one hundred and fifty dollars

Part One

a month. How to live, I ask you? My take-home pay, including overtime and various allowances, comes to two hundred and fifty-four dollars a month. How to live?"

"Can't you apply for an HDB apartment, for subsidized public housing? That's cheaper, surely?"

"I used to live in a one-room rental apartment in Bukit Merah. But when the Government found out that I was living alone, they chucked me out. I had put down my daughter's name earlier as co-resident, you see. Living alone, you don't qualify for HDB apartments."

"Seems unfair."

"Well, that's how it is. When you're alone, you don't qualify for *anything* in this life. It's nearly all over with me."

Kian Teck could think of nothing to say. The sound of traffic outside the park suddenly seemed louder.

"Don't know how long I can remain in that room. Just the other day, when I came home early, I caught the landlady putting out my things. She asked me to leave, and when I refused, she abused me. Wants more rent, that's why. We had a big fight. She threatened to call the police."

The leaves had begun to lose their green heart and already seemed to float on the sheer blue lake of evening. Time to go. Before driving away, Kian Teck glanced back. The park appeared to sink into the withering light as into a void, with a willingness and complacency that was stunning.

DURING THE FOLLOWING WEEKS, he got to know Old Ho fairly well. Kian Teck never remembered his full name, although the old man had mentioned it once. He had either not heard, or forgotten, and did not ask again. He passed Ho a ten-dollar note on a few occasions.

The chugging of a tugboat on the water brought back the presence of the sea, limpid in the early night, spangled with lights. The heavy air was rank with smells — brackishness of the water, odour of oil, putrescence of mud from the river and sea-bed, the aroma of spices from the eating stalls nearby: of cinnamon and pepper, chili and cloves, garlic and patchouli. Inhaling deeply, Kian Teck felt inebriated.

"You see, it has happened!" Old Ho continued.

With an effort, Kian Teck turned to his companion, who looked beaten with despair.

"I'm sorry, Ho. Where're you living now?"

"Staying with some people I know. A temporary arrangement. But I can't be happy there. They're only putting up with me."

Again Kian Teck could not find anything to say, and Old Ho too fell silent. The night sprawled over them, over the harbour, the whole city. The sky now conjured up stars, twinkling faintly. They could hear the gentle murmur of the sea nearby. The ships beyond wore an air of temporality, phantoms that visited for a limited time only, unlike the two men whose spirits were as earthbound as stones.

All of a sudden, Kian Teck wanted to shatter this maudlin mood, like glass into a thousand splinters. He felt a compulsion to abandon himself, to be wild, to be drunk with life.

"Come!" he commanded.

"Where're we going?" Ho asked, looking up, startled.

"In search of happiness!" Kian Teck announced, and started marching, a man who had no doubts. Old Ho followed him unresistingly, his blood quickening, the sluggish old stream beginning to surge as if propelled by a new engine. There was something awe-inspiring about the pair of them, walking with light steps away from the dark waterfront.

"Let's have some *satay* first," the younger man said, leading the way to one of the numerous stalls at the Satay Club alongside the Esplanade. These stalls had been re-sited from the dirty alleyway beside the Alhambra Cinema, itself also now torn down. The new structures purported to be designed in modern architecture, with a slight, unwilling condescension to native Malay tradition. Not surprisingly, they ended up as stylistic incongruities.

Half a dozen young touts buzzed around making loud, raucous pleas. Kian Teck waved them away. He walked up to a satayman and ordered twenty sticks each of chicken, mutton meat, and goat intestines.

They waited in silence. The younger man's lean and attractive face was a little taut, intense. He was taking in small sharp breaths of air, his nostrils slightly pinched, like a prizefighter in the ring. The old man sat watching him silently, wearing a bashful smile of complicity on his thick lips; his eyes had lost their habitual dreaminess.

The two sat like conspirators who had ceased to accept the common drudgery which was their lot, namely, a lifetime made up of hours — each like the one before and the one succeeding. But not now! Now, they'd seized the moment. Yes, a man must now and then have a night out.

The satayman was roasting the skewers of meat, fanning the charcoal spit with a palm fan in one hand and brushing oil, like lacquer, onto the browning morsels impaled on the stiff, thin sticks with his other hand. A tongue of yellow flame occasionally darted up from the smouldering charcoal logs to enfold the *satay*; there was a sizzling sound whenever a drop of oil, or melting fat, fell onto the hot charcoal.

Presently, the fragrant meal was placed before them — a large plate of *satay*, two small bowls of the chili-and-peanut gravy, a side dish of cut young cucumbers and raw onions, and a plate with two packets of *ketupat*.

The two men ate without ceremony. Sticks of *satay* were dipped into the thick gravy, their teeth stripped the morsels of chicken and mutton meat, and the tender tubes of goat intestines. The cucumber and raw onions were crisp and juicy. Before long, they had finished all the food. After consulting Old Ho, Kian Teck ordered two plates of *sup kambing*. Kian Teck loved soups. Late at night, he would drive out to buy Chinese mutton soup, *bat kut teh*, or turtle soup and bring them home in enamel tiffin carriers. At other times, he would take his wife Li Lian out to eat a supper of soup at a roadside stall.

An Indian Muslim in a parti-coloured sarong brought the soup. His grizzled beard glowed white on his black face. When he turned around, Kian Teck saw a smooth rounded cyst the size of a mandarin orange on the back of his neck, the skin stretched thin and shiny — moonlight bathing the dome of a mosque.

They sprinkled white pepper and stirred the light brown soup, the charred rings of small red onions, the chopped green scallion shoots, the greyish pieces of goat meat going round and round the plate. The grainy soup filled the palate with its voluptuous taste, with a tang of cloves and turmeric and cinnamon.

Afterwards they walked towards the car which Kian Teck had parked by the side of the *Padang*. City Hall was floodlit, designed to emanate an imperial aura, its large, tall, fluted columns highlighted, representing the grandiloquent dream, now vanished, of the British Raj.

They got into the car, Old Ho's bulk making the Toyota Corona seem smaller. Kian Teck eased his car onto the road and drove with a nonchalant expertise, sitting behind the lit panels on the dash-board as if he were piloting an airplane at thirty thousand feet through an empty night-sky. Through the windscreen, the vision of the city seemed to be vibrantly afloat, the lighted buildings weightless, hovering above the ground. It had an inexpressible beauty. To the two men, the city granted this fresh prospect of herself, in the nature of a gift, a dispensation, for which they had been singled out that night. She did so, like all cities, only to those whom she truly owns — her children.

They drove away from the sea front and headed north. They did not speak all this while. Old Ho watched his companion's face. Kian Teck's thin mouth was relaxed now, a man at peace with himself, and his eyes flashed an animation seen intermittently in the glare of oncoming cars.

Part One

His grip was light on the shiny steering wheel.

They turned into Orchard Road, and a little later, Kian Teck pulled up before the Hotel Singapura.

"I'm not properly dressed," Old Ho protested.

"Don't worry. Just come with me. No one's going to stop us tonight."

Old Ho responded with a nervous, almost childish, giggle.

They got out of the car and ambled side by side into the bright building. Someone was playing the piano at the Pebble Bar. The sound showered on them immediately, like a downpour of tiny fragments of glass, each keynote tinkling distinctly.

Old Ho was suddenly self-conscious, treading on the soft carpet. Luxury intimidated him. But no one stopped them. Kian Teck led him to the high stools arranged around the piano. Old Ho, who was quite short, found his feet dangling in the air, and, hoping he was not being noticed, attempted feebly to touch the ground with the tips of his toes. Also, he could not lean his great weight backwards. These were a fat man's intuitive grope for props, and he reeled without them. Quickly, he leant forwards, supporting his bulk on the bar counter. Then he felt less precarious.

The room was decorated in green with white, wooden-louvred doors, the carpet a green ambiance of ocean depths. Through the transparent plate glass of one entire wall, a blue swimming pool came into view. Although the room was air-conditioned, white ceiling fans whirled slowly and needlessly, more decorative than functional.

When a young waiter came up to them, Old Ho felt unnerved for a moment.

"What would you like to drink?" Kian Teck asked. Old Ho hesitated.

"I'm having a brandy," Kian Teck said, to encourage him.

Old Ho grunted, and, swallowing the resultant phlegm, muttered hoarsely, "The same, please."

"Two brandies. Remy Martin, VSOP," Kian Teck ordered. He swivelled round on his stool and scrutinized the room. The sweltering crowd had the look of a congregation at church, but they substituted an earnest jubilance for a congregation's aura of mellifluous piety. There was the same air of premeditation, of commitment. Details of the drifting faces dissolved in the smoky semi-darkness, except when an overhead light chanced to fall on a head. Then the hair shone and dazzled, but the face remained bloodless, vacant, the eyes eager, yet passionless. Kian Teck often ventured at night into bars like this. Somehow, he was drawn by the crowds of nocturnal transients with their collective, compulsive gaiety. At times, they seemed to him to be from another star. He looked at the solitary men drinking seriously by the long bar counter, studying their own reflections in the wall mirror behind the array of bottles. It can be dangerous, watching oneself drink all night long, for it creates a tendency to drink constantly, as if the action of lifting one's glass breaks the terrifying, impassive reflection. Kian Teck had made the mistake of sitting there one night, and got very drunk.

The brandies were placed before them. When the young waiter added water, the smouldering russet of the liquor stormed between the translucent ice cubes, volatile, combustible. They took up their glasses and toasted each other and "to happiness".[*] Old Ho's eyes had never seemed so vivid, glazed with night-fever.

"I've never had a night out like this, Mr. Ong."

"Call me K.T. My friends call me K.T."

"Honestly, I've never had a night out like this, K.T."

"Surely you must've. You must've seen better times before?"

"Perhaps. I suppose there must've been better times. We all think so, don't we? Yes, I must've forgotten."

For a moment the old man was lost, foraging for memories. When he stumbled upon them, they were faded, like weathered frescoes of an unknown era, and not embellished by time at all as precious moments are

---

[*] "*Kiong hee*" in the Hokkien dialect.

supposed to be, more brilliantly held in memory than the actual, lived moment! For him, it was like rummaging through an old, dirty drawer for articles which might be of value — and finding only cheap trinkets, broken combs, old bills, a stained colour postcard, twenty playing cards. He resurfaced from his search feeling more bereft.

"Did you ever go out drinking as a young man?" Kian Teck probed, genuinely interested.

"Yes, I suppose so, as a young man," Old Ho mumbled. He looked despondent.

"What sort of places did you go to?"

"What sort of places?" Old Ho blinked in his attempt to recollect. "Oh, not as posh as this. No air-conditioning. No carpets. No piano music. Only simple coffee shops which served beer or stout."

Kian Teck tried to imagine what Old Ho looked like as a young man. His face was so distinct, so formed, that it was impossible to think of him as other than what he was now. Some people are like that, so utterly real, so fixed in their present self that any other is unimaginable. Their other selves, versions, incarnations, are beyond reach, defy conjuring.

Then Kian Teck noticed Old Ho's wrist watch. Its glass was hazy, as if misted over with breath on the inner surface. From where he sat, Kian Teck could not see the hands. He wondered whether it still kept time, the tiny hands ticking round and round under the murky glass, registering, unseen, the lost hours and the lost days, the weeks and the years. Maybe it no longer functioned, and was worn for adornment, another component to complete the shabbiness of its owner, who himself bore the imprint of time lost? That fat, bewildered orphan of the night.

"No, sir. We didn't have places like this. Those days were simpler," the old man continued, his eyes losing focus, losing contact with the present. They were lost, submerged in bygone simpler days and simpler nights, remote from the phantom faces in this soft-lit room, from the sharp, arctic tinkling of ice cubes in tall glasses, from plaintive voices like the susurrus of tiny leaves in wind, and the nervous laughter of a middle-aged Malay woman when she entered the bar; all chimeras, all dissolved by those far-focussed pupils, liquescent, of the old man.

"Is it really true that the past was simpler?" Kian Teck asked. "Everybody says that. Is it true or only an illusion that our past, which we hoard, seems more golden? Maybe it's just that we're forgetful?"

Old Ho answered slowly: "I don't know. But I know that before the War — during the 'thirties and early 'forties, say — I could live well on my salary of twelve dollars a month. For a dollar, you could buy about thirty *katis* of rice. Now, a *kati* costs ninety cents. For fifty cents, I could take a friend to supper after a film show. For a dollar, we could even eat a decent meal in a respectable restaurant, like the restaurant in the Capitol Cinema. Even at the Raffles Hotel, a couple could dine well on two dollars. Of course, in those days, only Europeans went to places like the Raffles. They didn't mix with us."

"It's inflation over the years," Kian Teck replied. "Still, people earn more nowadays."

"Perhaps. But I can't live on my two hundred dollars now, as I could with my twelve then. I don't know. It doesn't make sense. Money has lost its value. Everything has lost its value. It doesn't make sense."

So much for progress, Kian Teck thought, looking once more at his companion — who had retreated into silence, to savour perhaps, in the deep tunnel of grey memory, those vaguely golden, stupendous hours of long ago.

There was half-hearted applause when the pianist finished his performance. He was a small Chinese man of about forty, dressed in a white shirt and a sober grey suit, with a plain, placid face, and the bearing of a clerk rather than an entertainer. There was no trace at all of exhibitionism, of flamboyance. Occasionally he sang to his own

Part One

accompaniment — "I Left My Heart in San Francisco", "Yesterday", "Raindrops are Falling on My Head", "Blue Moon", "You Belong to My Heart" — with unabashed sentimentality. An unromantic man, forced to sing romantic songs for his supper, for his living, whose music was swiftly lost in the tangle of faces and the rambling talk. His short fingers, surprising in a musician, ran along the ivory keys with a separate independence, the man simply an extension, an appendage, rather than the other way around.

The pianist gave a slight bow and a smile worked faintly across his lips. Then, gathering his bunch of music notes, he took his leave. No one offered him a drink in appreciation. Maybe he didn't imbibe, this misplaced clerk.

A new group of musicians were preparing to take over. Kian Teck excused himself and went to the toilet, which was situated outside the bar, by the swimming pool. The air was warm and moist, the black night above gouged by a few hard stars.

The toilet was bright, sparkling, it's atmosphere thick with the sweet perfume of disinfectant. As he peed, Kian Teck scrutinized himself in the big wall mirror. The harsh whiteness of the fluorescent light rendered his face pale, flat, as if it had lost one dimension. He saw a lean, tall man, with an air of ambivalence, of aloofness and openness, of seriousness and playfulness — a complex creature.

Then he noticed a short, almost completely bald man of about fifty, who had the sedateness of an old lady, studying him from a corner. He wore a ludicrously long green coat that hung down almost to his knees. It was the toilet attendant. When Kian Teck finished, he went to a basin to wash his hands. At once, the attendant sprang forward to turn the shiny chrome faucets, the hot and the cold water, and in another moment, presented Kian Teck with a paper hand-towel. Kian Teck accepted this without a word, and began to wipe his hands. The attendant was on the point of offering him a comb, but Kian Teck took out his own and briskly combed his hair. He placed two ten-cent coins on the plate.

"Th-th-th — thank you, sir!"

The stammer surprised Kian Teck. The man had seemed so composed, so impassive.

Just then, two other men came in, talking loudly about their women whom they had left behind in the bar. The confessional of the public urinal. Walking towards the bar, Kian Teck could hear the sound of the new band. The soft night leaned on the cold panes of glass that were opalescent with mist, the roomful of people within made remote, embedded in an ice cube. And there was Old Ho, meditative, with a timid watchfulness which made Kian Teck feel protective towards him. He wished he had not promised "happiness" so confidently and cockily earlier on. Through the thick furls of smoke he felt the old man floundering in there, and didn't want to let him down. He opened the doors and was sucked within, drowned in an instant.

"How's your drink?" he asked Old Ho.

"Fine, thank you."

"Let's have another."

They were all caught in the throes of loud music, and couples were dancing on the small square of parquet floor, jumping to match the upheavals of sound.

"Is this too noisy for you?"

"Oh, no. It's fine!" Old Ho said.

The drinks came. Again they toasted "to happiness", though this time Kian Teck did it with less bravado. He drank half a glass quickly, wishing for an early sorcery from the brandy.

"You know," Old Ho said, leaning closer, "sometimes I've really got it in my head to squander everything in one wild go. Everything that I've got left in one wild burst!" He uttered this with fervour, even vehemence, his words breaking in a rampage out of the white prison of his hours.

Part One

Kian Teck said, "Yes, we have only one life."

"Yes, one life!"

"We must live fully!"

"Always, I look forward to something, all my life, from the time I was small, always looking forward," Old Ho grumbled, as if to himself. "But that something never comes. Life goes on the same, day after day, week after week, year after year. The same."

"Yes," Kian Teck echoed, "an excess of sameness."

"I'd swap my remaining years of misery for a few months of joy, any time. What's the point of dragging out my life like this, day after day? I'd rather live extravagantly," Ho declared.

Kian Teck could have offered another view: that perhaps the extravagant man is the greater coward, while the cautious miser bears his life with courage and endurance. Wildness is a form of panic, and extravagance is just another side of wildness.

"The problem, however," continued Old Ho, "is a practical one: how to find enough money for the one wild burst? We, the poor, cannot save. I have nothing set aside, and for the likes of me, there's no credit. So it boils down to the problem of money, as always."

"But some people, without money, can be happy."

Old Ho laughed. "And I nearly believed it myself."

After a while, they decided to leave the Pebble Bar with its blustering foreign drunks, the pandemonium of its music, to pursue "happiness" elsewhere.

They came out into the open, the sky blacker now. Clouds were scuttling piecemeal in the lower sky. They got into Kian Teck's car which looked like a metallic carapace, shiny under the street lamp, and sped without speaking down brightly-lit Orchard Road. They passed the old Cathay Building, grey, gaunt, asquat Mount Sophia — which had always been a misnomer, for it was just a rise, built up with once-elegant houses, now decaying, like everything else — then went down Bras Basah Road, and turned sharply right at Queen Street, cutting across Stamford Road into Armenian Street. Kian Teck found an empty car slot, and reversed into it.

"Been to the Mayfair?" he asked.

Old Ho shook his head.

"Quieter here. There's no live band."

They walked up to the row of buildings, crossing a monsoon drain. The small hotel was midway down the block, the rooms upstairs, a Chinese restaurant and a cocktail lounge on the ground floor.

Both the men felt conspicuous when they entered, looking about like fugitives, until a young Chinese woman came up to them.

"Come in. There're seats over there."

They followed her willingly, and sat down on the plush leatherette sofa. The woman, in her mid-twenties and a bit on the plump side, leaned intimately towards Kian Teck and asked softly, "What're you drinking?" She spoke English with an attractive sing-song accent.

"Brandy and water," he said, and, glancing at Old Ho, added, "and the same for my friend, please."

She went away and returned with their drinks, slithering in beside Kian Teck, her body touching his. "Haven't seen you here before. Your first time?" She spoke to Kian Teck, and it was obvious that she would ignore Old Ho, although there was no offence meant, simply the hustler's instinct.

"I used to come here often, six, seven years ago. Place looks different now," he said, looking around, and not finding a single familiar face. Even the decor was different. But a few years back, Kian Teck and his friends had considered the Mayfair their own haunt. It had not occurred to any of them that one day they would stop coming, without any special reason, and another crowd of regulars would replace them. Now, Kian Teck felt like a stranger.

"So you used to come here?" she remarked.

Part One

"Yes, but I can't recognize anyone now."

"People come and go," she said.

"Yes, I suppose you're right. People come and go."

"I hope you'll come again."

"What's your name?"

"Lily."

"Lily-of-the-valley?"

They both laughed.

"Just Lily."

They're all called Lily or Violet or Rose, Kian Teck thought. After flowers. Petals of the night.

"What've you been doing all night?" Lily asked him.

"Looking for happiness."

She smiled, not quite sure if he were teasing.

"Looking for happiness?"

"That's right."

"And have you found it?"

Kian Teck glanced at Old Ho, whose eyes were focussed on his glass of brandy. "I don't think so," he told Lily.

"Do you know what you're looking for?" she persisted coquettishly, still concentrating on Kian Teck alone.

"Not sure. Perhaps you can tell us where we can find happiness?"

She laughed. "But I don't know *what* you want!"

"You look like someone who knows what happiness is."

"If I know, do you think I'd be sitting here!"

"We all look in vain," Old Ho said lugubriously, speaking for the first time.

"It's different for everyone, I think," Lily said. "For some men, it's a lot of drinks, and music, and a good woman."

"And for women?" Kian Teck teased. "Do they look for a good man?"

"Of course! But a good man is hard to find."

"Just like the song. But tell me, are good women also hard to find?"

"No! Plenty of good women, around. *I'm* a good woman."

"Happiness is hard to find. No one ever finds it," Old Ho mumbled. No one paid him any attention.

"But why are you troubling yourself looking for happiness?" Lily pursued, gazing curiously into Kian Teck's face. "For something so hard to find? Better to look for fun. Fun is easier to find."

"How wise you are! I'll call you Wise Lily from now on. But you're right, fun is easier to find."

"Sure it is! Drinks, a nice meal, and a good woman," Lily recited.

"Yes, good booze, good food and a good fuck. The Trinity. Let's have fun!" Kian Teck suggested.

Lily squeezed his hand. It made him feel good, feel like a good man. And she, a good woman.

"There's no such thing as happiness," Old Ho complained, looking very glum. Kian Teck felt exasperated with his companion. He's not helping at all, he thought. A miserable creature, impossible to cheer up. So he no longer paid any attention to him. Instead, he began to reminisce with Lily about his old drinking days. Lily leant closer and closer, her big breasts pressing against his side. They went through several rounds of drinks, and then it was time to go.

"Come again," Lily thanked him.

"Yes. I'll be back, Wise Lily."

Despite his earlier annoyance, Kian Teck insisted on driving Old Ho to his lodgings when he saw the man looking so lost. He did not have the heart to abandon him on the street, to find his own way home.

He drove slowly towards the slums of Jalan Besar. Old Ho was staying in a room in one of the rambling narrow streets in that area. It was late when they got there, and a silence hung over the street, the pavements empty under the bombardment of fluorescent street lamps. The night flowed and trembled below the clouds, and the old houses, in heterogeneous decline, seemed deposited out of time, sediments in the basin of night. Brokenness was everywhere, and smouldering decay, going on ceaselessly, in a dream-paced continuance.

After heaving himself out of the car, Old Ho vanished at once within the dark doorway of one of the houses, swallowed up, engulfed. This image was transfixed in Kian Teck's mind as he drove away.

HIS OWN APARTMENT WAS HUSHED, the pieces of furniture in the living room abandoned now by its human occupants. He went into the bedroom. His wife, Li Lian, had left a bedside light on. Her face bore the blissful imprint of sleep, her black hair lustrous. He changed into his pyjamas, tiptoed into the adjoining bathroom to clean up and to brush his teeth. Then he crept into bed. His wife stirred beside him and woke up.

"Is it very late?" she asked, sleepily.

"Yes. Sorry I woke you up."

"I'm glad you did," she said, snuggling close. He embraced her, felt the familiar warm grace of her body. He kissed her mouth, sweet with sleep, feeling an overflowing of graspable joy. Now he was truly home.

"Did it go well tonight, with the client?"

"Yes."

It was a discreet lie. When the lights were switched off, she turned to sleep again. He rolled her gently over to him, and bending down, kissed a breast. To appease his lie.

Later, through the hum of the air conditioner, Kian Teck could hear the sound of distant thunder outside, and then the sudden rain.

2

Pelted by the rain, Chan Kok Leong and Sundram made a dash for the foyer. They had come to see the late show at the Capitol Cinema. Before they went inside, Kok Leong announced: "I'm going for a pee."

He stood before the urinal, whose reek filled the small room. The square, white tiles were stained yellow; verdigris had accumulated on the copper piping. He watched his own yellow stream swirling around the half-dozen moth balls on top of the filter plate, together with some sodden cigarette stubs, their thin paper torn, the golden filaments spilling out like viscera. The piercing smell of the naphthalene moth balls pinched his nostrils. The old cast iron cistern framed high up in the wall clanked and clattered like a tortured animal as water flushed down through the pipes. Kok Leong gave an involuntary shudder as he finished and zipped up his fly, then washed his hands in the enamel basin whose cracks, fine as a spider's web, ran in every direction. He did not use the soiled soap, fearing contagion — a natural reaction in one who had suffered from the calamity of acne since boyhood. After wiping his hands with a clean white handkerchief, he approached the wall mirror.

His hair was hoary with rain drops. He combed briskly, with violent flicks of the wrist, waging a lifelong battle with his hair. He hated its waviness, and when younger, had tried to straighten it through long hours of hard combing, using a metallic comb specially bought for the purpose, one chosen because it looked more like a weapon than an article of toiletry.

Part One

But his efforts were in vain. He had once gone to a barber to get it straightened, but the man had advised against it; it was bound to spring out again in the heat and humidity.

Now Kok Leong stood transfixed before his own reflection, the pale face pitted with acne scars. He could not touch it up, make it up like a woman, with moisturiser, foundation, powder, eye shadow, mascara, kohl, to finally arrive at a composition suitable for the world. How marvellous it must be to be able to concoct a fresh life by making up one's face!

Kok Leong hated his face, his physique: short and thin, with skin riding shiny over the saddles of his ribs, hands small and delicate as a woman's; little wonder that from his earliest years he had been filled with self-loathing.

Finally, he emerged and joined Sundram in the crowded foyer. Outside, the rain had turned into delicate filaments, descending, soundless.

Sundram's broad brow jutted out into a question mark while the prehensile nose sat asquat his large, dark brown face, like an answer. When his eyes engaged you, you noticed the squint. One eye looked at you while the other fixed itself elsewhere, smouldering with passion or anger, you could never be certain which. What was striking about that face was not its ugliness, but its force and ebullience.

Chan Kok Leong and A. Sundram, short for Sundram, son of Arumugam, had been friends since their schooldays. They made an improbable pair, and contrary to all expectations, had remained friends to the present day. Kok Leong worked as an accounts clerk, while Sundram, drifting from job to job, was until recently a night janitor at a luxury hotel. But just the other night, he had confided to Kok Leong that he had become a burglar.

When Kok Leong first learned about this from his friend, he was not taken aback. He was not even surprised. For this total unpredictability of Sundram's was what attracted him to Kok Leong, plus the fact that, unlike other people, he could not be so easily placed. Years ago, Kok Leong had decided to become friends with this muscular, agile Indian boy when he saw the tattoo on his right forearm. It bore the initials "A. S.", for Arumugam Sundram. That it was this, rather than a girl friend's name, or the figure of a woman, or his mother, or a ship, or a flower, or some such thing, immediately endeared him to Kok Leong, who thought that it was marvellous that Sundram should be so enamoured of his own name, or — and this was equally marvellous — that he was simply afraid he might forget it.

Ever since Kok Leong had known him, Sundram had courted danger ardently. And Kok Leong's feeling for Sundram went deeper, was more intense, than anything he might feel for a girl. He sensed that no girl, in spite of the fact that it was Sundram who had brought him to his first brothel, could rival it. It was deep set, in the heart of dark stone.

But to what trait of character, what bent of personality, what quirk in Kok Leong, was *Sundram* attracted, which made him commit *his* friendship? What, if any, was the equivalent of the tattoo?

It was the knife. That red, Swiss-made knife that Kok Leong had bought when he was thirteen years old. He had bought it to fend off all the imagined terrors that had crowded in on him in the darkness — even going to the lavatory at night had held terrors for him. But once he clutched his knife, they vanished like magic. And the knife possessed a life of its own, clean, shining, like a brilliant spirit. He used to spend many hours at night just touching it.

So when he showed the knife to Sundram, Sundram understood, and it sealed their friendship, a friendship uninterrupted by all those dreamless hours in their workaday life.

THEY WENT INSIDE THE CINEMA. They had come to see a kung fu film. The hall was already darkened, the screen showing trailers and commercials.

Part One

They both disliked going in early to sit conspicuously in the lighted auditorium among the crowd, with time on their laps. They welcomed the obliteration brought on by the darkness when the screen lit up with images, swamping their minds. For two hours, then, they enjoyed every kick and punch, every thrust of the sword, and gloated over every kill as if they had meted it out themselves. Their favourite films were kung fu films and spaghetti Westerns.

After the show, the audience spewed out like aborted foetuses, stumbling into the world, blinded. Kok Leong and Sundram walked up Stamford Road towards Sundram's motorbike which he'd parked in front of the American Embassy in Hill Street. The road was wet and sleek after the rain, splashed with gold spilling from the headlights of passing cars. The sky above the trees and roof-tops was dark.

They passed an old Indian watchman, sleeping on his *charpoy* in the covered five-foot-way, lost in unshareable slumber, head wrapped in a white turban, feet uncovered, the soles clean and pink.

They reached Sundram's motorbike. With a brisk, downward kick on the starting pedal, Sundram made it roar into life. Astride that energy driven by Sundram, they rode along the almost empty streets. They had lost their individual identities, carapaced in safety helmets with the green plastic visors drawn down over their eyes. Their bodies brushed against invisible draughts of air as if cutting through a transparent lake, trailing ribbons and swathes of space in their wake.

On the pillion, Kok Leong felt his heart shift to the pit of his stomach, or to his sex.

Finally, they arrived at Hokkien Street. They sat at a table near one of the stalls lining the road, and ordered *prawn mee*. The stark yellowness of the spools of noodles, the sliced pink prawns and the brown onion whorls of the *prawn mee* stall made bright splashes of colour under the white glare of the unshaded light bulbs. Steam rose upwards from the wooden tub of soup stock, suffused with aroma, as the gold-toothed Chinese hawker woman prepared their supper.

The houses in that quarter of Chinatown were in a bad state of decay: dirty grey-stained walls, discoloured window curtains flapping in the light breeze like the old dresses worn by slum girls, potted plants in rows along the monsoon drains, growing in old zinc buckets and rusty Milo tins, sprouting green leaves, dirty and hard, like scales. The street was teeming with humanity, and yet it was all strangely subliminal, in that late night.

A big shiny car pulled to a stop across the street. A new, black Mercedes 280.

The doors swung open. A man and a young woman, both Chinese, got out and strolled towards an adjoining table. The man, Rolex-watched, paunch-bellied at forty, shouted orders. Kok Leong stared at the gaudy woman, her face heavily made-up, as she stepped on dainty heels towards the table. She stirred his animosity. Fucking bitch!

A plump, flat-faced young woman in a crumpled *samfoo* brought the bowls of noodles, which they ate with gusto. The woman at the next table laughed loudly, the laughter issuing erotically from her throat.

Later, as they were leaving, Kok Leong directed a look of hatred at her, but she remained unruffled, gazing blandly in his direction as if he wasn't there at all.

During the drive home Sundram turned on the throttle and the machine hurtled with great speed through the sleeping city. Soon he was left outside his block of HDB apartments, and stood there till the loud, God-like sound of Sundram's motorbike faded away entirely.

KOK LEONG LET HIMSELF INTO THE SMALL APARTMENT and walked past his father without a word. The old man was sitting at the dining table over his customary cup of hot chocolate, his thinning dome shining even in the dimly lit living room. He was alone, keeping watch over those few relic hours between night and morning. He had returned

Part One

not long ago from his night shift at the hotel.

"Want a cup of choc-choc — chocolate?" he asked.

Kok Leong shook his head, went into his bedroom, changed quickly. In the small apartment, the darkness seemed to pant as he lay down. The family, except for his father, hovering over his cup of chocolate, were all asleep.

A musical clinking of a porcelain cup came from the kitchen: his father washing up.

The old man had worked for fifteen years in the canteen at the British Naval Base at Sembawang, before being retrenched several years ago when the British withdrew from the garrison, from their crumbling empire.

After that, he couldn't find work for several months. Nobody wanted to employ an old man who had no qualifications. So when he was finally offered the job of toilet attendant by a hotel, he was glad.

However, Kok Leong, who was still in secondary school at that time, was deeply ashamed. A toilet attendant for a father! How he suffered in secret from anguish and anger.

Kok Leong's mother was a small, desiccated woman, but with that peculiar strength one finds in some thin women. She weathered trials and tribulations like a stone. Her only weakness lay in her gods. She prayed to every one of them with a democratic fervour. When he was a child Kok Leong was often dragged along when she visited various houses of worship. He remembered the Indian temples with their smell of fresh copra and coconut oil, heavy, cloying, and the scent of jasmines draped around the sleek neck of Ganesh, the elephant deity; the Chinese Taoist temples, dense with the smoke from incense and joss-sticks, haunted by oversized wood and stone effigies; the Christian churches, their air mellifluous with hymns and psalms. She would also bring her hands together in a pious gesture every time she walked past a mosque. She tried to placate every deity. It was the best form of insurance. And not just for the afterlife, she once explained, but also for this one, "For they can grant good health and prosperity".

Alas, her gods had turned a blind eye and a deaf ear. Her prayers went unanswered. She mostly prayed, the practical woman, for temporal benefits, for good health, for the monthly lottery, believing that there was a greater need for her gods' intervention in *this* life. Once only did they shower on her a little of their largesse, when she won a consolation prize of a hundred dollars in the Social Welfare Lottery. Still, it was a sign, a vindication of all her efforts, and she was so overcome with gratitude that she spent three-quarters of her winnings on gift-offerings to express her thanksgiving. There were so many gods, and there was no way of telling which one was responsible for this small beneficence. But that had been the only occasion. Life was one long, hard slog. And always, there was the problem of money.

Through the small window, Kok Leong saw the night sky growing threadbare, its intensity wavering.

Then his sister's cry gnawed away the remaining darkness. It came from the next bedroom, flooded the apartment, the whole building, the entire street, the universe. Kok Leong opened his eyes wide, staring at the fretted, dark ceiling. Throughout her eighteen years, her great animal cry had riven through him. No one ever knew why she did it, for she was dumb, a retarded quadriplegic.

Once she had cried for two whole days, on and off, and a doctor was called. He probed and examined, eventually deciding that she had a toothache. Her teeth were bad. She could not brush them herself, and daily, an old damp rag was used to clean them. Sometimes, her gums bled. On that occasion, when the doctor diagnosed a toothache, a young dentist who was prepared to make house calls came to perform the extractions at home, since she could not be taken to his surgery.

Every one said that Siew Wan had been a delightful baby, that she had been bright and full of smiles. Then everything went wrong. There were several versions, several reasons expounded to explain this. The one which haunted Kok Leong most, and which still sent a nameless shiver down his spine, was that she had been perfectly all right until she was kicked in the head by a cow's hoof while out playing in the street in front of their old home in Sembawang. She was about two years old then. According to this version, she had cried for half the night after this, and was feverish for days. Afterwards, she changed. Ever since that time, when he had first heard that story as a small boy, Kok Leong had been terrified of cows. Their big, round eyes, full of evil. He still had frequent nightmares about them.

Another version was that she had contracted a mysterious illness which the doctors could not diagnose, and she ran a high temperature and suffered convulsions for a week — and although she survived it, Siew Wan was never the same again.

She became dumb, and could neither walk nor use her hands, so that everything had to be done for her. She always had to be bathed, clothed, fed. Later, as she grew older, her hands and feet became deformed, the fingers and toes curling inwards like some bizarre flower-buds which never open to the sun. Also, because she had no sphincter control, she could not be toilet-trained, and even now, at eighteen, she always had to sit on a specially constructed chair. A round hole was sawed through the wood seat to fit the rim of a big enamel potty, and she sat on this in the day time, peeing and shitting at intervals, her *samfoo* trousers hanging limply at her feet, her faecal smell permeating their home. She was even fed while sitting on her potty chair.

It was after Siew Wan's affliction that Kok Leong's mother had become religious, wandering from temple to mosque to church, to pray for her recovery. They had consulted every doctor in town, Chinese *sinsehs*, Malay *bomohs* and whichever medicine- or miracle-man was recommended to them. But it was no use. Siew Wan was never cured.

About that time, Kok Leong's father took an action which made Kok Leong proud of him. In fact, it was the only time that Kok Leong had felt any respect for his father.

One day, the old man — he was not all that old then — went up to the family altar table and, in a burst of savage rage, swept all the prayer pots onto the floor, spilling the ashes, upsetting the joss-sticks and candles, and then hurled the ancestral tablets and the statues of Buddha and Kwan Yin, the Goddess of Mercy, across the room. He then stomped on them with his wooden-clogged* feet (for he had just had a bath) until they were all smashed into fragments.

So Siew Wan, the elder of the two girls, became the stigma of the family. All of them had been touched, marked, by her aberration. Secretly, they were filled with shame and impotence, anger and despair. They stopped speaking about her condition, and hid her away in a back room when visitors came to their home.

Now the apartment reeled with her crying, the night itself clotted around it. When Kok Leong was a boy, he thought that her cries, more than his mother's prayers, must surely reach up to heaven, if anything could. Yes, up to the stinking heavens. But by now he'd decided that there was only a void up there, which acted as an echo chamber, rebounding the cries back down to earth, to their very home — amplified.

After an age, Siew Wan's crying ceased and the world, with a lurch, fell back into place. Already the night had passed, as if an enclosing membrane had been lifted, and the first rays of the sun touched Kok Leong's room with bird-thread lightness.

Within his chest, at the very centre, Kok Leong felt the pulsating of his heart, and in the very core of this, with dazzling clarity, was his answer:

"Yes, I am capable of murder. Yes! Yes! Yes!"

---

*these wooden clogs, called *trompahs*, are used in the bathroom and toilets of most Singapore-Malaysian homes

3

The dawn might be shimmering silk for all he knew, but in the contrived limbo of his bedroom Ong Kian Teck was unaware of it. He woke up, mouth dry and bitter, and reached out for the glass of water standing on the bedside table. Every morning he found it a struggle to get out of bed. Li Lian, unlike him, would wake up and at once rise nimbly to her feet. He always marvelled at the alacrity with which she did this.

On this particular morning, Kian Teck lay in bed and watched her as she went up to the window and parted the curtains, allowing the savage discordance of daylight to pour in.

Later, at the dining table, he nibbled at his toast and recoiled from the fried egg, his stomach turning at the thought of puncturing the egg yolk with his knife or fork, bleeding that thick yellow goo all over his plate. He seldom enjoyed breakfast. During the early days of their marriage, his wife would try every morning to coax him to eat, but now she just grimaced. No longer funny. He thoroughly agreed.

He gazed at his two young sons, Guan Hock, eight, and Guan Hoe, four, and mused at their unjudging faces. For Kian Teck, his children mitigated against everything. He, who had never contemplated fatherhood! The sight of that wriggling pink of his firstborn, and then his second, all his begotten, had filled him with awe and joy. The various stages of their growth, sitting, standing, walking, and infant talk, were wondrous episodes. Yes, Kian Teck was devoted to his children. He would take them on Sundays to Changi, or to the beaches created along the reclaimed land on the east coast which stretched from Tanjong Rhu to Bedok. Sometimes they would hire a bumboat from Clifford Pier and head out for the Southern Islands. They would swim and fish from the boat. He knew of no better way to enjoy his Sundays.

Shortly after breakfast, Kian Teck left the apartment with the younger boy, Guan Hoe, whom he usually drove to kindergarten. Guan Hock attended afternoon school; he went by the chartered school bus.

Kian Teck consigned himself and his young son to the box-like lift and pressed the button for the ground floor. No one else rode down with them. Guan Hoe's tiny hand held onto his. When the lift doors opened, they strolled towards the car through yellow sunlight. On the way, Guan Hoe pleaded for presents. "Buy me an *Ultraman* comic, Daddy!"

He dropped off his son, then drove along the sea front, passing the Esplanade and Clifford Pier. He turned his head from time to time to his left, to catch a glimpse of the sea, that lilting blue, with the spanking new white ships in the sun, and the bumboats and *sampans* bobbing like sea birds. He would rather be out there, on a boat, adrift on the tide. Or in the air, a bird, lone, rocketing.

At the office, Emily Ho, his secretary, came in carrying a stack of files. And so it began. He dictated letters to Emily, a small, bony, pale Chinese girl with a bunched up face and small, close-set black eyes, magnified by large, round, plastic-framed spectacles. He attended to a few clients, sat in at a conference of senior managers, instructed subordinates, dictated more letters — his working day well and truly ushered in. Hours with their unique configuration, a web of codes, rites and rules in which he was enmeshed, a hapless victim. All else became secondary, laid aside, like his family's photographs, framed mementos sitting on his desk, peering out at him through a glassy separation, a separate existence.

Part One

A FEW HOURS LATER, ON THE SHADED VERANDAH of an old shop house next to a curry shop, a tiger-striped kitten stretched itself, then licked its right front paw. Lick, lick, lick. Kian Teck could hear the distinct flick, flick of the nimble tongue.

He was lunching with Peter Low and Gopal Nair at the curry shop in Bernam Street near the Port. These three had known each other since their undergraduate days in London, some fifteen, twenty years ago. They used to belong to a loose "gang", drinking and partying, going to concerts and films, and participating as a clique in student politics, attending all those meetings in Malaya Hall in Bryanston Square near Marble Arch. Malaya Hall was a students' hostel, a gathering place for the young from Malaya and Singapore. All this had taken place long before the political separation of Singapore from (what is now) Malaysia in 1965.

Sometimes they had chatted away late into the night, talking politics, girlfriends, films and books. Now, in spite of the fact that each of these three men had more or less gone his own way, they still made it a point to meet regularly for lunch, to talk of old times and present superficialities.

Peter Low had become a successful businessman, running an insurance company as well as being a director on the board of a couple of other companies; Gopal Nair had attained a junior partnership in an old established law firm in Singapore, was an amateur director in a local theatre group, and a Member of Parliament to boot. Nevertheless, none of them had changed essentially, except for growing a little older, acquiring a little more money, and fathering a couple of children (Gopal excluded — or "exempted", as his friends all teased him).

Their lives, views, careers, attitudes, beliefs and half-beliefs might be diverse, but they all shared one true uniting passion — they were curry fanatics! They met about once a week for lunch, nearly always at a curry shop. And they knew all the curry shops worth knowing. The one in Bernam Street, Klang Road, St. Gregory's Place, Race Course Road, the

Hospital Assistants' bachelors' quarters canteen in Outram Road, the curry shop in Cuff Road and the one in Tank Road.

"I don't have much will power," declared Peter Low, trying to sound convincing, but failing. Over lunch, he had been extolling his latest sexual exploits. His large, broad brow exuded sweat because of the curry. His hair was plastered down.

"On the contrary," Kian Teck said, "I think you possess great will power, Pete. Only, it's pointed in one direction."

Peter Low laughed lasciviously. And Gopal Nair also laughed, white tooth-paste-ad teeth flashing from his shiny brown face.

"Yes, you rascal, you!" Gopal admonished.

"My one track mind, you mean?" beamed rotund Peter.

"But a much used tract," quipped Gopal.

They laughed. Juvenilia. Always juvenilia when I'm with them, reflected Kian Teck.

"Still, it's a pity. And a waste. Imagine what could have happened if only my will had been directed towards something else? Something productive. I might have become a great scientist, for instance, or a great musician! Or a great statesman ..."

"Instead of being just a great prick," Kian Teck said, deadpan.

"Seriously," repeated Peter, when the laughter had subsided, "I sometimes consider all that I might have been, if only my will had been directed elsewhere. Architecture, poetry, philosophy, public affairs, any lofty thing, instead of dissipating away my life. D'you think I might've been happier?"

Kian Teck shrugged.

"*Deus ipse notavit*," intoned Gopal, as if he were on stage, or in court, or in Parliament.

"I mean, one is supposed to find a greater happiness, if one pursues loftier things in life," Peter continued doggedly, ignoring Gopal.

Part One

"Why, aren't you happy now, as you are?" Kian Teck asked.

"Is anyone happy as he is? Is that humanly possible?" Peter asked in turn.

"I'm sure Gopal is," Kian Teck ventured.

"What d'you mean?" Gopal objected, suspecting that what was said about him was somehow insulting; but he wasn't angry. He had a phobia against extremism, and, fighting shy of it, succeeded only in maintaining a constant state of blandness.

"I don't know about our friend, Gopal," Peter continued, "but I find that it's almost impossible for a man to be happy with what he has, with what he is. There's always something else he wants, or someone else that he'd rather be. No man likes to be in his own shoes. He imagines that the grass is always greener on the other side. He would rather be Onassis, for instance, or Rockefeller, or Paul Newman, or Muhammed Ali, or Mao Tze Tung, or Bruce Lee. For instance, right now I'd rather be that man over there with the girl with the big tits. Yum! Yum!"

They all turned to look. Yes, Yum! Yum!

"In other words," Kian Teck offered, "man is not made for happiness?"

"Yes, something like that," Peter agreed. "Don't you think so, K.T.?"

"It's an interesting notion — man not made for happiness."

"You fellows are beginning to sound like French intellectuals. You know, Camus, Sartre," Gopal said, pronouncing Sartre as *Satay*. He wanted it known that he had read the Existentialists and all their ilk, too.

"Speaking of French," Peter said, suddenly breaking into ribald laughter, "have I told you chaps about *pas de deux*?"

"You mean as in ballet?" Gopal asked.

"No, not quite. There are two sisters from Ipoh in town now. I've nick-named them *pas de deux*, because of what they do as a pair in bed."

"You mean they're lesbians?" Gopal's voice almost squeaked in excitement.

"No, Gopal my boy. *That* they're not. They're true blue

heterosexuals, like K.T. and myself."

"Why was I excluded?" asked Gopal, belligerently.

"I always thought that you were neutral," Peter said, mock innocently. "And I mean neutral in gender, not in politics. For we all know His Master's Voice's political preferences, don't we, K.T.?" Peter had once nicknamed Gopal "His Master's Voice", because Gopal Nair, like all his party colleagues, echoed the Prime Minister's words all the time. Lee Kuan Yew, lord and master.

"Careful, man," Kian Teck cautioned. "Don't you know you're talking to an M.P.?"

"You're right! I don't want to end up in jail!" exclaimed Peter, pretending terror.

"So, kindly restrict yourself to sex, please," Kian Teck implored. "More about *pas de deux*, if you don't mind."

"Yes. *Pas de deux*. Well, these two sisters hire out as a pair, and their modus operandi is this — while you diddle one sister, the other fondles your daddles. And it's great, man! I tried them out the other night, in River Valley Road. I *must* have them again next week, catch an encore before they leave. Say, would any of you chaps like to try? They're really fantastic! *Pas de deux*," Pete sighed, a reminiscent gleam in his moist eyes. "Can teach the Frenchies a trick or two. What a pair!"

So it was that the conversation turned around as usual to Peter's favourite subject. Peter could never get enough of sex, no matter how hard he tried — and *how* he tried! Most people, for instance, confine their amorous adventures, misadventures, habits, labours, call it what you will, to the night, for they all have the sane notion that sex is wicked, naughty, *naughty* — so they consign the act of making love, and sometimes the pretence of it, to the darkness. In hiding, as it were. From what? Original sin? From whom? Wives, husbands, and themselves. But not Peter Low, fat, short, mustachioed, long side-burned, with his thick ripe lips (the better to kiss you with), the tapered long nail on his right little finger (the better to ...), and other useful features. No, not him. The formidable Pete was known far and wide (and by his spouse, poor woman, although she never admitted it out loud) to indulge at any time of the day or night, at any hour, whenever providence provided or the opportunity presented itself (in his case, herself). And when opportunity did not present itself (herself), he would go seek it/her out. Not sit idly on his haunches, like other normal people would. No. "Faint heart never won fair lady," must've been coined just for Peter Low. So, true to form, Pete would, must, more than once a week at least, dart during lunch time into one of the many brothels and haunts he knew, to spend rather than to gain calories. His friends (envious they) wondered (like all envious people do, not in charity but in malice aforethought and afterthought) how poor Pete (notice *that*!) ever got on with so few calories in the day. But, not only metaphorically but also physically, he got on, our Pete. And he got in, and he got away. One simply had to admire him. And what an ingenious, prodigious, intricate, harmonious, effective, organized system he had!

He was on the closest of terms, bordering on intimacy, with the madams and pimps of the best brothels in town, who always kept him fully informed about the choicest girls, the prettiest, the ones with special talents or tricks, and the foreign ones. He was also a member of a couple of so-called clubs in Chinatown, where he could get a decent fuck, or a decent lunch, or a decent game of mahjong, or a decent massage, and if he felt so inclined, even an indecent massage. On top of all this, he shared a mess with a handful of randy business cronies in an apartment off Orchard Road, his own special haven from home and work. His own play pen. Here, he could throw parties, entertain clients, entertain non-clients, have a decent fuck, or a decent dinner, or a decent game of poker, or a decent massage, or, if he felt so inclined, an indecent one.

Peter's activities could be mind boggling. As if the list given above wasn't enough, he also frequented certain girlie bars (playing hanky-panky under the table in the dim red glow), hotel cocktail lounges, discotheques and assorted cabarets. He knew all the pick-up places, for let it not be said that Peter Low always had to pay for what he took. No! For there were girls and girls galore, who were willing to grant him their favours (and other things) without a fee, without a copper cent, gratis!

Looking at him, it was hard to imagine Pete as the ladies' man personified. He was short, certainly on the stout side, wore an untidy moustache, and had such moist, lascivious eyes (you know the expression, "he undresses me with his eyes"? Well, he had just those eyes!). He also wore rings (his favourites — jade and rhinestone, one on each index finger), and flashy clothes (right down to the fashionable platform shoes, which still did nothing to increase his height, for his shortness was an impressive one, unalterable even if he were to use stilts). But, defying all sense, belief, and fate, Pete was a ladies' man! How, it might well be asked, did he become one? What qualifications did he possess? What special traits? What particular distinctions? Certainly not his physical endowments, nor his accoutrements, which were really and truly in abominable taste. In short, as Yul Brynner said in *The King and I*: "'tis a puzzlement".

Once upon a time, in London, he told Kian Teck a tale, a true-to-life experience, which Kian Teck knew wasn't fabricated, for it was something that only Peter would be capable of. Typical for him, but unimaginable for the ordinary person.

Anyway, the story went like this: one night, he, Peter, caught sight of a young woman leaving a bar where he happened to be drinking with certain pals. He looked at her and — Wham! Instant chemistry! Sluices of juices! Without a word to his companions, or any hesitation, he got up and followed her. She walking ahead, he walking after. She boarded a bus and he jumped on in the nick of time, sitting at the back because the seat next

Part One

to her's was already occupied. Eventually (he did not know where the bus was heading), she got down at a certain stop. He also got off. She walked. He walked. She entered a house, he followed — into the house, up the stairs, to the landing with four apartment doors. Finally, just as she was inserting a key into her lock, he confronted her, face to face.

He: "I saw you leaving the Wellington's Arms. Followed you all the way here. Can't help myself. I want you. You're the most beautiful woman I've ever seen in my life."

At this point in the story, Kian Teck had laughed. Timidly, uncertainly, nervously. For, like most sensitive souls, he had felt embarrassed, as he would have been were he in Peter's shoes. He waited avidly to hear about the expected rebuff, the just desserts for such gall.

There was such a long pause that he finally had to ask Peter: "And then?" All the time preparing to guffaw.

Peter: "She studied me for a long while, then invited me in."

"No kidding?!"

"No."

"What happened?"

"Well, I poured everything out. I told her things about myself that I've never confessed to anyone before."

"Yes, yes, but what *happened* ?"

"We became lovers. Our affair lasted two whole months. It was too much for me. Had to end it. She became too possessive."

Kian Teck did not for a moment doubt Peter's story. He believed his friend, but, (typical of all vain men who think themselves endowed with good looks) he was constantly surprised at Peter's effect on women. Pete was so successful! During their student days in London, they sometimes went to various ballrooms and dance clubs. Their favourites were the Whiskey A Go Go in Soho, the Continental in St. John's Wood and the El Toro in Finchley Road. It was the time when the Cha Cha Cha, Rock and

Roll and the Twist were all the rage. On most occasions they went looking for girls to dance with, and, with luck, to go home with. If truth be told, Kian Teck invariably went in looking for romance, searching for the girl in his life, the girl who would instantly recognize him for what he was. Only when he failed would his motives degenerate to just wanting to dance and fuck. Then, any presentable, willing girl would do.

Kian Teck had never known Peter to be turned down by a girl, whereas he, who had always considered himself, without any false modesty, to be far more attractive to women, was turned down many a time, despite all his efforts to look just that bit slightly soulful, never allowing any randiness to show. All carefully calculated, but the inevitable result was that he only succeeded in looking sexless, bland, lonely and lost. Eyeing a beautiful girl who also seemed quite sensitive, he would make his awkward approach.

He: "Would you like to dance?"

She, examining him disdainfully, "No."

And, deflated, he would slink away, hoping that no one had noticed his disgrace. With murder in his heart. Especially when, a moment later, she would be dancing in the arms of a crude Cockney, or a hirsute German, or an oily Italian. A case of adding insult to injury, it was. Peter, on the other hand, never had such problems. How often had Kian Teck seen him walking towards a girl, swaggering across the room, wearing his randiness on his sleeve (trousers), so obvious it was, and, standing before the sweet thing, bend down to whisper a word or two. And up she would jump like a marionette, and in a jiffy, glue herself to his body, his lecherous arms a-feeling her here, and even there, the devil! Was it simply a question of tactics, then? Kian Teck often wondered. You mean sweet, young, sensitive things *really* fall for overt randiness in a man, rather than depth of soul and candy romance? What had the world come to? Anyway, to give himself a chance, he tried to adopt Peter's tactics. It took a lot of nerve and thespian ability to act the randy dick, the poor limp he. So Kian Teck

Part One

would swagger up to a likely prospect, bringing up the leer into his eyes, saliva practically drooling from his lower lip, and demand a dance. You should have seen the *looks* the prospects gave him! Nay, it didn't work for the poor drip. He decided that perhaps it was the moustache that made the difference, for girls (he had been told) could never resist the idea, and the reality, of being tickled while being nibbled and dickled. So, he grew one. Nothing stupendous, it must be admitted. But then, he consoled himself (he was good at this, as you may have observed), he had never been the hirsute, brute type — too civilized, he was. But again, it did no good. His moustache only made his face look lopsided. So he reconciled himself to merely being jealous of Peter, of whatever it was that Peter had and which God, or fate, saw to it that he, Ong Kian Teck, did not.

Now, years later, Kian Teck was wiser. He thought that perhaps he understood a little the difference between Peter and other men (he meant himself, Everyman). No doubt Peter's main preoccupation was sex, was desire, and moreover, a desire that was beyond measure. But here comes the crux: it was a desire without any urge for possession. He simply wanted to fuck. His great gluttony was for gratification, not for the draining of blood, lymph, soul and other liquids. And he was overt about it, honest about it. There was no lie, no cosmic humbug, no crap. Therefore, his desire had a certain integrity, a certain paradoxical sincerity, about it. So, girls and women tended to trust him. Repeat: *trust* him! Funny, but true. They, the dames, felt safe with our randy Pete, for after all, they knew that he was only interested in borrowing the use of their cunts. There were no hidden clauses, no legal fine print, to trick. As for other men, they want more, much, *much* more. To name only some — they want love, romance, faithfulness, devotion. Furthermore, Pete's desire was not accompanied by guilt, remorse, regret, shame, rain, and most important of all — despair. The rest of *Homo Sapiens Sapiens*, that stinking species, is stuffed full of all of these and more: guilt, remorse, regret, shame, rain and most important of all — despair. Yeah, *Homo Sapiens Sapiens* is stuffed full of despair.

However sad it is, Kian Teck, who knew all these truths and quarter-truths, could not emulate Peter. He could not change. He remained always what he was, in other words, Ong Kian Teck, a sometimes despairing *Homo sapiens*.

Time passed. Soon, their lunch break came to an end, and they had to go their separate ways. Outside, the day was on fire.

"See you all this evening, then," Gopal said.

They'd all been invited by the British High Commissioner to attend the Queen's Birthday celebrations.

His CHILDREN THREW THEIR ARMS AROUND HIM and kissed him goodnight. The dream-coloured evening was fading into night. Kian Teck sat on the leather chair in their lounge, twirling a brandy glass in one hand, holding a lit cigarillo in the other. He was already dressed. He could hear Li Lian getting ready in the bedroom. There must, he thought, be half a thousand women at that very moment doing the same thing, preening themselves before their mirrors, painting their eyelids green, blue, violet, indigo and other hues, and bedecking their ears, necks, arms and fingers with jewellery. He took a nip of brandy and drew on his cigarillo, expelling the pungent smoke as if to smudge out the thought of all those women, attempting with art and subterfuge, lotions and paints and pastes, to transform themselves, like frantic chrysalides, into fluttering butterflies. That his wife was one of them, irritated him, and yet, in common with all husbands, he himself wished for her to outpreen every other female, every other bollocks's wife.

He had already been to three such functions at Eden Hall, the British High Commissioner's residence, to honour Her Britannic Majesty's official birthday. After the first, he had sworn he would never go again. Each occasion was similarly, predictably, boring. And yet, here he was, a grown, sane and free adult, himself dressed and groomed (for the peacock contest, perhaps), ready to subject himself to it for the fourth time. Where was his will, resistance and integrity?

He rose from the deep chair and walked out onto the balcony. There was a half moon, bashful, beautiful, and he felt the lightly-blown air on his face, like a young girl's sigh. Wouldn't it be better just to sit out on the balcony, drinking his brandy and smoking cigarillos than to mingle with nits at that reception?

It was pleasant to look across the road to the grounds of the *Istana*, the President's official residence. Kian Teck and Li Lian had bought their apartment in this small block with the assurance that their view would never be obstructed.

The apartment was decorated in an eclectic style, a mixture of modern Scandinavian, traditional Chinese, and *Peranakan* — Straits Chinese — furniture. Original art by local painters hung on the walls, a couple of batik cloth hangings bought during a trip to Jakarta, a scroll of Chinese calligraphy, as well as old prints by Van Gogh and Cezanne, relics from his student days in London. Someone had once sneered that this common culture of the Singaporean professional was neither here nor there. Kian Teck was never upset by jibes like this, nor when he was labelled a "wog", a Westernized Oriental Gentleman. He was a product of his history, and if that made him a pariah, so be it.

"I'M READY!" LI LIAN ANNOUNCED, click-clacking in her high-heels.

"Let's go, then."

Outside, the early night was lovely, and he looked up at it with longing. He thought: "I don't have to go! Right this very moment, I can change my mind. I still have my freedom!"

Then he drove onto the main road. The issue settled! No, correction. Only one issue was settled. For there were plenty of them ahead, lying in wait, in ambush, ready to pounce at any moment. No wonder he was tired, being so constantly on the look out.

Driving along the Bukit Timah Road, he slowed down when he heard the tocsin of an ambulance. The closed, secretive, solemn vehicle rushed past. Well, he sighed, such is life. And death. And the state in between, which he suspected was the state he was in at that moment. Here we are (me and my made-up mate), heading for a party, whereas the other party in the ambulance (may Whatever or Whoever have mercy on him) is heading towards another appointment.

"You're very silent," Li Lian observed.

"Am I?"

"Yes."

Now, what on earth could he say to that? It was the sort of statement, transformed by repeated occurrence, into almost an inquisition. It exasperated him. How was he to answer? By the usual explanation? — "Sorry, dear, I was preoccupied. There was a slight hitch in the office this morning. Nothing serious, really." These might be truths, but are essentially lies, because they were not the real reasons for his silence. He did not know what the reasons were, himself. So he wished Li Lian had not questioned him. It was such a husband-and-wife situation. A routine aspect of marital life.

"I'm sorry," he said, "does my silence bother you?"

"No."

He knew she was lying. He turned to look at her face for an instant. Small, clean-lined, clear-toned, with the beauty of ..... he was lost for words. Porcelain? But she was beautiful. My wife, he thought, feeling contrite, for he loved her.

He had first met Li Lian at a dinner party. There was a lot of banter at their table, and he had noticed her quietness, her exceptional stillness. But there was laughter in her lovely brown eyes, frequently animated by a gentle, shy smile at some remark from the gathering, or at some private thought. Small and composed, yet she hinted at a certain capacity for mischief, and a promise of fun. He had wanted to get to know her. She had a wholesomeness that captured him.

Now he turned to her. "Sometimes, I simply have nothing to say."

"Well, recently you've been like this more often than before, that's all."

"Have I?"

"Yes," she replied, but without any combativeness in her voice.

Suddenly, they both smiled, looking at each other. He reached across and touched her hand lightly.

"I was thinking," he confessed, "how much I loathe going to this stupid do."

"We shouldn't have accepted. I don't enjoy these things either."

"What we get ourselves into! I'm sorry. Anyway, let's slip away early. Go some place just by ourselves."

Now it was her turn to reach over and touch his hand. "Yes, let's be by ourselves tonight."

Together. Conspiratorial. Close. Touched for a moment by romance, borne to them on tinsel-wings.

It took him a long time to park and then, hand in hand, they trailed up the path to the grand house, to be greeted with brief diplomatic smiles by their hosts. They proceeded through the carpeted hall and a long passage to a large, open lawn where the party had gathered. Close-clipped grass, flower beds, fan-shaped Traveller's palms and old rain trees, the last lit up from below by powerful arc lamps, their trunks grey and ghostly, their leaves glittering green trinkets. On the gilded lawn were figures clothed in ochres, reds, greens, purples, blues and swathed in silks and lamés — would-be paradisal birds, all.

A Chinese waiter in a stiff white suit came towards him with a tray. Kian Teck took the drink he offered. He felt an outsider in that official semi-solemnity, semi-gaiety, conscious of tasting a false splendour. He scoured around for a familiar face, but all the faces were familiar in a large anonymity, a herd-like homogeneity.

A large-boned European woman sauntered across his vision, long, yellow gown trailing down to her ankles, all wrapped up in fabric like a folded tulip. She joined a tall, thin, sharp-faced European man with straight black hair plastered down on his bony head and a neat little beard on a narrow chin, his eyes fierce, sardonic, his hands wrapped around a serviette-covered glass of whiskey-and-soda. He was talking to a young English couple. The red-headed, pale woman looked like a frightened mouse before a big, bad cat. Her husband, who wore horn-rimmed glasses, was a lecturer in English at the University of Singapore. He wore a calculatedly frumpy-looking suit like a badge, for he specialized in Mediaeval English and wrote novels about the East *à la* Somerset Maugham.

And there were others he had met before, the local citizenry, bankers and tycoons, politicians and senior civil servants, society doctors and architects and accountants, prominent or aspiring.

He took another drink from a waiter, and a little later, another.

Then Peter Low came towards them like a predator, shoulders hunched forward. His wife, Annie, trailed behind. Kian Teck, knowing Pete, was constantly surprised by her. He had expected the martyred wife, but Annie, small, firm-featured and bright-faced, was always self-assured, never cowed, never giving a hint of playing the soul-suffering wife to randy Pete.

A few acquaintances, including Gopal Nair, joined their company. They made decorous, inane conversation.

A roll of drums summoned. The British High Commissioner toasted the President of the Republic, and then the *Majulah Singapura* crackled over the public address system. Kian Teck, like everyone else, stood to

Part One

attention, semi-rigidly, glass of brandy clamped conspicuously in one hand, and face rigor-mortised, too adult to giggle.

Then came the response by the Minister for Foreign Affairs, representing Singapore, who toasted the good health and long life of the Queen, and *God Save the Queen* was played. The tune always evoked an image of fat, old Victoria for Kian Teck, her doughty body swathed in hot, black clothes, *her* shadow falling upon the gathering, upon the trampled lawn — not Elizabeth's.

Later, semi-drunk and semi-fed, with appetite killed and all dressed up with nowhere to go, they drove in separate cars with Pete and Annie Low and a small group of other acquaintances to the Coffee Shop at the Marco Polo Hotel, for more snacks and drinks.

It was only on the way home that Kian Teck remembered the night out alone with each other that he and Li Lian had planned earlier. An opportunity lost, tangled by trivia. Yes, another!

In the middle of the night, when Kian Teck was asleep, the minutes dragged on for Li Lian. Finally, she crept out of bed, went to the window and parted the thick curtains. Looking out, she felt the emptiness in their room rivering out into the sky, her world now the colour of air.

4

The mosquito landed on Chan Kok Leong's bare left forearm. He studied it, not moving a muscle. It raised its hind limbs, mere fragile sticks, and lowered its head, sting-equipped, to dip into his flesh like a fountain pen into an inkwell. He watched with fascination the elaborate organization of its faculties for its meal: a thin mosquito, empty bellied, just a shell of cells. Then he felt its sting, the clarity and precision of the sensation. Still, he would not move, feeling it pierce his flesh, drawing his blood into its small, tube-like belly. For a time, he was engrossed rather than angry.

Suddenly, he realized his supreme power. His will it was, to kill or not to kill, this insect. *His* will! His alone! Like a god, he gazed down upon the insect, and then, in this new and stern persona, whacked his right palm down upon it. The mosquito became a tangle of black in the small splash of red, so fragile it was.

Could it be satisfaction, this coldness he felt? If so, as he suspected it was, then his was green reptilian blood.

Now, near noon, the day was ablaze with a full sun. Barren brightness. Like over a desert. Or in his soul.

Kok Leong worked as an accounts clerk in an advertising agency. His was only a minor position, but still he was an accomplice, a member of a team whose function was to devise desires, clothe them in the alchemy of words and images into golden dreams. Golden dreams chased by millions of souls.

Part One

From the balcony of his apartment, high above the ground, Kok Leong surveyed the scene down below. There was a clear view of the Toa Payoh Sports Complex, and he could see the small figures in white shorts and sweat shirts running round the oval, bitumen track, the sunlight shining fiercely on all, their shadows tincturing the track like smoke, shifting shapes attached to the moving figures like thoughts. Running and jogging, treading the mill to keep the heart stout, the muscles supple, so that they could last a little longer, exist a little longer.

On evenings too, Kok Leong watched them with detachment, these runners and joggers, gritting their teeth in determination. After their day's labour, keeping in trim for the next day's labour.

At school, he had never tried to excel in games. He had never played soccer or badminton or basketball. The sporting urge, if that was what it was, that orthodox competitive spirit, was absent in Kok Leong, simply not there, just as some trees or plants are never apportioned flowers, sprouting only green leaves, just green leaves.

Suddenly, thinking about his school days, his mind pitched backwards, typhoon blown, blasted, and his blood broke through all the intervening years, a roaring flood of hatred.

It was his ugliness. It set him apart. Always, as a boy, he had suffered this feeling of unworthiness. He had wanted to hide. He used to examine his face, his features, and every single time, he hated it. He hated his parents for having given him life. Every time he looked at the mirror, the thought entered like a knife: outcast! Outcast! Yes, he had looked hard into the mirror. To peer long into it is to enter a special state of lucidity, or madness.

And one day, looking into the mirror, the world dissolved for Kok Leong, and the air swelled, swelled, and he felt he was afloat, lighter than anything, alone at last. How he gloated on his isolation. Also, there was in him an implanted time bomb, the fuse lit on a dark midnight of the soul, a midnight of the mirror, fizzing and sparking inevitably in a blue hypnotic logic towards the powder keg. But when would the lit fuse reach its destination? When would the explosion take place? The moment of liberation which Kok Leong awaited with greater passion and impatience than any mooning youth for his lover?

His eyes fell on his mother's potted rose plant in its frail wrought iron stand beside him on the balcony. It bore one incredible, pink rose, petals delicate beyond description. What an improbable beauty from such an unprepossessing, thorny plant! With a lightning impulse, he crushed its petals in his hand, sickened by its blandishment of colour: the whole operation enacted in the magnitude of his mind, that exclusive microcosm, that walled empire.

Now the world was broken, of crushed mosquito and petals, of blood and rose sap, bludgeoned by his own small hands that wanted to attack the earth and the sky.

He had fallen through the mirror. He had entered the heart of time, annexed it with his actions.

Way below, the joggers were going home, white dots in the noon sun, no doubt for the midday meal, the routine sustenance to keep the body alive for the next day. What a usurious rate man has to pay!

Kok Leong had striven hard to remain indifferent to the world of the white dots. He had carefully planned to exclude them, all of them, from his consciousness.

But one day, while gazing from his balcony, Kok Leong saw an old hunchback way down below him. He stared at the man in astonishment, in a kind of ecstasy. That ungovernable swelling of flesh, impossibly there! That lump, like a universe, on the man's back! Yes, deformities tend to expand into a universe. Entire. Kok Leong saw this, knew this, and for the first time, felt a commiserative pain for another man.

This event had occurred several years ago, but it was an indelible, authentic moment for Kok Leong, while most of his life, moment following moment, was merely diversionary.

One night, months later, when he could not sleep, Kok Leong recalled the hunchback, and in his mind, had this conversation with him. He had gone up to the man, and said, "I know how you feel!"

And the hunchback, straining to lift his heavy head, looked at Kok Leong with his rather large eyes, his forehead furrowed as a ploughed field, and replied, "Tell me, how can you possibly know? How can anybody possibly understand?"

His words were uttered with great effort, and he wrung his hands while speaking, as if the hands were at war with each other. Kok Leong was infected with a similar urge, his hands suddenly had an animal life of their own, and he wrung them in the darkness of his bedroom.

That ended the short, imaginary dialogue.

He then lay exhausted, and the soft sounds of his sleeping family washed faintly against the night like sea waves. Nostrils and mouths agape like wounds, orifices through which air entered and left, tangled in the vesicular nets of the lungs. Life-giving air, absorbed by the network of membranes in the chest cages. Physiological systems. He thought of this in the darkness, of the puzzle of it all, the mystery.

Much later, still unable to sleep, he had said: "Loneliness can never be understood. That is its nature." It was as if he were replying to the hunchback.

Meanwhile, the day had progressed, and by one o'clock, the town sagged beneath the afternoon heat.

Kok Leong's father came out onto the small balcony. He had just emerged from his hard sleep through the morning and the early part of the day, for, because of the unnatural hours of his job, it was his routine to sleep while others were awake. The day, as he joined his son on that balcony high in the sky, was bright with the shimmer of a million flashing knife blades, thrilling the air through and through. The sun silenced the two men.

Kok Leong looked at his father. A submissive, subjugated man, who had accepted his fate, accepted the dictates of the Government, the police, his employers, his superiors. He was the epitome of the universal small man, who no longer knew how to claim or clamour for his own uniqueness.

Kok Leong sometimes wondered what he felt, this small, bald old man? There he stood, stock still, facing the blinding light, his shadow a dark pool on the hard concrete. How different they were, genes and consanguinity notwithstanding!

No, he could not fathom his father, could only presume there must be discontent, although his father was a man who did not attitudinize, and therefore seemed artless and inarticulate. Even in the vise of a fate which offered little by way of money or prestige, he had always been, ostensibly, unbelligerent and unrebellious, a man who said little, who seldom complained. If only his father had shown more full-bloodedness, Kok Leong often thought. Whereas he felt *his* own dark blood coursing like lava. Black blood. As a boy he had been surprised when he cut his finger and discovered that his blood was only a common red. Just like the others.

After some time, his father turned around, his pupils pin-pointed from the sun. He leaned lightly against the railings of the balcony, his vertebrae bony piping against the iron railings, making a cross.

"Are you g-g-going out?"

"Yes," Kok Leong said.

"Your mother has c-c-cooked."

"I'm not hungry."

The old man nodded, or almost nodded, very slightly inclining his shiny dome.

Although they stayed on the balcony, they both had no inclination to converse further, and would remain so even if the two of them were the only inhabitants on earth, and the world empty and desolate beyond that high balcony washed by the harsh light.

Kok Leong spoke little, for words could never convey his feelings. He had found that out a long time ago. So much so, he regarded conversation as nothing more than the frantic and useless babble of voices, employed by normal people as a substitute for emotions. Only at night, in the darkness of his room, would he give vent to interior monologues, as if doing penance for his daily silence. Then he would be drunk and drowned by his own words, torrential swollen rivers, roaring through the deep, narrow gorges of his mind. Words like wild, rushing water, blind-forced, noisy, shattering the sky.

A short while later, his father went back into the apartment. It was also time for Kok Leong to go out, although he had made no clear plans. As he was about to leave, he noticed the crushed rose petals littering the floor around the base of the brown clay pot. Those pink petals, previously fleshy, crisp with juice, now lay scattered, wilted and lifeless. Whither the sap that had formed its fleshiness? Evaporated into the air?

He went into his room, sought out his shoes from beneath the low plank bed, and put them on. Then he went to the sink outside the bathroom to splash tap water on his face, on his hair. He patted his hair down as best he could, frowning, and dried his face with a white "Good Morning" towel. Although his mother nagged him for not eating the lunch which was already laid out on the dining table, he ignored her. He left, closing the door behind him resolutely.

There was a small, grassy plot between the adjacent blocks of apartments, and here, as he walked past, the few trees billowed their small leaves, green flame they were, and for a moment he thought that the deep shadow of one tree was infiltrated by phantoms. But they were only small children at play.

He stood there for a minute or two, out in the lewd, hot day, moved by some impulse, unfathomable, to stay. His sight soon got used to the shade and penetrated into that ample soft shadow, that hidden dream. He watched the young children playing, and mourned the loss of a childhood he never knew, and never shared.

Finally, he tore himself away with an incurable and endless ache, and continued walking down the mineral brightness of the street.

5

Ong Kian Teck woke with a start. A sun shaft in the room broke into fresh gold. It lay, a gleaming sword on the floor.

It was Sunday and he could lie awhile in bed, letting himself drift slowly with the minutes. A little later, Li Lian came into the room, with a deliberate air of preoccupation. She walked straight up to the built-in cupboard, slid open the panelled doors, carefully went through some drawers, picking out assorted articles of clothing, and then walked out again. She must have known that he was awake, and this conspicuous avoidance of glance or speech indicated a certain gulf between them. He thought, have things come to such a pass? There was a sense of either something ending, or of something beginning, he was not quite sure which. What was it, then?

Kian Teck had always considered their marriage a good one. They shared an intimacy, an understanding and an openness that was never forced, or false. And when he went away, on business mostly, he longed for Li Lian even a day away from her, missed her voice, her face, the way she walked across a room.

Without any apparent reason, all that had changed a dateless day ago. Now, small acts could hurt, like this morning, her simply walking into their room and deliberately not noticing him, avoiding him.

Suddenly, Kian Teck felt angry with himself, and leapt impatiently out of bed. He decided to take a cold shower, stripped, and stepped into the long bath tub, that replica of a stone coffin, the enamel flawlessly white (the better to see your dirt with, he thought) and perilously slippery. He stood with his bare feet apart, steadying himself, for he had visions of his skull cracking like an egg shell on the adamantine hardness of the tub. He turned on the cold faucet. With eyes closed as if to receive bliss, he felt the water drumming against his skin, and wished that the water could wash away this mood.

He dressed in casual clothes and went to the living room to look for his family. There was no one in the living room, but outside, through the open balcony door, oh how the sunlight danced! A fine Sunday morning, just right for their proposed outing to Changi beach. His spirits lifted.

He found Li Lian in the kitchen.

"Coffee?" she asked.

"Yes, please," he answered, adding, "where're the kids?"

"Playing in their room."

"It's nice outside."

"What's the time?"

He looked at his wrist watch. "Just past eleven."

She made no comment. What a conversation to inaugurate the day, he thought. Man and wife. He looked at Li Lian, her face tight, with that hint of tension around the mouth. What had brought forth this, he wondered, and after their labouring jointly all these supposedly holy years! "Speak! Speak!" Kian Teck silently called out. "Even the special palaver of mates, of inmates, private argot, anything!"

He drained the remaining coffee. "I'll go get the boys," he said. "Can we go soon? The day seems really nice."

"I'm about through."

As they drove off, the sky was a faultless blue, cobalt, like a dreamt-sea, such a one as a child might paint.

They got to North Bridge Road and he double-parked in front of the Islamic Restaurant, keeping the engine running. In town, there was a

Part One

conspicuous absence of franticness, of the workaday vibrancy, that resilient brawn and pulsation so essentially Singapore.

He darted into the restaurant and ordered *mutton briyani, kambing goreng, murtabaks* and a Madras chicken curry.

The drive to the beach took a long forty minutes, through middle-class, suburban Katong, Siglap, Bedok and Changi. The children babbled and quarrelled, without seriousness, but Li Lian and Kian Teck seemed staunched of words for each other. There was an edge to their silence, an iciness. On such a day, on such a day, he thought. Kian Teck felt tethered like an animal to a post, and yearned for the extravagant plantations of his dreams.

Arriving at the beach, they found a shady patch under the trees and unpacked, first making sure that their immediate neighbours were not armed with ghetto blasters. Mats were unrolled on the sand. He and the boys changed into swimming trunks, using their towels as sarongs to shield them as they wriggled out of their clothes.

The day was fine, and he began to feel good, although Changi beach hadn't the whitest sand this side of paradise, nor was its water the clearest — yet when the tide was up, it was satisfactory to swim in, and he was glad they had Changi. Anyway, which sane, reasonable, normal adult looks for paradise now? Only monks and priests, perhaps, or those unhappy souls with dark shadows beneath their eyes, with the hard diamond glint of search fixed in their pupils — not exactly models for emulation or envy. Better to be one of the common herd, head to the grass, with the green before the nose, and leave all quests for paradise to those who burn for it.

It could be worse. One must learn in this one life to be grateful for all small and tender mercies that chanced to come across one's path; otherwise, it's the mad house, or suicide.

He raced the boys, Guan Hoe with arm floats, to the water and plunged in, fairly athletically. And the sea received him, after that instant trusting abandon when his body, air-borne in a brief arc, entered the water softly; received him, with her eternal empathy and generosity, as if he were still to her a young and supple lover. He swam out a short distance, the water brushing against him like silk, and he savoured all that sweetness of sensation. He turned back to the shallows to be with the children, swimming with loose-limbed ease, infused with a natural gracefulness, almost like a fish, that slithering silver of exquisite, solitary beauty. Who fashioned fishes with such perfect artistry, if not God?

Kian Teck frolicked with his children in the warm water, moments as happy as any he had known, and, he knew, would ever get to know. Childish laughter sparkled like magic coins in the air, and over all soared the sun, sovereign brightness in all its splendour, unstinting in its gifts for the day.

After a while, they scampered out of the water, hair tousled and wet, ran up the beach to the shade and dried themselves. They sat on the straw mats and ate their lunch, their appetites sharpened. Afterwards, Kian Teck reclined on the mat to read the Sunday newspapers.

He adjusted his body as best he could on the mat which lay on top of uneven sand, and, physically comfortable, his mind fairly blank, unfolded the *Sunday Times*.

There was an article about the famine in Bangladesh. People, according to an agency report, were selling their wives and children to buy food, and some parents had strangled their children to end their suffering. Great hordes of hungry people were swarming the roads, dirty and bedraggled, weak and potbellied, heading for the cities. In overcrowded Calcutta, these skin and bones fought viciously over the rubbish bins.

Kian Teck put down the newspaper, resting it on his stomach, to hide the huge meal he had just consumed, and looked up at the holes of sky through the leaves as if he could find comprehension there. Masses of statistics. Numbed one's senses. Difficult to envision forty-five million people. Yes, the scale was overwhelming, diminishing the pain he ought to be feeling, in place of which there was a vague sympathy for the plight of all those blurred and shadowy figures. And great good *that* achieved!

Small, impotent concerns on a Sunday afternoon, lazy after a nice swim and a great lunch.

He flipped through to the woman's page. There was an advice column on "How to cope with unexpected guests." There was also a piece entitled, "Understanding Bisexuality". He turned to the leisure page and read about the Costa Del Sol: "Paradise for sun and fun seekers in southern Spain".

A group of young Malays strolled by laughing gaily, dressed in bright colours. Malays can wear primary colours, and in startling combinations, with *élan* and grace, whereas the same colours would look outlandish on others. They posed for photographs nearby.

Kian Teck wondered whether they realized that posing for photographs on a Sunday afternoon by the beach, as they were doing, was done out of a realization of their own mortality, and that in the face of impermanence — of the day, of the week, of life — one craved photographs?

Under the trees, stirred by a light breeze, the minutes dropped like leaves. Kian Teck closed his eyes. He could hear the lapping of the small waves and the sound of leaves fluttering above. And the sound of the sea, or of wind blowing through foliage, or of falling rain, any sound of nature, soothes, because it makes man instinctively feel a part of nature too, and part of life's rhythms, the swelling and ebbing of tides, growth and decay, birth and death, and the stars at night.

He watched his sons playing in the water, greyish already because of the fast receding tide, the silt rising through the former blueness. Out at sea, the *kelongs* perched on their stilts like tall spiders standing on long, thin limbs. Catches were poor nowadays, with pollution from the nearby reclamation of the sea by a land-hungry populace. They were reclaiming land for the new airport. He could see dredges at one corner of the bay, dumping red earth, which bled into the salt water. Fish were being driven away.

"Would you like a cup of coffee?" Li Lian asked. She was reclining on a canvas beach chair, reading an Agatha Christie novel.

"Yes, please!"

She rose, went to the basket and poured out a cup from the thermos flask. She moved with such neat nimbleness, did everything with this quick grace. He remembered how he had been attracted to this small, fair and bright girl when he first met her at a dinner party. She sat with such an admirable stillness, while inanities were being passed round the table. She said very little, but how brightly her eyes lit up her face! There was a kittenish quality about her, independent, self-sufficient, and how he had wanted her when he saw her closing her eyes and stroking one side of her nose meditatively with a small and slender finger. And when she noticed him watching, gave him that first intimate smile.

She came towards him with the cup of coffee. He had wanted to smile, out of affection and gratitude, but their fingers, momentarily touching over the passing of the cup, discovered no correspondence; and she went silently back to her chair, both of them making no claim.

He sipped the hot coffee, savouring its sweet tang on his tongue and inhaling its roasted aroma. He heard the crisp rustling as she flipped a page, suddenly sparking an annoyance in him. Her act of reading was a rebuff. She sat aloof from him, wrapped in silence, in an inner room of her mind, occasionally turning a page with precision. She always had this aura of economy, of impeccability. In comparison, Kian Teck was extravagant and untidy in his actions.

By late afternoon, the sky slowly turned silver, on which a fine latticework of casuarina needles imprinted themselves, lines of sepia, no longer greyish green. Birds now crossed the sky, on their way elsewhere.

Along the whole stretch of the beach, people were departing, the day

Part One

done. Time to return home, to await the next day, the next week. In fact, a sense of the future had already intruded upon a day which, earlier, was mostly focused on the present. There was an air of regret, of melancholy.

Reaching home, they bathed, changed hastily, and went out to dine nearby at the hawkers' centre at Newton. There was a big Sunday crowd. The children went to gawk at toys and comics. Kian Teck sat beside his wife at their customary table in front of the *laksa* stall.

"Would you like a *rojak* ?" he asked.

"No, thanks. I'm not particularly hungry."

"We could share one."

"I'm not hungry."

They seemed circumscribed by the surrounding air — milkier than usual beneath the hanging lamps and impregnated with the piquant fragrance of cooked food — feeling dazed with a kind of torpor which prevented more than conventional conversation. Intimacy was banished. They sat in a slightly startled silence, with an intimation of despair, as they watched other people, other families, whose natural togetherness made their own a travesty.

The food arrived and the children were brought back to the table. They were both relieved when the meal was over.

Back home again, the children were made to brush their teeth and change into pyjamas. Only then were they allowed to watch TV — they were just in time for *Hawaii Five O*. Kian Teck opened a can of Tiger beer, walked out to the balcony and sat in the rattan rocking chair. He lit a cigarillo. The sky was black except for an aureole, tinctured zinc, around the low moon. The trees in the compound below were almost indistinguishable from each other, coming to terms with the night. We will have to come to terms with the end, in the end, Kian Teck thought, ruefully.

The TV poured forth an avalanche of noise, like an electronic rainstorm blasting at him, jolting the wreckages of mind and heart.

Ought to be languorous, Sunday, all of it, delicious and long in passing, each hour precious, slowly savoured, instead of this state of unwelcome agitation.

Soon, however, the television programme was over, and the children trundled off to bed.

He was rocking gently, indolently, taking periodic sips of beer, rocking to and fro, to and fro, his chair creaking slightly as the arcs of cane rubbed against the ceramic tiles of the balcony floor. He seemed to be waiting for something. What was it?

There was no clue in Kian Teck's rather blank face, from which a pair of dark brown, almond-shaped eyes glinted a puzzled questioning, his thin, lower lip jutting outward slightly in anticipation, his body curled to fit the curve of the chair. He was simply waiting, for nothing in particular, for an event which still had no configuration, and which, he suspected, could only be recognized and comprehended after its occurrence.

Li Lian returned quietly to the sitting room. He sensed her presence at once and felt a sudden ravaged need for her, but she had already switched on the TV. It was too late. She sat curled up on the soft sofa, a tidy, orderly bundle, riveting her attention on the flickering screen, shutting him out. He abandoned every inclination to draw near.

Late that night, lying side by side, he felt worn and haggard, as if he had gone through some great ordeal. The darkness was gathering more densely around them, pressing down with its weight. They hugged their silences separately, encapsulated, as if silence was something they prized.

After a while, Kian Teck cleared his throat, as though unaccustomed to and apprehensive of his own voice, and asked, "Is anything wrong?"

"No," she replied. "Nothing." But there was a catch in her voice.

He let it go at that. But for a long time he could not sleep, his eyes opened to the interminable night.

When he did, he dreamt. First, of his children. They were babies with huge, imploring eyes and emaciated limbs, crying piteously in hunger, their cries piercing his very being. He couldn't bear to hear them crying, and involuntarily his strong hands circled their small throats to stop their cries, gripping tighter and tighter. He woke up with a jerk, his heart thumping, his brow damp with sweat. For a while, he tried to stay awake; he didn't want to sleep in case the dream resumed. But he did fall asleep, and dreamt another dream. This time, he was walking by a deserted seashore in a glittering dawn, and the crashing of the surf roared in his sleep.

6

The *muezzin* was wailing the *Azan*, calling the faithful to prayer, his ululation haunting the evening. Somewhere in the neighbourhood, a dog was barking.

Chan Kok Leong sat sipping coke at a coffee shop, listening inattentively to that plaintive strain of Arabic, the long trails of sound spiraling, dangling in the air, embellished and amplified by a public address system which crackled sandily — the intrusion of technology. There was a certain completeness about him, sitting alone by the old, marble-topped table with blue veins running across its cold surface. He watched the feeble light fading away and listened to the breeze sweeping down the street off invisible hills, propelling the cars and pedestrians, the world and time itself, in its secret language.

After a while, the *muezzin* concluded his wailing, the prolonged traceries of his voice, spun earlier in space, disentangled, lay sunken in the lake of memory.

Then the shiny, black face of Sundram floated towards Kok Leong. When he arrived within the light of the coffee shop, his hair gleamed, his squinting eyes, lucent pellets of tar.

Sundram sat opposite Kok Leong and ordered a cup of coffee. The coffee shop proprietor was a thin Chinese man in his sixties with thick hair cut close to his scalp, standing upright like a low stubble of *padi*, the gray tufts, new wire, rummaging in the crop.

Part One

Sundram sported an aquamarine-green T-shirt tucked into a pair of blue denim jeans. His bare arms lay like logs on the flawed white marble top of the coffee shop table. Kok Leong could not help looking at the fancy lettering, "A S", tattooed on the right forearm. Sundram's presence was atavistic, his neck and head exuding a smell, not at all repellent, of coconut oil, his skin glowing under the yellow of the electric light.

Kok Leong sensed a certain excitement, bordering on exuberance, in his friend. It was those eyes, squinting defiantly at the world, whose apertures permitted Kok Leong a peep into the inner vista of a mind strange-seeded with extraordinary thoughts, theorems, like a private hot house filled with exotic flora.

The coffee shop was in a shabby, pre-War shop house on the Bukit Timah Road, near the Singapore University. Most of the customers were labourers, gardeners, car park attendants and undergraduates.

The walls were a dirty green, the paint work peeling like flaps of skin. Any effort to refurbish the place had been abandoned long ago. Perhaps that was one of its attractions. There was familiarity in the hanging wooden wall clock with its hazy glass face, its golden-coloured pendulum disc swinging monotonously to and fro, measuring time with each swing. Other walls were hung with mirrors etched with faded inscriptions in Chinese characters, huge posters advertising soft drinks, and trade calendars. An enormous glass-fronted ice box stacked with slices of cut fruit and canned drinks stood against one wall, like a sci-fi effigy of some deity.

The two friends surveyed the early night outside, soft, opened to them like a ripened fruit, or a fresh wound. It belonged to them. Daytime moved with a different pulse, a pulse they seldom felt themselves in step with. The bright sun, the surfeit of nature's bounty, the sensual riches, paralysed rather than stimulated. Whereas the night was vast in its darkness, unknowable, harbouring fantasies.

"I did a big job!" Sundram confided. Sparks of excitement ignited his eyes.

Kok Leong looked at him questioningly.

"Two nights ago. House in Balmoral Road!"

"What happened?"

Sundram's answer was sudden, loud bark of laughter, breaking like cannon shots over the slovenliness of the small coffee shop.

"I took almost two thousand bucks! And an expensive watch! And jewels, man! Jewels!"

Kok Leong was impressed.

But that wasn't all. Sundram hadn't finished his accounting. He agonized a long while over it. How to describe what he had gone through? He felt stricken, like a dumb man with an overwhelming inspiration he could not articulate. There were flashes in his mind, like lightning, as Sundram relived the event in silence.

IT WAS EXACTLY 2.30 BY THE LUMINOUS HANDS OF HIS WRIST WATCH when Sundram stole into the shadowed garden of the large, two-storeyed bungalow. He slid quickly beneath a rain tree, stationing himself beside the thick trunk, his senses alerted to any danger. But he was certain his entry had gone unnoticed, and the quietness lay undisturbed like a still pool. He waited, knowing that patience was an essential attribute, an essential part of the entire action. Everything was essential in this operation, intrinsically, like the components of a perfect mechanism. His understanding of this was also perfect, so he could wait under that tree without impatience, experiencing a sense of mastery that perhaps only the artist possesses, gathering and ordering various diverse parts and faculties into a single, cohesive power.

The sweep of night sky, that drunken darkness, wrapped him in its cascading fall, while he steeled himself, standing very still in the whirling core of the universe with stars, clouds, trees gyring around in a fundamental

Part One

and harmonious choreography. He gave himself wholly, collaborated unequivocally, without any anxiety or doubt.

He donned a pair of dark glasses to hide his squint, pulled a black beret over his hair and moved towards the house, guided, impelled by a precision of intent, if not of actual thought — his actions essentially unpremeditated, but intuitively expert.

The large house itself lay under a propitious trance, invested with an air of conspiracy for the coming ritual, as if sharing with Sundram the force of an intoxication.

Positioning himself in one corner of the house, he made a routine check. The pencil torch and the switch-blade (very much like Kok Leong's Swiss knife) were secured in his back trouser pocket. He was ready.

The next instant, without hesitation at this crucial juncture when nerve can fail, he climbed the drain-pipe. He did this with all the discipline of a gymnast, his hands' clasp about the tubular pipe sure and strong, and his feet, in canvas shoes, wrapped around with a steady grip. Without any haste, he climbed upwards until he reached the upper floor and hauled himself over the ledge of the open window. And he was in.

He paused, motionless. It seemed to him that all was quiet except for the impulsive stampede in his chest. He waited patiently for this to subside. Each time, in a similar, smouldering darkness, the wild horses in his chest would ride out their vehemence, their urgent, lightning passion, and leave a gloss of sweat on his dark skin.

He looked about him, slowly. Glints from star and street lights showed on the knuckle of an armchair, the corner of a table, the porcelain rim of a flower pot. This must be some kind of verandah, he guessed. Sundram took out the knife and, pressing the mechanical catch, flicked the blade open. It emerged with a sharp, distinct click! It worked perfectly, hence could be trusted. For, in this activity, trustworthiness was equated with simplicity, with an unfussy functionalism. He held the knife in his right hand. In his left, the slim pencil torch with the fresh batteries. He switched this on. A circle of light fell near his feet, the brown-stained wood reflecting the moon of light on its varnished surface. He trained the small circle of light about, still standing by the window ledge. He felt a breeze blowing at him from the outside, but did not allow this to distract him.

The light fell on a set of wicker chairs with wide backs where the cane had been twisted and trained into various curlicue patterns, the tension of the arcs mastered by tiny nails. Sundram noted their intricate design without any emotion. He had little taste for fancy things. The light then found a low, glass-topped table with a red glass ashtray and a bowl of yellow orchids on it. A few indoor potted plants decorated a corner, arranged together to attain a green luxuriance. And then the pencil of light found the door which led within, into the dark bowels of the house.

When he was satisfied that he was familiar with the surrounding terrain, he moved silently, adroitly, towards the door, meandering around the furniture. As he moved, the light threw shadows, magnified, of the chairs and the potted plants against the walls, the shadows moving in an opposite direction to the light; spurious, ghostly figures, sometimes dissolving, sometimes reassembling together like partners in a macabre dance, fused in an eerie collaboration, on the walls around him.

He reached the door and gingerly tried the brass knob. With a gentle turn, it opened. He stepped quickly inside the inner living room. Again, without moving, he trained his torch around. It was a large room, luxuriously furnished, with soft sofas upholstered in rich, flower-patterned fabrics. Thick, hand-woven silk rugs, both Persian and Chinese, were strewn on the polished hardwood floor.

Sundram took his time, examining the room minutely. There was a teakwood cabinet with a door of clear paned glass, in which gleamed bottles of liquor, whose rich, warm colours almost seemed to reveal their bouquet and taste; a floor-to-ceiling wooden bookshelf filled with the multicoloured bindings of hard cover books ran the entire length of one wall, and a stereo console was built into a brown-stained, wooden sideboard. The other walls were adorned with paintings and objets d'art. Sundram evaluated the worth of every article, selecting mentally, without rush, what he was going to take away.

Suddenly, voices from within a room at the far end disrupted his casual perusal, and then a shaft of light shone from under the door of what he presumed was the master bedroom. Sundram moved swiftly to one side, but before he could get very far the bedroom door opened and someone switched on the living room light.

Sundram stepped forward, brandishing the switch-blade. He found himself confronting a plump, old Chinese man with rumpled gray hair, wearing a pair of blue-and-white striped pyjamas and gaping at him in horror.

As he stared at the intruder, a broken word began to form on the old man's lips. It was a moment charged with challenge as the two men stood face to face in the opulent room. They both knew that either they would have to fight, or else one of them would have to give in — it was as simple, as merciless, as that. They had to make up their minds.

Sundram would not give in, that was plain enough, and this constituted victory, for the other man immediately capitulated. Sundram could now master the other without force, but with only the threat of it.

"Keep quite!" Sundram commanded. The vanquished's mouth opened weakly, his pink gums glistening with saliva, but he made no sound. He just stood there, trembling pathetically.

At that very moment a shrill, wavering female voice called from within the bedroom behind them, and the old man made a half turn of his head in that direction.

"Go in! Tell her to shut up. Or else ..." Sundram threatened gruffly, flashing the knife.

The old man obeyed, retreating into the bedroom. Sundram followed and quickly bolted the door behind him. The sharp sound of the iron bolt shooting in must have startled the woman who let out a cry.

"Quiet!" Sundram barked.

She looked at her husband with fright in her eyes, and then at the knife in Sundram's hand. She started to whimper softly, and pulled up the bed sheet as though to protect herself.

"Keep quiet and no one gets hurt," Sundram said softly. In the same tone he asked the old man, "Where're your neckties?"

Unable to understand this unexpected question, the quivering old man regressed into a deeper silence. Such a strange request! Ordinarily it might be considered funny, but now it only served to increase his terror. For a lack of comprehension accentuates terror.

"Where're your neckties?" Sundram repeated, a little more loudly this time.

Still unable to comprehend, the old man affected a more docile stance so that his acquiescence could not be mistaken by this sinister stranger.

"I want *neckties*," Sundram demanded, raising his voice slightly. "Where you keep them?"

The old man pointed with a trembling finger. "That closet ..."

Sundram walked across and opened the closet door. A row of neckties were draped over a string tacked across the inside of the door. He pulled out a couple. Next he opened a drawer and found a pile of handkerchiefs, all neatly folded into squares, uniformly white.

"Don't be afraid. I got to tie you up, understand?" he told them conversationally.

He went up to the old man and tied his hands firmly behind him. Then he went to the woman and tied her up. Her muscles were soft. Lax flesh, which had long ago surrendered its firmness to age. He could feel the underlying bones of her arms, like slender pipes. Her skin was dry,

Part One

spotted with brown age freckles, shedding fine, powdery flakes because of his firm grip. He tied her hands behind her back and then stuffed a handkerchief into her mouth. His face was very close to her's, and he peered into her eyes, their pupils dilated with fear. She stared back at him in awe.

Sundram turned to the old man, asked: "Where you keep money and jewellery?"

The old man, still standing up as if he were a private on parade, remained silent. His wife, though, made sounds, muffled by the gag in her mouth.

"Tell me quickly!" Sundram hissed. He paused, scowling malevolently to let his words sink in, "Or you'll get hurt!" He brought the knife up to the old man's face, the sharp tip of steel touching the soft knob of his nose.

"It's in my wallet, in that drawer over there," he whispered.

"Keep quite! One shout, you and your old woman will feel my knife, understand?" Sundram growled, frowning horribly.

The old man nodded meekly.

Sundram went up to the drawer and found the brown leather wallet without difficulty. He quickly flipped it open and fished out some notes, about two hundred dollars. He stuffed them into his trouser pocket, threw the wallet onto the floor by the bed where it landed just in front of the old man.

"There must be more in the house. Tell me where?" Sundram snapped.

"That's all we have. It's the truth," the old man wavered.

Without warning, Sundram gave him a hard slap across the face which nearly sent him reeling.

The old woman was trying to say something through her gag. Sundram looked down at her sternly. He thought for a moment. Making his decision, he stuffed a fistful of handkerchiefs into the old man's mouth, that weak oval with the bald, wet, pink gums; he had removed his dentures earlier, no doubt before going to bed.

Sundram then turned to the old woman lying on the large, white-sheeted bed. "I bet you know where the money and jewellery are hidden," he said. "Now, I'm going to kill your husband unless you tell me where they're kept. I'll really do it. So, don't lie, or try to fool me. You understand?" he threatened.

She nodded quickly, like a frightened bird.

"I'm going to take the handkerchief from your mouth. You're not going to scream. You know better than to do that. And you're going to tell me quickly where the things are."

Again, she nodded.

"Good!" Sundram removed the wad of wet cloth, stringy with saliva. "Tell me!"

"The money's in a tin box behind the shoe boxes. Bottom of the closet," she answered breathlessly.

"And the jewels?"

"My dressing table, right drawer. A thin red leather case ..."

"I hope you're not lying."

"I'm not lying," she protested and began to weep, so Sundram stuffed up her mouth again.

He went to the locations she gave, and found the money and jewellery. Satisfied with this haul, he stuffed the money into his pockets and wedged the case of jewellery into the waist band of his trousers.

Before leaving the room, he warned them against raising an alarm, then switched off the lights and closed the door. Using the pencil torch to guide him he found his way downstairs to the hall doorway. He opened the front door gently, stepped out, and walked away from the big house.

Sundram removed his dark glasses and took off the beret. He walked to his motorbike which he'd parked earlier in the secluded compound of a bungalow on the next street, hidden behind a thick bamboo hedge. He

Part One

wheeled the bike quietly onto the road, started it, and rode away.

The bike charged down the road, the wind lovely, working against a feverishness which had suddenly risen in him. Torrents brushed past as he slammed into the air, the engine pummeling the night with its roar, hurtling down street after street as if reaching for a jewelled hinterland. In fact, he had entered another frontier the moment he had confronted the old man with his flashing blade and realized the fear he had evoked. Suddenly, he burst into loud, jubilant laughter.

After a while, Sundram grew conscious that the black, unremitting sky had become eroded by an ambivalence of light, a signal that the night must soon dissolve into dawn, into light which cannot be withheld. A state of equilibrium settled into Sundram's mind and he turned in the direction of home, acquiescent, satisfied.

RETURNING TO THE PRESENT, Sundram found Kok Leong still gazing at him avidly. Although he knew that his friend wanted to hear more about that night, Sundram realized that the nature of his adventure was such that unless the totality of the experience could be conveyed, it would be worse than pointless to try.

"So what happened, man?" Kok Leong asked, impatient, excited.

"I broke into this house. I was discovered. So I threatened them with my knife."

"You used your knife?"

"I had to tie them up and gag them too. Then forced them to tell me where they hid the loot."

"You used *force*?" Kok Leong's voice rose, hardly able to contain his excitement.

"Sure, I socked the old guy, told them I was going to stab the bastard, then the woman got frightened and squealed."

"You actually *stabbed* the old man?"

"No, lah! What for? I already got what I wanted."

"You *didn't* use your knife?"

"Only to frighten them. And they sure were frightened like hell," Sundram said, laughing.

"So they were frightened of the knife?"

"Sure, man. Come! Tonight I take you out. We go and eat some nice curry, and afterwards maybe go to a girlie bar or a disco and smoke some *ganja*. I brought some *really* good stuff."

Sundram was already on his feet. He paid for the drinks and strode out like a Colossus to his motorbike. Kok Leong followed, mesmerized. He sat pillion as they rode into the oncoming night.

So Sundram *had* used the knife, Kok Leong thought, excitedly. The glint of the stars was like the glint of his own knife. Yes, his knife, cold, hard, could outshine all the stars in the bloody universe!

7

When Ong Kian Teck jogged around the park, he was assailed by the rich fragrance of freshly cut grass thickening the late sunlit air. He inhaled deeply, savouring the smell. A big brown dog lay in simple contentment across the footpath, and Kian Teck had to manoeuvre his feet around it. Let sleeping dogs lie.

His children were playing beneath a tall rain tree, teasing with tender finger tips the creeping touch-me-nots which grew in stubborn clusters amongst the fat, green grass. The boys were fascinated by the tiny leaves which folded back reflexively at the merest touch. Shy, or sly? Kian Teck himself had often wondered, when he was a child.

His calf muscles were beginning to hurt and his breathing was becoming conscious and laboured. He decided to rest.

All the while Old Ho had been sitting on one of the stone benches. Kian Teck hadn't seen him for some time and felt slightly guilty about his indifference. He approached the old man.

"How are you?" Kian Teck called out.

Old Ho looked up at him with his large, morose eyes, not answering.

"Haven't seen you here for some time. How's life treating you?"

Old Ho gestured emptily.

Kian Teck realized he needn't have asked.

"Better take your boys home," Old Ho finally said, gruffly, then loudly cleared his throat, thick with phlegm. Kian Teck watched the act of swallowing and felt a responsive saltiness on his own palate.

"See that group of young Malays?" Old Ho pointed. "They're out to make trouble."

Kian Teck turned around and saw a group of five Malay boys. They appeared harmless enough to him. "Why should they want to cause trouble here?"

"Because of me!" Old Ho said, breathlessly. As he spoke, short gasps of air were wrung from his musty lungs, smelling of the stale sweetness of his diabetes. Kian Teck half expected a visible, viscous, green mist to emerge each time a breath was forced out of the old man.

"See that boy with his arm in a sling?" Old Ho continued.

Kian Teck nodded.

"Yesterday afternoon, I saw him fiddling with my plastic bag which I'd strapped to the back seat of my bicycle. Caught him red-handed! So I shouted *'Pencuri ! Pencuri !* Thief! Thief!' — and ran after him. He ran away very quickly and I had no hope of catching up. But he fell down by the drain outside the park. As you can see, he must've hurt his arm then. Today he returns with his gang. Earlier, they came and taunted me, calling me *'Dirty China Kwee'*. I was alone, and scared. They took the small torch from my shirt pocket and threw it into the pond, laughing all the time. I could do nothing. As you can see, they're still here, waiting to get me. So you better take your children away."

"Don't worry. There're so many people here, they won't dare to do anything. Anyway, if you really think they'll create more trouble, why don't you go home now?"

"But I can't! It's not time yet! And if the supervisor comes to check and I'm not here ..."

"Surely you can explain to him?"

"But you don't understand! He doesn't like me! He tries to find fault with me all the time. I've always been polite and respectful, even though he's not very well educated. I've always done my best. But he simply doesn't like me!"

"Perhaps you're mistaken. After all, he has no cause to dislike you."

"No, you're only trying to be kind. Nobody likes me," Old Ho whined.

Again, Kian Teck tried to reassure him. He felt both contempt and pity for the old man.

"What shall I do, Mr. Ong? Should I make a report to the police? But if I do, they might return another day and get me ..."

"Perhaps you should make a report, I really don't know," Kian Teck offered. This was hardly helpful. Old Ho's obvious dejection and fear embarrassed him.

Soon afterwards, he called out to his children and went away, leaving the old man to his tormentors. Somehow, although the sun was still shining brightly, the park had taken on an air of danger: Old Ho had contaminated it with his anxiety.

LI LIAN WAS IN A SOMBRE MOOD. He was about to tell her about Old Ho, but she ignored him and stalked off to the bathroom with the children, a firm set to her mouth. Kian Teck felt like someone who has gone to see a friend off at the railway station, but arrives just too late; he can see the train pulling away, and he has lost his chance to say a few warm words, which now jostle in his head.

He fetched a can of cold beer from the fridge and moved towards the open balcony, sat down on the rocking chair with the sententiousness of a lone drinker, and removed his shoes and socks. His naked feet look red and babyish. He wriggled his litter of toes.

An army of dark clouds had amassed like thick smoke, piling atop the dipping sun to make a ceremonial pyre of the residue of the day. He could almost hear the roar and crackle of flames. In the garden below, shadows had returned in a silent crawl to the base of the trees, seeking shelter within the greater shade. To the oncoming, wished-for, ministering darkness, Kian Teck protested: "I've committed no crime! So why? Why?"

The family sat down to a quiet, quick dinner. Afterwards, the children ensconced themselves on the sofa to watch TV. It was a one-way transmission, not a communication, and Kian Teck often felt irresponsible for allowing his children to be so exposed. There they sat, like zombies. But he found it hard to control the situation, and became more or less resigned to it, not without a twinge of guilt. Weak, was he? Probably, probably.

Li Lian was washing up in the kitchen, the tinkling sounds of dishes knocking against each other coming through to him as a litany of complaints. So he retreated, can of beer in hand, out to the balcony again. He reclined on the rocker and lit a cigarillo.

A low, half moon had risen over the trees and the distant roof tops. From the garden, various insects made their nocturnal cries, swarming upwards, these sonic pulsations of the tropical night, kindling thoughts and desires.

Then an insect screeched from the bushes its lone, operatic cry: such an immensity of sound from so small a creature, as if its whole being were being transformed into sonic waves! Kian Teck could almost feel its throes. With eyes half closed, he sighed to the night as if in pain.

But he wasn't in pain now, was he? Whatever it was, it didn't fit into the definition of pain. Unlike Old Ho, for instance, or poor Robert Sim, the accounts controller in his office, whose only son, aged two-and-a-half, had been killed in a motor accident the previous week. That look on Robert's face when he returned to the office, drained and abstracted in shock, *that* registered pain. Recalling that face, Kian Teck was ashamed to confess, made him feel better! Shocking! Perverse! Indeed, indeed. But he had discovered that sometimes, when one is confronted with a host of problems, there is a certain measure of solace to be found in

Part One

knowing about the pain, the plight, of others. Terrible? Yes. But true. One reads about a bereavement, or about a bankruptcy suit, or about some poor sod being given a stiff prison sentence, and thinks, "My God, I'm glad *I'm* not in that poor bugger's shoes!" And, reading about a suicide in the Sunday papers at a picnic by the beach, with the sounds of life all around you, the sun caressing your back with its golden warmth, how you congratulate yourself with: "At least I've not been driven into doing *THAT!*" Without any sense of shame, you may even be patting yourself on the back, proud of having a stiffer spine. And you return to the picnic and the joviality with renewed vigour. Yes, there is always someone bearing a heavier burden, someone suffering a pain more extreme than one's own, and in comparison (a ceaseless human passion, this), one is relatively better off, or less worse off — they're both the same.

But is pain necessary?

Famine and starvation, and mass graves found in Cyprus, and Typhoon Fifi killing one thousand people in Honduras. What cosmic pain!

He tilted the can, now light as a shell, to his lips and savoured the last drops of the rich, tasty beer. He rocked gently a while, trying to make up his mind about whether or not to open another. The lightness of the hollow can in his hands helped him decide. He went into the kitchen. Li Lian was no longer there. She was watching TV with the boys.

There was a perfume-like scent in the air. Li Lian must have sprayed the kitchen with Sheltox, that canister of insecticide. Only atoms in the air, yet so lethal to insects — even big, hard-shelled cockroaches! And man made it smell like flowers. Consider to what degree man sinks — to infuse insect-killing sprays with the smell of sweet flowers! To kill with an agreeable scent! What perversity! What a ludicrous technology!

Kian Teck quickly took a fresh beer from the fridge and returned to his rocking chair out on the balcony. He rocked slowly, opened the cold can and drank a bit of the beer (bad for the liver!) and then lit up another cigarillo (bad for the lungs!). He caressed the tube of rolled, brown tobacco leaves with almost a loving hand. The thick smoke rose, aromatic, poisoning his lungs with deliciousness. He considered it all right (and with what gravity he did that!) for a mature man, who knows what he wants, and the attendant risks he's taking, to kill himself by what he ingests and inhales. At least it's a conscious act.

Rocking gently to and fro, he suddenly laughed softly, the sound actually more of a chuckle than a laugh. He remembered having read somewhere that scientists were alarmed by the discovery that the atomized particles from all the atomizing, aerosol sprays — insecticides, hair sprays, deodorants for the armpits, anti-perspirants, etc. — had gradually and relentlessly infiltrated into the upper atmosphere, the ozone layer, lying there like (he imagined) a glistening film of perfumery; and that this film of atomized particles allows a greater penetration of radiation by the sun, with unforeseen effects on mankind. So each time we spray our kitchens, or our hair, or our armpits, or any other part of our anatomy, we're actually adding to this accumulating layer of various pleasant scents that glisten there in the upper atmosphere and which, one day, will harm us all. Maybe our hair will fall off, or there'll be a great increase in skin cancer. Imagine! What cosmic humour!

The children ran out to kiss him goodnight. He hugged their small, firm bodies. After they had gone into their bedroom, Li Lian went in to read them a bedtime story. The TV was switched off. The sudden silence washed against him then, like cool water. He allowed his mind to disperse, to wander, but it could find no destination, nowhere to go to, and soon returned, all in the time it took to break a dream. It returned to inform him: "I am where I am, I am only what I am," again and again. Like a mantra.

LI LIAN CAME OUT ONTO THE BALCONY and stood there looking out at the night, her back towards him. After a while, without turning around, she asked, "I want to know what's going to happen to us?"

A commonplace question, he reasoned, but nevertheless, one which was impossible to answer. Some questions are like that. So he made no attempt to answer, truly not knowing what to say.

The few seconds before she spoke again seemed abnormally long, as if time had been stretched and warped out of its usual sequence.

"What's going to happen to us? Can't you even tell me?" she repeated.

Kian Teck stubbed out his cigarillo, as if he was mustering himself, as if he meant to be serious. He thought for a moment before saying, "I don't know."

She gave a short laugh, shaking her small head from side to side. It made him feel bad, inadequate, as if he had failed to meet some responsibility rightly his.

"I've given up wondering why," she said, shaking her head from side to side again. "I've given up, you may say."

"But I've done nothing! I've committed nothing wrong," he protested.

"If you mean adultery, I believe you," she said, quickly.

He thought he caught a trace of sarcasm.

"Then, why're you complaining?"

"Forget it," she said, as though his question was unnecessary, if not offensive; it wasn't worthy of a reply.

"Anyway, since you've taken my faithfulness for granted, what're you griping about? I've done nothing *wrong*."

"Your silences!" she hissed. Her fierceness disconcerted him. The air was charged with danger now.

He knew that, and yet, inexorably, he fueled it by laughing. "Ha! That's beautiful! So, I've committed the sin of silence! So *that's* my great crime?"

He could not see her face, yet suspected that her pale cheeks had flushed pink, her lips swollen, full and quivering, her eyes hot with incipient tears.

Still looking out, and as if addressing the few distant stars, she remarked,

A Dance of Moths

"Though it may seem funny to you, your silence *has* fouled up our relationship. Maybe you don't consider that a crime."

Slightly remorseful, he said softly, "I can't explain it, can't explain myself. My silence ... how or why ... I myself don't know."

"I'm left out, shut out completely. You're so tightly wrapped up I can't come near you. I feel useless, unwanted."

"I'm sorry. I don't want us to be like this. I don't mean to hurt you. More than anything, you must believe me when I say that. Only, it seems to be beyond my control. I'm helpless."

"Can't get through to you," Li Lian muttered, almost to herself. "Tried and tried, but there's this impenetrable wall, this great silence. I feel always outside, always on the periphery. There's a barrier I can't cross into your very private world. I'm excluded from it."

Kian Teck sighed. If only he could explain it to her, to himself, but the whole thing was beyond his own understanding. He could feel the chasm yawning between them, and yet he remained seated in his rocking chair.

"Why, K.T.? Why?"

Again he sighed. "I don't know. I really don't know. Can't you believe me when I say that I can't account for it?" he asked her, despair tingeing his voice.

"But *why* can't you share it with me?"

"You think I don't want to? I hate it! Hate this ... this silence, this ... I don't even know what to call it!" he said with some heat, rising from his rocking chair to walk towards her by the balcony railings.

"A thing with no name," she remarked ironically, shaking her head from side to side for the third time (an action which affected him more than her words). "Yet it could change our lives! Seems incredible, but it *has* changed our lives, hasn't it? I don't understand it. Don't understand anything any more."

"I don't love anyone else. You know that."

She gave an abbreviated laugh, apologising quickly. "I'm sorry. Can't help myself. You see, I find it rather funny. Tell me, is that a roundabout way of saying that you love me? Or perhaps I should take your words at their face value — that you're not in love with anybody, including me? Tell me!" And when he didn't reply immediately, asked again, "*Why* don't you tell me?"

"You know I love you?"

"Then why don't you show it? Why don't I feel loved?"

"Don't I show it?"

"When? When?"

"You mean I *never* show it?"

"When? In the bedroom? When we make love? Now that's a funny word too, 'To make love.' You think that just because you make love to me, it means that you love me?"

"Oh shit!"

"No, don't be angry. There's no reason to be angry. You can calm down and tell me. Why are you so angry?"

"You're being unfair."

"Why?"

"What are you trying to do?"

"Get at the truth?"

"Get at *what* truth?"

"I don't know."

"Well, I must say this is just great, really great! You know that?" he exclaimed.

"You're angry with me again. I don't mean to make you angry. Please don't get angry."

"It's my turn to ask you now. What's going to happen to us? It doesn't depend entirely on me, you know," he said.

This time she turned to face him. There was a pinched tension around her small mouth, her eyes glittering with a bemused defiance. She studied him clinically, as if she was doing so for the first time in her life. He was discomfited by it, but looked her straight in the eye. The pinched lines around her mouth relaxed into the ghost of a smile, as she answered: "I don't know what's going to happen to us. It seems neither of us know." After a short, teasing pause, she asked, "What do you intend doing about it?"

"It's not up to me to decide."

"So you think that *I* should decide?" she asked, pitching her voice higher, her strange amusement almost erupting into overt laughter.

By now both of them were intent on hurting each other, relentless and reckless in the execution of their quarrel.

"If it pleases you, why don't we let the devil decide for us?" Kian Teck asked, sarcastically.

"But where is he?"

"Oh, I'm sure he's around here somewhere, probably quite close by."

"I thought you're the man of the house, therefore *you* make the decisions."

"Not any more. We men have abdicated. Haven't you joined your sisters in the women's lib movement yet?"

"Up till now, frankly, I haven't had the time."

"Well, now you have. The time."

"Meaning what?"

"Any bloody thing you like!" he exploded.

This time, Li Lian remained silent. She felt they had crossed a certain line she had perhaps earlier desired, because it might mean a change, bring about an improvement, but now that the given moment had arrived, she hesitated, even wanting to recoil from it. It was a good wife's sense of practicality, comprising both her strength and, in a way, her weakness. She abandoned the quarrel.

Her silence left his own simmering belligerence in suspension (they were near to annihilating each other, were they not?). He was ready to counter-attack when the expected assault did not materialize. Also, when she chose silence, her eyes, with hardly a flicker, lost their hard glitter and grew soft. And though poised, he had no heart to attack, even if he did not desire a truce either. A truce would make their quarrel a farce, a small marital tiff. So, what was he to do with this abeyance, this stasis of flung, hurling words?

Even the insects had ceased their chirruping. Was this peace then? He felt diminished and flat. They stood apart on the balcony, emptied of something, they both believed at that moment, to be irretrievable.

It was over. Although the night air was warm and mellow, Li Lian shivered slightly, like a rippling stream tossed silver, guarded by the moon in the deep privacy of the jungle. It was not what Kian Teck had expected — torrents of recriminations tumbling, thunderous, like a heavy fall of water crashing onto his head, onto the hard carapace of his un-feeling. His soul shrunken, he felt immeasurably sad.

It was over. Neither of them made any move towards a reconciliation, to reestablish communion, intimacy. The moon shone above them, a ghostly crescent.

He walked towards the entrance to the living room, empty can of beer in his right hand. "I'm going out," he said, without any invitation in his tone.

She leaned slightly over the balcony, looking down at the airy space above the dark garden, seeming not to hear him at all.

Kian Teck turned quickly into the apartment. He dumped the empty can into the kitchen bin, collected his wallet from the bedroom, put on his shoes, and without once looking back at his wife, walked out and closed the door.

He pressed the summons button for the lift, shifting his weight from one foot to another, feeling a certain tension, a certain unsettledness. He was eager to be out.

A Dance of Moths

The ride down (abandon control all those who descend), the whoosh of it, caused a fluttering inside his head. Crossing the garden to his car, he didn't look up to see if Li Lian was still standing there, leaning out. As the car shot out of the driveway, he gave vent to pent up laughter, laughing to himself in his shut-in, air-conditioned car, not so much out of glee, as from a feeling of foolishness.

KIAN TECK SAT ALONE IN THE PEBBLE BAR, his head resting on the backrest of the cane chair, his eyelids half-closed, his lips loosely arranged around a languid smile. The pianist was playing "September in the rain." The notes descended like rain drops: cool, diamonded. Earlier, feeling lonely and lost, he had phoned Peter Low to join him. Now he waited, hidden in a corner, like a man who did not know his place. He appraised a couple of drunks, jocular in their happiness, and thought that he might as well be consummate in his drinking.

After a while, he began to feel quite at home in that green room, where voices whirled and pitched, incessant as the sea, back and forth, back and forth, its waves washing against his mind. Yes, he felt quite at home there, in a room which no one could rightly claim his own. He was relaxed, beer-blissed.

Presently, when the pianist completed his set, the band arrived, trooping in like a pack of boy scouts. An extravagant outpouring of music soon flooded the stuffy room. Shock wave upon shock wave of loud sound penetrated Kian Teck's skull, almost physically, like a pneumatic drill. In time, however, he got used to it.

"Tie a yellow ribbon round the old oak tree."

Everybody joined in and sang, gay, abandoned, with a hint of frenzy, the songs littering the brain like confetti. Still they did not quite reach, touch the real source, the soul, located beyond the translucent wrappings of their singing. When Peter strode towards him the atmosphere changed for Kian Teck, the intricate, delicate tissues of its being snapping like coloured paper ribbons when a body crashes across their soft tangle.

There was a leer in Peter's eyes. The moment he sat down, sliding into his seat like a playful bear, he confided, "There's a juicy one over there, by the piano bar."

Kian Teck turned to look at an attractive Eurasian girl with lanky legs and a generous figure sheathed in a tight yellow dress. The material was silky, with a sheen like a glazed snake's skin.

"Ooooooh, how I'd love to ..." and smack, smack, went Peter's lips wetly, swollen with lust. Peter's lechery was highly contagious. He made Kian Teck suddenly feel horny.

Peter ordered a Black Label-and-water from a waiter, then, turning to Kian Teck, who was distracted by the girl in yellow, remarked, "No point drooling, man. She's stuck with her boyfriend: that *Ang-moh kwee* in the blue batik shirt."

Kian Teck's romantic ardour (for that's what he would have liked to call it) was dampened, and he felt a sense of loss, a deprivation. (Well, we can't always have what we want, can we? But why not? Why not?) Sighing, he tore his eyes (and mind) away from the girl and regarded Peter. That bloody bastard looked so settled there, so much more at home than Kian Teck could ever be. He had a certain naturalness, which made him seem never out of place, anywhere, in any situation.

"Well, tell us why you're all alone tonight," Peter asked, as if there were two or more Peters present, in the manner of Her Britannic Majesty, or of His Holiness the Pope, or of any cheap, dime-a-dozen, self-inflated president of a newly independent, impossible-to-govern country. "C'mon! Tell us!"

Should he? Kian Teck wondered. Oh well, nothing to lose. "Li Lian and I broke up."

His own expression was befittingly solemn, while Peter's broke by perceptible degrees into hilarity, that damned, insensitive prick!

"Hoo! Hoo! Hoo!" he hooted, laughing raucously. Needless to say, his laughter was of the loud, crude, everybody-turning-around-to-see, variety. Asking, "What happened?" when he could speak at last.

Kian Teck had no desire to answer that. Not after Peter's despicable reaction. He maintained a dignified silence.

"What happened? Did you finally leave Li Lian for another woman, you devil you? Hoo! Hoo! Hoo!"

Kian Teck shook his head, still silent, trying hard to keep calm.

"Hoo! Hoo! Hoo! So *she* left you for another bloke!" slapping his big (the better to ... etc.) thighs.

"Screw you!" Kian Teck exclaimed.

The whiskey arrived. Peter swirled the glass in his hand, the russet liquid dashing against the geometrical ice cubes. When it got sufficiently chilled, he drank it with a glucking sound, like a basin of water draining down a pipe, his Adam's apple riding up and down.

One more, the music throbbed against them —

> "So goodbye yellow brick road,
> Where the hounds of society howl.
> You can't plant me in your penthouse,
> I'm going back to my plough."

Peter contemplated the pool of russet in his glass, and occasionally glanced up at Kian Teck. After a long pause, he resumed, more seriously, "What really happened, K.T.?"
"I don't know, Li Lian's been upset of late. Over what, I don't know for sure. Something to do with me, of course. Shit! I don't know ..." He was vexed. At his rambling speech, his clumsy explanation. His *attempt* to explain. And to a clown!

But immediately he felt chastened at his own conceit. Yes! Who the hell did he think he was? What made him think he was so special? And

Part One

who gave him the right to judge Peter? Clown? He *himself* was the clown!

Peter offered him a cigarette. Kian Teck lit it, the smell of scorched sulphur smarting his nostrils. He held on to the burning match, watching the flame advancing down the stick, the stiff wood blackening and curling. The flame died just before reaching his finger tips, the pulpy flesh waxen, like a corpse's.

"The two of you seemed such a happy couple!"

Kian Teck laughed. "Seemed," he said, giving another quick, nervous laugh and then shaking his head slowly from side to side. Like Li Lian, he suddenly remembered.

"I guess one mustn't judge by surfaces alone ..." Peter ventured.

Yes, thou shalt not judge. At all. At all. Judge not and ye shalt not ...

"But you and Li Lian seemed so close! You know ... well-matched. To be honest, I rather admired your marriage. I mean, you were so self-sufficient, the two of you. As for myself ..." Here Peter flourished his hand in illustration, in emphasis. "Well, you know how different I am. I simply will *not* be tied down to one woman. No, sir! But still, I admired your marriage."

"And all of us other married guys envied you *your* freedom, the way you flaunt your women around, as if it doesn't matter. I still wonder how you do it, how you bring it off, you bastard," Kian Teck replied, trying to sound flippant.

Peter gave a little laugh, at once delighted, because the conversation had at last turned round to a topic he was always familiar with, happy with. Namely, himself. He had attempted to rôle play the part of friend earlier on, turning on the seriousness, pumping out sympathy for his friend's problems, but all the while knowing that he'd far rather not be around. He had found it boring, to be honest. A bit soppy. Morbid. Anyway, he was glad to change the subject, and felt sure it would do his friend good as well. Keep him from moping, the poor shit. So Peter sniffed his whiskey, his knobby nose dipping beneath the rim of the glass. Inhaling that rich bouquet recharged him, kindling a twinkle in his eyes.

"It's all a question of honesty," he propounded, puffing out his chest so that his flesh stretched against the fabric of his shirt. "A question of being true to yourself." He waited patiently for the response which, expert actor that he was (and there's no greater actor than a lover), he expected, like a cue.

And it came.

"What do you mean?" Kian Teck asked.

Peter was delighted. His eyes twinkled the more.

"Shit!" he exclaimed. "Everyone, everything conspires to trap you into becoming what you're not. I mean the usual prick-less, ball-less married man, always snivelling back to his wife, chasing the occasional piece of ass on the side, on the sly. I say, *shit!* Be honest. Be yourself. In my case, it happens that I'm a lover, man, so *let* the whole world know. See what the fuck they can do about it. After a while, you'll find that the world accepts you on your own terms."

"How does your wife react to your playing around, *that's* what I would like to know?"

Peter was expecting that too, of course. Another cue right on time. "Oh, she knows about it all right, like everyone else, but she says nothing. I don't hide it from her, and she doesn't dig. So, it's like an acceptance. It's peace. Of course," he added, pausing to sip his drink, keeping his audience waiting for the punch line, "you must have the nerve!"

Peter's right, Kian Teck thought, a quick jigger of excitement dancing in his mind — one must have the nerve! Whereas he himself had lost his nerve! And with it, a certain sureness of touch, essential to deal with situations, with life itself. When one has the nerve, one rides situations with a natural gracefulness, with an appealing effortlessness. To lose it is to become uncertain, clumsy. Is to fall. But he wouldn't grant Peter the gratification of this admission.

"What you mean is, a thick skin, don't you?" he said.

Peter laughed swaggeringly. "And that too, why not? A thick skin doesn't do anybody any harm, I think. On the contrary, it's the thin-skinned ones who're to be pitied. They get hurt all the time."

However, Kian Teck could not to let him get away with that. "It seems to me that a thick skin also prevents you from sensing how you're hurting others."

"Maybe. But *you're* not the one who's smarting. That's preferable, isn't it?"

Again, Kian Teck wouldn't let this argument pass without comment. "Perhaps," he paused, as though thinking this one out seriously, "your wife accepts you for what you are because she's a masochist?" he asked, poker-faced.

"And I'm a sadist?"

"Yes!"

Peter laughed, but there was no braggadocio this time, only a hint of anger. "Well, and what are *you*? A sadist or a masochist? More likely the latter, I should say."

It was getting ugly. It had started off innocently enough, two old friends teasing and jabbing at each other like school boys, but now a dark shadow was about to fall, threatening to make them despise and fight each other. Time to stop. Kian Teck was the first to step back from the abyss. "I'm going for a pee," he said, rising. "I'll order us another round."

"Sure. And get me a pack of Dunhill, will you?" Peter asked, also making his retreat.

"OK!"

Friends again.

As Kian Teck approached the girl in yellow, he slowed down deliberately. Her face, skin and hair shone with a vitality that thrilled and attracted him. He caught her eye and she smiled with a casual friendliness. Then he saw his own reflection briefly in the looking glass wall. It startled him. His image appeared eager, expectant and lost. Such a stray-dog look.

At the counter he ordered the drinks and a packet of Dunhill cigarettes. He pushed against the clear glass door and emerged into the open air by the swimming pool.

Kian Teck remembered that when the Singapura Hotel first opened, some time in the early 'Sixties, it was the "in" place, and he used to go there with Li Lian and Guan Hock, who was a baby at that time, on Saturday afternoons or Sunday mornings for a swim. They had joined the Poolside Club. In those days, one had an uninterrupted view of the sky from the patio. Now, newer, bigger structures on either side partially blocked out the view. Time and progress. The fickle crowd no longer considered it the "in" place, but were drawn towards posher, more expensive places: the Shangri la, the Mandarin. These luxury hotels are grander than any palace: thick carpets, ornate glass chandeliers, sumptuous decor, and muzak perpetually filling air already charged with the smell of wealth. How man craves luxury and grandeur! Everyman yearning to live like an emperor for a few days, or for a day, even if he has to pay through his nose for the privilege.

Kian Teck walked into the toilet to pee and then went to wash his hands, but the old toilet attendant was once again a few steps ahead of him and had already turned on the water faucets. Kian Teck squirted a few drops of liquid detergent soap onto his hands and immersed them in the warm water. The attendant held a large paper towel in readiness for him. After drying his hands, Kian Teck dropped a fifty-cent coin into the saucer by the sink.

"Thank you, s-s-sir!"

Kian Teck nodded. He had never felt comfortable in the presence of the handicapped: stutterers, cripples, the blind, the one-eyed man, the squint-eyed, the cleft palate, the deaf and dumb, the dwarf. Ever since his childhood, when he was told that it was rude to stare at the unfortunate, he had tried to avoid them. For instance, when he had to speak to a person with a squint, he never knew which eye to look at, which was the good eye that regarded him, holding him in its field of vision, and which was the other, focussed elsewhere, at a corner of a room, or a window curtain. He always had the feeling that he was looking at the wrong eye, a mistake which, he imagined, angered the person with the squint.

Anyway, Kian Teck, able and whole of body (though not perfect of course), always felt guilty and ashamed in the presence of a handicapped person. Not for himself, but for "God! God! God! where *are* you?" he would ask, although he professed to be an atheist. God, God, he would cry, when confronted with one of nature's aberrations. So he left the toilet as quickly as possible.

He rejoined his friend. They drank silently, both cautious after their near quarrel, listening to the music. The band was singing:

> "Imagine there's no heaven,
> it's easy if you try.
> No hell below us,
> above us only sky.
> Imagine all the people,
> living for today ..."

"Where're you staying?" asked Peter.

"What?" Kian Teck asked, startled, his mind still with the music, the song.

"You said you'd broken up."

"Oh! Well, maybe I was exaggerating a bit. I *do* feel we're in the process of breaking up. But I'm still staying at home. We've not separated, or anything like that."

In fact, it had never occurred to him to think of leaving.

"Oh, I see," Peter said.

No, he didn't see, Kian Teck thought, imagining what Peter must make of all this wishy-washiness. He felt ashamed, angry with himself. A blunderer, yes! Someone who couldn't manage properly, unlike Peter whose life was neat, open, honest. While his own was all confusion, uncertainty, an unmanageable glob of mess. God, he was fed up with himself.

They did not speak again but listened till the song ended:

> "You may say I'm a dreamer,
> But I'm not the only one.
> I hope some day you'll join us,
> and the world will be as one."

The band boys began to pack up their instruments, their engagement over for the night. The song had come to an end. The evening too. And for that matter, thought Kian Teck, life too, will come to an end. Songs, nights out, life, everything is limited, is finite, and will come to an end. But one does not ponder over this. No. One perpetually procrastinates. Was it out of fear?

One day, when Kian Teck was a student in London, Gopal Nair, that Hindu, had set him a riddle: "What causes death?" he asked.

Kian Teck had thought seriously, strenuously, but could not come up with an answer. He was a little annoyed about it. "I give up," he blurted out finally.

"It's birth!" Gopal said.

Ahh, these Hindus! And Taoists! And Buddhists! And Christians! Great riddle-setters, they!

"Too late to go anywhere else tonight, K.T." Peter said.

"You're right. Let's call it a night."

"Perhaps we can paint the town red some other night, eh? But give me a bit of notice, man! So that I can fix up the chicks."

Part One

"Yeah."

Kian Teck settled the bill with his Diners Card.

Outside, Peter said, "Let me know when, OK?"

"Yeah. I'll call you. Goodnight, Peter."

"Goodnight."

Peter drove off in his cream-coloured Mercedes. Kian Teck walked over to his Toyota. His wrist watch read 2:10. There was hardly any traffic along Orchard Road. The air smelt cleaner. There was a milkiness in the night light, and a curved moon, quite white, its disc nibbled neatly, sailed low over the transplanted, misshapen trees lining the road.

He drove at a great speed, his right foot stamping down hard on the accelerator, the tires screeching like a wounded beast as he cornered sharply, swiftly, driven by a strange compulsion. He felt a forbidden exhilaration in this mad speeding, his hands deft on the steering, in control of the car — not of his life. He arrived home.

What has no limit? What's it like: endlessness? Riddles, riddles. Senseless riddles in the late night. There was an odd bickering sound made by an insomniac insect from within the condensed shadows of the bushes. Kian Teck walked with a mechanical gait into the apartment.

His wife's loose, wandering hair etched the snowy pillow with the vividness of fire. He knew she was still awake. Her face, turned away from his side of the bed, harboured a secret alertness. He slid into bed and lay there quietly, unsleeping, all night long. Till dawn mimicked the blank whiteness of the moon.

8

The pale, virtually transparent torso of the baby spider, come from some sunless vista, dangled before his face. Turning his head slightly, Chan Kok Leong could clearly see the silken thread by which it had suspended itself, daredevil acrobat, the thin strand spun from its own belly.

In the dark, crowded discotheque, the flickering strobe lights revealed the dancers for a moment, then lost them again, the girls like undines, throbbing and dancing to the music as if no other world existed beyond these walls. Flashes of light, dazzling like desert snow, touched the skin of darkness in this room gilded with artificial galaxies.

Kok Leong shut his eyes and saw white spots against his eyelids. He pressed his lids against the marbles of his eyeballs, massaging with finger tips to bring out a burst of colours. But it did not work. Yet when he closed his eyelids against the sun and rubbed them, he would see dizzying colours — a red curtain shot through with zig-zags of greens and purples and golds, bristling electric snakes. Now, only white spots. Where have all the colours gone? He had a wild intuition, totally unfounded he knew, that all the colours in that dark void of a room had somehow drained into his glass of Coca Cola. Also sunrises, the scent of roses, the breath of green leaves in the afternoon, the brown rivers with their odour of ooze, the far off, violet archipelagoes of evening, the rat-gray canals, the sky, silvery fishes, and girls' dresses, all, all dissolved in that glass of Coca Cola. He imagined so strongly a taste of multiple colours that he could not resist lifting up the glass. He drank. It tasted only of Coca Cola.

A sudden crescendo of cymbals, like a gust of startled birds rising in flight, signalled the end of the music. Sundram was making his way back to their table with a girl in tow on his brown rope of an arm, his broad, shiny face trophied with sweat. But the girl was dry, cool-skinned, unscathed by the exertion of the dance. Perhaps for her, dancing wasn't an exertion. Kok Leong had watched her on that tiny arena of a dance floor, looking independent for all her movements, for all the shifting dynamics of her arms, legs, neck, the music washing over her like water, her body light, floating, almost air borne, rippling in response, unlike others who seemed all tangled up, struggling in conflict, tossed and plucked beneath the webs of the music.

Her name was Cynthia de Souza. Slim and tanned, a Eurasian of Portuguese extraction. They had gone to a social escort office to fetch her. She was the only one that they booked out from that bright room filled with dressed-up girls. The three of them had dined at the Coffee House in the Hyatt Hotel and afterwards had a few drinks in the lounge on the Hyatt's mezzanine floor. Sundram had hired a car for the night. Before coming to this discotheque, they had cruised around for more than an hour, Sundram and the girl smoking a couple of joints, while Kok Leong sat alone in the back. He did not smoke.

The limp, creased tube was passed between Sundram and Cynthia with an almost religious solemnity. None of them spoke. They drove along tree-lined streets, the trees whooshing past like phantoms in the street lights, the sweet smell of marijuana trapped within the compartment. Kok Leong watched Sundram as his friend entered into a deep silence, into privacy, into holiness. After a while, he felt himself sharing the same journey. The trees kept flying past, carried on the wind like birds into a sacred wood, timeless, while the car, rushed, rushed into the body of night.

"Another vodka and lime, Cynthia?" Sundram offered.

She nodded.

"How about you?" Sundram asked Kok Leong, turning to his friend.

"I still got my coke."

"OK. A vodka-lime and a Scotch-on-the-rocks," Sundram told the waitress.

"You really don't drink," Cynthia observed, gazing at Kok Leong curiously.

Kok Leong shook his head, in slow motion. It was so heavy, an iron ball.

"So you don't drink and you don't smoke grass," she remarked.

Kok Leong remained silent. He would not explain. It was nobody's business.

"No, he doesn't drink," Sundram replied in his stead.

"And he doesn't dance," Cynthia pursued.

"No, he doesn't," Sundram said, his skin sleek with sweat, odorous, resinous. Adding, in a lazy drawl, "He's happy enough."

Cynthia shrugged her shoulders. What was it to her?

Actually, she was happy enough herself, in a state of listless contentment after the marijuana, the flame still brightly jewelled in her head, a flame that extinguished all others: desire, anxiety, anger, ambition, sorrow, love. She had dared, had entered the present, and it belonged to her, uniquely, exclusively, however makeshift, however fleeting it might be. She was keenly aware, although without despair — that was the miracle — that these moments would last only so long and no longer. She knew this. Knew she would be swamped. But while the moments lasted, she felt a certain contentment.

Their drinks arrived. Sundram drank his noisily, swallowing molten fire, the shiny black globes of his eyes turbulent. Soon, the music returned, and the tireless lights flickered their summons. A few assorted couples

Part One

regathered on the dance floor. It was muted, moaning music this time, to which the dancers swayed slowly, pressed close together, their pores charging whatever small space there was between their hot bodies, as if they would be welded by the acetylene of concupiscence, would be fused. Furnace of loins, soft tits like floury snow.

Kok Leong suddenly realized that the baby spider was no longer dangling in front of him. Could it have fallen onto the floor, or maybe onto his lap? Or could it have climbed back, up its own spun-strand to the hidden rafters above, with Herculean will?

"What's the time?" Cynthia asked abruptly.

Sundram looked at his watch, turning its white face to the light shining from behind him.

"A quarter past one," he said.

"Oh," she said, mildly surprised.

She sniffed the air tentatively. It gave no kick. The effect of the grass was wearing off. A certain restlessness intruded into her gestures.

"You impatient to go?" Sundram asked.

"Not really," she answered, in a considering tone.

"Hey! I've booked you up till two, you know," Sundram reminded her reprovingly, a hint of hurt in his voice.

"Sure, man, sure you did," she answered nonchalantly.

Then Sundram leaned towards her, so close that he was smelling her hair, and whispered into her ear. Kok Leong thought he was nibbling it. She gave a cynical, knowing giggle. Implying an acceptance, an abandonment.

"Get me another drink," she said, unabashed now in her pursuit of simple things to pleasure her — a drink, a cigarette, a dance, a kiss, a fuck — to gratify either herself or another, she hardly bothered to distinguish. Give, give, give, take, take, take — what's the difference?

When her vodka-and-lime came, she drank it up quickly, in a few desperate gulps, then plunked her empty glass on the table with defiance. Sundram smiled, and immediately asked the waiter for a refill.

Kok Leong took in everything, adding every bit, every scrap, into that locked casket in his head. After years of accumulation, it had the same quality as disused pools, the cess dumps for a melange of unwanted items.

Again Cynthia brought the glass up to her lips, the volatile, yellowish liquid swaying slightly from the motion, and drank half the contents in small quick swallows, like a bird. Then she flung back her head defiantly, her long black hair, coltish, splayed like a skein of electric energy. She glared at Kok Leong with hostility. Was it, he wondered, because he had overheard Sundram's proposition earlier on? That whispered suggestion, intimate, but indelicate to other ears? Or was it because, by just being there, he was a witness, was even, in a way, a party to it?

Kok Leong diverted his gaze to Sundram. A smile still hovered, lingering, like licquorice, on his full lips as he gazed at Cynthia. As if in anticipation of the kisses they would impart and receive. In the dark, tasting her lips, her flesh. How would she taste? Kok Leong wondered.

"I don't trust men who don't drink," she burst out suddenly, as if she had thought about the subject for a long time. Kok Leong knew she was trying to pick a quarrel with him. He looked straight at her, without replying, curious that she should be so rattled, she with the cool, dry skin.

"Ah, leave him alone," Sundram said, lazily. "Don't pick on him."

But she would not let it be. "Why are you so afraid to drink?" she asked Kok Leong aggressively.

"I'm not afraid."

"Hunh!" She hissed jets of sharp air through her nostrils.

"Anyway, it's my own business."

"Sure, man," Sundram said. "No one's going to interfere with you."

Kok Leong didn't quite like this patronizing tone. "Don't worry about me. I can take care of myself," he insisted. "No one can make me do what

Part One

I don't want to do."

"Oh, a big shot, eh?" She was being bitchy. But he wasn't offended, wasn't angry. Only surprised at her lack of cool. He had thought more of her.

"C'mon, babe. Let's dance," Sundram suggested.

She drank up all her drink, rose from her chair, and with a final glare at Kok Leong, followed Sundram onto the crowded dance floor, deliberately swaying her bottom with a wanton air. He smiled to himself. I suppose she'll make a good lay, he judged. A body, only a body. That's all she is. He thought he heard her sharp laughter, hinting of wildness. It made him feel alone again. He looked at the bit of coke stagnant in his glass, no longer bubbling. He too, felt a certain lassitude, felt himself sinking deeper into a state of passivity. It was like a hangover from marijuana, which he had tried only once. The problem with grass is that the good effect leaves you after a while, and you're back where you started from. Only somewhat worse off. He made an effort to look for Sundram and Cynthia, but they were swallowed up by the crowd. Once or twice, though, he caught glimpses of Cynthia, of her smooth skin, flashing into sight as the kinetic lighting shone on her, but only to lose sight of her the next moment. Could she not feel the light on her skin? Brushing against her like kisses?

The pulsing rhythm of the music rocked the room with sheer energy. Kok Leong watched the bodies pitching about, obedient to the seismic beat, yielding their spirits into the smoky darkness. Pivoting feet, tilting necks, swan-long, a miscellany of arms unfurling as if to soar. Like a storm of bats in a dark cave when evening is about to end, twittering their fracas, blasting their restless, reckless trajectories with stark courage, seeming not to calculate nor care whether they bounced into each other or crashed onto the hard surface of a rocky wall. And these dancers were the same.

Bats, however, have a built-in radar. Perhaps he had been born with this too, Kok Leong mused, this built-in radar that kept him from crashing into contact with others, that allowed him to cruise the parabola of the bluest air?

Once more Kok Leong caught a fleeting glimpse of Cynthia. She rose up and then plunged in and out of the light like a dolphin at play. To hold her, press against her sweet flesh, he had only to ask her for a dance. To dance with her: it was achingly simple. But he would not do so. And suffered a nameless anguish.

Suddenly, he longed for a gust of wind to lift, carry these dancers away, like white paper kites into the far sky. But they danced on and on, indefatigable.

Then he felt a tickling sensation on the back of his right hand. He looked at the baby spider crawling on his hand. Abruptly he felt revolted at being touched by it, and swung his hand down, flinging the spider violently onto the floor. He hesitated a second, then stamped hard on it. Thump! Lifting his foot, he saw only a patch of wetness on the wooden floor. Not even red blood. The crushed body of the tiny spider must have clung to the sole of his shoe. He ground his shoe against the floor. It hardly made a crunch. Then he lost interest.

His attention was jolted by a loud commotion. Raised voices reached him from the direction of the dance floor, angry shouts, and then a girl screamed. The movement of the crowd was formless, different from that of the dance, and even in the shadowy darkness he could sense bodies lurching about wildly. Another scream rose above the ugly, angry shouts. Just as he stood up, trying to discover what was going on, the place was suddenly floodlit, the polar whiteness of the lights blinding in the abrupt transition. This instant shock froze everything for a split second, catching everyone off guard. People stood arrested, as in a frieze. Then, as if it were all choreographed, the action which had earlier been hidden by the dimness and disembodied by the sudden, drenching light, came together

Part One

again, the components fitting piece by piece like a jig-saw puzzle — it was a fight.

A young Chinese pitched himself forward to throw a punch at a white man whose face was putty coloured beneath a reddish-brown shock of curly hair. They yelled at each other, their words indistinct. A few men were trying to separate them, while everyone else fled from the scene.

Sundram and Cynthia walked back to the table, Sundram with an air of imperturbability, while Cynthia's expression spelt disapproval, and Kok Leong noticed that her pupils were slightly dilated with fear. It gave him a strange satisfaction: to know that she was afraid.

The people looked like pale crustaceans stranded in the harsh light, washed up out of the night, their milk-white faces raptly focussed on the fight. They were immobilized by fear, by a sickening disgust, their demeanours assuming an inscrutability, as though they could seek refuge in the blank map of their faces.

Suddenly, the fighting erupted with renewed fierceness, and the two men tumbled down from the dance floor. Kok Leong saw the white man fall near his feet, and with astonishing quickness, his opponent yanked up a chair and with a mad, bellicose grunt whacked the prostrate figure powerfully on the head. He then gave a few vicious kicks to the writhing body before he was pulled back. All this happened right in front of Kok Leong, causing feelings to rush like a drug through his blood stream: wariness and excitement, in quick, changing succession, in spurts. Although Kok Leong braced himself, his insides coiled into knots. He hardly breathed.

The crowd fell back from the figure lying on the floor, and in the ensuing quietness Kok Leong could hear him moan. The victim had curled his body into a tight crampedness, wrapping around his pain. Wordless sounds issued from his broken mouth, through which trickles of blood wormed down his chin and face, now wan and drawn.

Kok Leong's heart thumped in his chest; he felt as though his rib cage would give way to this fist-like thumping.

"Let's *get!*" Sundram called, pulling Cynthia away.

As he got up to follow, Kok Leong felt a little dizzy, and lurched slightly from side to side. He thought he was going to throw up. Then, while he stood still to steady himself, he abruptly gave the injured man a hard kick, the entire action completely unpremeditated, almost involuntary. Though he knew he was doing it as his foot shot out, in his mind it was like an act done in slow motion, moving trance-like as in a dream. It was almost as if someone else, not himself, had executed that cruel kick.

Kok Leong emerged into the open. Sundram and Cynthia were waiting for him in the meagre light of the car park. The eerie siren of a police car floated nearer through the night. He looked up at the moonlit, starshot sky and felt the world spinning on and on and on.

A Dance of Moths

Part Two

1

Outside, the world was filled with sound — yelps of children at play, blare of a radio, tap tap tap tap of a ping pong game, sounds of a car shifting gear — in short, the sounds of living.

Ong Kian Teck felt his brow frequently with his palm to find out if his feeling of feverishness was real, or only imagined; but it was difficult to assess with another part of one's own body. To measure reliably, a neutral object was needed. Yes, the self can never be trusted. Never!

Time passed in surges, morning into afternoon, evening into night. He had no notion of the time. How long had he been lying in bed? Three days? It had begun when he woke up one night shivering with a chill. Li Lian said he had a fever and gave him two panadols with a glass of milk she had warmed up, but still he shivered and tossed all night. The following morning, he was drenched in sweat and his limbs ached. When he tried to get up, his head throbbed. The doctor came and diagnosed a viral infection, left some medicine, and instructions to call him should any new symptoms crop up.

At first, Kian Teck thought that he was having a relapse of the infectious hepatitis he had contracted two years earlier. The severe chills resembled those of that earlier episode. When he had suffered that first bout of hepatitis, he turned a deep yellow, which made him feel like a fruit gone rotten — poisoned by his own internal secretions. Funny thing, the body. If it stops excreting its usual quota of waste material, of urine and shit and foul breath, then it poisons itself.

The air felt shallow, and Kian Teck grew conscious of drawing it in. He felt exhausted, simply breathing in and out. He could hear the soft whispers of his family washing against the closed door of his bedroom, accentuating his seclusion. He had been isolated, quarantined. He accepted it placidly, as he accepted his exemption, however temporary, from the usual daily routine. Barred from him, normal life seemed a strange, distant affair. He felt as if he were exiled to another country.

Daily, the invasion of visitors. His mother, his two sisters, his maternal aunt, his mother-in-law — the family's female brigade, answering the call of duty, to give succour to the sick. They trooped in, one by one, two by two, solemn and grave as soldiers advancing upon the enemy, armed with hampers of fruit and biscuits and cartons of Brand's Essence of Chicken. At least he was spared flowers, he thought.

Anyway, they came and sat by his bedside by the hour, gazing at him as if he would disappear if they so much as took their eyes off him. He could not return their unshifting gaze, but stared up forlornly at the ceiling — which he was getting to know better than his own palm — and further contributing, by the faraway haze in his eyes, to that non-permanent, evanescent, unanchored, ready-to-depart look of his. Which, in turn, increased the intensity of their gaze upon him, really pinning him onto the bed. He did not know from which he suffered more — the aches and discomforts of his illness, or this suffocating solicitude of women. They sat around him and chattered brightly about dearly departed (but not forgotten) members of the family, the latest gossip about who had run away from whom, or with whom. His mind grew more blurred after each visitor, so that he usually collapsed into sleep as soon as they left him.

It got to be that he became quite annoyed. A sick man ought to be left in peace. A selfish indulgence perhaps, but when one is ill, one becomes a true egotist, and the world and everything in it could burn for all one cared.

Kian Teck sighed. He had a vague sense of the night racing away, and of featureless hours. He peered through the liquid, lemony light at the sheen of the shellacked cupboard, then at the mirror of the dressing table, which, from his angle, reflected no images — it was just an oblong hole. The sounds of the TV, although the volume was toned down in consideration for his illness, were obscene: facetious, bizarre, hinting at fictions totally foreign to him. Learn to submit, learn to submit. The reiteration echoed in his mind, and lulled him to sleep.

The sound of rain darted into his shallow sleep, inserted itself there, and became active, participant in a formless dream. Then the dream and wakefulness blurred into each other, as the sky is sometimes indistinguishable from the sea, the horizon so awash with rain, a homogeneous grayness. Out of which a silhouette loomed.

It was his wife.

"Your mother's here," she said.

Sleep thawed away. He saw the rain beating on the window panes, the drops trickling down the smoke-tinted glass like tears. Through the smoky glass and the sleek smears of rain, the sky had the colour of slime. It was the late afternoon of another day.

"Can I send her in?"

He wanted to avoid meeting his mother, feeling simply not up to it.

Li Lian seemed to be aware of his feelings, and offered to send his mother away; she could say that he was still asleep.

Although tempted, he shook his head.

"No, send her in."

"I'll tell her not to stay too long," she volunteered.

He hauled himself up on his elbows to lean against the headboard of the bed; in this propped-up position, he felt better able to cope with the situation.

Li Lian returned with his mother. The rectangular, steel-rimmed

Part Two

spectacles, thick-lensed, were twin ice cubes engraved on the old woman's face, and the first things to catch his attention. They made her eyes seem hazy, submerged, swimming below the surface of the glass, so that it was difficult to read their expression. Kian Teck had never been able to fathom her feelings by studying her face: joy or pain, he never knew which she was experiencing. Even when his father passed away, that year before he left for his studies in England, he had searched her face but found it impossible to discern her reaction. Had she loved her husband, his father? He could not guess at her true feelings with any certainty. At times, he wondered what she had been like when she was young. Did she later train her facial muscles to disguise her feelings, or was she born with the face that he knew, which always expressed a state of placidity, a preparedness to deal with life's crises without revealing any surprise? And because she seemed so imperturbable on the one hand, and so circumspect on the other, he had always assumed that she was a person of strength. A still centre, while the storm of life raged around her.

Li Lian fetched a chair and planted it beside his bed. His mother sat down; Li Lian left the room.

"How're you feeling?" his mother asked.

"I'm all right."

With her sitting so close to him, he realized that she had become an old woman. White hair threaded with occasional strands of a wispy, dirty, mousy colour, and thinning so that the smooth, pale skull showed through. It gave her a look of fragility. Below the frugal snow of her hair, her brow and cheeks had lost their earlier firmness. So this is what will accrue to us over the years, he thought, our skin and flesh surrendering resilience and suppleness, sagging year by year. The irreversible deterioration of the body. This old woman had been young once. A baby once. He tried to conjure up an image, and almost laughed, it was all so funny.

"Li Lian said the doctor came by today."

"Yes."

"He told her you're much the same."

"I'll be well soon."

"This doctor, he doesn't know what you're suffering from, does he?"

"It's just a simple fever. That's all. Now don't you go and worry."

"Is he any good?"

"The doctor?"

"*This* doctor."

"Well, he's our usual doctor. As good as any other, I guess."

"Then why doesn't he know what your sickness is?"

"He knows. It's a viral infection, that's all. I don't know where you get the idea ..."

"Not much good if he doesn't know what your sickness is."

"Ah, Ma!"

"Doctors," she said, disdainfully. A judgment passed.

"Ah, Ma!"

"Li Lian says you're not eating."

"It's no harm. I'll get my appetite back."

"Why is she unhappy?"

"What do you mean?"

"What's wrong with you two?"

"Nothing."

"You quarrelling?"

"No!" he answered too loudly, although she didn't seem to notice.

The conversation then drifted to other, inconsequential topics, and Kian Teck began to feel sleepy.

As she was leaving, she said: "Think of the children."

That was all she said, but after she left, her words echoed, ricocheting from wall to wall, striking him inwardly, straightforward and unanswerable.

Unseen surges of wind drove the rain slapping, knocking on the window

Part Two

panes with a sound like fine sand being thrown in haphazard showers, miniature storms against the drumskin of the mind. His mother's words, the rain, him in that sealed room. To ward them off, he shut his eyes, but blindly they reached in, traversing the convolutions of the brain. Turmoiling, they went on, and on, until the crashing of thunder augured a distant convulsion.

HE WAS SITTING ON THE ROCKING CHAIR out on the balcony. It was just after ten in the morning, the sky booming with light. He was convalescing, the sickness having run its course. Still, he had not yet fully regained his strength and all his usual faculties. His sensory system, for example, seemed to have been replaced by an infantile model, and was now hardly able to cope with the light and sound of an ordinary day. There was a lingering insipidity which made enthusiasm seem unbecoming, if not improbable.

The children were at school and Li Lian hadn't returned from the market. A glass of warm milk and a copy of the day's *Straits Times* lay on the small, glass-topped, circular table beside him. He felt no inclination to pick up either.

The ball of sun blazed in a clear sky. The whole city appeared to waver and plunge beneath the heat, bustling with traffic, as men and women engrossed themselves in the business of living. He could picture the scene in a thousand offices — typewriters clacking away, people talking urgently into phones, computers whirring. And he had been a participant, until recently! Was it all meaningless?

He was getting to feel a bit hot and thirsty, the sun already spilling onto the balcony. He gave his tongue a few weak sucks. Overcoming a slight repugnance, he reached out for the glass of milk and drank half its contents in gulps, then licked the untidy lines of milk trace from his lips, like a kitten. How sickness can bestow on one the state of childhood, or even of the animal! And like either category, he was puzzled by the world of the grown-ups. But he would re-attain it soon, would recover, be normal again. This obviousness, this inescapability, did not fill him with keen anticipation.

The sun had crept up onto his knees, and he felt it singe through the thin cotton fabric of his sarong. He retreated into the sitting room, picking up the half glass of milk and the folded newspaper. He selected a recent copy of *National Geographic* from the magazine rack and sat down to read.

The printed words danced erratically before his eyes and he felt almost dizzy. He put the magazine down for a moment, then studied the pictures. There were some beautifully photographed scenes of Vermont — picturesque, white clapboard hamlets nestling in the enfolding valleys, through which a small road unwound, empty of cars. It must have been autumn, for the trees were blazing with oranges, reds, yellows, while the pines alone were green, like the meadows. There were photographs of distant, soft hills, vaguely blue, and of lush grass scored by morning shadows, of birch trees etching the skyline, of thick carpets of green underbrush, so fresh that the iridescent hoarfrost could be seen on the blades of grass and on the leaves. Yes, the pasture is decidedly greener on the other side.

Kian Teck's eyes had a dreamy look, enchanted by the scenes of Vermont. He felt marooned in the apartment, gazing at the sun-drenched balcony and listening to the distant stir of life. A sudden, brief gust of wind entered, lifting the curtains which flapped and ballooned, issuing a caressing whisper before dying down. It comes and goes, the wind, just like that, but I can't get away, Kian Teck thought, melancholy either over the wind's departure or his own immobility. One of the reasons Kian Teck liked *National Geographic* was that it encouraged him towards thoughts of escape. All those quaint, faraway places with strange-sounding names — Bhutan, Senegal, the Great Barrier Reef, Martha's Vineyard, Timbuktu,

Part Two

Aspen, Kabul, Seychelles, Provence, Istanbul, Alexandria — so many alluring places that he could only daydream about.

Kian Teck shut his eyes, trying to hoard impressions of those places in his mind, but they eluded him, rushing by like way stations on a speeding train which never stopped. He still felt the slow wash of his recent fever, when time lost its narrow, calibrated progression and expanded like the ocean, with no landmarks from which he could read his bearings. He put the magazine away and retreated into the bedroom.

Lying down, gratefully resettled, he faced those intricate, fine, cracked lines of paint work on the ceiling once again. They suggested various shapes to him— here a tall, thin woman in a flowing skirt, windblown, and there a galloping horse, a ship, a funny, fat man with an unfurled umbrella— all friends that he recognised. When he was bedridden, they had encompassed his world.

Now he found convalescence disagreeable, even more difficult to bear than the actual illness itself, a kind of twilight zone where he was neither sick nor well. He was hesitant and yet eager to get back to normality, irritated by a sense of guilt and remorse. At least, during the acute phase of his illness, his inactivity had been compulsory. Now, he felt like a cheat.

The twittering of birds, ubiquitous, filled his room, rising from the cloud of green leaves in the garden below. He listened to them, sharing their furtive mood as the day grew hotter and they had to shelter in the small trees. It was simply too hot to fly. A glance out the window confirmed a white, bleak sky. Overcome by the glare, he closed his eyes, willing up a vision of a quiet country road which would take him into a cool, green wood. The birds sang happily. He fell asleep.

THE LIGHT CAME IN THROUGH THE OPEN WINDOW, almost reaching the foot of the bed. For a moment, Kian Teck had difficulty clearing his head. It was filled with birdsong, and then it seemed to be playing a trick on him, for the birdsong began to sound like human voices. Also, a shape was moving about the room, phantasmagorically. He rose up in bed. Then everything became clear.

Li Lian was putting some clothes back into the cupboard. The voices he had heard were those of his children, playing in the living room.

Li Lian turned and noticed that he was awake. "Sorry. Did I wake you?"

"No. Time I got up, anyway."

"Good for you to sleep."

"I've had enough of it these past few days."

"You're not fully recovered yet. You should get as much sleep as you can, while you can."

"The children back?"

She nodded. "It's getting on to one. Lunch will be ready in a minute. I'm making some soup *mee hoon*. Think you'll be able to eat a bit?"

He hadn't had an appetite for so long; there was a perpetual flavourlessness in his mouth. Now, at the mention of soup *mee hoon*, he experienced a tingle of taste on his tongue.

"I think I can eat some."

"Good. I'll see to the cooking then."

She moved nimbly, was immediately out of the room.

For a while, he sat listening to the sounds of his household — his wife in the kitchen, his children playing outside his bedroom — listening to them with the absorption of a man looking into a pool, the surface glimmering with a tender light, luring him.

She must have returned from the market, Kian Teck pondered, quite some time ago, and had begun preparing their lunch. Then, she must have washed and ironed the clothes, which he had caught her placing back into the cupboard. So much work. He reflected on the fact that a man usually regards himself as the breadwinner, and, by extension, the

Part Two

only worker in the family. He tends to disregard his wife's work, which is a mysterious domain to him. It's unfair. No wonder they call us male chauvinist pigs, he mused.

The door opened. His children paused by the doorway, regarding him with a slight bewilderment, with a trace of reproach. After all, he had been almost a stranger while he was sick.

"Lunch, Daddy," Guan Hock ventured.

Kian Teck smiled, and rose to follow them.

AN ODOUR OF DAMPNESS LIFTED to Kian Teck's nostrils. For some time, the rain had been falling so quietly that the mind no longer registered its existence, until a gust of wind swept down and then the rain strafed the asphalt and the bonnets of the cars parked across the road from the curry shop, beating staccato with its salvos.

The remains of their lunch still lay on the formica-topped table — the four large sheets of banana leaf littered with bits of rice and vegetables and various other curries. The lunch that day was in honour of Shamsuddin Ahmad, an old friend who had come down from Kuala Lumpur on a short visit. Peter Low and Gopal Nair made up the rest of the company.

The wind had gone on its course, and the rain filtered down noiselessly again. It was one of those tropical drizzles which descend from a cloudless sky, called *serein*. They watched it in silence. Between the low blocks of apartments across the road, they could see Farrer Park, where puddles of water lay here and there on the grassy field, sleek as pools of mercury.

"I'm quite content to let the Government run the show, so that I can devote myself to the really serious things in life, the important things," Peter Low proclaimed.

"And what are they, Peter?" Shamsuddin asked.

"They're the four Ms: money, mating, *makan* and *minum*. To make money, to fuck, to eat and to drink; these are the most important things in life."

"You left out one other thing, which, I may add, you seem to excel in," Kian Teck said, dryly.

"What's that?" demanded Peter.

"Shitting. Both human and bull."

Everyone laughed.

Kian Teck thought it all rather puerile and a waste of time, this idiotic playfulness. Then his attention was drawn to a small bird amongst the tree branches, a solitary gray bird, hopping from branch to branch, occasionally shaking off the water from its feathered body with little shudders; with its quick-turning head, alert rather than nervous, happy as can be.

"I told you all about Sime Darby, didn't I?" demanded Peter. "What about you, K.T.? Did you take my advice?

"I bought a thousand."

"So you've made five to six thousand dollars. Now, wasn't that easy?" said Peter, smugly.

Recently, Kian Teck had begun reading the Market section of the *Straits Times* avidly each day, and in the early evening he listened to Radio Singapore to catch the latest price movements. And *how* the price had climbed! When it reached more than nine dollars per share, he had bought another thousand shares on a sudden irresistible urge to gamble, thereby extending his bank overdraft even further. But it did not worry him, as he had already made a fair bit from his earlier purchase. Thereafter, the price continued to climb, and with it, his mounting excitement. Only three weeks or so had passed, and he had made a tidy profit of some eight thousand dollars! Yes, it was easy. Ridiculously easy. He had some difficulty in imagining that the figures represented real money, real cash. Quite a lot of money, in fact, eight thousand dollars. It would normally take him

Part Two

over two months to earn that sum. In a way, this experience seemed to have made his daily work seem somewhat ludicrous. Luckily, he was aware of the pitfalls of this trend of thought. It could alter his values, lead him astray.

"So, you owe me at least a dinner," declared Peter.

It was reminiscent of their student days in London, Kian Teck thought, staring rather blankly at the rain. Yes, grey rain on the grey pavements of London, and the ardent conversations, as if life depended on them. Endless hours spent arguing over pint glasses of golden, tepid beer at one or the other of their favourite pubs, or at someone's flat late at night, talking earnestly in a corner while perhaps a small party was going on. Talk, so much talk, as if words could succour their arid little souls.

Soon afterwards, lunch ended, and they each went their separate ways.

IT WAS NIGHT. KIAN TECK WAS STANDING ON THE BALCONY of Gopal's living room, which looked onto a fine view of Kallang Basin and the harbour. Although the sky was fairly dark, Kian Teck could make out the mouth of the river almost directly below, and the tall masts of the coastal junks, the Macassar junks, which carried cargoes of charcoal and timber from Malaysia, Thailand, Burma[*] and the Indonesian islands. They huddled together, a congregation of shadows. Beyond the basin towards the eastern anchorage of the harbour, other ships scattered their lights onto the iridescent ink of the sea. Landward, towards his left, the oval of the National Stadium glowed emerald green, surrounded by huge light pylons. A soccer match was on. But although he listened for the roar of the crowd, all he heard was the murmuring flow of conversation behind him from within the living room. It accentuated the silence of the junks berthed below.

Kian Teck felt he ought to join the company. He walked in, without much anticipation or enthusiasm, and made for the kitchen. He took out

---

[*] Now Myanmar

a can of Tiger beer from the large metal bin filled with blocks of half-melted ice. His hand was momentarily wet and numb. He dried it against the sides of his trousers.

He wandered towards Shamsuddin who was talking to a couple of other men. One was an architect whom Kian Teck knew, a portly, middle-aged Chinese, his hair standing in tufts like teased cotton wool, his eyes glinting as he spoke. "The trend is towards greater authoritarianism everywhere in Asia. Indira Gandhi's action is not unique," he said, his voice low, sombre.

"But is there any real justification for her to suspend the Constitution?" asked a thin American named Grey. He was with the USIS, and widely suspected of being a CIA agent.

Standing there dumbly, Kian Teck felt like a weak swimmer, the chorus of voices swirling round the room like the sea when it breaks against rocks by the coast, curling around. He floated, wavering.

Gopal came towards them, bearing a tumbler of brandy for Shamsuddin.

"Oh, that's super, Gopal. Thank you," murmured Shamsuddin as he gracefully accepted the brandy.

Shamsuddin had acquired an Oxbridge accent half a year after arriving in England. Some time after completing his studies, he had been posted to the Malaysian Mission at the United Nations, in New York. There, he had adopted a Manhattan, a mid-Atlantic inflection. "By the way, Gopal, your denizens here seem to be complaining of a lack of freedom. I can't elucidate why," he said, pleasantly.

"Oh?" Gopal remarked, his bushy eyebrows jumping upwards like a pair of bat wings.

"Perhaps, as their Member of Parliament, you might care to ... ?" Shamsuddin asked, urbanely.

The company laughed. Kian Teck did not join in. His eyes roamed

Part Two

around the room. Peter Low was chatting up a bright flower. They were seated on a divan at the farther side of the room. Another girl was with them, a white girl with flowing dark brown hair, wearing a long white cheese-cloth blouse and a pair of faded blue denim pants. When her face, basking momentarily in a shallow pool of light from one of the small ceiling lamps, turned towards Kian Teck, he saw that she was very beautiful. He walked across.

"Hi! K.T. Meet Serene Lim, Joanne Wood," Peter introduced.

"My friends call me Jay, though my name's Joanne. I'm from Connecticut," she said, extending her right hand to Kian Teck.

"My friends call me K.T., though my name's Kian Teck." He took her hand briefly, shook it.

"I've met you somewhere before," the other girl, a pretty young Chinese, interposed, craning her neck around Jay's left shoulder.

"I'm sorry. I don't think I've had the pleasure," Kian Teck replied, politely.

"What do you do?" she insisted, still leaning forward.

"I'm in advertising."

"Where?" her pupils gleamed, vying with her iridescent painted lids. Kian Teck mentioned the name of his firm.

"I've been there! Two or three times. I'm a model. Your firm engaged me for a film commercial. It was for jeans!" Serene was exultant.

"Well, you'd better be nice to me, Serene," Peter said. "If you're nice to me, I'll get my friend here to get you more assignments."

"Hunh!" Serene pouted her well-defined, ruby red lips, each like a slice of ripened, glazed fruit. "Why should I do that? I might as well be nice to your friend. Then *he* can get me some assignments, what."

A short while later, Kian Teck found himself alone with Jay. He was pleased. He was also pleased that it was Serene and not Jay who was Peter's prey for the night.

Jay's full figure and breasts filled him with a visceral longing.

"You're just travelling?" he asked her.

"Yes, you might say that," she gave him a smile. "Travelling."

"Have you been away long?"

"Two years."

"*Two years!*" he exclaimed, and sighed audibly. "It must be terrific, to be free, to see the world leisurely."

"Why? You could do the same, if you really wanted to, if you really put your mind to it."

"If only it were so easy," he sighed again. "I'm married. Have two children. Boys," he said. He did not know why he volunteered this personal information. It just slipped out naturally. He continued, " I don't mean that I regard my family as a trap. I won't use that as an excuse for my inability to act. But it's a statement of fact. What I mean is, no matter how resolute one is, one has to act within the sphere of the fact — that one is a husband and a father. I'm expressing myself badly," he ended miserably, feeling rather foolish.

"I don't think so," she said.

"I'll fetch us another drink," he offered.

This time, before he left the kitchen to return to the living room, he gulped several quick swallows from the cold can, each swallow going down his gullet, a bolus of ice.

He saw her standing by the sofa and talking to a young Indian couple. She was laughing. She tossed back her long, brown hair, her slender neck bending, white, desirable. That moment, Kian Teck resolved he would sink into her, on a field of grass, under a hot, spinning sky.

2

It was midmorning. Masses of clouds, processional like priests in billowing white cassocks, moved in stately grace across the light blue sky.

Chan Kok Leong felt pinioned under the sky, earthbound as he tramped restlessly from the living room to the balcony, from the balcony to the living room, back and forth, back and forth. On one occasion, he saw some human figures below, slowly crossing the grassy quadrangle between the tall blocks of apartments. They reminded him of the cockroaches which scurried across the kitchen floor at night. Inhabitants of a wasteland.

The kitchen door flew open. At once there was a smell of human shit, not quite masked by the scents of carbolic soap and pitch-pine which his mother used to disinfect the floor and scour his sister's potty.

Mrs. Chan and his maternal Third Aunt entered. Third Aunt was a large, effusive woman in her late fifties. She had bosoms as big as water melons and three folds of fat beneath her chin.

"Hey, Kok Leong! What're you doing at home? Everyone's gone to the parade!" his aunt thundered in her hearty, sing-song voice.

It was National Day, a public holiday. As usual, the family spoke in a mixture of English and Cantonese, a commonly-used Chinese dialect in Singapore.

"Hello, Third Aunt!" Kok Leong replied animatedly.

She was his favourite relative. She overwhelmed him with her jollity, with her great, unshakable spirit, which seemed to swell from within like a choir and organ music from a cathedral. It had survived many vicissitudes, many tragedies, among which was the early death of a faithless husband who had left her with three young children to rear alone. She had done it all by herself, taking on a dazzling variety of jobs and tasks throughout the years. Successively, and sometimes simultaneously, Third Aunt had helped out at a fresh-fish stall in the Killiney Road Market, been a four-digit runner for a syndicate of criminals, a smuggler of pornographic photographs, magazines and films into, and from, Malaysia, a paid escorter and recruiter of gamblers for the casinos in Jakarta, a part-owner of a dressmaking establishment (the Chinese sign hanging over the entrance to the shop house in Katong boasted of "Shanghai Tailoring"), run a *laksa* stall for a while at a hawkers' pitch near the General Hospital in Tiong Bahru, and was the lover of an old Chinese brothel keeper in Race Course Road — to whom, moreover, she was never faithful! There was apparently nothing she couldn't, or wouldn't, do. Against such a prodigious talent, Kok Leong simply had no chance. She had worn down his hostility and disdain a long time ago. So when she glowered at him and boomed at him with her great voice, he gleamed back at her with unabashed amusement and affection.

The armchair almost collapsed as she planted her heavy weight on it. She was wearing a preposterous, multi-coloured silky *samfoo* which showed off rather than hid her rippling fat. He wondered whether she ever patronized her own fashion establishment. Shanghai tailoring, indeed!

"So, why aren't you cheering at the parade?" she demanded.

"Why aren't *you*, Third Aunt?" he quipped.

"Ha-hah!" she laughed. "Me? In this heat! My fat will melt! Ha-hah!"

"That'll be one way to slim down."

"*Ai-yo*. What for I go and do that? Loose all my fat, loose all my beauty. If I go and loose all my beauty, I loose all my men! Ha-hah!"

Part Two

As usual, her elder sister, Kok Leong's mother, did not know whether to join in the laughter or not. She was not overly embarrassed by this coarse talk, but, just to be on the safe side, she would say an extra prayer to her gods, in case one of them might be offended by this display of vulgarity in her home.

"So, how's business, Third Aunt?"

"Which business?"

"Your latest one."

"Well, not bad, not bad. I've been going to Jakarta quite often. All these suckers wanting to gamble, so I take them. Get a nice commission from the casinos. How about coming with me some time? I'd like to show you around."

"But I'm not interested in gambling."

"Who's talking about gambling? You think your Third Aunt is going teach you bad ways? *Cheh!* I wouldn't want you to end up a gambler. Anyway, Jakarta is more than just a gambling den, you know. There's lots to see. Some people say it's very crowded, very poor and dirty. That's true. But that shouldn't stop *you* from having a good time. There's lots to do in Jakarta," she said, winking at him suggestively.

Kok Leong wasn't shocked by her. After all, he had come to expect anything from this outlandish relative.

"I'll show you a good time, Kok Leong," Third Aunt continued persuasively.

"I'm just not very interested in travelling."

"What's wrong with you young people nowadays? Not interested in travelling! My goodness! Why, I might be a fat old woman, but I still enjoy gallivanting all over the place. I have lots of fun. Ah, you! I don't know *what's* wrong with you," she sighed gustily.

At the beginning, when he was a lot younger, Kok Leong had marvelled that such a fat, gross woman could enthrall *anyone*. Yet she did; she managed to entice her brothel keeper, a purveyor of women (presumably younger and more attractive than her, at that), as well as several other men, whom she occasionally alluded to, who swarmed around her like bees. How could such a fat old woman attract, indeed *dazzle*, so many men? It certainly was one of life's great mysteries. For one had to admit that she did not conform to any popular notion of the desirable woman. Oh no! Third Aunt was no slim, sloe-eyed beauty, no stunner, she.

Kok Leong studied her, bestowed there upon the chair like some comic parody of enthroned majesty, arrayed like a large, exuberant flower, radiant, glossily coloured. She might be no beauty, but she certainly commanded one's attention. And once she had your attention, she simply devastated you with her personality. Her nephew was one of those whom she enthralled. To him, she was the grandest of the grand.

"It's a good idea. Why don't you go with your Third Aunt? You've not been anywhere. You should see a bit of the world," said Mrs. Chan.

Kok Leong hardly heard his mother. It was as if she wasn't there at all, so overshadowed was she by her younger sister. Mrs. Chan was aware of this, but she was neither resentful nor jealous: Third Aunt never provoked such trite feelings in anyone.

"Why should you think there's something wrong with me, just because I don't want to travel?" Kok Leong asked. "What's so great about travelling anyway? It's only a change of scenery," he challenged his aunt.

"It's shocking that a young man like you should have so little appetite for life," Third Aunt said reprovingly.

"Maybe that's how I keep slim, and not grow fat like you. What for I want to grow fat like you?" he teased her.

"Terrible! What for this, and what for that? That's all you ask. How can you have so little interest in life? Why, you're half-dead, although you're less than half my age! I feel like *shaking* you up, you get me so mad!" Third Aunt lifted her arms as if she were going to carry out her

Part Two

threat. There was something babyish, or doll-like, about her arms, with their pendulous sags of loose fat. She wore a large, oval jade ring mounted in gold on her left ring finger.

"I don't know. Running about like an excited hen from place to place isn't such a great way to show that one's alive. As I've said, what's so special about a change of scenery? When you yourself remain the same, remain unchanged? Seems like a waste of time to me, a waste of energy," replied Kok Leong, disparagingly.

"To you, I suppose everything's a waste of time, a waste of energy. No interest in anything. What for you stay alive then?"

"Well, what choice have I got?"

"*Ai-yo!* Kok Leong!" she cried out, raising her voice and popping out her eyes in playful outrage. "You really have such black thoughts! Where you learn these terrible things from?"

"It's my natural genius," Kok Leong answered, abruptly.

Third Aunt shook her big head sadly. She turned to her elder sister. "How come he grow up like this?"

Mrs. Chan sighed. "Nowadays, old people don't have any influence over their children. I don't know what happened. We tried our best, but we can't control our children."

"You should've hit their backsides harder when they were young. Smack some sense into them. Like my children. They sure got walloped a lot. Now they grown up, they behave nicely. At least, in front of me, they do. What they do behind my back is another matter. Ah, who cares? Let them do what they want. And let us old ones do what *we* want. Perhaps that's better."

Mrs. Chan sighed and shook her head. She was about to say that perhaps if they'd prayed more, things would have turned out better. But she kept this to herself for fear that her sister might laugh. Third Aunt had always ridiculed religion.

"Or perhaps," Third Aunt continued, with a mischievous glint in her eyes, "Kok Leong will change when he gets married. I think a good woman ought to change him for the better. Anyway, you're old enough to get married, Kok Leong. Tell me, have you got a special girl friend yet?"

"*Cheh!*" he said, contemptuously.

She laughed. The glint flamed brighter. She was obviously enjoying herself. "Why so shy? Tell me about her, lah," she coaxed in a girlish voice.

"Smelly cunts! Not interested!"

"*Choi!*" she exclaimed, and then laughed, "Ha-hah!"

"Kok Leong! You shouldn't say such bad words* in front of your aunt," Mrs. Chan chided gently.

"Smelly cunts!" he repeated.

Third Aunt roared even more with laughter. When she managed to control herself, she returned to her teasing.

"Don't tell me," she asked, mock-serious, "you're not interested in girls?"

"*Cheh!*"

"*Cheh?* Then why you say '*cheh*' to girls?"

"They don't interest me."

"What? Girls don't interest you, ah? There must be something wrong with you!"

"There's nothing wrong with me."

"But it's not natural! I don't believe you. I think it's because you're too shy. What you say, your Third Aunt introduce you to some nice girls?" she wheedled.

This time, it was he who laughed. "You're beginning to sound just like Koe Low Pak," he said.

Koe Low Pak, or Venerable Tall Uncle, was Third Aunt's lover — the brothel keeper. Kok Leong had met him a few times. The first time was when Koe Low Pak visited their home with Third Aunt during the Chinese

---

* Kok Leong used the Cantonese equivalent, i.e. "*Chow fah hai*"

Part Two

New Year festival several years ago. Subsequently, they had returned on certain festive occasions. Kok Leong also met him when he went, occasionally, to dine with Third Aunt. He was always intrigued by this "bad character", and his opinion of Third Aunt was greatly enhanced by the fact that she "had the gall to openly parade this bad hat," (his mother's words). He discovered a tall, thin, taciturn man in Koe Low Pak, who never had much to say, and when he did, it was always about his atrocious paintings of Chinese deities, a hobby which he pursued, a side line. He had even sold some of his vulgarly colourful paintings to Chinese temples in the rural areas of Malaysia. But there was nothing at all flamboyant about this tall, old man who kept a cheap brothel in Race Course Road, the garish products of whose brushes adorned small Chinese temples in places like Jemaluang, Bentong and Ulu Langat. Still, Koe Low Pak could be said to cater, in his work, to both man's venal as well as his spiritual needs.

"Oh no! I certainly am not going to match-make you with one of Koe Low Pak's girls!" Third Aunt said.

"I think you both should stop saying such things. How can you talk about such girls to my boy?" Mrs. Chan protested.

"Boy! Ha-hah! Kok Leong's no boy! Don't you know he's a grown man? And there's nothing wrong in talking about Koe Low Pak's girls either. Kok Leong should've had enough experience with women by now. If he hasn't, then it's high time he did!"

"He'll learn in good time. There's no need to encourage him to go with bad women," Mrs. Chan said.

"One would think you want him to be a saint! Which I'm sure he's not."

"For goodness' sake, stop discussing me!" Kok Leong interrupted them disgustedly.

Just then a strident cry burst from the kitchen. It became a wail, and, like an avalanche in the monsoon, crashing down the deforested hill slopes, thundering down tons of mud, dislodging rocks in its wake, it shattered the conversation.

"It's Siew Wan," Mrs. Chan sighed, yet made no visible move to rise from her chair. "She was crying almost the whole of last night," she said, addressing no one in particular.

The crying dominated them like a mountain: implacable, immovable. They all sat very still, solemn in that uneasy, expectant air, each waiting for the other to make the first move.

"I'd better go and see to her," Mrs. Chan finally said, with another long sigh. She got up and walked with a defeated air out of the room, dragging her slippered feet.

With the opening of the kitchen door, the wailing, accompanied by the steamy odour of shit, ballooned to fill up the living room. A large house fly buzzed around the half-empty cups of coffee on the oblong table. Kok Leong and his aunt sat watching the fly darting to and fro on its restless errands.

"Oy! Oy!" he could hear his mother soothing Siew Wan in the next room. "Oy! Oy!" But the wailing did not let up.

"*Ai yah!*" Third Aunt broke her silence at last, shaking her big head slowly and sadly, like a cow. "She still cries often like this?"

Kok Leong nodded.

"*Ai!* What a fate! I'll join your mother. See what I can do," she declared, getting up with some difficulty, pushing up her great weight with her small hands, gripping the edge of the chair for purchase. For a moment she swayed on her feet, then sailed through the doorway into the kitchen.

After a while, Kok Leong heard Third Aunt talking baby talk to his sister. Siew Wan was now eighteen years old, and yet most people attempted baby talk with her. This was what was happening just then in the kitchen, he imagined, with Third Aunt urging, "Hush, hush! Good girl, good girl!"

And all the while Siew Wan would be sitting on her potty chair (the enamel rim leaving an imprint on the soft map of her buttocks) and howling like an animal. She simply could not be reached. People, Kok Leong noticed, tended to become embarrassed, frightened or angered by this unresponsiveness, which they could not understand. And many a time a visitor would emerge from an encounter with Siew Wan wearing a puzzled and aggrieved expression. Sometimes, they grew resentful; it was to be expected, for most people like to communicate, to captivate their audience. Often, the unspoken question hovered over them: "Can she think?" She did not seem to be quite human: more like a strange, wild dog. And people are suspicious of strange, wild dogs.

Kok Leong had lain awake almost all the previous night, tormented by his sister's ceaseless crying. When he finally lapsed into a brief sleep, it was already near dawn. He had a bad dream: he was lying paralysed on the hard ground, strangely inert, when he heard the thudding of hooves, and looking up, he saw a bull charging towards him, its hooves rising and falling, rising and falling, as he lay mesmerized, unable to move, until it seemed to be just above his head, the cloven hooves flashing cruelly against the sky and then crashing down, stamping down as if to crush him. He had woken up in terror, drenched in sweat.

Now, down by the road, noon shadows were compressed and stunted. A drowsing cat sheltered in the shade of a tree, forming a small mound of tawny fur, smooth, rounded, as if completely boneless, without muscles and sinews, like the roll of a wave at the rise. People wandered about, their faces eyeless in the stark, white sunlight.

Kok Leong heard the apartment door opening and then closing, and voices. It was his father and his youngest sister, Siew Kum. They had returned from the National Day Parade. They entered the sitting room with Third Aunt. The faces of the old man and the young girl bore traces of drained excitement, of exaltation ended: the parade was over, the moment was over, and life remained the same.

Mr. Chan was wiping his face with a large, white handkerchief, still neatly folded, with which he gently and carefully dabbed his gleaming forehead — his movements as punctilious as a young bride's at her dressing table —as if he didn't want to soil the perfect whiteness. He had earlier splashed his face with tap water in the kitchen.

Siew Kum went to sit astride the rounded arm of the sofa chair, dangling her thin legs. She was about to turn fifteen, and was wearing her white school uniform for the day's celebrations. She was a small, pale girl with her straight hair cut short. Her eyes were hidden behind a pair of large, round spectacles with transparent plastic frames. Her lenses were those thick ones with distinct concentric rings. Siew Kum wasn't a comely girl; certainly not a pretty one.

"How was the grand parade?" Third Aunt asked genially.

"No different from la-last year's. They're all the s-s-same. It was too hot," Mr. Chan said. He finished mopping his face and replaced the handkerchief neatly into his shirt pocket. He wore a light-green Hawaiian shirt and a pair of dark grey cotton trousers and still had his black leatherette Bata shoes on. He wore no socks, his hairless, bony ankles looking like the small knobs on lean tree trunks.

"Did you like it, Ah Kum?" Third Aunt asked next.

Siew Kum continued swinging her legs, her eyes vague, blurred behind her lenses, following the pendula of her swinging legs, undistracted by Third Aunt's question.

"Kum! Third Aunt was t-t-talking to you!" Mr. Chan admonished gently.

"It was boring," Siew Kum said, without looking up.

Just then, Mrs. Chan came in, her eyes wracked and distraught.

"Siew Wan's quiet now," she said.

Yes, Kok Leong thought: she has stopped crying, she has returned to her inchoate silence.

Part Two

Third Aunt shook her head slowly, synchronizing with the swinging of Siew Kum's legs, as if movement could soothe, while Mr. Chan placed both hands on his lap, not knowing what to do with them. He sat stiffly as if he were posing for a formal portrait, his eyes fixed straight ahead, expressionless.

"Shall I serve lunch now?" Mrs. Chan asked. "It's all prepared," she said. But no one responded. She turned her head slightly, looking out. "It's hot. You all must be tired after your walk. Can I get anyone a drink?"

"I'd like a-a glass of ice water," Mr. Chan said.

"What about you?" she asked Third Aunt.

"No, thanks! I'd better be going." Third Aunt hauled herself up from the chair.

"But you must stay for lunch!" Mrs. Chan insisted.

"No, lah. I've already promised to eat with a few friends. They want to gamble in Jakarta."

A few moments later, Third Aunt took her leave, rolling out like a grand ocean liner, debonair.

Mrs. Chan returned to the kitchen, having decided to lay out their lunch.

Kok Leong went out to the balcony. Down below, he could see Third Aunt walking along the white throat of the road. He stood watching until she disappeared from view.

3

The sky had lost the afternoon's lavish light. They were on their way to Johor Bahru. When they reached the causeway which connects Singapore to Johor, it was already evening, the darkness pouring down, spreading wide over the land and the sea, smearing until it skimmed the tops of the jungled hills.

"We're here!" Ong Kian Teck said, marvelling at how he had got Jay to come with him. A couple of days after Gopal's party, he had invited her to lunch at Muthu's Makan Shop on Race Course Road. She had enjoyed eating off a banana leaf, using her fingers. He couldn't recall much of their conversation, but they had become friendly, and had laughed together. He expressed a wish to see her again.

They drove into Johor Bahru after the short wait to clear first through immigration, and then customs. Soon, they were on a road which ran beside a narrow stretch of sea, the strip of water smooth, gleaming in the darkness. There were views of the Sultan's fine *Istana* and the royal gardens. At intervals, they passed umbrella-shaped structures of wrought iron from which light bulbs were suspended like clusters of exotic fruit, or props in a musical show. The road was lined with acacias, casuarinas, eucalyptus trees.

They passed the red bricked General Hospital with its unkempt grounds and some withered-looking trees, then Kian Teck turned into a small winding road which led to the Straits View Hotel.

Part Two

They finally reached the hotel's car park at the top of a small rise, the wheels grinding against the gravelly, pebble-strewn surface. When Kian Teck had locked his car, they walked across the desolate-looking lot, shoes crunching on the coarse ground.

As they came to the dingy foyer, Jay stopped suddenly. "Hey! Look at this!" she cried, pointing to a large board with various coloured photographs pasted on it. It advertised the floor show, featuring "The Twin Fireflies from Korea" — two sisters who danced the "Dance Erotica", "Candy and Dr. Dragus" — a beauty and the beast couple, both gone somewhat to seed, and "Sexy Suzy, fresh from her triumphs in Las Vegas". According to the billboard, music would be provided by the famed rock band, "The Fish baits", five young Malays with shoulder-length hair, all dressed up in red jump suits with glittering gold sequins sewn on the lapels and cuffs; and finally, the local songbirds, Daisy Chan, Lee See See and Djamila.

"What have you brought me to?" Jay asked, laughing.

When they went by the reception counter, the desk clerk looked up at them for a moment, then returned to the comic book she was reading. Kian Teck read the title of the book upside down: *A Child of the Hills*, it was called, the cover depicting a white woman with long, windswept blonde hair, standing alone beside a solitary, wind bitten tree, wearing a light, loose shawl wrapped around her thin shoulders, her gaze directed at the far distance. A thin, plain Indian girl in a red frock, reading a romance comic, daydreaming of the dark and handsome stranger who would come and sweep her off her feet, take her away from dull and dreary old Johor Bahru. Suddenly it occurred to Kian Teck that, with his American girl beside him in this cheap hotel, he was putting flesh to a daydream. And he felt guilty.

> "You're a dirty old man
> You can't keep your hands to yourself.
> A dirty old man
> Go mess around with somebody else ..."

When he had gone to pick Jay up at her friend's apartment in Orange Grove Road in Tanglin, she said she had bought him a present. It was a couple of cassette tapes, one of which was selection of songs by "The Three Degrees".

> "Dirty, dirty old man,
> Yea— aa-a
> Dirty, dirty old man ..."

They went through the restaurant onto the lawn. At Kian Teck's insistence, a young Chinese waiter brought them over to a table laid out in the open air, near the trees growing along a slope above the coast road. The young waiter lit the small red candle lamp on the table.

On the far side they could see the sea-girt island of Singapore across the Straits of Johor, with the tall chimneys of its Senoko Power Station and the smaller red bricked chimneys of the sawmills in the Kranji Industrial Estate.

"Do you get away often?" Jay asked.

"Not often enough. Singapore's so claustrophobic and hectic. Guess I'm starting to feel the pace," he said.

"Perhaps it's only the city, only urban life. And one city is much like another."

"Ah, but our city is also our country! Everything is encompassed within our tiny shoreline. We're so bloody tiny! No room to breathe!"

The young waiter returned with their drinks. A Tiger beer and a Bacardi-and-coke.

Part Two

"This is our first toast, therefore we must toast something really important," said Kian Teck.

"Something important? How about freedom?"

"Yes! To freedom!" retorted Kian Teck.

They clinked glasses.

When they'd each had a few sips in a friendly silence, he said, "You know, freedom is a very dangerous notion."

Jay did not seem to find this interesting. Instead, "Tell me, what do you desire most of all?" she asked, looking at him intently.

"What do I desire most of all?"

"Yes."

There was a pause while he tried to give this his consideration.

"That's a difficult question to answer."

"Why?"

"Because ..." and his answer trailed away. She's right! he thought. Why should it be difficult to answer? She was looking patiently but expectantly at him. "Because," he tried again, "it's always hard to make a choice."

"Surely you can discriminate between your desires?"

"I find it difficult. Perhaps I don't know what it is I want, or else I'm simply too greedy to name one exclusive choice," he said, slowly. Then, "But it's so nice out here that I'm beginning to wonder why I bother to live in Singapore at all!" he suddenly exclaimed.

"Are you really tired of living in Singapore?" Jay continued questioning him, persistent.

"I'm sick of life in the city, all that senseless rush and envy, acquisitiveness and competition. How can any sane person stand it? Life's so fast that everything becomes blurred. I'm beginning to feel as if life is passing me by, that I'm constantly missing something terribly important."

"Are you going to do something about it?"

"My, how direct you Americans are!"

"Are we?" she asked, flashing a smile.

"Yes. Maybe that's why you're so affluent. So certain and efficient, while the rest of us wallow in indecisiveness; we beat about the bush — to coin a phrase." He tried to sound light-hearted.

"You're teasing me," Jay scolded.

An abrupt whirr of wings interrupted their conversation as several birds suddenly rose from the dark depths of a tree, from its black branches. In a while, the birds could not be seen in the sky, but a memory of the sound of their flapping wings remained. For a moment, speech was superfluous. A soft wind ruffled the yellow candle flame, making it waver like a wing about to take flight — but although it danced and struggled, it remained tethered to the wick. A turgid drop of wax slid down the sleek side of the red candle, a pendulous, voluptuous tear. The candle created a cosy well of soft light.

Jay leaned forward, putting her elbows on the table. Her beauty filled Kian Teck with an immeasurable joy.

"You're very beautiful," he said.

Jay looked down for a moment, absent-mindedly doodling with a fore finger on the table cloth. She seemed to make up her mind suddenly, looking straight into Kian Teck's eyes, "There's some hidden charge in you, which I felt when I first noticed you at Gopal's party. You were with your old friends, and yet I sensed that you were really far away; as if you were alone on an island. You aroused my curiosity."

"Why? Do you like lone men on islands?" Kian Teck was determined to keep the mood light.

"Perhaps," she said, laughing with her eyes. "Anyway, I never did like men who're sheep."

"And did you ever want to join a lone man on an island?"

"Depends on who he is."

Part Two

The band inside the restaurant was now beginning their night's entertainment, threatening to shatter their mood. The night seemed a little bruised.

They held hands, with his right, her left, their fingers intertwined, her thumb describing a circular caress on the back of his hand. They seemed content just to hold hands, sunk into one of those silences which are like submerged islands, barely perceptible beneath the rippling current. From where he was sitting, Kian Teck could see the languid silver of the straits, and also the half moon climbing the sky, silver like the sea, as if the moon had sipped from the straits its liquid of silver.

Later, their dinner was laid on the table. The young waiter was assisted by a young Chinese waitress dressed in a pink *samfoo*. When they had finished placing the dishes before the guests, the young couple withdrew.

"The fish looks good," Jay offered.

"Yes, but as if it's seen too much," Kian Teck remarked, looking at the pomfret's protruding eyes — two perfectly rounded white marbles hanging somewhat loosely in the orbital sockets, the rest melted from the cooking so that all that remained were just mucilaginous shreds. The fish was bathed in a clear sauce, sprinkled with thin strips of ginger, sliced red chilies, carrot discs and chopped-up green scallion shoots. The shells of the crabs were steamed a bright red, the flesh almost snowy white. The fried *kai lan* was a deep green, and crisp.

Soon after they started eating, the singers appeared, one after another. Each rendered about four or five songs, mostly Mandarin or Malay pop, with a few western ones sung with atrocious pronunciation. Kian Teck gave them only a cursory glance, hardly hearing them. The restaurant was gradually filling up.

Then there was a sudden crescendo of drum beats, and a young, wavy-haired Indian went up to the microphone. He spoke with an overpowering friendliness, a born master of ceremonies.

The lights in the restaurant were dimmed and then a spotlight focused on the figure of a white woman with shockingly bright red hair, wearing a long red gown covered in red sequins which flashed and sparkled as she moved. The music started — tritely, Ravel's *Bolero* — and she began to dance, slowly, sluggishly, and although her eyes tried to look dauntless and provocative, the effect was diminished by her sad, clownish, made-up face. Moving about the dance floor, the spotlights following her, never letting her out of their focus, "Sexy Suzy" listlessly stripped off all her clothes, becoming a swollen, milky-white insect, a queen ant, an exhibit trapped, exposed, by the harsh light The placid faces of the audience either showed no emotion, or looked bored. Most continued eating their dinner.

"She's grotesque," Jay whispered.

He thought there was both pathos and dignity in that florid, white body under display, and was moved by the dancer's eyes, filled with the fatigue of a thousand years. "Fresh from her triumphs in Las Vegas"? Sitting in the cool garden under the open sky, Kian Teck felt miserable and ashamed. He wondered about her age, what had been crammed into her life, and when her face would become open and alive. He imagined her sitting over her first morning cup of coffee with a cigarette in her mouth, simply looking out of a window at the sky, at the street, at people going by.

"I was just thinking that it would be nice to take a bottle of brandy with us and drive out to Sedili," he suggested.

"Sedili? Where's that?"

He drove fifty miles through the darkness on the lonely road buttressed by jungle and rubber estates, with both of them swigging eagerly from the bottle of brandy. When they arrived, Kian Teck parked on the grass verge and they scampered down the broad, flat, deserted beach. In the scanty light, he could barely pick out the white scales of the waves as they rolled relentlessly towards the shore.

Part Two

Up towards where the car sat like a beetle, the fringe of vegetation was a mass of blotchy shadows under the brooding, indolent half-moon. The tall casuarina trees stood out from the rest, billowing in the air, their fine leaves the colour of smoke, rising, unfurling, ghostly.

Barefooted, they padded on firm sand, with it's glittering, phosphorescent coruscations, like tiny fire flies, left by the tide. Up near the clumpy vegetation, they saw occasional pieces of driftwood, bleached white by sun and salt water. Many looked deformed, petrified, with withered branches and broken roots clutching at emptiness. They lent the beach a derelict air.

Kian Teck walked back to the car, unlocked the trunk and took out some old newspapers. When he returned to Jay, he found her sitting on the sand, her body arched forward, her chin cradled on her bent knees, one hand absent-mindedly tracing doodles on the soft sand. She looked a bit dreamy, inwardly engrossed. He spread out the newspapers carefully beside her.

They sat side by side, looking out to sea: the spume, livid white, rising from the sullen grey water. He felt a sudden shiver running through her and turned her face towards him. He kissed her mouth hungrily.

She stretched out on the newspaper, the stiff sheets crackling crisply. Naked, her skin was subdued gold save for the paler areas on her breasts, and on her pelvis, with its detail of dark pubic frizz. He wanted to feast his eyes, to stroke and caress, but knew this first time needed a consummation before everything else.

And he fucked her furiously, piling down down down into her as she curved up up up to receive him.

Afterwards, he lay collapsed, flat on her, their bodies warm and slippery with sweat, the plop plop plop internal piston of her heart tattooing its beat against his own. They lay together like that for a while, surfacing slowly, the night around them reconstituting by bits.

"Can I have a cigarette?" she asked.

He probed around for his clothes and found the packet in his trouser pocket. The lit match flickered in the night, shot the warp and weft of her hair, her eyes. They smoked in silence, the sky, the clouds, the sea, the wind encroaching on them.

At length, they rose to get dressed. And at once, the newspapers on which they had made love lifted in the breeze, flapping whitely across the darkness over the ribbed sand like souls, no doubt to be crucified, festooned across tree branches up the beach, and eventually yellowed by the sun. Before they walked away, they saw the tell-tale stormy pattern left by their recent passion, a turmoil on the sand.

4

Friday, one p.m. Chan Kok Leong came out of the office building and was at once sunstruck. The light poured, flooded, drew in around him, seeped into his brain in white implosions — flash flash — his mind soon white as the sky.

A besotted crowd scurried along the streets, driven by the slamming of the heat, insubstantial, transfigured, as though their souls had migrated.

Kok Leong was standing on the curb at the top of Shenton Way across the street from the Telok Ayer Food Centre, waiting for the traffic lights to change. I'm being consumed by the sun, he thought, as sweat was wrung out of his body; he imagined its vapours rising upwards between the sterile skyscrapers, reaching forty, fifty storeys to that tintless sky above.

The Telok Ayer Food Centre was conveniently close to his office. It used to be one of Singapore's oldest markets, the Telok Ayer Market, before being converted recently. At one time, in the frantic sweep of the Government's urban renewal programme, it had been threatened with demolition, but was spared in a rare moment of civic sanity, and now, gazetted as a national monument, graced the concrete jungle of the downtown financial district — a pretty Victorian structure of wood and elaborate cast iron filigree work, painted in white, black and pleasing pastel colours.

As soon as he entered, a mishmash of smells ambushed him: of mutton fat and chilies, of fish and garlic, of sesame oil and pig's liver, of roasted coffee beans and *murtabak,* of cigarettes and shrimps, of curries and rock oysters. It was, in short, a palace of a thousand delicacies.

The large interior was a maze of food stalls. Kok Leong sat at a vacant table and ordered a bowl of fish ball *tung hoon* and a bottle of chrysanthemum tea. He sat waiting for his food, gazing around him indifferently.

The place was packed with office workers, a vast congregation of clerks and peons, typists and stenographers, receptionists and telephonists. Most of them came there for lunch in groups.

His chrysanthemum tea arrived, a bottle of urine-coloured liquid. He poured it into a glass crammed with chunks of ice, and swirled the glass in his hand. When he felt the chill on his fingers, he began to draw sips through a white plastic straw, and a faint, almost timid, fragrance reached his nostrils, of flowers amidst the carnivorous smells. A young lad brought his bowl of *tung hoon* and a tiny side dish of freshly-cut circles of red chilies bathed in a thin, brandy-coloured soya sauce.

A demure young Chinese girl was sitting at the next table, her small, bud-like lips folded around the stem of a pink straw, slowly sucking up Pepsi Cola in a continuous flow into her avid mouth. Her companions were two other young girls — one, whose face he couldn't quite see, as she was bent over her bowl of noodles, busily eating, intent, hectic with chopsticks, appearing capable of gulping down the world, while the other was pretty and proud, assured of attention. One could tell she was used to being pampered by men's eyes. She wore a smile jauntily on her face, the very flower of a smile it was, but not directed at anyone in particular: it was for everyone, even for Kok Leong.

A big, rough-looking Chinese man of about sixty wearing the faded blue cotton shorts and shirt of dockyard workers came and sat at his table, without asking permission. He called loudly in dialect for a *Hokkien soup mee.* Kok Leong noticed the unkempt hairs on his upper lip, the slightly

Part Two

protuberant eyes which looked harassed, as if disturbed by some turmoil inside his head. The whites of his eyes were shot with spidery clusters of angry capillaries. His thick fingers were stained brown.

The two of them sat silently next to each other, total strangers whose paths had never crossed before, and who had no intention now of developing any relationship. They were simply sitting at the same table at a particular, random moment in time, that's all, two satellites, each journeying on a different orbit.

Then a girl from his office came to the table. The food centre was so crowded that people tended to sit wherever there was a space. They exchanged the merest, most minimal glance of recognition. She was simply a girl who worked in the same firm, though in a different section. What was her name? Kok Leong wondered. Emily something? Emily Ho.

He heard her give her order, also for fish ball *tung hoon*, to the boy, speaking slowly, precisely, with just sufficient economy of words to convey her needs. Must come from all that precise typing, those pages and pages of neat words, mused Kok Leong. She sat upright, holding herself very stiffly, careful to appear purposeful, formal.

Kok Leong had finished his meal. He ought to leave now, but for some unaccountable reason he was reluctant to do so. When the young help came to collect his glass and empty bowl, he asked for a cup of hot coffee. Emily Ho had begun to eat.

The old man had slurped up the last of his noodles, and, hunger appeased, belched so loudly that Kok Leong half expected clouds to spurt from the bulging sack of his stomach. Food had taken that edge of embattlement, of anger and fear, off the old man, and he seemed better prepared than before to continue the day, to live it out. He rose heavily to his feet, beckoned to the hawker and paid for his meal, taking out a crumpled dollar note and some coins from his shirt pocket.

"Well, good luck, you two! Have a good day," he said in Hokkien, with a small, shy, broken smile. It was an unexpectedly touching thing for this big wreck of a man to say, and both Kok Leong and Emily Ho were too startled to respond. The man was already walking away. For once, Kok Leong felt ashamed of his own silence and suspicion.

After the old man's departure, Kok Leong and Emily remained in their seats, feeling abandoned. The silence between them was strained, and their consciousness of each other began to grow.

"That was a strange old man!" Kok Leong blurted out, finally.

"A mad man!" Emily Ho replied curtly. They both spoke in English.

"No, not mad. Only strange."

"I know these mad, old men!" Emily Ho exclaimed.

Her note of vehemence discouraged Kok Leong from arguing. "I don't know him," he said.

"He was just a bum!" She seemed peculiarly fierce.

"No, I don't think so. He works. Can see from his body, from his hands." Somehow he wanted to defend the old stranger.

"So what?" Emily declared, her small head tilting upwards slightly, brisk and quick like a bird, her spectacles glinting at him, a flash of animosity in her dark pupils. She pinched her small, pursed mouth even tighter, a reflexive contraction, a defensive closing in. Kok Leong could sense her hardening, tightening. For some reason he wanted to prise her open, slip in the knife edge before the clam closed its shell, but he was already a little too late. He felt himself shunned, on the outside, their brief conversation apparently over. For some reason, this made him panic. He suddenly wanted words, words. *He* wanted. He!

But what if he were mistaken? What if there was no real source, no core, what if she were like a block of homogeneous ice which, when melted down, becomes mere water? Some human beings are like that. Nothing inside them at all. But something about her sparked an interest in him, a fascination. At the same time he knew that this could threaten his self-

Part Two

control, he himself so prone to unknown, unpredictable upheavals. Maybe it would all end badly.

"Do you eat here often?" he asked, painfully aware of the inanity of his question.

"Sometimes," she replied, bored with his clumsiness, and not bothering to hide her slight contempt.

He had always been niggardly with words, and, lacking a good command of them as well, had never been adept at social interaction. But there was about her a certain untouchability that he admired.

"I'm not any good at talking," he declared, with involuntary urgency, intoxicated by a stirring within.

Emily looked up at him sharply, but the intensity she saw in his face surprised her into silence, though her normal reflex would have been to rebuff. In the first place she had not planned to strike up a conversation with this young accounts clerk. He was so peculiar, with his wavy hair, his suspicious eyes piercing at you, his pimply, pale face and his slender, girlish physique. He was looking at her in a very odd way.

"I'm not good at it myself, not good at conversation," she said at last. Having finished her meal, she aligned her pair of chopsticks neatly across the rim of the empty bowl.

"Yes, I noticed that you're a very quiet girl."

"Is that unusual?"

"Yes. Most girls talk a lot."

"Do they?"

"Yes."

"You're very quiet yourself."

"When one has nothing to say, one listens to others, who seem to have plenty to say."

"I think they only talk a lot of nonsense."

"Yes," he said. "People do talk nonsense most of the time. They bore me to death."

Kok Leong felt that he had not been mistaken about Emily. Already, he regarded her as a fellow survivor, a fellow-combatant.

Just then the young hawker's helper came up to their table to collect the money for their meals.

"Let me pay," he offered.

"No, thanks. I always pay for myself," she insisted.

"Perhaps I can buy you lunch some other time. I would like to." And when she didn't respond, he added, "I've never asked any other girl before."

"Do you always eat alone?"

"Yes."

"You're a strange man. Most men don't eat alone."

"Most girls don't eat alone either. We have something in common."

They walked to the entrance, and hesitated, looking out across the street at the intense white sky, peering at it with circumspection, like divers moments before they have to plunge off a high cliff into the soaring air. Yes, they would have to plunge. There was no avoiding it.

"It's still a little early," he said, to cushion their plunge. "We have time. Let's have a stroll before going back to the office."

"It's so hot!"

"We can cross the street and walk under those trees to Clifford Pier."

"All right."

They emerged into the open air, quickly crossing the street to the pedestrian mall adjacent to the fenced godowns by the Telok Ayer Basin. The trees, transplanted alongside the concrete footway, were still small, but already their leaves were plump and glistening waxily in the strong sunlight. The shrubs of hibiscus and oleanders in their concrete tubs bore a concentration of flowers in various shades of pink and deep red. One particularly luxuriant oleander struck Kok Leong with its burst, with its proliferation of petals of a soft pink, so delicate, so fresh in the harsh heat. Oleanders, Kok Leong remembered from a botany lesson in school, secrete a toxic juice. So these delicate, pretty blossoms bore a poison. One could be fooled by nature.

Near Clifford Pier, the air, drifting in from the sea, had a pleasing freshness. They walked on a bit and there it was — the sea, with its surface sheen, its amplitude. Hundreds of small ships and boats squatted and skimmed on the glossy skin of the water. The sea, with her monstrous bliss, her innate, natural health.

"Can't hear the waves," Emily said.

"Waves?"

"Waves. Can't hear them," she complained. She preferred a sea stitched with waves, whipped whites frothing on top of turbulence the colour of cold iron, of water roaring, roaring. She was already turning away from this placid harbour, without a backward glance.

Kok Leong followed her, eager, for he sensed that she had something to say, something of importance. He waited, walking beside her, dogging her, but she had retreated, back into silence, her face shut. What face was this that seemed to hide something from the world? Was there a deep wound perhaps, inflicted when she was very young, that she kept hidden? Kok Leong wondered. Perhaps silence was a kind of solution she had found.

Emily said little. In answer to his queries, she only replied that she lived alone, boarding in a room with a family in Upper Serangoon, and that she liked going to the movies.

Movies? He was a bit surprised. There was a lot more he wanted to find out about her. For instance, why was she living alone? Was she an orphan? And this wound of hers, who had inflicted it on her? Who was instrumental, who was responsible for it?

Later, Kok Leong spent a long time thinking about these puzzles. All afternoon, he thought about her.

Was Kok Leong in love then? He must have been, for he was in a state of grace. And the proof of this? Why, in nature herself, for nature had become an accomplice. Through the wide glass window of the office, the afternoon waltzed with a graceful slowness, the dance of air as it rose and ballooned out. Later, a hazy blue displaced the whiteness.

And when he rode home in the early evening, a blueness also drifted into Kok Leong's mind, spontaneously, and looking at the sky from the moving bus he saw a dozen birds high up, cruising freely in the soft air, buffeted by unseen winds.

5

A month had passed since their tryst on the nocturnal sands of Sedili. Since then, they had snatched a few furtive nights, when their bodies thrashed against each other wildly, deliciously, rubbing together like fish. They had shared many sensual delights, and many simple ones. They had explored and improvised without caution or shame. Her sexual playfulness was a new intoxication for Kian Teck. Mate of one mate, before this.

Yet, after each assignation, after each rise and fall of passion, nothing very much remained, and he was piqued by the fact that memories were never sufficient, tangled as they were with time. Indeed, memories were not what he required. He found himself still burning for something else, tugged by an unknown pulse. Was he to chase after phantoms all his life? What the hell for?

Leaning against the sofa cushions, Kian Teck opened his eyes, turning his head slightly to look at Jay, her hair glossy in the dim light, her eyes liquid green. They were at a party Jay had been invited to.

"I like your eyes. Green. So quaint. So unique."

"They're hazel, and not so unique where I come from."

"Hazel?"

"Yes, hazel. A kind of green," she explained.

"How strange, to have hazel eyes. Do you see the world through a green veil?"

She laughed.

"Through a green jewel?"

Her face fell on his neck, her hair prickling, her ripples of laughter on his skin.

"I know what! Through a green ocean!"

She licked his skin.

"How strange it is!"

" What is?" She raised her head.

"Everything." And a little later, asked, "Do you have a cigarette?"

Jay took one from her rather large, shapeless, cloth handbag, and lit it for him. He inhaled deeply and released the smoke slowly through his nostrils, sensing the sere of scorched tobacco streaming across the small acreage of pink, moist, mucous membrane.

He continued. "We might think we're know-alls, but we live skimming on the surface of an iceberg, with a vast unknown beneath, submerged, that we're stupidly ignorant of, or are too frightened to want to know about. Or underneath it's like a deep dark hole, full of mysteries, filled with passions, with emotions and superstitions, and with unformed thoughts and desires, a lot of which are ill-defined, but are considered ugly and lewd shapes that should be kept hidden, like naked worms under the mossy wetness of stones. We hoard them, don't want them revealed."

"My! How sombrely you speak! I think you like to peer into this deep, dark subconscious hole of yours."

"All holes fascinate me," he bantered (*à la* Peter Low), "and," he said, his tone changing, "precipices. I like the wobbly feeling, the queasy sensation in the stomach, whenever I lean over ..."

"But most of us do that, now and then," she protested.

"No. Some don't. The Efficient don't. The Efficient do not bother with their subconscious. For them, the Id rules firmly. Hence they can achieve, can progress, can conquer ..."

"By the Efficient, you mean Americans?"

"Not only them, my darling. For aren't we all Americans now, in this day and age?"

A couple of people were dancing on the small square of space at the centre of the room, fenced by a swarm of blotchy faces, all wearing the forced, phony gaiety of parties. A man had come up to ask Jay to dance, but she declined. From his accent, he was either Swiss or German.

"You're wandering alone again," she said, turning to Kian Teck. "My lonely, eternal wanderer."

"Sure I'm not one of your bland men?"

"Don't fish for compliments," she said. Then added, "You know how to suffer."

Kian Teck was about to laugh out loud, but held himself in check at the final moment. Serious, he said, "I'm not so sure I do. Is suffering an art?"

"You're asking the wrong person. I'm totally unlike you. I've no yen for suffering. All I know is that some people do and some don't."

"Some are fat and some are thin," he recited. "Some eat meat and some eat vegetables. We have them all, in this God-given, diverse, great world of ours."

"Why do you want to suffer, Kian Teck?"

He considered this, gulping down the last dregs of his vodka. The cigarette felt like a cinder in his tender fingers and he dropped it into the glass. A hiss. Like a single falling star, its scintillant death-sink in the sky. Incendiary extinction. Hisssss!

"Because it's easier," he finally answered. "It's easier than not to suffer."

"What have you been drinking?"

"Vodka, gin, brandy, beer, vodka ... This is a very posh party that you've brought me to. By the way, who is our generous host?"

"Some young Yank. With one of the big merchant banks. You drink too much."

"Now you're nagging me."

"You seem to drink so *recklessly*. I don't understand you."

"Nothing to understand. Simply got to fill my bottomless pit. The dark pit we talked about, remember? That you said you liked?"

"Oh, Kian Teck!"

It was both a rebuke and solicitude.

"You know, kiddo, you're terrific," he told her. "You really are. You have this style, this incredible undemandingness, that is so rare. You're so alive!"

"You're alive too. Only ..." and she looked at him wonderingly, "... there is this recklessness. You're consumed by it!"

"Ahhh! Fire! Fire!"

"You're too much!"

"My glass is empty. Must get a refill."

He attempted to get up, but was a bit clumsy, the sofa so deep.

"I'll get it for you," she offered.

He handed her the glass. "You're an angel. Please make sure it's Stolichnaya. The real stuff. Not Smirnoff, nor any of that émigré shit!"

"You're impossible!"

"Have always been!" he shouted after her as she walked away, heading for the bar at the far end of the glittering room.

After her! Quick! With an offering of words, a bouquet of apologies. But the words remained unspoken, clotted in his throat. What could he tell her? How could he tell her, his bronzed lover, that in spite of her, he still felt empty? How could he tell her that? There was a great deal that couldn't be explained. He felt he did not have the energy to initiate this rush of words. They had to be wrenched out of him. On the rack, most likely. Bone-soft, he was tempted to just let things slide, let his life and all that revolved so madly around it, fall apart, fall away. After the fall, maybe peace. *Pacem in terra.* Now? Only tedium, tedium! *Omnium est!*

In the duration, a new record, a new sound. Soul music. Black female voices rolled and pitched high on the oily waves of euphony, in the cinnamon-scented sweaty night, musk and perfume, heady and erotic, but with an inner core that drilled you with their hysteria for life, with their liberated energy, pure and smooth, on top, on top of the ruling rhythms — of drums that gunned at you, and brassy reverberations that blasted at you, that would make you celebratory. In an instant, celebrants got up to dance, their bodies rippling and stirring like a school of fish in night-water. The sounds reaching Kian Teck were overwhelming, and he sank back in the sofa, to listen, to watch, and felt the blood beating in his own heart.

Jay returned with a filled glass. She handed it to him, then tried to coax him to dance. He demurred, offering instead a somewhat bruised smile, battered by hours, worn thin by use and abuse. But Jay's keen, green eyes rejected his smile, and turning her head this way and that, with a certain resolution, a bit of hauteur (for every lover is quick to take offence), she finally settled for their young Yankee host, and walked up to him.

Kian Teck took a large swallow of vodka and watched the dancers moving in a silver-blue cloud of smoke, their bodies withdrawing into a dream-like a slow glide of swans. Never still. They were never still. He closed his eyes. His thoughts, slow-moving clouds.

The dancers seemed to be enacting a rite in which he had no rôle, no part. Distant and unapproachable. As distant as the stars which he could see through the wide, unpanelled glass of the window. Outflung nebulae they were, materializing in the black night outside, so remote, millions of light years away, and so alien, they made him feel un-needed. What had his life to do with these scraps of crystal? What had it to do with the universe?

He thought of the unseen Mariner space module that the Americans,

Jay's people, had sent up, to probe Mars. Even at that very moment it was silently whizzing through space towards Mars at a thousand miles a minute, or some such incredible speed. Mars? What had Mars to do with him?

What am I doing here? he asked himself. What plagues me?

Then the loud music sang in him, his pulse obedient to the beat, though through the tide of the song, the flow of melody, speaking voices intruded (they had seemed so ... irreconcilable!).

His eyes peeled open. Soft fruit blinking in raw air. For a moment, he felt lost. Indistinctly, he saw blurry figures sliding across the floor. Was he dreaming still? Everything lacked clarity. It was as if he had been sleeping, but for how long he could not tell. For a minute? Or two hours? Six years? He could not tell. It came to him that he had been truant — Rip van Winkle!

But how could he count the hours in this hourless night?

What could ratify?

Outside, the stars were frozen still. Far removed.

Then out of the wavering crowd he spotted Jay's eyes, rending apart the dream, or sleep, or whatever it was. Through a haze, she came towards him.

"You're ghastly pale!" she scolded.

"I'm a ghost," he told her, solemnly.

"Are you all right?"

He nodded. But his head felt as if it would crash down, snap from the stalk of his neck.

"It's late, Kian Teck. I think we should go."

"Have you danced enough?"

"I didn't come here to dance."

"Why did we come? I've forgotten."

"You wanted to meet people."

"I did?"

"Let's go. Please."

Part Two

So he drove around Tanglin. All the tall hotels and luxury apartment blocks had lost their hard shapes, floating, dissolving in the rich, warm darkness above the street lamps. The lamps poured their gold onto the trees and shrubbery by the roadside, creating gilded, inner pools of artificial afternoons (that a Debussy faun could browse in) amongst the leaves, mingling glows and shadows, scattering, melting into many layers, many levels.

As Kian Teck motored through the silent streets, Jay gently unzipped his fly, dipped in her hand and drew out his cock. Then bowed her head low and took it in her mouth. She sucked him as he drove. He was conscious only of the warm, rhythmic, smooth motions of her inner cheeks and tongue, ripples of silk on his cock, and he wished it would never stop. Never stop. Never. Never. Never.

Then, as he surged, he held his breath, before groaning "Aaagh!" and spilled his seed into her mouth.

A little later, he dropped Jay off at her friend's apartment in Orange Grove Road and headed for his own home.

Emptied, he cursed himself: "Is it not enough? Insatiable, rotten pig!"

The car slid quietly into the driveway. Kian Teck got out, locked the car door and walked across the garden, treading noiselessly on night-grass.

Glancing up, he saw no light in his apartment. Only a couple of others were lit in the entire building, making it look like a mammoth skull with light filtering blindly through empty eye sockets. A bony relic.

The stars were still there, embedded in the black face of the sky, but they were fixed and unchanging, so familiar that they held no surprises, no wonder. No, there was nothing new in the sky.

Suddenly, he staggered, his head dizzy with nausea. He leaned against a small tree in the garden, but the spinning would not go away, and he felt chill shivers running up and down his skin. At last he stooped low and vomited and retched and vomited again, his system attempting to expel all that foulness from his insides. Emptied, he felt wan and weak, his forehead coated with cold sweat. He rested for a short while, leaning his head against the tree. Then he stumbled slowly home.

Far, far away, Mariner continued its silent rocketing through space.

IT WAS ALREADY HALF-PAST TEN when Kian Teck woke up the next morning. The slowness of Sunday hung in the air. The curtains had been drawn and the whole sky opened up, powerfully torn asunder, so that light flew everywhere. It darted into his bedroom, leaving its yellow imprints on the window sill. It obliterated every trace of the night, including the false disasters of his lingering dreams. Dreams? But which the real and which the false? Which? The one faded by distance (the length of the distance itself lovely), smoky, like old photographs, sepia-tinted, or this one, in which he was immersed at present, so light-blasted?

But could one hope to re-enter a dream? Could one hope (similarly) to re-live yesterday, re-explore the past, take up all those lost opportunities proffered before but rejected, travel at last down all those undiscovered side-lanes (so out of the way) that one had shunned, had deliberately missed? Yes! All those sins of omission, because of one's foolishness, or impatience, or cowardice, or just plain ordinary weakness. Could one do that? Only by a miracle. Or madness. Otherwise, they were all forbidden. *Verboten!*

So, generally forbidden to retrace one's steps, there is left only the now, the imminent, the future (whatever its length) which one has to negotiate, still endowed with one's foolishness, impatience, cowardice, and plain ordinary weakness. Yes, one's ordinariness, as opposed to uniqueness. Yet others seemed so unruffled by this same knowledge, so un-scornful of themselves! Quite unlike him! Actually, he decided, he deluded himself that he was marked, that God's finger (for want of a better way of putting it) was on him.

He rose up slightly in the bed, supporting himself on one elbow, and stretched out the other hand (like the beggar he really was) for the handy glass of water. Ah water! Water! How he needed water. To dilute the alcohol. Last night's drunkenness was still in his bloodstream, which danced and flickered, the crowded corpuscles like tiny hooked fish flashing in the tide, jostling against the vessels' walls, particularly in those that delved deep inside his head. It was all too much, and he let his head fall, leaf-light, on the snow-white pillow, feather-puffed soft.

The drawn curtains hung stiffly in two solid columns one on each side of the wide window; the air in the room, dead. And the brightness served to accentuate the barrenness within. All was foreign — the roomful of air, the assorted pieces of furniture, and time; all somewhat defunct, having lost their identities. They seemed to be waiting for someone to claim ownership. Yet Kian Teck doubted whether their identities could ever be restored. For he himself no longer had any rights. He had lost his authority, he guessed, maybe forever. He had no illusions about this. There they lay, like vessels to be filled, for life and buoyancy (the very stuff of which identity is composed) would come only when someone poured in a measure of grace, a touch of love, an act of kindness. Yes, loving kindness. The grace of loving kindness. That was what was needed. That was what he could not give.

Lack of authority brought about inertia, so he simply lounged in his bed, waiting (like the air in the room, the furniture and the hours) for something to happen.

He heard the door click open and saw Li Lian coming in. He watched her walk across the room towards the bathroom, tense, as if trailing electrical static behind her, sparking the air. It made him nervous.

It had been many weeks now since they had really talked to each other. In fact, not since his illicit tryst with Jay at Sedili. Illicit? Now *that* was a strange word. And adultery. As if marriage was still sacred! Which, of course, it was not. Just old-fashioned, Christianised, westernized shit! Foreign notions.

And yet, Kian Teck could not help feeling guilty about his deception — for simply, that was what it was — and his transgression of, not so much the rules, but the living spirit, of marriage. (Sometimes he wondered how old Peter could breeze through it all!) And he had discovered that deception was not fool proof. His wife knew. No one had told her, he was certain of that. They never spoke about it, never discussed it. But a silence had fallen between them, a void they could not close. On his part, he knew it could not be filled with lies, and he did not tell any. On her part, she did not recriminate, did not pick an open quarrel, but went about with a vigilant air, and sealed herself in. She carefully guarded her private world from him, so that, recently, (as if by poetic justice) it was his wife's silence that Kian Teck found unnerving, as she busied herself with the children, or went about doing her household chores, with muted accents, behind closed doors. It intimidated him to such an extent that without consciously thinking about it, he made himself as unobtrusive as possible. Small as a mouse in the house.

So there existed a constant tension between them as they gave each other quick, stealthy glances, taking care to avoid looking directly into each other's eyes. They became quite adept at this. And when they had to speak to each other, they restricted themselves to topics which did not break, but preserved, this distance between them, their selective vocabulary merely empty echoes in the void. The worst was when night was upon them, when they would lie next to each other in the same bed, but so cold and apart (clamped in their shells) that they might just as well have been a continent apart. They had discontinued love-making. It was (paradoxically) one of those unspoken but intuitive agreements that only two people who shared a long relationship could reach. So he would lie next to her, and feel her growing colder and harder with each passing night, like the process of scarring (tissues hardening as the wound closes), and he had not found a way to salve this wound, of which he was the cause, this great hole of hers that he could fall into and get lost in. There were some nights when he had desired, but dared not touch her, thus losing the opportunity which only their bodies, their flesh, could grant them if they had acted — the boon of forgiveness.

He had grown insomniac, restless most nights, and more and more, he took to drinking to prepare for the nightly ordeal. He was now drinking with a compulsion, driven by his apprehension of their silent, chaste bed. There were nights when he got up in the late hours and went out to raid the drinks cabinet in the dining room. Avid gulps of brandy straight from the neck of the bottle.

Early one evening, when Kian Teck had taken his children to play in the Kampong Java Park, he had strolled (lapsed jogger he) near the rim of the pond. It was a clear, still evening and the pond was a smooth mirror that reflected without distortion the sky, the rolling white clouds, the old, tall *tembusus* growing on the bank. He saw the lovely pink brow of twilight inclining over the water. Truly, a mirror. He leant over, trying to peer at the fertile depths of the pond, and at those hidden things, fishes, weeds, beneath the surface, with their unseen, deep (suspicion of) sleep. But his attention was distracted by several insects, long-legged, which skimmed across the surface of the water, like ice skaters. They moved smoothly, swiftly, criss-crossing the pond and setting tiny, trailing waves in motion, lines rather than waves, so fine, in their nameless dance, darting here and there, but never touching, or meeting at all, their movements never in unison. Watching the, he thought how he and his wife had become like these water insects, moving independently of each other, skimming on the surface of each other's lives, and never meeting any more (two balloon-worlds receding). Thus he interpreted the meaning of the long-legged water insects (suddenly recalling an apt line of Yeats's ... "Like a long-legged fly upon the stream/ His mind moves upon silence.")

He watched them, waiting for them (a wish, somewhere?) to sink down into the depths of the water, claimed by preying fish, but they just continued moving blithely across the surface, oblivious of any danger. Finally he turned away from the pond, despondent.

Li Lian came out of the bathroom and he glanced sideways at her, at her stride, which, though small, flowed strongly and brightly. She was wearing a yellow T-shirt and a pair of beige jeans. Bright as a flower.

"Are we going to the beach today?" he asked, before she could leave the room.

"No. I'm taking the kids to Mother's."

"They don't want to go to the beach?"

"We'd planned to go to Mother's earlier in the week." Her demeanour, he detected, meant it was final, but she said, to soften, "I can't let Mother down. She's not been too well."

"Is it something serious?"

"It's her back. Her rheumatism. It's getting bad."

"So it's only her back?"

"Yes, but I must get the boys ready now."

Even on the subject of her mother's health, it seemed Li Lian would not be drawn out. Not that Kian Teck was truly concerned about his mother-in-law. But she really was OK, a harmless, mild-mannered old bird. Never made any demands on them. She lived quietly with Li Lian's spinster elder sister in a large, ramshackle pre-War bungalow on the East Coast Road, just beyond the old Marine Parade. The house once faced the sea, which had been reclaimed during the past couple of years, and high-rise HDB apartments, built by the Government, had sprung up on the reclaimed, flat land. It was an old, wooden bungalow, one-storeyed, but raised a few feet on concrete stilts, in the fashion of the seaside

Part Two

bungalows of those bygone days when life was more sumptuous and gracious. Now widowed, the old lady had taken in four or five lodgers. Old bachelors, as if to go with the large, antique pieces of furniture, so strongly built and of such fine hardwood that they had withstood the years, the white ants, and the generations of children. The large garden was full of old fruit trees, *rambutans*, mangoes, *chicku* and *chempedak*; they shed a perpetual miasma of over-ripe and rotting fruit into the warm air, which lingered in one's nostrils. The children loved the place, loved running about the large grounds, playing amongst the trees, munching the air swollen with the scent of ripened fruit in the warm and brooding glow of the afternoons. They also loved to roam through the big rooms of the house — some of which had not been used for years — with their stale, musty air, and cobwebs in the corners of the high ceilings, and the broken furniture, hunting for, or being hunted by, ghosts. Grandma never scolded, even when they made a racket, but sat in her rattan armchair and smiled gently, her face white with the "cooling" *bedak sejuk* rice powder, serving everybody *Nonya kuehs* and tea from the silver tea set at four o'clock. Yes, Grandma was a nice old lady, in her *sarong kebaya*, and with the long gold *chucok-sanggul* hairpins in her *sanggul*, her grey-chignoned hair.

So Li Lian and Kian Teck used to take the kids to visit their grandma, usually on Saturday afternoons. But this was a Sunday, their own day, and yet Li Lian was taking them to Grandma's. It wasn't stated in so many words, but he was not invited to accompany them (big, bad Daddy that he was). He was being left alone, abandoned to the Sunday.

Soon after his family had left, Kian Teck (who was attentive to the minutest sounds of their going) got out of bed. He went from the bedroom, across the living room, into the kitchen and got himself a glass of cold water from the fridge. He threw back his head and drank it all down in one go (he had to hurry, now that there was no need at all to do that!). Then he walked about the empty flat, like a vagrant wind, blowing from room to room, sweeping in and out and about without any aim. Outside, the day lay in wait, hard and bright, that suddenly excessive day, with its stretch of superfluous hours. He winced from the glare and found that he had no will, no aspiration, to go out. What was there to aspire to anyway? Only somehow to contrive to while the excess day away. That was all.

So be it! He decided to have a wash. Get ready. Be prepared. Etcetera. In the bathroom, he filled up the washbasin with water and submerged his face in it. Then he saw his face in the mirror, dripping wet, his eyes with their tangles of angry blood vessels. God, I'm getting careless with myself, he thought. God, this degeneration of the body, this green liver of mine! Green liver? It's probably *purple* by now. He could taste disgust on his soiled and furry tongue. Must look after yourself, man, however imperfectly you do it. Otherwise ...

Otherwise?

The question was left unresolved that Sunday.

Sunday?

Yes, Sunday. And then, Monday, and then Tuesday, Wednesday, Thursday, Friday, Saturday and back again to Sunday. They'd just keep recurring, these days of the week, like thirst, like hunger, like sleepiness, like the urge to piss and shit, like lust, like the urge to fuck. What is life but a cycle of these urges and habits?

Sunday. And yet, one day is, and should be, indistinguishable from another. Sunday. There was really nothing that made the day a Sunday. The day itself did not give any clue. It was only man-imposed. Why? What for? It was unnatural. Animals, for instance, don't distinguish a Sunday from a Monday. They do not care, nor ask, for one day to be different from another. At least, they *wouldn't* ask! Man, the only asking creature in the world! Yes! Ask! Ask! Ask! Arse! Arse! Arse! Ach! Ach! Ach! and — cocking his right fore finger like a gun and aiming it at the side of his head — *Ack! Ack! Ack! Ack!* he drilled it full of imaginary holes.

Part Two

EARLY MONDAY MORNING FLASHED BETWEEN THE BUILDINGS as Kian Teck drove his new car towards the city. It was a Chevrolet 350, British Racing Green, automatic transmission, power-steering, with built-in air-con and remote control knobs for raising and lowering the windows of all four doors. Posh, beautiful. He hummed to himself as he drove. The car made no sound. The tinted glass windows were wound up, the air-con whirred gently, insulating him from the world outside.

All in all, Kian Teck had every reason to hum. He was enjoying his brand new car, he had made a tidy sum of money playing the stock market, he had his golden-girl lover, and his family was still with him. What more could a man want?

Yes, his marriage was still intact, although, admittedly, the undertones of its continuity had gone through a change (only a shift of sea-bed, dimly perceived from a boat drifting along the shore, changing from aquamarine to green and darker greens, with flickering faint shadows). But then, what doesn't change with time? Nothing stays the same. Yes, their marriage was like a rock. Only, now the undercurrents were pulling in a different direction from that charted previously (perhaps it ought to be declared a slightly unsafe zone?).

But, driving his brand new car, he felt sure he could negotiate those undercurrents, which seemed somewhat slack. Yes, he felt safer in the big new car. Less assailable. For nowadays, in our consumerist age, it's the make of his car that maketh a man.

He had actually (secretly) desired a Jaguar XJ6. Gosh! That sleek design! Those exquisite lines! Above all, its discreet opulence!

But he simply did not possess that essential insouciance, the required daring and flair. Truth was, he had enough virtue left in him to understand the vulgarity of ownership, of possessing the symbols of riches. So he had vacillated between keeping his perfectly serviceable old Toyota and buying a Jag. Finally he compromised, and settled for a Chevrolet 350. He had succumbed, had capitulated to greed and desire. For the first few days he had suffered misgivings driving around in a car which was so expensive, luxurious and ostentatious. He felt shy, ill at ease, uncomfortable, embarrassed, guilty, foolish, unworthy — in short, like a usurper, as if he had no right to own such a grand thing. When he drove around he felt self-conscious, not knowing whether he was exhibiting his car or himself. A show-off!

To counteract this feeling, he found himself compelled to go around concocting and offering excuses to everyone, even if no one asked him to do so, even if no one was really interested or cared a hoot about his new car.

He told his wife that the old Toyota was beginning to give trouble. The engine. The body work. You know these Japanese things, he said, they look nice but the truth is they're not made to last. Li Lian hadn't bothered to ask him why he'd changed the car, much less accused him of doing anything wrong.

To his friends, and office colleagues, he gave a big intellectual discourse on how things were simply not made to last nowadays. Cars, radios, TV sets, watches. Nothing lasts. We live in the great disposable age, he propounded, the age of planned obsolescence. Everything has a built-in obsolescence, so that the gigantic wheel of industry can keep on turning. If things last, why, whole economies would collapse! Man must consume, must discard, must dispose of things in order to maintain a high standard of living. So, he had to dispose of his old, beat-up Toyota, he said, although no one was interested.

He repeated the same things to Jay, adding that even love and marriage have a built-in obsolescence nowadays. And man too! Then he clowned, by intoning like the character in the TV series: "Mr. Ong! Your life will self-destruct in just twenty-eight years, six months, five days, seven hours, four minutes, and eleven seconds from now! If your death should be discovered, God, and everybody else in the department, will claim no responsibility. They will just not know you. They will deny everything ..."

So, for days Kian Teck went around boring the hell out of everyone. Luckily for his friends, he eventually got used to his car and felt quite at home cruising the great green thing around town. The moral is that one can get used to practically anything. In other words, everything is habit-forming — from a new car to a new wife, from poverty to riches, and from love to murder. Man is excellently endowed.

His run of good fortune had changed Kian Teck, made him feel that perhaps it wasn't so impossible for a person to become rich. Hitherto, like most wage-earners, workers and peasants — in other words, like ninety-nine per cent of the world's people — he had thought it beyond his understanding how a man like Howard Hughes or John Paul Getty, or Mellon, or Runme Shaw, could each amass a personal fortune in the hundreds of millions! Four hundred million dollars! Such a ludicrous, unreal sum!

On the other hand, Kian Teck used to ruminate, consider a country like Indonesia. The per capita income there is around two hundred US dollars per annum. So, by simple arithmetic, it would take twenty million Indonesians working collectively a whole year, to attain a sum that just matches this one man's fortune! So, what is this talk about justice and equality? With this astronomical gap between the rich and the poor, how could there be peace on earth?

But these thoughts seldom concerned Kian Teck nowadays. That particular Monday morning, driving his brand new car towards town, he was preoccupied with the prospects of the stock exchange. He no longer bothered himself with the world's perennial problems and disasters. The rapidly unfolding drama of the Watergate scandal, the deteriorating state of affairs in South Vietnam, Laos and Cambodia,* the instability of the Thai coalition government of Seni Pramoj, the situation in Portugal and

---

* Now Kampuchea.

in the Lebanon crowded the newspaper headlines that year. And Kian Teck's attitude when he read them now was, *fuck the world!* If mankind insists on clobbering, robbing and killing one another, there was nothing he could do about it, so fuck each and every one of them. Let them do what they wanted to. As far as *he* was concerned, these events were relevant only because they might affect the price movement of the shares.

At the previous Friday's close, the market had been generally steady, with small, selective gains in the industrial and property sections. His Cold Storage shares had an aggregate gain of eight cents throughout the week, and Town and City gained six cents. On the financial and banking sections, his holdings of ten thousand UOB shares gave the best results, gaining fourteen cents, closing at four dollars and twenty-eight cents. He wondered whether he ought to let UOB go. He'd already made a fair profit. Well, he'd see when the market opened. And talk to Kay Fong, his broker. Might just take the profit and pick up more Town and City. The latter would rise some more. These were Kian Teck's thoughts as he arrived at the office.

His secretary, Emily Ho, came in to discuss the day's schedule and he was able to ease into his workaday rôle with routine smoothness. And so the morning disappeared, hastened along by his work as he kept his appointments with clients, went over various projects with his team of subordinates, checked out the final layout for a glossy brochure, adjusted the copy of certain ad inserts, and made sure that all those coined phrases, captions and jingles sounded sufficiently apt and convincing to entice the public mind.

While he was busy playing this rôle, there was an inner — and expanding — world which he kept in his head: the world of the stock market. Throughout the morning he made periodic phone calls to his broker, Goh Kay Fong. Already an esteemed and important client, Kian Teck had access to Mr. Goh's private, unlisted line. They were now on first-name terms, although, strictly speaking they were not friends, but had a relationship that was rather special, that was perhaps even more intimate than friendship. Goh Kay Fong was a small, bony man in his mid-thirties who wore a pair of black, horn-rimmed spectacles and who always spoke in a soft but deep voice, a sagely, reassuring voice which hinted at authority, at a calm and judicious intelligence, and a certain mysterious acquaintance with "intimate sources" which he could, as a special favour, reveal only to his favoured client, Ong Kian Teck. One could easily become addicted to such a voice. Kian Teck looked forward with great eagerness to their hushed, intimate conversations on the phone; he enjoyed indulging in that special argot of the stock market.

So, with this inner world in his head, Kian Teck could sometimes ignore the exigencies of the other world: of wife and lover, of love and lust, of guilt and ecstasy. They faded away as he became mesmerised by the ups and downs of the market. The truth was that he had now discovered something almost akin to religion, or to the passion of the artist — he had discovered the keen, obsessive joy of gambling, of laying long odds. So much so that whenever he played the market correctly and saw the prices of the shares he had bought soar, he grew convinced that he possessed a talent for the game of chance. He was fascinated by what he thought was the clear, clean logic of the stock market, and was more than gratified to find that he had the gift to analyse, to decipher, to predict its movements — movements quite unlike the vagaries and messiness of the other world, the world of the emotions.

Gambling, he thought, had the simplicity, the purity, the order of higher mathematics, lofty and supreme. Yes, Kian Teck believed, with the superstition of the gambler, that he had the uncanny gift (and no one questions gift horses) of analysing the odds, and this made him heady. He felt that wealth could be conquered, could be *his!* And not only wealth, but all that went with it: power, position, etcetera.

Yes, they could be his, he felt sure, if he were bold enough and had enough faith in his own skill (he, a buccaneer now, an Errol Flynn of high finance, no less). And if someone had asked him on that Monday morning whether he believed in himself, Kian Teck would have emphatically said, Yes! Yes! And again, *Yes!*

6

During those first weeks, images of Emily would sometimes appear to Chan Kok Leong at night, intensified, when the small apartment was awash with the heavy breathing of his family, lost in sleep. Images of her eyes, her small-boned hands, the slight angular bracing of her shoulders, the way she spoke, would fill him with tenderness. Yes, Kok Leong was in love.

But first, a nightmare.

One night soon after their chance meeting at the Telok Ayer Food Centre, he dreamed that Emily was being disemboweled with his own Swiss knife, the blade flashing silver, cleanly cutting open the soft walls of her belly, a torrent of intestines spilling out, gleaming pale in a matrix of blood. Kok Leong woke up terrified, drenched in sweat, and, filled with nausea, he rushed into the kitchen and threw up into the aluminum sink.

That was the only bad moment. Usually, when he thought about Emily, he was filled with a tenderness he had never experienced before. Until this happened, he would not have believed it possible that he could feel this way.

One evening, on his way home from work, Kok Leong was caught in a sudden drizzle. He did not run away from it, did not seek shelter, but enjoyed feeling the fine rain, gentle as caresses, on his upturned face.

And one night, after dining with his family, he went for a walk, although he did not plan to go anywhere in particular. He did not feel the need for companionship, was content to be on his own, thinking his own quiet thoughts. Actually, so vague and amorphous they were, they were hardly thoughts, just processes of a mind at rest, sailing like clouds slowly across the sky. Kok Leong wandered wherever his mood took him. He toured of part of Toa Payoh, walking by the empty wet market where smells of fish, raw meat and vegetables still lingered. He walked past small provision shops and coffee shops and restaurants. There were people everywhere, ordinary people, doing ordinary things, and Kok Leong felt that he shared something with them.

Sometimes, observing his father enjoy a cigarette over a cup of hot chocolate late at night, his old eyes watery and contented, Kok Leong would almost smile. He was vaguely conscious that his smile, if it materialized, would actually be directed at Emily, although she was far away in Upper Serangoon. He would be alone and yet somehow feel that he was with her. It was a miracle!

He had been out with Emily five times in as many weeks. Twice, they lunched together. They went to the cinema a couple of times. And there was that night when they had dinner at an open-air seafood restaurant in Bedok. After dinner, they had gone for a walk on the reclaimed beach at Marine Parade. That was what Kok Leong had enjoyed most of all, walking by the sea, that early night, under the stars with Emily. The whole world seemed different: the night sky, the soft murmuring sea, the vibrant air. It made him tingle inside, as if there were a cluster of tiny bells somewhere within him. It made him feel romantic, although of course he didn't think of it as such. Romance was only a word, and what he was experiencing could never be adequately described by words alone. All said, however, Kok Leong, for want of a better way to describe his state, was feeling romantic, and the world was transformed by the luminosity of his love. A cliché? Perhaps. But when one is in love, calling that a cliché means very little. After all, all love songs are clichés: "Rose, Rose I love you, with an aching heart", and "You are my everything", and "Drink to me only with thine eyes". Take any love song, in any language, from any age — they're all nothing but clichés, their words and sentiments, banal. But they are so only to those who are not in love, and especially so to those who've never been in love. There are so many sour, hardened, dried up people in this world who consider love vulgar, people who live within locked rooms, staring up at blank ceilings, counting each barren minute. And yet, besides love, what are the rest but abstractions? Philosophy and religion, science and technology, mathematics and economics, all abstractions, arranged only by the mind. And however stupendous an invention the mind, when it's working alone it cannot understand the pleasures of existence, the pleasures of being alive. Whereas love heightens and intensifies and makes wondrous every small thing, charging it with sacred beauty.

Kok Leong and Emily walked along the promenade which skirted the seashore. There was a white moon. On one side stood the gleaming tall blocks of HDB apartments and the regularly-spaced street lamps of globular glass, on the other, the sea, across patches of sandy beach. A wind starting up from the land was quietly stroking the sea. They could see across the stretch of water to the vast clusters of lighted ships in the harbour, and behind these, in the distance, the city skyscrapers jutting up ghost-like, dissolving as the light withdrew from the sky. The city seemed so very far away, while nearby, the sea uncoiled its waves, gnawing at the sand, groping with a primaeval patience.

"Let's sit down for a while," Kok Leong urged.

Emily nodded.

They walked a little distance out onto the beach and sat where the sand was dry and powdery and it was a little darker than the lit path. There, on that dim spot of beach, Emily had spoken for the first time about herself, although what had prompted her to speak, Kok Leong could never be sure. Perhaps it was the setting, the sea, the open sky, although she had once told him that she did not care for beautiful scenery, for pretty landscapes. It began when he asked her a simple question.

"Where exactly do you live?"

He knew that it was somewhere in Upper Serangoon, but he had never been to her place. She had always insisted on finding her own way home.

"A small house on a small road near Yio Chu Kang," she replied, brief and to the point.

"It's quite far from here then," Kok Leong probed.

"No, not far."

"This family you're lodging with, are they all right?"

"I'm only a lodger. I have my own room. My own freedom. I don't bother them, they don't bother me."

"You're alone then?"

"Yes, I'm alone. Since childhood, I've impatiently counted the days when I'd be old enough to live on my own. To be independent, to be free at last."

"What about your family?"

"I don't have much of a family left."

"Are they all ... ?" he left the question tactfully unfinished.

"I'm an only child. My mother died many years ago. There's only my father."

"Do you see him often?"

"As seldom as I can. I hate my father. I know what people will think, what they will say. But I don't care. I've always hated him. He's a good-for-nothing! A weak, selfish, greedy pig!"

"Did he mistreat you?"

"I don't know what you mean by that. I hate him. Doesn't *that* say something?"

They heard the sea groping the shore, wave after wave, as if to retrieve something it had lost, or wanted. There was only sand, dead seaweed, discarded bottles, cans, broken pieces of toys, and black, soaked planks with rusty nails sticking out.

After a long while Kok Leong said, "I'd always thought of my father as a nobody. Only now do I begin to see him for what he is."

"What do you see?"

"Just an ordinary old man, who works, who is poor, who is tired and worn out. I don't blame him as much as I used to."

"What happened?"

"Nothing. I mean, I don't know. Before, I used to despise him because I thought he was weak and ineffectual. Now I know that being weak and ineffectual are not so uncommon in life. But there's one more thing. It's very important. Now I see that he does not despair, and therefore he does not deserve to be so despised."

"I despise *my* father!" Emily insisted.

"You know," Kok Leong continued, seeming not to hear her exclamation, "he works as a toilet attendant in a hotel. A toilet attendant! I used to be so ashamed — for him, for us, for me. But my old man, *he's* not ashamed of himself and he does not cringe. Only, he's a little sad, perhaps. A little worn out. A toilet attendant! Somehow, it doesn't matter so much now, to me. To him, I guess it never mattered very much. It was just another way to make a living, that's all. Isn't his attitude amazing?" he concluded, turning his head to see Emily's reaction.

"I've never found adults amazing," Emily replied curtly. "Not in an admirable sense. Even as a little girl, I never thought much of adults — especially when I had my own parents as examples. My father was very selfish; he never cared about anybody else; I don't think he really cared about my mother, or me. He only thought about himself, and wanted everything for himself. And so greedy! Such a glutton! Even now, I can't wipe away my memory of him during meal times, gorging himself, stuffing all that food into his mouth, as if he was terrified that others might steal the choice bits. My memory of him is with his mouth stuffed with food, and spit dribbling down his chin. A pig! A revolting pig!" Emily said, with a look of sheer disgust on her face. She was a little girl again, staring open-mouthed at her father eating dinner at home. Later, she'd learnt to shut her own lips, tight as a zippered purse.

"What was your mother like?" Kok Leong asked.

"My mother? She died when I was ten. A frail creature, foolish and romantic." She spoke dispassionately, describing an insect, a fly, perhaps — or a butterfly? "When I was a small girl, I used to watch her as she sat in front of her dressing table, looking at herself in the mirror, and taking a long time doing her face, combing her hair. She must have fancied herself as a flower of a woman, or a butterfly, and dreamed of dancing at the Great World ballroom or some such place. Sometimes, my father took her out, but those occasions were as rare as they must have been memorable. I think my father took her out not more than a dozen times during their life together, but my mother lived for those moments. They were the real highlights of her life, the flower season, the butterfly season — or hours. They were too brief to be called seasons. All the same, she would sit there for hours, making herself up in front of the dressing table mirror. I thought, even then, and I've no reason to change my opinion now, how vain and frivolous woman is. To spend so much time staring at her own image! And my mother couldn't even be considered a beautiful woman. I think our sex is prone to frivolity."

Time was washed away by the rolling of the waves. The field of lights radiated by ships in the harbour across the water grew palpitant, tremulous, Emily's mother lost amongst them. A jewel shimmering momentarily, during one of her hours, one of her dances.

"But she died unhappy," Emily continued. "For we got poorer and poorer, and there was no more dancing, no more dressing up. Life became more and more grey, more and more grim. We were in financial difficulties when she died. I never knew what she died of. She seemed to succumb very quickly. To whatever sickness. Perhaps it wasn't a sickness. Just a lack of dancing." Emily sounded bitter.

"Didn't you ever ask your father about it?"

"No. I wasn't interested. I'm still not interested. She was never close to me. I was never pretty as a baby, never a flower, you see. So we had no communication. It was as if we were of two different species." Again, she spoke without emotion.

"My own mother never went dancing," Kok Leong said. "I don't think the thought or desire ever occurred to her. What she does though, is to pray a lot. To anything!" he went on, uttering a small laugh of pity. "She prays to any god, to any deity. Even to a rock or a special tree! All it needs is for someone to tell her that a particular rock, or tree, is holy, or that a spirit dwells in it, and she'll go and make offerings. And after all these years, she still hasn't given up! That's perseverance for you!" he concluded, wonder tingeing his voice.

"Well, adults never learn anything," Emily said, but her voice held contempt.

"Perhaps there really isn't very much to learn? About life, I mean. Is there?" he was diffident, made anxious by her assurance, her contempt.

"Even about the most basic things, they never seem to be able to learn!"

"What do you mean?"

"Well, the fact that life is tough, is hard; the fact that no one really cares one jot about you, that you must fend for yourself. I learnt all this very early in childhood. Yes, I learned early."

"What you say is true. We all learn early, and children know a lot. But adults don't acknowledge this."

"Didn't you hate adults when you were a child?" Emily asked.

Kok Leong considered how to answer. He tried to remember how he'd felt.

"I did!" Emily said, without waiting for his reply.

"I guess I must've hated them too," he said finally, recalling how lonely he had been as a child, how angry he had always felt.

"How I used to hate adults! They ruled the world, they ruled our lives. Always ordering us about. Don't do this! Don't do that! Forbidding us. Punishing us. As though they were gods! I longed to escape from their domination, but when I was a young girl, I didn't have the means to revolt."

Kok Leong thought back again to his own childhood, back to that time when his family lived in Sembawang Village, outside the British Naval Base where his father used to work. They had lived in a small, one-storeyed house by the main road. He recalled how, on rainy afternoons, the children were confined indoors, their small faces at the barred windows looking out wistfully at the rain, and there was no sound of laughter or ringing voices at play down the road, only the rain falling and the sad, wet, hissing sound of tyres on wet tarmac from the passing trucks, cars, and buses. Yes, Kok Leong remembered those young prisoners of the afternoon rains, remembered those hours when nothing happened except the monotonous patter of the falling drops, and faces were white and cold and silent with the loss of expectation. He remembered how he himself, aged five or six, used to sit on the low window sill, his small hands gripping the iron bars, those long, slender, vertical rods spaced at intervals across the wooden window frame, and how his legs dangled out through the bars, and how he sometimes thought that the rain would never stop, that the world would become a world of endless rain, and there would never be another sunlit morning ever again. Those heavy afternoons hung in rain, those small white faces, those neighbourhood kids. What were their names? He had forgotten. Faces and names deposited behind the great sheets of rain, obscured, opaque, abandoned, and then dissolved, lost, and only the rain remained in his memory.

Then the present intruded, disclosing on one side trees and tall lighted buildings poised in air, in the night's breath, and on the other side, down

Part Two

the stretch of sand, the sea upsurging, brimming black like oil; while above them pressed the design of stars and the lone moon. Now, in the darkness, there was no smell of rain, only the whiff of the salt sea and the warm scent of the sand, all held together by time, tenuous and alive: the soft, full night, the star-encrusted sky, the sea's regular susurrus, and memories of young faces drained by sheets of rain, and Emily seated close beside him.

How right it was!

Life!

"And now, I myself am an adult!" Emily continued. "It was what I wanted all along — to grow up. When I was a child, it seemed to me the only way of escape. My longing for escape, for independence, drove me on. I shut myself in, in case I should expose myself to them, and my dream of escape."

Kok Leong suddenly remembered his nightmare. The guts spilling out, bloated with gas, gleaming, opalescent. He turned his mind away, away from the frangibility of it all, and the horror.

"Now that we're grown up, do you think children regard us in the same way?" she asked.

"Possibly."

"But ... !" and her voice trailed away, lost in perplexity for the moment, and she dug her bare toes into the soft sand, digging, digging. Digging for what?

Sand had also got into his own shoes. The loose grains felt like rocks.

"I thought that when I grew up, I would never become like them," she continued, mournfully.

"But you're not," he insisted.

"What?"

"You're not like the others," he consoled.

"Oh I hope so! I hope so!"

In her yearning, Kok Leong found the little girl in Emily. He looked

180

at her small feet, her toes buried in sand; he looked at her face and saw the acne scars in that small patch of flesh above her chin, and found that even this blemish was touching. Proximity to her did not diminish for him his idealized Emily, did not lessen his enchantment.

"I've never wanted to be like them," Emily said, barely suppressed fury in he voice, now. "The antics of adults! So grotesque! So repulsive! If only they knew how they appear to a child! So pompous, so inflated with their own egos, so dishonest and foolish. Yes, above all, so foolish! But they're all blind. And the things they say, the things which gush out of their mouths! All lies, deceit, hypocrisy. They seem incapable of stopping themselves, unconscious of how they might appear, and to children, no less!"

Kok Leong saw her point, although he did not share the heat of her anger. He was too intoxicated by that flowing, yielding, deepening night.

He watched two old men strolling slowly by the sea's edge. They did not speak to one another. One was tall and thin, with a head of short, snowy-white hair; he wore a thin, white cotton singlet and a pair of khaki shorts which were baggy and reached almost to his knobbly knees. The other was shorter, stouter, with a dark blue cloth cap on his head, his belly slightly protuberant under a yellow T-shirt, his white shorts grubby. They each had a fishing rod slung over a shoulder. They must have been fishing in the shallows along the shore towards Tanjong Rhu, mused Kok Leong. The shorter one swung a transparent plastic bag filled with catfish in one hand, while the other man was carrying a woven rattan fish basket.

"You're very quiet," Emily observed, perhaps a bit self-conscious after her tirade.

"I was thinking about what you said," he lied. Her silence urged him to continue. "I understand just how you feel. I've felt the same way. But I'm simply not used to talking about it. Or about anything, really. I guess I'm just not the talkative type."

"Me neither!" Emily exclaimed. "I don't understand what came over me tonight!"

"I've always felt a deep anger, and even a hatred, for everything. Like you, I wouldn't want to reveal my feelings, normally."

"How strange that we should meet. That we should sit here and talk like this!" she said, and to cover up her embarrassment, uttered a little laugh.

Kok Leong nodded in agreement.

Afterwards, they sat in silence as the night overflowed from the sea, from its immense, secret darkness, lying out of the reach of one's eye, if not of one's mind, while over the trembling water the city lay, flickering faintly, willing, accepting out of exhaustion this inflow. And as the night advanced, it also carried the young couple away.

It was time to go.

And as they turned away, they left behind them the sea's quiet slurring on the sand, like a gigantic snoring animal. Even when he could no longer hear it, Kok Leong knew that the sea would continue lapping the shore. The sea would continue, without end, and perhaps, without a beginning.

Without end. Without a beginning. Memories. Back and forth. Washed up, and then receding. Memories. While Kok Leong lay motionless on his narrow bed, in his dark bedroom, considering each image meditatively as it sprang clearly into consciousness, and, as soon, one after another, dispersed. One and one and one. Rising and falling to the slow music of the passing night, the night flowing past, bearing him along with it, away and away, away to where wordlessness reigned, and he was undone at last.

7

Night was slow in coming, taking its own sweet time, and there was nothing Ong Kian Teck could do about it. Not a thing. Except wait. He was too tired to think. He had gone alone to Kampong Java Park around six o'clock, and lain down prone on the prickly grass, under a tree whose name he didn't know. It had a grey, gnarled trunk and twisted branches and small, oval-shaped leaves. So much that he didn't know! He only knew he was all washed out, flat on his back, staring up. He fastened his sight on the great masses of white cumulus clouds which almost wholly covered the sky, watching how they tumbled and churned, all in motion, in turmoil furling and unfurling, sometimes plunging into themselves. And he imagined them to have been conjured up by some great disturbance, or by ire, by duress. That wild, white, aerial cauldron was real, like what was happening inside him, but it surged without any clamour, without any sound. While he had sighed, and said, "That's life," or something to that effect. He had heaved a sigh and said, to the tree, "It's often like that, life."

So now you talk to trees? You only share your thoughts with trees?
And why not?
What else is there?
Otherwise, there would only be
Silence.
From where he lay, he could see the clouds, close-pressed, not admitting

a niche of blue sky anywhere, the blue blotted out by the white clouds. Oh, there must be a way out of every day, even a day like this, he thought, but without belief. Belief too, was blotted up by whiteness.

In whatever
way it may
There must be
a way out!

Had it been a clear and transparent day, there would have been a great sunburst at this hour. There would be a moment, however transitory, of swelling light, when the leaves would grow green with fire, the day fall burningly, and a scorched smell rise from the earth; or a wind would ripple the grass, and lovers stroll hand in hand, and water stand in rings on the pond, and birds, small, up in the air carry time away. And closing your eyes against the light, against the curve of sky, your dreams could explode into gold. For we feed on the sun. Leaves. Earth. Man. We burn. But when Kian Teck tried closing his eyes, his dreams did not explode into gold and he thought that there was no way out of the day, only the oncoming night falling into night falling.

In fact, light was now contracting perceptibly, withdrawing from the world, and everything, leaves, grass, birds, people strolling in the park, the oval pond, grew less distinct in shape, less defined, less physical in that remorseless withdrawal of light. Yes, it was a remorseless process, and not random, not one of chance. As the night descended, Kian Teck felt that he too was losing his hold, around whatever it was that he had arranged his life. He rose from the grass and sat up, hands dangling between bent knees. His head felt light, swam. The far-off trees and distant buildings were already lavender shadows, no longer asserting their form, their particular composition. They were about to float away, so fast their erosion, their going.

The last joggers passed him by, the die-hards, their feet nimble in white running shoes, flashing left, right, in the air, left, right, metronomical, mechanical toys.

It was time to go. Time to pack it in. Everything indicated that. The last pair of joggers had already run out of sight, gone towards the car park on the other shore of the pond. A thin mist rose from its surface reminding Kian Teck a little of winter in London, of his student days, when he used to wander about Hampstead Heath like a ghost within the mist which sighed from the earth into the cold air.

Yes, it was high time to go. Vacate the park. The trees, the flowering shrubs, the distant buildings were all vaulting through space, and a part of him shared the same sensation of vaulting through space, a thing so easy to do that it seemed not to need a miracle, or a magical power, or strength; whilst another part of him, that part which did not have much self-esteem, knew that it exceeded his capabilities, his limits. He was not mad enough, although something was surely falling apart. So get up and go. Vacate the park to the lovers who would come later in the night.

And just as he got to his feet, his eyes, even in the dimness, fell on a disused condom. A bald, wrinkled, deflated balloon. Still holding a suggestion of the opalescent discharge, the trapped cloud of sperm, in the small knob at the end. And just beside the buttress roots of the gnarled tree trunk, near this comical remnant of past passion, he saw the torn, glossy wrapper. Durex Gossamer, *"Sensitol lubricated"*. Which pair of lovers, he wondered, had lain, fumbling for each other on the previous night, under the soft shadows of this tree, with only a shawl of stars above them? Or was it a clumsy boy who'd urgently ploughed into that slit with the aid of "Sensitol"? And afterwards crassly abandoned the used condom on the grass? (Like Kian Teck himself, in his present insomniac nights, slipping down into sleep, lubricated by Soneryl.) Whatever it is, man likes to ease the passage with a little help, a little lubrication.

Well, cynical creep, time to be off, he reminded himself. The day is finished, *finito*, done, carried away by the dry and silent draught of time. Eternity moving on. Don't you feel it? Yes, eternity. And your span of it. Therefore, accept. Accept the moment that comes and the moment that goes. Go, then! Don't drag your bloody feet, avoiding it. The precipice. Freedom. Yes, freedom! It's yours at last. Don't you remember? Now that Li Lian has taken the kids away? Don't you remember? After last night's confrontation, she'd taken the boys away with her, to live with their grandma in Katong. They would spend Christmas there, they'd been told. So you are free. Free.

What if the rooms are now silent, with your wife gone, your children gone? You're free. You'll no doubt get accustomed to it. It only takes a little time. That's to be expected.

So Kian Teck began to walk away from the park, leaving behind thousands of leaves which only waited for a breeze to rise, to shiver and unfold their wings. He headed for the city, pollinated now by myriad globules of lights strung out to celebrate the coming Christmas. Mankind determined to have a fête.

The night perceptibly slowed as Kian Teck returned to his apartment, hoping against hope to find his family still there. But they were gone. Absent. Not even a footprint anywhere. Only silence ripened in the empty rooms, filled them to the brim so that Kian Teck could not breathe, but gulped for air. Quickly parting the sliding doors, he went out onto the balcony. The sky was now empty of clouds (where oh where had they gone?) and only the remains of a moon hung low over the tree tops, the moon having been bitten by an animal. Only a slice of it left. Kian Teck also felt his life bitten into. A great big chunk of it eaten away. He was no longer whole. (But when had he ever been whole, or holy?)

He took a quick, cold shower and changed into fresh clothes. Then sat on the long sofa in the sitting room and lit a cigarillo. He sat there without moving, only his right hand bringing the cigarillo to his lips, then away, slowly. After a while, the confrontation with Li Lian on the night before came back to haunt him, their words whirling around, white-winged, flying about him while he sat still, without moving, to receive them, to trap them. Wings of white words, the returning migration of birds, swarming back, but all eventually caught in the net cast by his stillness. Held fast, they orchestrated again into distinct sentences.

"I'M LEAVING," LI LIAN SAID. He had only just returned from work.

"What do you mean?" he asked, knowing full well what she meant.

"I'm leaving. I'm taking the kids. There's nothing more I want to say to you."

(Sitting now alone, recalling, the birds held fast, he distinctly remembered how she'd paused at that point, the length of that pause now causing flowers to unfold their black petals to the darkness.)

"I don't want a scene," she had insisted, her face white, not with facial powder, but a clear, pellucid whiteness, like a patina of ice.

"Can't we talk?" he asked. Although this time, he knew, there would be no idle talk of this and that while they both waited for the opportunity to begin. What was coming was a flood, an ocean.

"What is there left to talk about?" she asked, bluntly.

"Ourselves?"

"I'm afraid it's too late for that."

"It's not too late!" Kian Teck expostulated.

"No. It's too late." Li Lian was firm, cold.

"Please be patient with me."

"Patient!" It was the first time she had raised her voice. Her face seemed whiter: ice thickening. "Do you know how long I've been doing just that, been patient with you? While all this time you ..." she didn't bother to finish the sentence.

Part Two

"I think I can understand how you feel, but I'm begging you to stay. There's so much at stake."

"No, I don't think there's much at stake now. Not for me. Not any more."

"Sweet, I'll do anything you want me to, I promise!"

"Oh you're mad! Mad! And blind as well! You don't understand at all!"

"But I do!"

"No you *don't*. You don't even understand the simplest things. For instance, you don't understand that it's not a question of your doing what I want you to do; I don't want you to do anything at my bidding. I don't want to authorize you, or tell you how to lead your life. I don't want to demand anything from you that you can't give wholeheartedly, of your own volition. And I don't want to command. Your life's in your own hands. Don't you understand that?"

"All right then, help me. Can't you help me?"

While she had been talking, Li Lian had been moving aimlessly about the room, going from the armchair to the bookshelf, and back to the armchair, and then towards the TV, but now she sat down on the armchair, like a bird alighting on a floating log after a long flight all night above the dark waters.

"We're getting nowhere. *Can't* you see that?" she sighed.

"But we must go on! To stop would mean ..." he flailed out an arm dispiritedly, to signify something final, adding, after his arm had completed its arc, "death."

"You're being melodramatic," Li Lian retorted, flatly.

"I find it perplexing how you can sit there so calmly!" he exclaimed.

"I told you earlier that I don't particularly want to create a scene."

"But how can you be so calm about it all?"

"Calm? You call this *calmness*? I don't think that's a very apt description of my state. If you care to know, I'm tired out, exhausted, worn out, drained.

It's been going on for so long, for so long. I can't even remember how long or when it started. And you accuse me of being *calm!* I can yell blue murder, I can scream like a mad woman, go into hysterics — but I'm drained of strength. I guess, finally, I'm too tired out. I can't endure any more," she concluded, perched on the chair, a bird on its log as the water swelled and sank. It had been a long journey.

"Do you think that leaving me and taking the boys with you is the solution?"

"Is it a solution? I myself don't know. Does a solution exist? A solution in which no one suffers? I don't believe so. I'm simply going away. I can't take it any more. Do you know what it's been like for me?"

He was about to say yes, but she cut him short: "Stop! Don't say any more, don't say that you understand. Not at this moment. Don't say pat things, or try to soothe, or tell lies. Not any more. It's too late now. It's time for the truth. And one thing about yourself you should know — you don't really understand me. You've never *tried* to understand me. You've never really listened to me, or wanted to hear what I have to say. I do have needs, you know, to say things, to express myself, to voice my doubts, my fears, joys. But you never wanted to listen, never wanted to know. For you, there's only *your* life, *your* problems, that you needed to talk about. And you wanted me, and perhaps others, perhaps this girl of yours, to understand you. You *use* people. You used me, but you never gave yourself in return. You never shared. You took. You never paid any attention to me, you know that? Many times, I thought, oh he's bored with me. Many times I thought, oh he doesn't care about me any more, doesn't care enough. And you know, the funny thing is, I blamed myself. I told myself that I'm boring, that I'm getting old, that I'm no longer fresh, no longer pretty, no longer interesting or attractive. That's feminine masochism for you, if you like. *No,* don't interrupt, please! Let me go on, then I'll shut up. You needn't worry. I'll shut up. You see, I've lost confidence in myself. And I'm getting old. I'm thirty-two, and I'm a little afraid. I needed to be reassured; I needed love and attention; I needed you, you, my husband. But I sat and waited, and you didn't say anything. Didn't *do* anything. Day after day, night after night, I waited. But there was nothing, nothing. I know what loneliness is, I a wife and a mother! But d'you know, since our marriage and since having the kids, I've not been myself. I've been a wife, a mother, I have a few hen friends who don't interest me. I've been fulfilling a functional rôle as wife, mother, and friend to a handful of spoilt, rich, foolish females. And that's *all* I've ever been. I found that I was losing myself. I began to wonder whether I *am* myself any more. By that, I mean myself, as a person — an individual named Ong Li Lian, with my own thoughts, feelings, ideas. It sounds such a small thing, but it's important to me. I'm slowly going out of my mind, going insane, and you hardly even notice. Right before your very eyes. We live together, we're husband and wife, and you do not notice anything. I think that frightens me more than anything else. It means that you do not care, that there's nothing between us any more. So, it's come to this. It's taken a long time. So please don't say that I'm impatient. Time is running out for me. I want to live my own life, and not be dependent on you. There might just be enough strength and courage left in me to make this attempt. We shall see. But I *must* make the attempt. I can live at my mother's place with the kids for a while. I can look for a job. I want to pick up my own life once more, find my own interests, make new friends. I want to have contact with life," she said, and, uttering a small, self-deprecating laugh, continued: "Well that was a long speech. I'm sorry. I'll shut up now." Tears began to brim in her eyes, and Li Lian picked up a paper tissue and dabbed them.

Oh he had been blind, blind! Her soul, Kian Teck realized, had eluded his grasp, far more, he now knew, than had Jay's. In comparison, Jay was an open book, plain and simple. While he did not know his own wife!

We've been made strangers, he thought, by our marriage, by domesticity and career-building, by our functional rôles, as Li Lian said, playing husband and wife and parents. We provided for everything except for the soul. Hence the sterility of our marriage. Her words moved him right to his very innermost being. He was fed up with deceit, with evasions.

"I'm so sorry," he burst out at last. "So sorry. You said that I didn't know. Actually, I knew, I knew, but I failed to do something about it. I failed you. I did nothing, because I didn't know what to do. More likely, I've been too engrossed with myself. I don't know why. It's not simple to put into words. I don't know why I did all those things. This girl ..."

"I don't want to hear about her! Please spare me that," she cried out. "For your information, I've known about her for a long time. I know more, more than you think. Don't mention her to me, or start apologizing about her!"

"All right. I won't defend myself ..."

"No one asked you to!"

"I am what I am! I have become what I've become, and only God knows why this is so," Kian Teck exclaimed.

"You sound like God Himself, the way you speak those words: *I am what I am!* You're simply too much, you know that? I ought to laugh in your face, or just get quickly out of here. I don't know why I bother to go on sitting here," she said. She walked to the ash tray on the coffee table and placed the sodden, crumpled-up ball of tissue in it. When she returned to the armchair, she said, "I want to ask you something, which I'd like you to answer in all honesty."

Kian Teck looked up at her, and into her eyes, for now they must communicate or this would be the end. He was willing to open up his soul to her, although he was not quite sure what there was in his soul to expose.

"What," she asked, "is it that you're searching for? Tell me, what great

Part Two

thing, what great, shining truth are you always looking for? Your mind always somewhere in the clouds, up there in the rarefied atmosphere. Tell me, I'm really curious to know," and as she spoke, he could see that despite the mockery and irony of her tone, she was being minutely observant.

Earlier, a moment before she had asked him, Kian Teck had suddenly wanted to say exactly what he felt. He was desperate to be utterly and completely understood. Now, with her question waiting to be answered, he was no longer sure that he could express himself lucidly.

"My sweet, I don't know! God, I don't know!" he exclaimed in some despair. "I've asked myself a thousand times over, a million times over, what it is that I want. Is it fame and fortune? Or what? But I don't think it's only fame and fortune. I honestly don't think so. Yet, what *is* it? Why am I so restless, so dissatisfied and so bored?"

"But we've *all* experienced states of boredom, of restlessness and despair. It's universal, I should imagine," Li Lian replied. She sounded bewildered.

"These states of mine, alas, are virtually perpetual. It's seldom that I can avoid them. And yet I have so much! I have you, and the kids, and a bright career. That should suffice, should be enough for any ordinary, sane man. What can I say? I go around feeling like someone to whom the banality of his life has finally dawned. How did this happen? I don't know. I thought, and you may laugh at this, I thought — I'm going to die one day. Yes, one day, it'll be the end. I'm going to die! And this fact, this knowledge confronted me, made me realise that life is banal. If it has to end, life is meaningless. So, perhaps out of desperation, I became restless, scared of missing something, scared of wasting possibilities, and I felt I must plunge into life, dive in headlong. And when I found that I could not do that, could not do that always, then came the moments of inertia, of boredom. The highs and the lows. *God,* I'm tired. If I could have my way now, I'd want my life to be simple and sweet. I'd want my happiness to be complete and flawless. And if I'm granted this, I will be whole again. I want to be grateful for all things, if I only knew how. Do you find any sense in what I'm saying?" he asked, searching his wife's face with an intensity he had never expressed before.

"What can I say?" answered Li Lian. "To live as we did, to bring up a family, is our lot, is enough purpose. I'm not an intellectual, and maybe that's why I can ask *why*, and of what relevance, is there in all this search for an answer? Or maybe, an answer to the riddle that is life — of what relevance is it to *me*, to my true and simple daily life? Of what relevance is it to the kids? It's not that I'm such a simpleton that I don't sometimes question my own life. But I'm not given to this childish, crazy philosophising about death, etcetera. Death will come, eventually, to all of us; even the simpletons, the stupidest among us, know that. But we don't go around feeling sorry for ourselves, or use that as an excuse for unhappiness! The reasons for happiness or unhappiness, for me at any rate, are simple: some things in life make us happy, such as love, good health, kindness, and so on. And unhappiness is caused by misfortunes like sickness, pain, poverty, bereavement, war. I hope I'm not making light of your tormented search. I only think that it leads nowhere, that in no way can it bring you any happiness. I'm sorry to disagree with you. Obviously I am, and can be, of no help to you. Perhaps that's why you go to somebody else. Someone who can understand and sympathize with your torment. I want no part of it. I want an ordinary life. No wonder things are falling apart for us!" she concluded, bitterly.

"But I *do* want to change! I want to change! I want to live in peace, in tranquility, in acceptance. *Please* believe me. I'll try not to ruin our lives. Give me another chance."

"How like a child you are!" Li Lian exclaimed, exasperation underlying the fatigue in her voice. "You wish that life could be a fairy tale, one that is without any suffering, with a constant happiness that lasts forever and ever. But life's not like that. Life's not a fairy tale."

Kian Teck laughed. "I really used to think that if it's not what you call a fairy tale, that's only because we don't make the effort to transform it into one. Yes, I used to think that I could make this life into a fairy tale. Isn't that funny?"

She listened in silence, sadly shaking her head.

"I know I must change my attitude, change my life," he declared.

She remained silent a little longer, looking out at the night beyond the open balcony, and when she returned her gaze to the room again, she said, "I cannot cope any more, Teck."

"Do you doubt that I have the spiritual strength to change?" he asked her, slightly belligerently.

"Oh, I don't know," Li Lian sounded weary. "Don't ask me. I don't even understand or care about what we've been talking about. It has no relevance to our life. To my life, I mean, to my daily life. Perhaps it's because I'm a woman who sees things in a practical light, first, and I'm more practical than you. Dreams are dreams. And life is simply life. A day-to-day affair. It may be dull, boring, as you said. Anyway, I don't think I can cope any more."

"Well, what else can I say? I'm guilty, I know, for causing you all this pain, all this time, and I can't seem to make amends. I honestly mean it when I say I'll try to change. I *want* to change, to regenerate myself, if only I knew how. This concept of man's free will ... we only flatter ourselves. We think we can choose freely, from an existing multiplicity of choices, but in the final analysis there is only one choice, the one that has all along been lying in wait for us, that we have to choose finally. We are only granted the *illusion* of choice. It flatters us. But in the end, after we've exercised our so-called free will, our actions return to haunt us, to punish us, to make us feel foolish and guilty. They have a rebound, a backlash effect, and consequences which we cannot fully foresee."

"I'm afraid I still haven't grasped your point," she said to him when he stopped talking. She sounded rather irritated now.

"It's impossible to come to the point. That's why I ramble on and on. Although it appears to be all up to me. To be answerable about the unanswerable! To account for the unaccountable! It's one of life's great jokes, and life is certainly rich in jokes, one must admit!"

"I don't follow what you're saying at all. You're amazing! Such a dreamer, you are! And, on the other hand, how practical I am. But I can't really blame you; I knew that about you before. In fact, I fell for you partly *because* you were a dreamer. And now I complain. I'm sorry."

Yes, his roots of bone, instead of upholding him, trembled and shook to the fluted dreams. And with what disaster!

"Please stay. Don't leave me."

"No. I have to go. I might not know the meaning behind all that you've told me, but I'm afraid I've learned to distrust all those dreams and abstractions of yours, that have contributed towards making my life so insufferable. I've grown to be more sensible. Besides, my being here with you, living with you all these years, it hasn't helped you a great deal, has it?"

"That's not true! Your merely *living* here means something. I mean, it matters a lot to me. More than you can imagine."

"I will *never* understand you!"

"Ah, there's not much about me to understand. After all, I'm only a man, as simple and as complicated as they come. I'm only a man."

"No, I distrust you too much now. I distrust your words as well as your silences. Which, to be frank, seemed to me as if you were putting them on, to make some impression."

Kian Teck burst into bitter laughter.

"I don't mean to insult you, or your depths, your profundities," she said, sounding rather contrite.

"To hell with these so-called profundities, the sheer idiocy of these so-called profound questions! I only want you to stay with me."

"No!"

"Please, Li Lian."

"No!"

"What will I do? Life without you and the kids is too terrible to bear thinking of."

"Oh, you'll be all right," she said, bitter, sarcastic now. "Just carry on. Continue your search, your quest, or whatever, with someone else."

He could see the arrangements of his life (and they're always unfinished, endless, these arrangements) in disarray, about to disintegrate. Anyway, there was going to be a shift in the pattern and design of the components, of the elements, to an extent that he felt he might not be able to deal with. He felt he had to make a desperate attempt to prevent that from happening.

"Sweet, we can't wind the whole thing up, just like that, after all these years? Although I admit that we've made a messy job of it these past few months, it hasn't been as bad as we've made it out to be. I can't believe that we can wind it all up just like that? What about the children?"

It wasn't entirely a soft pitch, he thought, bringing in the children, for he loved them. But still, to bring them up as a factor showed that he was also a bit of a louse. He was aware of that. Yet, this attempt to keep things together had to be made.

"You, know," Li Lian managed to say calmly, "ours is not the first marriage to have failed. Many marriages nowadays have broken up, have 'irretrievably broken up' — I think that's the term— on the grounds of 'irreconcilable differences', or 'incompatibility'. Apart, of course, from the old-fashioned grounds like adultery, mental cruelty, and so on. Well, there are all sorts of grounds for divorce nowadays. It appears to be very simple, almost like going shopping in a fancy supermarket, only one goes to a lawyer's office instead. Yes, one sees a lot of divorces nowadays. Do you remember the Leongs, John and Mary, and Lim Koon Choy and his wife, whose weddings we attended? Well, they're all divorced now. In fact. we've outlasted them! And they all seem to have survived it, the divorce, I mean. The children too, they seem to take it in their stride. So we shall manage, somehow."

"You've really boned up on divorce, I see. Almost an authority," he said, sarcastically.

"Yes, I have," she replied defiantly.

"I can't believe that we're really finished for good! I simply can't believe it!" He was serious, this time.

"You better believe it! You're too much! Now you can whine 'Stay! stay!' But what about all these years? What about me? I can't overlook them. Don't expect me to. I'm only human, in case you haven't noticed. I've been confused, hurt, jealous, miserable, lonely! I can't forget so easily. I'm not that noble. I'm not above it all ... being jealous and angry. So don't whine and ask me to forget everything. It's not that easy. I've lost the power to endure any more. Don't you *understand* that?" she cried out, both anger and agony in her voice now.

He should have wept for his sins, wept hard. He should have wept a torrent of tears to atone for the pain and anguish he had caused his wife. But he remained dry-eyed. A lost cause. One of the damned. Gone case.

"Can't you forgive me?" he implored, looking into her eyes earnestly.

"I don't know, I don't know. The wound's too fresh; it still hurts too much. Or, as I said, I'm not noble, not that forgiving a person. I'm made of flesh and blood. A common, ordinary, weak woman."

"Oh, but you're not ordinary, Li Lian. You're not! You're wonderful!" he exclaimed.

Li Lian could not suppress a smile, remembering how she had fallen for his earnestness, his appealing, ardent airs, when she'd first known him. But too much had happened since then. She had developed a little immunity. One of nature's processes for self-protection, self-preservation.

"You know," she said after some reflection, "you're a born romantic."

"Am I? I think of myself as a clown, more likely," he said, feeling sorry for himself.

"No, not a clown, but a true romantic," Li Lian insisted. "A serious romantic, one of the real, true blue ones. One of the originals. You would like to wander through a life filled with enchantment, full of wonder and magic, soft guitar music under the stars and the moon."

He laughed. He did not know whether she was mocking him. "You make me sound like a love-struck maiden, a Juliet," he said.

"Perhaps, but that isn't so bad. I was one myself, once, a love-struck, swooning maiden, when I was young and you were courting me. How lovely it was then! Everything was wonderful, the world was an enchanting place, life itself was an enchantment when I was a girl, falling in love with you, and being loved in return; the two of us, young lovers, holding hands, stealing kisses .... How lovely it was. But how was I to know then that it wouldn't last, that romance is short-lived, that it would disappear, and we'd grow older, grow apart rather than closer together? How was a young girl to know all that? To know that soon there'd be no more holding hands, no more stolen kisses, no more tender affection? Yes, it was nice, when we were just young lovers, joining our hands in public, for the whole world to know. But how long ago has it been since we've done that? Ah, so long that I can't even remember the last time you held my hand! We made an undertaking, a covenant, but vows and promises, and love and kisses, cannot withstand the wear of time. Everything wilts, like roses."

"I love you!" he declared, but his irrepressible imagination was seeing those roses Li Lian mentioned, once startling, velvety red, now faded, their petals limp. "I love you!" he repeated.

She gave a sad little laugh. "How long ago it's been since I heard you say that!"

"But I've always loved you, you know that!"

She looked down, with demure shyness, at a spot on the floor.

She looked just like she did that day, oh so many years ago, when he had first whispered those words to her. "I love you," he'd spoken close to her ear, while they were strolling along the Esplanade in Johor Bahru, where they had gone to spend a Sunday afternoon. She had looked down on the ground, with a demure, shy smile on her lips. When she finally looked up at him that day, her eyes were lit with joy.

"Why can't you believe that I still love you? I thought it could be taken for granted," he now said to her.

She looked up at him, but this time her eyes were lit with a different flame. "How do you expect me to take *anything* for granted? How, when you've given me so few signs? A woman needs to feel that she's being loved *all* the time. And the man has to show her, he has to be demonstrative. But no, we're not demonstrative any more. We hide our love from the public, as if love between husband and wife were something to be ashamed of. In fact, we seem to hide this love even from ourselves. Tell me why, just like so many husbands, you seem ashamed of showing love for your wife?"

He sighed. "You know that's not true. I'm not ashamed."

"You say it isn't true. But I only know that, somehow, love has vanished."

"Why are you saying all this? Simply because we husbands are not demonstrative to our wives?"

"What's wrong with being demonstrative? Are we all dead or something? Incapable of showing our true feelings? When we were courting, then you were demonstrative enough. That was the best phase of our life together, our courting days, when we were young and madly in love. And I felt, early in our marriage, so terrific, so happy, so bride-sweet. Do you know what I mean?" Wistfulness softened her eyes, momentarily.

"But it did not last," she continued, "because, suddenly you seemed to have something else on your mind. Some problem, I used to think, some crisis at the office. Life was hard, I kept telling myself, with so much to do, such a great load to carry, and he has more important things on his mind, the poor man. It was the hard struggle for a career, I told myself. He has no more time for holding hands. For *years* I told myself that. But it's not true! It's not true at all! I was a fool. I was mistaken. You should never have allowed those problems and crises to crowd your mind to the extent that there was no more space for me. Now I realize that it was simply that you didn't have me in your mind at all. Or in your heart. Whatever. It's the same — I'm left out, cast out. A woman, a wife, moving around in the lonely track of home and domesticity. Oh God! God! Why do you allow this woman, this wife, to grow old?" she wailed.

Kian Teck reached out to touch her hand, to comfort her, but Li Lian swiftly snatched it back.

"Sweet, sweet! You're still beautiful, you're still young and lovely, you haven't lost your beauty at all," he said. "I too have aged, have grown older. Perhaps that partially explains the desperation that I've been feeling. I'm not a young man any more. But no one can return to their glittering youth. No one. And it shouldn't matter."

"It matters to me! To me!" she raised her voice, vehement. "It's different for me! I'm a woman!"

He waited for her to calm down, waited for her to continue. In those moments, time lost its colour, and he was drowning in an ashen maelstrom, going under, going under.

"It's all right for you. It's easier for a man. You can find someone else; some young girl; some pretty, fresh, adorable thing. And then it'll be easier for you to hold her hand, to steal kisses, to whisper sweet, romantic things. Yes, then you won't find holding hands a chore. Let's face it, what romance is there left for me after ten years of marriage? What can I expect? I was a fool!" she was very bitter now.

"Oh Li Lian, Li Lian! I'm sorry! I do love you. I do! I want to make it up to you. Let me have another chance. Please?"

She fell silent, more tired than sombre; her face pale, thoughtful. "I'd like a cigarette," she asked after a while, she, a non-smoker. Kian Teck reached out to the low table for the carved ebony cigarette box (a wedding present from someone or other), extracted two Dunhills and lit them. He offered one to Li Lian. So they sat, in that room, each with a cigarette which they would bring up to their lips at intervals, draw in and puff: gestures merely to fill in the time, a diversion from their confrontation, a distraction from the business of living. In that mutually devised silence, they reappraised what they had said to each other, what each had disclosed. The frail strands of cigarette smoke drifting up in the room-enclosed space led them to explore an illusion, an illusion which they both believed in for a moment, for a spell — that lost connections could be woven back together; by smoke, no less. Smoky threads to repair lives, to stitch over wounds.

"You must stay!" Kian Teck made another plea. "I'll be lost without you, without the kids. I'll be truly lost. I'm very tired, very confused. Please don't leave."

Li Lian, unaccustomed smoker, had let the cigarette go out, half-smoked, in her fingers. Only moments later did she realise that the thing in her hand was dead. She leaned forward from the big armchair and dropped the butt into the red, cut-glass ashtray: another wedding present. It's interesting, thought Kian Teck, this custom of giving wedding gifts, of launching young newlyweds on the long road of matrimony with the ashtrays, cigarette boxes, silver cutlery, fancy lace table mats, glass goblets, liquor decanters, bedspreads, fondue sets, "His and Hers" towels, perfumery for the bride, male toiletries for the groom, photo albums blankly waiting to be filled in, trinket after trinket, loads and loads of them. Perhaps people realized that marriage was a long and arduous road, a perilous and tempestuous journey, and that these gifts and trinkets might come in handy some time, that they might help make the passage a little easier, a little more pleasant?

"And another thing I've been wanting to ask you," Li Lian said at length, breaking into Kian Teck's musings, "this latest craze of yours — I'm sorry I can't find another word for it, a softer word for it — but can you explain why you've become so extravagant lately? This big, new, expensive car, all those flashy new clothes, the Italian shoes and sandals and leather belts you've been buying, squandering money on yourself as though you were an oil sheik or something! And when I happened to see the price tag on one of your gaudy neckties, a St. Laurent, I think, and saw that it cost over sixty dollars, I nearly had a fit! Sixty dollars for a necktie! That's a lot of money. I could almost buy a really good dress with that. A necktie! Anyway, I wanted to ask you whether we could really afford all those luxuries and extravagances, but I was in no mood to nag you. Though I was anxious, naturally, about our finances. But I didn't want to nag. Are our finances in such a healthy state? Are we *really* that well-off? I know you told me once, rather off-handedly, that you've made money on the stock market. But isn't it dangerous to gamble so heavily? I'm still anxious to know. Whatever might happen, there are still the kids to think of."

"I've simply become an old dandy," he said, trying to laugh it off. "A sign of creeping old age, and my comic, pathetic attempts to fight it. In a kind of madness, I've succumbed to dandyism."

"If you only knew how foolish you look," was all she said. "But that doesn't concern me now, if you want to get yourself up as an old peacock. What matters is that we have a family, and I think we ought to be careful, to be sensible about our money. Tell me, are we *really* so well-off?"

"Like I told you before, I've made some money playing the stock market," he said, abruptly. The truth was that Kian Teck had begun to lose money in the past few weeks. Suddenly, the market had dropped, and he was aghast at how quickly and how much he had lost. It was worrying him a great deal, but he had made no mention of this to Li Lian; nor was this an opportune moment to bring it up. He was in deep enough trouble as it was.

"Sixty dollars for a necktie! You men are truly worse than girls! I suppose you did it to impress this young chick of yours," she said sarcastically.

"She's not a chick. She's quite a nice kid."

"A *kid?*" Li Lian laughed, humourlessly.

"Anyway, I'll end it now. I promise."

"You can do what you like, it doesn't concern me any more. My feelings have grown quite numb."

"No, I'll end it. Honestly. I know what you've gone through. I know now that what really matters is the family. You and I. She was just a fling."

"Just a fling!" she screamed, suddenly abandoning her poise. "You can sit there and tell me straight to my face that it was just a fling! What gall! You're an even greater liar and bastard than I thought! You men are monsters! Animals! Full of nothing but lust, wishywashiness, lies, deceit. And the truth is, you're really a coward, on top of everything else! I hate you. Right now I feel as if I don't know you at all, though we've been married for ten years! I was blind! Blind!" Li Lian was furious.

"Now, would you rather that I told you that I love this girl? I don't really think I do, incidentally. I didn't want to hurt you by saying that my relationship with Jay was serious, that's all. I *don't* want to hurt you." Kian Teck tried to keep calm, reasonable.

"But you've made a great job of it. I don't care any more. I'm leaving. You can go to hell! You're a monster! An animal!" she yelled, her face flaming.

"Oh, come off it!" Kian Teck shouted, stabbed by a sudden anger. "Come down off your fucking high horse! You bloody women! You call husbands 'animals', 'bastards', 'crude', 'lustful', 'deceitful'! Every dirty name under the sun, eh? Well, if husbands are what you paint them to be, then it's because you bloody wives have made them like that! You've all connived and contrived to make us like that. And don't think you women are so bloody innocent and pure, either. It takes two to fornicate, in or out of wedlock. You women are co-conspirators. You're all prepared to do it for whatever you can get from us — money, a pet-dog of a husband who goes off quietly every day to work his balls off, so that a certain standard of living can be maintained for you bitches. While *we're* the ones who slog, day in, day out, even if it's at a soulless, meaningless job. I've sat here all evening listening to your accusations, which you hurl at me with great relish. That I'm cold, unromantic, undemonstrative; that I don't give you enough attention, enough love and tender affection; that I don't walk with you hand-in-hand. But what about me? How much love and affection do *you* show me? For years I've slogged, worked like the devil, tried to be a good husband and a good father, but how often do you show me your love and affection? For your information, I'm *starved* of love and affection — if you really care to know. I'm lonely as *hell!* Confused, tired, troubled, lost! Oh, shit! *Go* if you want to! In fact, let's both get to hell, or kill ourselves, anything! End everything! I don't care! Fuck everything! Marriage! Life! Everything! Fuck! Fuck! *Fuck!*" he stormed, out of control. Then he shot up from the sofa and headed straight for the table lamp (yes, another wedding gift, from Uncle John and Aunty Mary) which stood on a small, square wooden table in a corner of the room; it had a green Thai silk shade over a white porcelain base. He flung it onto the floor where it crashed, white shards flying, then he kicked at it in blind fury, shouting all the while, "Finished! All finished! I've had it! I've had it! *I've had it !*"

"Stop it! Stop it! Please stop!" Li Lian pleaded, crying weakly, tears streaming down her face.

The lamp was broken. The shade torn, its wire frame bent and twisted, the porcelain base in jagged splinters and shards strewn around the floor. Kian Teck stared at the result of his assault, panting hard like an animal, half expecting the broken lampshade to bleed — if not bright red blood, at least white light, or something. But it just lay there in its smashed white bits, unprotesting. Kian Teck too, his violence gone out of him, felt dissipated, spent. He stood there, above the wreck of the lamp, listening, and then only half-listening, to the quiet snivelling of his wife. Then silence. And stillness. Both husband and wife were stifled in the suddenly cramped room.

"Why must you do this?" Li Lian finally asked. "Tell me, why do you have to destroy, to resort to this senseless violence?"

"Why?"

"Yes, why? Tell me simply."

"Tell you simply? My God! Don't you know, woman, that there is no simplicity? Open your eyes! Look at this crazy, fucked-up world of ours! Just *look* about you! War, famine, starvation, poverty, pollution, motiveless murders, motivated murders, individual murders, state murders, an endless list. Just read the newspapers or watch the TV. They lay it on thickly, day and night, entertaining us with their accounts of such mayhem and madness that I wonder why the sky hasn't collapsed yet upon the whole stinking mess!"

"And, of course," she said, herself once more, "you have to take this personally. You think no one else notices anything except you, because you're so special, so unique. I suppose you think the whole thing's a personal affront, and you're angry because this so-called crazy world interferes with, intrudes upon, spoils your dream, of Nirvana or whatever. But let me ask you this, who says it has anything to do with you? *Who?*"

"God!" he replied.

"You don't mean God. You mean you, you, Ong Kian Teck, saintly sufferer!" she accused.

He laughed, collapsing onto the sofa, onto its soft cushions.

"Why are you like this, Teck?"

He felt tired, tired, sinking into the oh so soft depths of the sofa.

"I don't know," he replied, momentarily surfacing from tiredness, from the soft sea.

"You don't know! To every question, you reply that — *you, don't, know!* Are you going to go through life just saying, 'I don't know! I don't know!?'"

He was too tired to say anything.

"When you die," Li Lian continued, "they might inscribe this on your epitaph: 'Here lies Ong Kian Teck, the man who doesn't know' !"

When she saw that he was going to just go on lying there, saying nothing, she went on: "If you are really concerned with the messy state of the world, why don't you try to do something about it? Instead of just moaning, paying lip service to this so-called great suffering of yours? We all suffer, the world over, scratching for a living, bringing up children, feeding them, and so on. It's our lot. No doubt the world's in a mess, but if you feel like you do, *do* something about it! There are many causes you can support, can enlist in. You can be a politician, a statesman, or a priest. Do something! It might rid you of your self-pity."

"You know, what you said a moment ago, about the epitaph? It's delightful. The more I think about the inscription, the more I like it. It suits me! 'Here lies Ong Kian Teck, a man who lived and died without knowing why. Born on such and such a date; died on such and such a date.' I think that reads rather well, and is suitably pseudo-profound, don't you?"

"Oh, *why* are we still talking? It achieves nothing. I'll go now," said Li Lian in reply, sounding truly exasperated.

He sank deeper into the sofa, seeming unflappable, unperturbed.

"Have you nothing to say?" she asked, ready to rise from the chair.

At first he simply shook his head, then said, speaking softly: "Go. You deserve better. Go, if that's what you want to do, if that's what you must do."

"About the children," she explained, "of course you can visit them, any time you like. You're their father, and they do love you."

He was about to say that he loved them too, with a deep, abiding love, and one he felt that laid no conditions upon him. To them, he only had to be himself. But he could not speak, being on the verge of tears. He simply nodded.

"I'll go and fetch something I've left in the bedroom. Then I'll leave." Li Lian got up and retreated into the bedroom.

Alone, impaled on the sofa, Kian Teck watched the evening shadows floating and trembling in the room, and the thought came to him that these same shadows would be there tomorrow, and the day after that, and the day after *that*. He imagined the shadows whispering something to him, in thin, rasping voices, just beyond distinction. Or were the voices coming from his own heart?

Li Lian soon came out, carrying her handbag and a leather vanity case. She stood still for a second, looking down at him, and then said, "Goodbye!"

"Before you go," he said, "let me tell you a fable."

She looked impatient, all set to leave.

"It won't take very long. Please?" Kian Teck sounded serious.

Li Lian put her things down but remained standing. It was obvious that she had no intention of sitting down, of lingering any longer than strictly neccessary. Perhaps she feared being trapped, he thought.

"It's a fable which I shall call '*A dance of moths!*' It grew from a story that a friend told me," he began. (Jay had told him about her experiences while travelling overland through Pakistan, India and Bangladesh.)

"There is a certain season in the year in Dacca, in Bangladesh, when these white moths, they're called jute moths, appear. They come in great numbers, a storm of them, swarming, covering the whole place. They usually emerge at night, when the lamps are lit. Then they rise, seemingly out of nowhere, materializing from the darkness, and fly towards the light. They head for the light and then they fly round and round the lamps as though in a trance, in a mysterious compulsion, and finally, driven by a strange passion, they fling and hurl themselves at the light — where of course they're burnt alive. All of them prepared to die, prepared to have lived for only a few hours, participating in their brief death-dance. The next morning, their dead bodies litter entire floors, making them white with their corpses.

"And we are just like these moths! We too are fatally attracted towards the lights, the flames, around which we dance and dance. I'm not referring only to the light of the sun, but also to other kinds of light, or things symbolic of light. The neon lights of the cities, the strobe lights of the discos, the fun palaces, the shopping centres, the hypnotic light of TV and the cinema, the sparkle of jewellery, the posh restaurants, the rock concerts, the exclusive parties, the military parades. And things, things which emit an irresistible light. Ah, how they attract us! The brightness! It is because our souls are dark, because we have no light within us, that we propel ourselves towards these external lights, these materialistic lights. We fly around them like moths, driven by hunger and passion, prepared, like the moths of Dacca, to live only for the duration of the dance, and then finally to die — for, near the flame, near the blinding brightness, we have no knowledge of, and hence no fear of, death. Death also has no meaning, and we shall die without knowing why. Our fate is that we are never to find out why."

When Kian Teck stopped speaking at that point, Li Lian picked up her case and left without a word.

So HERE HE WAS. Kian Teck recalled every moment of the night before, the night when his family left him. Now, alone in the apartment, he watched the shadows trembling, just as he had predicted, while outside, the night pulsated, as if filled with the beat of a thousand drums, and with the mad cries of the frantic dancers, raving, hysterical, hedonistic, whooping and singing and calling out to him to come, to come! And like one in a trance, Kian Teck rose and went out to join the dance.

8

One Sunday morning in late December, Chan Kok Leong walked home so sluiced with the light which brimmed over the sky, that, entering the small apartment, he could almost feel the light falling off his shoulders, the sparks shedding from his body like rain drops. He, a carrier of light!

In the kitchen, he caught a glimpse of his mother and Siew Kum, his youngest sister, holding up Siew Wan. Their arms were tucked under Siew Wan's armpits. With her other hand, his mother was patting talc onto the pink, plump buttocks of his paralysed sister. He was moved by the intimacy of the scene, though it was one he had often witnessed before. The smell of talc and fresh shit stuck in the air. He quickly went inside his room and shut the door.

He had risen early from a shallow sleep and had gone out for a stroll. It was an airy, quiet dawn, most of their neighbours still asleep. He walked slowly for about an hour until he saw an open coffee shop. It was the first time that Kok Leong had visited that coffee shop, which, besides the usual collection of dining tables inside, also had a few formica-topped tables surrounded by wooden stools laid out in the open on the pavement outside it. Two young trees, an acacia and a lean *ketapang*, grew on a small patch of bare, brown earth facing the shop.

He sat down on a stool at a table out in the open, and asked the serving boy for a cup of sugared black coffee and two slices of bread and *kaya*. It was around seven o'clock by now, and about a dozen men sat around the

A Dance of Moths

scattered tables. The place seemed to be a bird fanciers' haunt. Bird cages hung from the branches of the acacia and *ketapang*, or from stout steel wires strung across the open space. As he sipped the hot, rich coffee and munched into the soft whiteness of bread spread with sweet and fragrant *kaya* jam, Kok Leong heard the intermittent singing of birds, mainly *merboks* and tiny 'white-eyes', in their elaborate bamboo and wooden cages. Apart from the strangely pleasing cacophony of birdsong, it was a quiet and peaceful place, for the men seldom spoke. They seemed content to just listen to their birds. He noticed one old man, thin and slight of frame, scanning the Sunday edition of the *Nanyang Siang Pau* through rimless spectacles, his small, bony head shiny and smooth through the thin, neatly-combed grey hair. While he concentrated on the Chinese newspaper, his brow became deeply furrowed. Once, when he looked up for a moment, Kok Leong caught the old man's eyes. They were watery and opaque behind his glasses, as though he were scanning another world and not the reality of that bright morning, stitched intermittently with birdsong.

After this breakfast, Kok Leong left the coffee shop. On his way home, he bought the Sunday newspapers. The sun was brighter, the morning warmer. And he felt an inner coherence.

THEN THE SCENE OF SIEW WAN BEING HELD UP LIKE A MARIONETTE in the kitchen.

As soon as he entered his bedroom and closed the door, he removed his shoes, placed them under the bed. Then he lay down, propping his head on a pillow. For a while, he did nothing but stare at the whitewashed ceiling, then let his eyes trail around the room. The walls were also whitewashed. Besides the narrow wooden bed, his room held a big, brown-stained bureau and a simple iron-framed chair with a light-blue formica seat and back rest. There were no other pieces of furniture. Kok Leong kept everything he owned in the bureau; his red Swiss knife he kept inside a drawer. On one wall was a small, square unframed mirror and three blue plastic hooks, from which a towel, a pair of trousers and a light green T-shirt hung. His shoes and a pair of rubber slippers were placed side by side beneath his bed. There was nothing else. No pictures or prints or even a calendar on the walls, and no photographs. The single electric bulb, suspended by a short white flex from the ceiling, was covered by a globular, white, Japanese rice-paper lampshade with thin strips of bamboo forming the frame. It was an ascetic room, reflecting its occupant's tastes. Kok Leong had never cared much for things, for possessions, and over the years he had accumulated very few belongings. Only a few clothes, towels, handerkchiefs, a comb and toothbrush, his knife, and other simple, utilitarian articles. There was not a single book or magazine in the room. He only read the papers, having come to the conclusion long ago that he would not gain much from reading books. Books were filled with a kind of useless knowledge, in his opinion. So what was the point of knowing about things which were useless?

It was a room where he could be himself, where he could concentrate and focus his thoughts with greater precision. Also, its barrenness augmented rather than constricted space. Kok Leong would have hated a room crowded with nonessential paraphernalia.

Sometimes, he would draw his chair to the window. If he opened the glass louvres, it gave onto a view of the neighbouring apartment blocks and, at one corner, a glimpse of the Toa Payoh Sports Complex with its bitumen track, its oval of trimmed green. He would sit and look at this compressed view of the world, watch the days and the nights pass by — the gradual emergence of light at dawn, its hardening into morning, or the day unstiffening, then the swift extinction of light in the evening. Nothing really momentous, just the passing of time, which moved so inexorably that sometimes he feared losing himself to its passage. And, at other times, it was not fear, but rather an exultation which he felt, to be swept along, a tiny grain caught in an avalanche.

On that particular Sunday morning, Kok Leong resisted reading the newspapers which were piled thickly beside him. His mind kept returning again and again to that scene in the kitchen, of his mother rubbing talcum powder onto Siew Wan's buttocks, and Siew Wan's face registering no complaint, her body held up by the armpits, like a limp rag doll, although her mouth, with the few, yellow-stained broken teeth in it, gaped wide like a great, big wound. It was as if some unknown force had stolen away her cry, her voice. What she thought or knew, Kok Leong could not even guess at, but her silent face spoke more powerfully than anything she could have put into words, of an inexpressible pain. That pain was so terrible that no cry could possibly do it justice.

And so pain, as well as pity, sorrow and shame, were emotions which, although shared by every member of his family, were either not expressed at all in their home, or only obliquely. Indeed, if a stranger had witnessed that same scene in the kitchen that morning, he or she would have condemned them all for lack of feeling, of emotion. In other words, their phlegmatism and stoicism would have been perceived as callousness. It was true that most of the members of his family no longer openly rebelled or raged against improvident fate which had brought this tragedy into their lives, nor did they, overtly, seem to be repelled by the hideousness of it all — the odour of Siew Wan's shit, or the sight of her body seized by a fit as though she were being electrocuted, with saliva, and sometimes even blood when she bit her tongue, dribbling from the corners of her mouth. They could be accused of being inured to pain and hideousness. But that would not be the truth.

Time, instead of eroding and blunting their feelings, instead of wearing them thin over the years, had, rather, wracked and ravaged them, had rendered them highly sensitized, taut, like thinly-stretched wires that vibrate with every passing wind. Thus, if his mother and youngest sister had seemed to serve his stricken sister without any expressions of disgust or protest, nevertheless they suffered, and bore, like the rest of the family, this stigma in their souls and psyches. Perhaps this servitude to Siew Wan, which his mother and Siew Kum had just rendered, this labour of theirs, meant the triumph of a greater love? And there was, implicit in their acts of service and of acceptance, something akin to heroism in that family, and love which had triumphed over affliction, day in, day out, for untold years, love which they kept alive in their household. Service, acceptance, love. And above all else, Siew Wan, the stricken one, the most innocent.

This understanding came to Kok Leong on that Sunday morning. He lay in bed, his eyes trailing across the whitewashed ceiling and then moving in circles around the bare walls of his simple room, focusing on nothing in particular, indeed seeing nothing, and after some time there was only a sensation of the day shedding its colours, thickening the air into which his thoughts had dissolved; and the whole thing did not settle, did not set solid, but drifted out of the window into the greater world outside. He had lost his inwardness.

The sound of conversation flowed into his room, seeping like water through the space beneath the closed door, washing against his motionless body lying colourless on the white-sheeted bed. Slowly, he began to stir, inflated again, like a balloon effigy, by the source of life outside. A while later, he got up and went out, carrying the pile of unread newspapers.

Kok Leong's father was genteely sipping a cup of hot coffee, while his mother watched him solicitously, wifely. Siew Kum was stretched out on the rattan sofa, reading a comic.

"Do you want a cup of coffee?" his mother asked him.

Kok Leong nodded.

"How about something to eat?"

"I've already eaten, early this morning."

Mrs. Chan went to fetch the coffee. Not a sound came from the kitchen except for the faint clinking of a cup. Siew Wan was keeping her stony silence, either sitting on her potty chair, or else asleep on her plank sleeping platform.

Siew Kum violently flipped over a page of her comic, her young face glum with concentration. Mr. Chan made a sloppy, slurping sound as he drew in the hot coffee, his lips bloated and pink. Some old men have lips the same as babies, pink and fat.

Kok Leong went up to his father, whose face was lowered over his cup, like a bull grazing, and placed a copy of the *Nanyang Siang Pao* on his lap. The old head acknowledged this with a weak nod.

He had noticed that recently, his son had begun sharing the Sunday newspapers with him. Mr. Chan was surprised by this act at first, and even now he was a little shy whenever it occurred. It was such a small thing, but it meant so much. And it also explained so much. The old man knew that. One evening when he didn't have to report for work, his wife had spoken to him about a certain change which had come over their son. His wife said that she had already discussed the matter with Third Aunt, and Third Aunt had merely suggested that Kok Leong had probably found a girl friend. But Kok Leong himself never mentioned it, and he did not bring any girl home. In fact, he never brought any of his friends home. He must have had friends, but no one in the family had met any of them; only Siew Kum had seen any of his friends. She told her parents that she had once seen someone picking up her brother near their home, an evil-looking Indian man with crossed eyes, who rode a big motorbike.

SOMETIMES, LATE AT NIGHT, when few people entered the hotel toilet, Mr. Chan would think about his only son. He would sit primly erect on his chair in the corner, his mind wide awake in that quiet hour when the only sound was that of flushing as the pipes automatically ejected a fan of water at regular intervals onto the smooth, glazed, tiled wall of the common urinal. During these moments, Mr. Chan really believed that his toilet was the most peaceful place on earth. There, he could deal with some of his personal problems. He thought of his son often, in the quiet of the night. Even when Kok Leong was an adolescent, Mr. Chan had worried about him. For instance, he knew when he had lost his job with the British forces and took on his present work, that Kok Leong, who was only twelve or thirteen at the time, had been deeply pained and ashamed. He sensed, as Kok Leong grew up, that there was a steely spring wound up tight within him. Mr. Chan was aware of this, but felt there was nothing he could do about it. After all, what could he have done? He was a shy, quiet man, not gifted with the art of forging personal relationships with words. In fact, words had to struggle into form each time he attempted speech, fractured by the uncontrollable stutter which had been with him for as long as he could remember. It had set him apart, even in childhood. So, even though he knew about his son's anguish and anger, he did not know how to assuage it; he did not know what to do. He simply waited, and watched, and waited, and grew old.

Everyone took him for a weakling, a pathetic figure of a man. Few people respected him, his son among them. He knew that, but he felt that they were not to be blamed; it was quite understandable. Mr. Chan had few illusions about himself. He knew he was not cut out to be a showy rebel. He was not a brazenly brave and angry man fighting against adversity, fist raised in the hot air, raging at the world, shouting at injustice, cursing fate. He was not like that at all. It wasn't because he didn't have any revulsion against poverty and the humiliation that went with it; being poor himself, he hated poverty as much, and maybe more, than the next man. However, to him, life always had limited options, and only offered him plain choices. For instance, when he was retrenched from the British Naval Base, he fully realized his predicament, that his age and lack of qualifications placed him in a most precarious and disadvantageous position, and he feared that he might not get hold of another job. He had a family to feed and support. The choice was plain enough: he had to take on anything that came his way, accept whatever work he could find. He had to put his shoulder to the yoke, whatever people might think of him, for emotions, and even personal feelings, were luxuries he could not afford. It was a practical problem, a vital problem, and he had grappled with it the best way he could at the time. That he had to work as a toilet attendant, an occupation considered socially the lowest of the low, (in fact, not so far removed from the "*jamban* men" — the night-soil carriers — of even earlier days) did not bother him personally. Status and rank did not matter. So, for years he accepted the confines, and earned the disapprobation, of his lowly status in society.

To him, it was only simple, practical common sense: he had to earn his daily bread, his daily bowl of rice. But because he was a quiet and shy man, people mistook him for a weakling, and believed that he had no pride; while the truth was that it required an intact will, a certain unshakable strength, to accept life the way he did.

However, that is not to say that Mr. Chan was not an observant man, a man who took no notice or had no interest in others. On the contrary, he was an astute observer of mankind. Sitting quietly in his chair by the corner, with little to do, he watched mankind drift in and out, night after night, for his work was not at all strenuous or time-consuming. Indeed, ironically, it was the sheer ease, even bordering on laxity of the work which he found most difficult to bear, and if Mr. Chan had been a complaining sort of man, which he was not, he would have complained about boredom, about the lack of exertion, both mentally and physically, of his task — for a man, any man, is capable of doing more.

Mr. Chan had a lot of time on his hands. He was not allowed to read while at work, so he was forced to be a spectator. Knowing it would offend them, he tried hard not to let the customers realize that he was watching, observing them minutely. So he cultivated certain tricks, or traits, like an actor playing a rôle, realizing, of course, that he could not attain the ideal rôle, which was to be invisible. Instead, he tried to be as unobtrusive as possible.

Nightly the customers came in, their eyes blazing with alcohol, dewy with dreams and romance, or bleary with weariness. They trooped in, one by one, to piss, to shit, to vomit, and then to line up by the big wall mirror under the bright, white lights, washing their green and greasy faces, combing their hair, studying themselves in the mirror — all of them incorrigibly expectant, ignorant of the simple fact that mirrors never deceive, but rather, show up all their vanity, eagerness, fears, their hopes and despair. As they stood before the large mirror, they lied to themselves, deceived themselves, that they could fix up, could reassemble, their faces and expressions, when it was their souls that they really wanted fixed and reassembled. But mirrors only reflect the souls of those brave enough to want to see them, which most people do not: they are content to be blind. All this Mr. Chan knew, through all the years of sitting in his corner and observing them.

And yet, in spite of this knowledge, this insight, there had been occasions when he too had confronted himself in that large mirror, late at night when the place had emptied — he would catch his own reflection, in spite of his lack of pretensions, and he would examine himself, curiously, speculatively, passionately, for, like other men, he too was capable of fooling himself. On those occasions, he saw himself as a small, balding old man, the lights throwing a shine onto his dome, onto his sloping, smooth forehead and the stub of his flat, wide nose. There were not many creases or wrinkles, but age showed itself in that certain pastiness of his skin, in a certain delicacy and fragility, and also in his eyes, which had been large and brown and moist when he was a young man, but were now hazed over, with the slightest mist that time had laid over them. A small, prim old man, slightly officious in his green uniform. This was what the mirror evoked, but there had been certain nights when it seemed as if he were able to reach beyond this, locating behind the image and seeing loneliness where his soul might be: a recognition that was disconcerting, for he had believed so firmly in his own intactness that he did not realize that a man can be alone from choice, and yet have to suffer for it.

Sometimes when Mr. Chan returned from work and sat alone at the table in the kitchen over the customary cup of hot chocolate, with the lights off, the household asleep, and all was quiet, he would brood over his loneliness, while the air was still and translucent, glazed with lateness, when time moved so ambiguously that one was hardly aware if it moved forwards or backwards in that interregnum. On a few occasions, Kok Leong, coming home late, would walk past the kitchen doorway without giving so much as a glance or uttering a word, to his father, and sensing his son's movement towards his room, Mr. Chan would be almost tempted to believe that he was truly invisible after all.

So when Kok Leong began to change in little ways, such as by sharing the Sunday newspapers and sometimes even buying him a copy of the *Nanyang Siang Pao* because his command of Chinese was better than his English, Mr. Chan felt a melting warmth diffusing through his soul, and he felt less lonely. There was no gravity in Mr. Chan's heart that Sunday morning as he sat sipping his hot coffee in the apartment.

MEANWHILE, KOK LEONG HAD GONE OUT to sit on the small balcony. His mother had fetched a cup of hot coffee for him, which he placed beside his chair. The sun was higher now and the air quite still. Way below, he could see the occasional passerby, and the small trees lining the streets, motionless, their leaves a stunning green, basking in the light.

He began reading the *Sunday Times*, while in the background he could hear his mother talking softly to Siew Kum. Suddenly, a small

Part Two

headline leapt into his vision. "Burglar caught red-handed."

Kok Leong read the story quickly, hardly breathing. It said:

> At the Third Magistrate's Court yesterday morning, a young man, Somasundram *s/o* Arumugam, 22, unemployed, was convicted of attempted burglary. He was also charged with carrying a lethal weapon. He pleaded guilty to both charges. The prosecuting inspector, Inspector G. Pillai of the Kandang Kerbau Police Station, told the Court that on the night of Dec. 18th, the culprit was seen by someone who thought he was behaving suspiciously in the garden of a bungalow in Stevens Road. This person called the police. A squad car, led by Sergeant K.H. Tan of the Kandang Kerbau Police Station, was dispatched to the scene. The police officers arrested the culprit, who was caught trying to prise open the back door of the bungalow with an iron crowbar. He was searched, and was found to be carrying a torch light, a chisel, a small coil of wire, and a knife with a six-inch blade. He was wearing a black beret, a pair of dark glasses and a pair of cotton gloves.
>
> The accused pleaded guilty to the charge of attempted burglary, and also admitted, while being held for questioning, to at least a dozen other burglaries that he had made in the past couple of months. He was sentenced by the Magistrate, Mr. M. Ramalingam, to three years' imprisonment and six strokes of the *rottan* for burglary and possession of a lethal weapon.

Kok Leong put down the newspaper. He thought of poor Sundram, locked up in Changi prison. Kok Leong couldn't imagine what it would be like to be locked up in a cell. Suddenly, he shivered slightly, in spite of the hot sun. He looked steadily at a distant point in the sky, which was cloudless and pale blue. A bird warbled, just audibly, down there among the trees, reminding him of that early morning, of his walk in the cool dawn and the coffee shop. But now, he couldn't understand why the caged birds sang.

A Dance of Moths

Part Three

1

The year had ended. Through December and January monsoon clouds made the sky dull pewter, the city constantly under shadow. The festive season saw days which were huge blurs of torrential rain, and at night the sound of the rain, ferocious as battering rams, was audible even above the hum of the air conditioner. It was a bad time for Ong Kian Teck.

In 1974, Singapore, like most of the world, went through a severe recession, coupled with inflation, caused partly by the steep rise in oil prices which the OPEC cartel demanded. For a while, there was a "Save Energy" campaign on the island, and the threat of petrol rationing. The economy went into a slump, the stock market dived, Kian Teck lost a great deal of money and found himself in debt. He had large overdrafts at three different banks, all of whom constantly hounded him. He had already sold his new Chev 350 and bought a second-hand Volkswagen. So late December through to the early months of 1975 was an anxious time for him.

Living alone, apart from his family, Kian Teck's daily life had lost its cohesion, its core. He drifted about with an emptiness he could not fill, either with work or play. He no longer had any appetite for reading, listening to music, talking — or even for thinking. He missed his family, and realized how much he loved them, needed them. Without them, he was now disconnected from the universe. He knew now that loneliness would be his greatest punishment.

Part Three

He visited his children once or twice a week at his mother-in-law's house. Because of the monsoon weather, he could only take them to the cinema or to supermarkets, where he bought them toys, comic books and ice-cream. The supermarkets were doing a roaring trade in spite of the economic situation. People seemed to be consuming as much as ever, a hard habit to kick, as Kian Teck himself realized while buying all those worthless toys which would break within days, or which the children would get bored with within a week. But he continued to spend on them, out of love, indulgence, and guilt.

Guan Hoe, the younger boy, often asked why his daddy was not staying with them, while his elder brother, Guan Hock, said nothing. Guan Hoe was easily distracted at the shops, while Guan Hock maintained a silent reproach: or so Kian Teck thought, feeling chastised before his elder son who would stand a little aloof while faced with the toys, his arms hanging by his side, with a gravity which was the result of hurt, of knowledge, of growing up. Ah pity, pity all those who reach the age of knowledge, an age usually more bitter than sweet!

Li Lian did not deliberately try to avoid him whenever he visited, but she was cool. She had turned him down twice when he suggested a reconciliation. At first he had been hopeful, thinking that time would heal the rift, but as the weeks and months went by, he gradually gave up entertaining any hope. Li Lian appeared implacable.

Still, there was Jay. She kept him company, although, out of an unexpected sentiment, for which perhaps there was no longer any validity, he had resisted inviting her to move in with him. His home, though empty, was still sacrosanct.

ONE NIGHT, SOON AFTER THE NEW YEAR, he quarrelled with Jay. It was over some trivial matter, but he got quite heated about it. He was driving his yellow Volkswagen at the time. Suddenly, his car rear ended the one in front as he halted by the traffic lights. Kian Teck knew he was at fault. The other driver got out to survey the damage. Kian Teck followed suit. The bright-red Colt Galant had a slight dent on the back fender. The Volks was unmarked. Kian Teck at once offered his apologies to the Colt's owner, a tall, thin Chinese man with a slight stoop, sporting a "mod" hairstyle.

"Sorry! It's my fault!" Kian Teck called out.

The man did not reply immediately, but glowering, continued to inspect the damage to his car.

"It's only a small dent, luckily," Kian Teck said, quite cheerfully. "About fifty bucks to repair, I should think. Here's my driving license and papers for your insurance claim." He took out his wallet.

"Shit! I won't claim fifty bucks from the insurance company!" the other man exclaimed, his face, flushed with rage, a lemony-yellow colour (like Kian Teck's Volks). Anger seemed to ripple in small tremors off his upper lip. "I won't claim from the insurance company," he hissed, saliva splattering in a fine spray onto Kian Teck's shirt. He was clearly very agitated.

"Why not?" Kian Teck asked, careful not to raise his own voice. After all, he *was* in the wrong.

"I'll only claim if the damage is over a hundred dollars!" the man spat out, his voice even more furious.

"So what do you want me to do?" Kian Teck asked, trying to be reasonable, but unable to suppress a smile; in a macabre way, the situation was becoming quite comical.

"I won't claim for fifty dollars!" the man repeated, raising his voice by several decibels.

"Look! I'm sorry. I know I'm to blame. But kindly write in to the insurance company. After all, that's why we pay our exorbitant premiums!" Kian Teck was beginning to feel annoyed.

Part Three

"I won't!"

"OK. Let's forget it then," Kian Teck retorted abruptly.

"Oh, no! Oh, no!" the other shouted angrily, shooting out his rather skinny hand and grabbing hold of Kian Teck's shirt sleeve. "You pay me now! In cash!" he demanded, another blob of saliva splattering onto Kian Teck's hair.

By now Kian Teck was more than a bit irritated. He knew that Jay was watching and listening, and this annoyed him further. In a flash, he made up his mind. He gently disengaged the other fellow's grip from his sleeve and still politely, said, "OK, OK." Then, taking the man's hand, "Now my good friend, you just stand over here a moment," he urged softly, leading him onto the grass verge beside his red Colt Galant. "You just stand here a little while, OK?"

The other man, looking nonplussed, stood obediently on the verge.

Kian Teck returned to his Volks, reversed a few metres, revved up the engine, and put it into first gear. Then he suddenly drove forward, accelerating, and smashed his car hard into the back of the Colt Galant. There was a rich sound of crushed metal. Disengaging, he reversed a little, then, as he straightened his car and drove slowly away, he leaned out and said to the man, "Well, now I've solved your little problem, haven't I? You can now file in a claim. I'm sure it'll cost more than a hundred bucks, OK?" Smiling tigerishly, Kian Teck then called out, "Goodnight!" and waved as he drove off. The man's eyes were as wide as a fish's. His mouth had fallen open, but no sound came from it.

"You're mad!" Jay admonished.

"I was only obliging the chap. He *asked* for it."

"You're a mean bastard, you really are!"

Kian Teck laughed.

"The poor man! How can you find it funny? Such a childish prank! Such a low-down trick! How *could* you do it?"

"OK. It was a mean, dirty trick. OK. But don't make such a big scene out of it, all right? Don't be so fucking sanctimonious!" Kian Teck was fast losing his temper with Jay.

She shook her head in dismay. "Why did you do it? What do you get out of it? So senseless! So disgusting! I don't understand *why* you have to be so violent!"

"OK. So I've sinned. So, in the fullness of time, I will be punished. The day of reckoning will come, and I shall burn. God will punish me," he retorted lightly.

"You're punishing yourself!"

Kian Teck suddenly felt crestfallen and foolish. Yes, he thought, Jay was right. His behaviour was abominable. It wasn't at all funny, what he'd done to that poor arsehole.

"You've been under too much stress lately. Get away for a spell. Have a breather. It'll do you good," Jay continued.

"Where to go?"

"Why, anywhere!"

Her prompting excited something in him. He felt it thrilling in his blood.

"Yes! Why not? I've got quite a lot of leave. Let's get away from here!"

Jay laughed.

"I mean it, girl! Come with me to Zee Casbah!"

"OK. Let's!"

They both suddenly felt light-headed, felt already free as birds. Within minutes, they had decided to go to Bali. It was near by, it was quite cheap, and it was both exotic and different.

That first sunset over Kuta beach, everything silvery-blue, the broad sky, the sea, the gleaming wet pools like glossy mirrors left by the tide on the

Part Three

flat beach. They sat on the sand watching a small *prahu*, with its white triangular piece of sail-cloth, skating across the water, and the dark figures of swimmers playing in the roaring surf, gambolling down in the water like a troop of ducklings.

In those dying moments of the day, the Balinese people living nearby assembled on the beach like a congregation for some mystical benediction, to witness the sun going down again, just as it had done for millennia. Then, quickly, it was all over. Night flowed in fast and thick. When Kian Teck and Jay returned to the village, they were treading through darkness.

Dining at a small restaurant in the village that night, he heard the strains of a *gamelan* orchestra carried through the air, a distilled shower of fine tinsel, fabricated, yet wholly magical. The night was gilded at once, enriched, as if paradise were possible.

Jay looked at him with her green eyes.

"Do you know what I'd like to do with you?" she asked with a smile.

He shook his head.

"I'd like to smoke grass or hash with you, go on a trip with you on the magic mushroom."

"Why me?" he asked, his voice sounding strange, formed below thought, discordant to the snatches of the distant music still fluttering like tinsel moths, wingings, forming and unfolding.

"I want to get you stoned," she said, hissingly, her eyes green burnings, scintillant.

He laughed softly. "Why not?" he conceded.

"We can get some. I know how."

She knows so much, he thought. So smart, many of these young people nowadays, street wise, knocking around the world on the cheap, trying everything, experiencing. Yes, she knows so much. How and when and where. But what about *why*? Does she know that too? Perhaps she doesn't need to. The rest of it, yes. How to, and when to, and where: they're useful to know. Not why. That's of no use. None at all.

Jay brought him to a small hut where they shared a magic mushroom. They returned to their *losman*. The darkness within the small room was so intense, it seemed solid; but the darkness was extinguished instantly, with the flick of the light switch. It was a simple, neat, unencumbered room with a high ceiling of yellow thatched grass, arching up like the twin cusps of a tent, a very typical Balinese design. It held two narrow beds separated by a small bamboo table, and a small hardwood cupboard. There was a square, wood-shuttered window, with a blue cotton curtain strung on a strip of wire half way down.

Jay moved silently and sat cross-legged on her bed. She placed a small brown-paper wrapped parcel before her, took out a packet of Dunhills and a box of matches.

It is time, he thought.

She took out a cigarette, rolled it gently between her right fore finger and thumb along the whole length of the cylindrical tube, then tapped one end lightly on the cigarette box and began to withdraw the shreds of tobacco bit by bit, extracting with her finger nails, emptying the last shreds by tweezing them out with a match stick. Now only the shell of paper, the empty tube, was left. She unwrapped the packet, a small handful of dried, greyish-green grass.

All the while Kian Teck watched in fascination. She was like a little girl totally absorbed in her toy, riveted by her work — an inappropriate word — with a serene secretive concentration. There was an air about her, not of criminality nor of wrong-doing, but of innocence. When she finished, she told Kian Teck to switch off the lights but to leave the window open.

He did as he was told.

"Come, sit by me," she said, her voice solemn. A priestess.

He groped his way to the bed, and sat down. Time froze. He waited for the induction.

Part Three

Jay lit a match, illuminating her face; it had a soft glow, a bit strange, like a foreign landscape seen in a dream, her gaze lowered to the white stick of marijuana in her hand. She raised this slowly to her lips and lit its tapered tip. Tiny, crackling sounds in the hushed room as the flame singed it. She put out the match with a wild, flinging motion of her hand. Then, eyes closed, she drew on the joint. She took it out, holding her breath for a long time, drawing in little inhalations, her nostrils sniffing, and then she broke into a slow smile, directed not at him, nor at something near at hand, but at something welling within.

Kian Teck took the joint and placed it between his lips. He closed his eyes and drew in deeply, trying to keep the smoke down, but it was a bit difficult. He was scared lest he lose even a bit of it, and swallowed at the end. There was a dryness in his throat. He returned the stick to Jay. She inhaled deeply again and passed it back to him. They exchanged the joint three, four times before she spoke.

"Are you getting it?"

Her voice seemed to come from a great distance, where her spirit had withdrawn.

"I'm not sure," he said. He really didn't want to talk at all, trying instead to experience, to catch, any feelings of change the drug might bring on.

"Relax. Let yourself go. Relax," she intoned, passing the joint back to him.

This time he took a deep, eager, greedy draw, and waited expectantly. In the pitch-black room there was nothing for him to select, no object to concentrate on. After a while, he felt himself going out, out into the blackness itself, and everything was black, the blackest black, an infinity of blackness into which everything receded, his mind as well, and strangely, it was beautiful, wonderfully beautiful! It spread around him, enfolding him. He seemed to exist in another dimension, where thoughts evaded him.

"Are you getting there?" a voice asked.

He knew it was Jay, but he could not answer her. He felt as if he couldn't move, and when he tried, the motion of his hand making an arc in the darkness was slow, slow and holy, a vague process, as if not of his body, the sap of his body siphoned away — but it was beautiful! Then he sensed the air outside rushing fast as wild horses, and just as fast, stars were falling down the silent face of the night, and when he swayed his head, multiple glittering moons suddenly rose silvery above a turquoise sea, followed by a yellow sun, round and perfect, over a desert-like landscape, and then it got white, now as sand, now as the sparkle of snow, brilliant, dazzling, iridescent, and then rhythmical lights in various forms drifted past his vision, his mind, and evanesced, then ceaselessly recomposed, a lyrical repertoire of wonders, so remote one moment, the next so immediate he felt sure he could reach to touch, and then, in a moment of whiteness again, he did not know any more where his own body ended and the crystal whiteness began. He felt weightless. And could not put any meaning to, could not interpret, what was happening, and it did not matter any more. Kian Teck felt unbridled, freed, as the universe whirled, careened away from him, and he was submerged.

2

Late one night, unable to sleep, Chan Kok Leong thought about Sundram. He could hear the sound of rain far away, falling in another area, and his memory flung him back to his childhood. He was again sitting on the window sill, clutching the iron bars, his thin little legs dangling outside, as the rain fell. Those weary afternoons of rain which made prisoners of children. Kok Leong shivered on his hard bed. The wind howled outside. After a while, his mind scattered and raced with the wind.

Saturday afternoon came, bright, hot and humid. The city lay dazed under a relentless spell of heat. The passengers in the crowded bus were stuporous. Sitting by the window, Kok Leong shared a seat with a fat, old Malay woman whose warm flesh pressed close against his, but for once he did not move away. In fact, her presence, the touch of her, was strangely, unaccountably, comforting. From time to time she turned her head in his direction, looking out of the window. Once, when their eyes met, she smiled at him, and when he returned her smile, it transformed their relationship from that of total strangers to that of people who have shared a smile. And when the fat Malay lady left, getting off the bus at Joo Chiat, Kok Leong felt a little bereft, as at a friend's departure.

The bus reached Changi and Kok Leong got down at the stop near the prison. Three women also alighted at the same stop. Perhaps they were mothers, wives, sisters or girlfriends, coming to visit their men locked up on this hot day behind those high walls. None of them spoke, or even looked at one another, each woman hiding behind a terrible timorousness. They seemed like ones afraid of giving others a contagious disease, like lepers slinking from friend and neighbour and stranger alike. Weighted by his own thoughts, Kok Leong had fallen back, walking behind them. He let them lead the way. It was his first time there.

Suddenly, a shrill, deafening screech shattered the air. A lone jet plane raced across the cloudless sky, trailing a long, white, vaporous tail. He stood watching as it sped away and away, as though trying to pierce through the sky, driven by boldness, madness or a desperate terror, he wasn't sure which. But on and on it flew until it was no longer audible, a mere mote now in the light-blue haze, scintillating one last moment as the sun reflected off a wing, then vanishing completely, freed from time and space at last. What's it like, up there? Kok Leong wondered. What's it like to be so free, so exonerated from the ground, and so far away it seemed it would never return to earth again? Kok Leong remained immersed in that trance, that dream, till it fragmented when he found himself in front of the high walls of the prison, against whose solid massiveness dreams were bound to be broken up.

Kok Leong entered through a small side door set beside the enormous, main doorway. He imagined the clangour those huge doors would make when their heavy, iron leaves were shut and their iron bolts shot, the metallic sounds of finality reverberating through the entire neighbourhood. It sent a shiver through him. He was now inside a small yard which led to the security office where he filled in a form, surrendered his identity card, and was given his visitor's pass. Then he was led through a maze of corridors until, finally, he was brought into a room to wait for his friend's arrival.

It was a large, bare room, the walls moon cool with whitewash. Here, a crowd of relatives and friends were trying to communicate with the prisoners — who were seated in a long row on the other side — through a perforated transparent plastic barrier. There was no privacy at all. Personal and family matters had to be openly discussed, and intimate words exchanged for all to hear. For those too shy, or too stricken, to speak, there was only the silent communication of eyes; but every word, every look which passed between prisoner and visitor could be heard and seen.

Kok Leong was led to a seat. His brow felt like ice, his brain numbed — so much so that after a while he no longer heard the voices in that large room. However, the stony silence in his mind was soon shattered by the sound of leather boots resounding with military crispness on the cemented floor as a warden led Sundram in.

The two friends sat facing each other. Kok Leong studied Sundram's head of bristling black hair, his face alight against the backdrop of the whitewashed walls. There was no trace of strain on Sundram's face. The same inextinguishable fire rose out of the depths of those squinting eyes. At least, thought Kok Leong, he still has this fire, whatever else has been taken from him.

"How're they treating you?" he asked Sundram nervously, his voice almost a whisper.

"Fine," Sundram laughed, a short burst, stifled swiftly when eyes were instantly trained on him. Eyes of birds.

"The *makan's* OK." Sundram spoke in his normal hearty manner. "I get curry almost every day. A lot of rice. And bread in the mornings, from the prison bakery."

"You don't find it hard, being locked up?" Kok Leong asked, anxiously.

Another short burst of laughter, like sub-machine gun fire in the white, white room where blood could spurt red like flowers opening their petals.

"They don't lock me up all the time! At first I thought they would, but I'm allowed out of the cell from morning till evening."

Kok Leong's face must have shown his surprise. It seemed to amuse

Sundram, who grinned.

"I work in the laundry. A bloody big laundry, too! It's like a bloody *factory* in here. Everyone's put to work. Laundry, bakery, carpentry, bookbinding, all sorts of things. But they pay us peanuts!"

"You sleep alone?"

"No. Three of us in a cell. One Malay, another Indian bloke, and myself. Each of us has a mat on the floor. We have to keep the place clean and tidy," replied Sundram, adding nonchalantly, "it's not too bad."

As Sundram discussed his experiences of prison life, Kok Leong felt comforted by the evidence that his friend hadn't changed, that imprisonment had not succeeded in breaking his spirit — which, Kok Leong now realized, was probably unassailable in the first place. Sundram was always *utterly* himself. Even in prison he was always himself, independent, fitting naturally into the new external environment. He did not cultivate other traits than those that were already his. He did not feel the need to evolve a new style. Prison life, therefore, did not bother him. He simply dispensed with what is called "freedom", in what is called "the outside world". In that way, although he was locked up, Sundram was in fact freer than a lot of other men. It was his nature. He did not depend upon, nor care for, the sanctions of other men, of society. His fulfillment did not require this.

Some men, like Sundram, are born to be free, while others are born to be enslaved, whatever their external circumstances. We all invent stronger prisons for ourselves: subtle, ingenious forms, from a lifetime of deliberation, of method, with such impenetrability that there is no way into, or out of them. This, Kok Leong realized, with a sudden lucidity which outshone the whiteness of the afternoon. He knew that he himself was no exception, that he too was an inventor of a prison, of which he was the inmate.

It was then that Kok Leong realized that hatred was his special prison.

Part Three

He was walled in by hatred. How am I to free myself? he wondered.

But the self is not easily subject to change. It might be easier to move a mountain than to effect a change in the self. Unless one were struck, as it were, by lightning, by a momentous force, by drama — then, sudden prospects of change might be possible.

But usually our days are not made for drama, for recklessness. Instead, we are diminished and drowned in an ocean of days, moving so slowly, so inexorably, that life itself seems a motionless monotony.

Yet Kok Leong wanted to hold onto a glimmer of hope: that, somehow, he could storm his way out of his prison. He breathed more sharply, sucking in air through his nostrils as if it could charge him, energize him, then letting out the hot air through his teeth-clenched mouth, like a boxer before a fight. So Kok Leong strained, and it seemed possible that his prison could burst open, and that all the poisonous hatred within him would be flushed out.

Then Sundram stirred, uncoiled his tall body, rising to his feet in one slow, stately movement. Looking up, Kok Leong saw the strong neck of his friend, like a bull's, and that implicit simplicity etched on a face which bore no trace of his imprisonment, no trace of humility. Yes, thought Kok Leong — not contemptuously, more in wonder — he is just an animal.

It was time to part. So Kok Leong left Sundram, who, accompanied by the grave-faced guard, was roaming either into or out of a dream while he himself, emerging from that large, white, visitor's room, returned to the world beyond the high concrete walls.

DAYLIGHT WAS ALREADY DRAINING FAST into the cool hollow of evening. The day's heat had gone, the texture of the sky now soft. It was strange, therefore, to realize that the impulse to fly no longer animated his bones. He didn't know why, but he had already lost his yearning to be free.

When he got off the bus from Changi, Kok Leong wandered about town, awaiting the dream-fall of night, the darkness descending in a long, unbroken fall over the city until the city was overcome, as if by some black mood of the waters.

Later, a moon struggled to rise, a flat, silvery disc, or rather, three-quarters of a disc — like something fashioned by a craftsman who had, in the end, run out of material, leaving his handiwork unfinished. Nevertheless, it seemed, to Kok Leong's eyes, to have arisen out of a dream. Perhaps Sundram's dream was a part of this; and his own, too. Each of them possessed by a dream. Then the stars came out, glittering, delirious, wild.

Kok Leong walked past a young Chinese girl with blood on her mouth — a shocking red. But it was only lipstick. There were other people on the street, a strong tide of them, walking to and fro, floating, finding the current irresistible. It was easy simply to ride along, following the tide. That Chinese girl who had attracted his attention, what dreams burnt in her young heart? Some of the older men, he saw, were limp with exhaustion, their backs bent by the day's toil. Yes, it was sad, in spite of the shop fronts, the cinemas, the street lamps spewing forth mouthfuls of light.

He had intended to eat, but after a while he turned away from the town, following the not-long-risen, imperfect moon home. During the bus ride, Kok Leong thought how all the nights in his life were stretched out like endless lines of lamp posts that lead nowhere.

It was with a certain numbness that he entered the apartment, his being so shrunken he felt he might never surface again.

His mother and Siew Kum were washing dirty dishes in the kitchen. Siew Wan was probably asleep, in a dream he could not hope to decipher.

"Have you eaten already?" his mother asked. "We've had our dinner, but I could warm up something for you. "

Kok Leong shook his head. "I've eaten," he lied.

Part Three

Then he retreated into his own room, locking the door behind him. He walked to the window, pulled out the blue chair and sat down. He did not switch on the light but left his small room in darkness, sitting there watching the stars and the hundreds of lights from the other blocks of apartments, both near and far. After he'd stared at them for a while, the lights seemed to ripple on crests of invisible waves, the whole night itself trembling as if it were a living thing. He thought he heard people's voices coming through that cavernous darkness, with a rattling sound like dry leaves fluttering in the wind, tangling with the stars, the whole scene filled with such mystery and wonder that Kok Leong watched with a slight breathlessness, breathing in all the twinkling of the stars and the lighted windows in one hungry gulp, he was so hungry! He felt so outside of things, sitting there and watching, and waiting ... for nothing in particular. Only knowing that he felt small and insignificant, that he felt alone and lost. Freedom? Who needs it? he mused. Yet something was imminent, the moment pregnant. And Kok Leong waited breathlessly for the storm to break, waited for the lightning.

THEN IT STRUCK!

He must marry Emily!

That night, Chan Kok Leong went to bed hungry.

3

Ong Kian Teck sat alone, naked on the sand, bathing in the liquid light. His book lay unopened on his lap as he watched young men riding the surf on colourful boards skimming the crests of the waves. They were poised, fluent, so much in control, ruling the waves like gods. Kian Teck wished he could surf. It seemed so easy to do. Must be a great feeling, he thought.

Nearer shore, some swimmers were leaping like horses in the water. Others swam with sweeping strokes, a slither of dolphins. How he cherished that moment, when everything was exalted to rightness.

Later, he opened his book on Chuang Tzu's writings and read:

> Uncle Lack-Limb and Uncle Lame-Gait were seeing the sights at Dark Lord Hill and the wastes of K'un-lun, the place where the Yellow Emperor rested. Suddenly a willow sprouted out of Uncle Lame-Gait's left elbow. He looked very startled and seemed to be annoyed. "Do you resent it?" said Uncle Lack-Limb.
>
> "No — what is there to resent?" said Uncle Lame-Gait. "To live is to borrow. And if we borrow to live, then the living must be a pile of trash. Life and death are day and night. You and I came to watch the process of change, and now change has caught up with me. Why would I have anything to resent?"

Kian Teck put the book down on his lap, almost unconsciously covering his genitals, but when he realized what he was doing, he deliberately

Part Three

removed the book, placing it on the sand beside him. He wanted to indulge in nudity, not cover it. He laughed to himself a little, thinking of the passage he'd just read. It made sense. He thought he understood Chuang Tzu, and was gratified, pleased with himself — but he wasn't a hundred per cent sure. Well, no one can be a hundred per cent sure about anything, he mused. Except fools. Although he knew it was only meant as a metaphor, the vision of a willow suddenly sprouting out of Uncle Lame-Gait's left elbow suddenly seemed hilarious. Stunning, in fact. And the words: "The living must be a pile of trash." Are we, then, all trash? Do I really believe that? He decided that he didn't. And then again, he did. And then, those other words: "And now change has caught up with me. Why would I have anything to resent?" Somehow, while flaunting his own nakedness in the light and the air on this foreign shore, Kian Teck felt that the words rang true for him. But what he enjoyed most of all about Chuang Tzu's book was the pervading hilarity, rather than the so-called Truths, or Wisdom — or whatever.

"The living must be a pile of trash. Life and death are day and night..."

He scooped up a handful of coral sand and let it trickle in a stream through his fingers. He examined a few grains closely. Simply bits and pieces of broken shells. So this beach is a cemetery of once-live corals and shells! he thought. And what I'm sitting on now are countless millions of skeletons, carcasses of creatures once alive! Yes! — "The living must be a pile of trash." — Yes! In time, we too shall all be dead, a pile of trash, a pile of coral sand.

"And life and death are day and night ..."

He reflected on this, gazing down at his hands while the sun warmed his cool flesh. He could see the blue veins running beneath the pale skin of his arms, coursing towards his heart.

Suddenly, a shadow fell across his belly. He looked up and saw the smiling face of a young Balinese man.

"*Selamat pagi!* Good morning!" the man greeted him cheerfully in English and then sat down beside Kian Teck without an invitation.

At once, Kian Teck was conscious of his limp prick and the sad sacks of his flaccid balls, but he did not try to cover them up. Anyway, he was only a little embarrassed, a little ashamed, and since any move he might make to hide them would only emphasize his shame, he did nothing. It was the most modest thing he could have done, under the circumstances.

And the smiling intruder seemed to have politely accepted the situation. Nevertheless, it was an anomalous, unequal situation, Kian Teck felt, though he was not sure who held the advantage, the clothed or the unclothed.

"My name is I. Madé."*

"My name is Ong Kian Teck."

"You having a good time here in Bali?"

"Yes, I am."

"How long you been in Bali?"

"I arrived yesterday."

"You will stay longer?"

"I hope so."

"I hope you have good time here. Have good impression of Bali."

"I'm sure I will, I. Madé." After thinking about it for a second, Kian Teck asked, "How do your friends call you?"

"Wayan. I. Madé my caste name."

He had a broad face, with a wide brow and a flat nose beneath wavy black hair, brilliantined and carefully combed. His skin was a rich brown, like ripe tobacco, and he sported a thick black moustache. It adorned his youngish face above the full lips and perfect, white teeth. A smile flickered perpetually in the depths of his black eyes. Yes, Bali, the land of smiles, Kian Teck thought.

"Have you been to Kintamani? To Tanah Lot?" Wayan asked.

---

* pronounced "*Ee Madeh*".

"No, not yet."

"There are many places to see in Bali. Bersakih, the mother temple."

"Yes, I've heard of it."

"Perhaps I can make trips for you?"

Well, another tout, Kian Teck thought, a bit disappointed. "Are you a tourist guide?" he asked, rather pointedly.

Wayan laughed, reacting to the tone of the other man's question. "I not tourist guide, but I take you if you like," he said, with simple dignity.

"What do you do, Wayan?"

"I looking for work." Wayan laughed again. "Any work," he continued. "All Bali looking for work."

"You speak good English!"

"No, I only speak a little. I only learn a little in school. I try to learn from tourists, who show kindness to teach me."

"You speak well enough. Why can't you find work?"

Wayan shrugged. "There's not much work, and there are many people in Bali. I know nobody in high position, you know?"

Kian Teck nodded. Same old story. Everywhere. Of string-pulling, of influence-peddling.

"How long have you been out of work?"

"Three years." Wayan turned serious. The flickering smile in the depths of his eyes swiftly faded. He didn't say anything for a few minutes, then, gloomily, "Since I finished college, three years ago."

"You're a college graduate and yet you can't find a job?" Kian Teck sounded incredulous.

"Before college, I worked in small *losman* on Sanur Beach. Very little money. But I was happy. I gamble everything. At cock-fighting." Wayan paused again, lost in memories. Then, brightening like quicksilver, he grinned at Kian Teck, "You seen cock-fighting?"

"No."

"If you like, I take you."

"Perhaps."

Wayan fell silent for a moment, his mercurial temperament recalling other memories. Eyes cast down. A finger doodling on the sand, his chin resting on the raised arch of his knees. Kian Teck waited for him to continue. "I was young and foolish. I spend all my money. But I was happy. Then I got married. Now we got three children."

"But you are so young?!" Wayan looked barely twenty, and Kian Teck found it hard to imagine him a father.

"Yes, I have three children. One boy, two girls. Now I not feel so young." Wayan lifted his chin, his gaze straying out to the sea which was animated by grey-green shadows. Then his pupils contracted as if around the grit of some pain, like an oyster, and his face closed. A long silence fell, so that Kian Teck thought Wayan would not speak about it again. But, in time, the young Balinese went on. "At first, I try very hard to get work. I try everywhere, in Sanur, in Denpasar, in Kuta. Every day. And every day I come home with nothing, and my wife look at my face and know. Every day I go out, I come home with nothing. We had no money. We borrow. And we borrow. I was young and strong. See my muscles?" Wayan flexed his right arm, tensing his biceps. He slapped it with his left hand. Smack! Smack! "See? Hard!" he exclaimed, his voice fierce with anger and almost hissing with pride, but a pride eroded by knowledge, by experience, by frustration. "But I can't get work!" he cried, and then repeated, his voice losing strength, becoming only a weak, sad echo, "But I can't get work!" He was bewildered again into silence.

Out there, beneath the demure blue of the sky, a couple of naked foreign surf riders rode gracefully on the big, sculptured crest of a wave, sheer and brilliant. One could sense their youth, their health and exhilaration. They came in closer and closer until they gradually sank in the shallows. A young European woman, bikini-clad, her skin embossed

Part Three

gold under the torrent of the sun, walked across the sand, across the spaces of the thoughts of the two seated men, and at that moment it was difficult for Kian Teck to share the bitterness of his new acquaintance, until Wayan picked up his story again.

"I got tired of going out every day, tired of finding my wife waiting for me at home, with that asking look in her eyes. There was no work. So I began to stay at home. I hate to get up in the morning, I hate to go out. So, I sleep all day. For many, many months, I sleep all day. I lie in bed, try to sleep, never want to go out of the house. Just sleep and sleep. I hate to see the sun coming out every morning. I only want to sleep. It was very difficult. Was terrible. People say Wayan lazy man. They pity my wife, my children. They all say I a lazy man. A man young and strong, but no good, because he no go to work. He only like to sleep all day, never think of his family. After a long time, I think like them too. I no good, I lazy. I think I will never get up. No more strength to get up. I was like that for a long time. A long time." Wayan's voice grew softer, as if he were talking to himself.

For some reason, Kian Teck thought of Old Ho, whom he hadn't seen for quite some time. He wondered what had happened to the old chap, and made up his mind to look him up again when he returned home.

Home? He felt a distinct pain. It seemed so very far away, although he had only been gone one day! Home. Carried away by the peerless wings of time. It seemed altogether another life, to him now sitting on this strange shore, alongside a stranger whose long silence made him suddenly feel conscious of his own nakedness, which now seemed a mere frivolity. Without a word, Kian Teck stood up and pulled on his trousers.

"You come alone?" Wayan asked, cautiously, seeing the other dressing, wondering if he were leaving.

"No." Kian Teck was terse, his thoughts elsewhere.

"You like buy pretty shell necklace for wife?"

"I didn't come with my wife," he said and sat down again. He put his head through the neck of his T-shirt. Pulled it down to cover his chest.

It was a time for confessions, that ripening day.

Kian Teck sat quiet as a stone in the still, hot sunlight. Wayan went on with his story, telling how he'd been forced to pick up various odd jobs, how he now peddled souvenirs on the beach to survive. He was carried away by his own words, spinning out his life, an engrossing activity.

But Kian Teck was no longer really listening, and did not retain details of the rest of the story. Finally, he bought a shell necklace from Wayan for a few hundred rupiahs, either out of sympathy or to purge himself of guilt, he wasn't quite sure which. He held in his hands the pretty shell necklace, bleached almost perfectly white, an ornament of dead shells to adorn and to give pleasure to a young maiden, a girl friend, a lover. Kian Teck knew then that he would lose Jay.

Then he realized that Wayan was speaking to him. He asked, "You like hire motorbike?"

What an exciting idea, Kian Teck thought. What a *truly* exciting idea! The open road! A motorbike! And so many unexplored places! All at once, he felt a great longing for the feel of the wind, the wind which would strip off his flesh, which would blow away all thoughts from his head. So he made arrangements with Wayan I. Madé to hire a motorbike. When he left the beach, his steps were sprightly.

WHEN KIAN TECK FINALLY RETURNED, roaring back on the bike like a god to the *losman*, he almost expected a welcoming reception of cheers and accolades. Like a drunk, he expected the world to share in his intoxication and exhilaration, which of course the world did not. He parked the motorbike in the pebble-strewn yard.

A few people had gathered in the small restaurant; Jay introduced them to him. There was a young couple from Sydney called Penny and Hans, who both looked pale and thin and frail. Later, Kian Teck learned that they had the "Bali belly," a form of diarrheoa which commonly afflicted visitors. There was another man, a European, small and bony, with long black hair and a rather luxuriant beard, who was greedily puffing a cigarette. His colour was like white bread, grainy, but there was no hint of frailty about him. His eyes gleamed and there was a sense of quickness, an animal reflexiveness, about him. He spoke English with an unusual accent, and Kian Teck discovered that he was originally from Brazil. His name was Francisco da Silva.

"Whatever possessed you to get a bike?" Jay asked Kian Teck in a tone of slightly amused amazement. "Do you *really* know how to ride one?"

"Well, the answer to your first question is: the Devil! And to your second: no!"

Francisco laughed, extracting a quick enjoyment out of this; one suspected he would, out of any charged situation. He laughed with his mouth open, displaying brown-stained teeth, all small and sharp, like a fish. A piranha, perhaps, Kian Teck thought. He grew interested in the Brazilian.

"How much did you pay for it?" asked one of the young Aussies, the one called Paul.

Kian Teck didn't reply. He wasn't keen to oblige, to divulge.

"How much did the bugger charge you?" Paul insisted.

"Eleven thousand rupiahs for a week," Kian Teck reluctantly admitted.

"*Eleven thousand rupes?!* You got fleeced, mate!" Paul laughed with undisguised glee. "Eleven thousand rupes!"

And Bill, Paul's other Aussie friend, chipped in: "You could've got yourself a brand new Honda 125 for eight thousand rupes. Or nine thousand, at the most."

"You should've asked us first. You can't trust these bloody natives.

They'll rob the *skin* off your back, if you're not careful. Bargain, bargain, *bargain!* If they name a price, halve it!" Paul rattled on.

They are all like this, Kian Teck thought, rather ruefully. Always showing off their little bits and pieces of knowledge, and proud that they're so smart, so tough, not to be taken in by "the natives". They reminded him of the saying about how some people knew the prevailing price of everything, but the value of nothing. It was silly, really, but nevertheless he was irked. He should have been comforted by the fact that he wasn't like them, and that he wasn't so dumb either, that he knew, when Wayan named his price, that it was too high. He could have bargained, but after their conversation on the beach, he couldn't bring himself to do so.

On a fine morning a few days later, Kian Teck went with Jay and Wayan I. Madé to a cockfight in a small village on the road to Tanah Lot, not far from Denpasar. Wayan acted as their guide. The cockpit itself was on a piece of barren ground by the side of a small stone temple. A makeshift cane-and-grass awning was erected over the patch of ground, with supporting poles and beams of cut bamboo trunks. The place had a festive air. Women sold cooked food and soft drinks while children gambled at *tikum-tikum*, the wheel of fortune. As the sun rose high in the sky, the place gradually filled with villagers from the surrounding areas. Many brought along their own fighting cocks in special cane baskets which they placed around the perimeter of the arena.

Before the first fight began, several men strolled towards the centre of the pit with their caged cockerels and squatted around, gossiping with each other. They examined their rivals' birds, assessing the weight, feeling the muscles of the back and the shanks carefully, seriously. Then an agreement was struck and two cocks were chosen for the first fight. One was a multi-coloured cockerel with red, brown and yellow body feathers, and magnificent long black tail feathers. The other was plainer, yellow and white, looking less imposing because it had no tail feathers. The owner of the multi-coloured cockerel was a young man in a tie-dyed T-shirt and brown jeans, while the other belonged to a man of about fifty with close-cropped hair, wearing a shabby green shirt over a green-and-brown checked sarong. The crowd exchanged bets under the supervision of a referee, a venerable-looking old man. Then the owners tied gleaming steel stilettos with string onto the feet of their cocks, winding the blue nylon string round and round. When these preparations were completed, their cocks were taken into the adjacent temple for prayers.

On their return, the air of excitement grew more intense. Loud cries of bets being offered rose into a storm: "*Breng! Breng!*" the crowd called out for the multi-coloured cockerel, and "*Puteh! Puteh!*"

At last, the fight began. Squatting on their haunches in the centre of the earthen pit, facing each other, the owners held the birds firmly between their hands for a few moments. Then suddenly, in one tense movement, eyes still locked, they thrust the cockerels at each other, swiftly plucking out feathers to goad them on.

The men then moved back, and a hush fell over the circle of spectators. The cocks stood alone in the small cockpit, the ground embossed with discs of gold as the sun bored through the lattice-work awning. The birds manouvered around each other slowly in a circle, one walking clockwise, the other, anti-clockwise. Then, facing each other, they stood poised, very still, a ring of feathers flaring out like flames around their necks. They shared the silence, and the sun, while the brown faces of the spectators were lost in absorption, all eyes riveted on the contestants. Suddenly, the two cocks flew at each other in a rush, their wings flapping, everything happening almost too quickly for the eye to follow, flashing steel blades, brilliant colours of feathers whipped into a storm. Everyone watched breathlessly as the two cocks clashed in the air once, twice, blinded by fury and blood. Then, abruptly, one lay down on the ground — quite motionless. It was the colourful cockerel, now mortally wounded, blood oozing in a dark red stream from its pierced breast onto the barren earth. Yet it did not cry out in pain. It simply lay quietly, waiting for death, while the other cockerel stood watch, bound to his enemy in the brotherhood of contest, in victory and in defeat. Yes, the afternoon was theirs. But no more would the fallen one run happily on the green hillsides, his brilliant feathers flashing in the sunlight. He had won his death.

And death is a thing that happens. How does a man die? Kian Teck wondered. And, when the time came, would *he* know how to die?

Wayan laughed. He was happy. He had won his bet. Some people wandered away to buy soft drinks from an old woman with dry breasts, bare above her bright sarong. Later, the fights started again. That afternoon, the men gathered once more at the cockpit, thirsting for blood to be shed onto the sun-baked earth.

"What happens to the dead birds? Their owners seemed to love them so much?" Jay asked.

Wayan laughed, replying, "Cut to pieces and cooked. Good dinner tonight!"

On another day, Kian Teck went to witness a Balinese cremation.[*] Jay accompanied him, but protestingly.

"Why do you want to see it? Why are you so morbidly curious?" She sounded both disgruntled and anxious.

What there was to see, he did not know, but there was a death, and, should a miracle take place, he might be there to witness a soul setting out. Who knows, it might cast some light?

Light there certainly was, that peerless afternoon. It was mid-day. And apt. Morning or evening would have been too benign, the one too crisp-

---

[*] The Balinese, an exception to most other Indonesians, are mainly Hindu and therefore always cremate their dead.

Part Three

fresh and the other too slack. It should happen under the harsh sun, thought Kian Teck, at noon, which exposes everything. Noon, when all mysteries vanish, or are understood.

And death, it appeared, was a public occasion. A large crowd of local villagers and gawking tourists had gathered on the wretched piece of ground chosen as the cremation site. By the time Kian Teck and Jay arrived, the funeral rites had already begun. Kian Teck watched the spectators, both native and foreign, male and female, young and old; he saw how the sunlight rinsed their eyes of mundane affairs and how they grew filled with apprehension in the face of this great and abstract mystery. Man, who was born, who lived, would also die.

And Kian Teck observed how the villagers, out of their simplicity, had invented elaborate rituals in order to try to arrive at an understanding of death. While the more sophisticated modern man, he realized, would reduce everything to essentials, to a bleak puritanism — a plain wooden box and an electric oven! — and thereby deprive himself of consolation, and understanding. For ceremonies *do* console. After all, man must laugh and dance and sing and cry. And in order to forget (ourselves, and that life is easily annihilated), and be forgiven, and to forgive (God?), it is necessary to be very simple, very good, like these villagers.

A TEAM OF MEN, YELLING AND SHOUTING in the great din of gongs and cymbals, were dragging the corpse, in its shroud of woven palm fronds, hither and thither in some obscene tug-of-war, pulling it first in one direction, and then, with a sudden shift in momentum, in another. Even Kian Teck found this a little bit frightening. Though, actually, what was really obscene was his fear itself.

After a while, the men placed the corpse into a shallow, freshly made earthen sarcophagus. A couple of men then hacked the palm shroud open, their *parangs* making horrible, loud thuds. The lack of gentleness was shocking. After all, there was a human body wrapped up inside! When the shroud was opened and the body finally exposed, the strong, sweet odour of decomposition pricked Kian Teck's nostrils. But he went closer.

It was a thin, old man. He had died some eight days earlier, Kian Teck was told. His eyes were sunken, and only an opaque, soft, jelly-like substance remained at the bottom of the socket cups. His chest had caved in, his flesh was wasted and grey. A paltry old thing. And yet, Kian Teck thought, those hands once fondled the swell of a woman's breast; and those loins lusted to thrust between a woman's thighs. And now, there he was, with nothing to show what his life had once been. Yes, there it was.

Then came the time to say the words which had to be said. Not only to bring grace, to bestow blessing, to console, but simply because silence was more terrible. There is a time in a man's life when priests are called for. And so, that afternoon, the village priest came forth to perform the funeral rites. He was a tall, thin, middle-aged man with distinguished, aristocratic features; long black hair, a lean and handsome face, graceful hands and fastidious gestures. He wore a bluish-grey, short-sleeved shirt over a brown-patterned sarong. A beautiful young Balinese woman held over her left shoulder a woven rattan tray bearing an earthen water jar and flower petals — bright, orange marigolds, purple orchids, tiny red roses — for the priest. She had vivid, live-coal eyes. Was lovely, lovely. When she lowered the tray the priest dipped his hands from time to time into the jar and then anointed the dead man with holy water and scattered flower petals over him. And like petals his words fell, scattering over the assembly, who tried to look solemn and conduct themselves with the appropriate feeling, grace and decorum.

But a small village boy, perhaps he was a grandson? went up to stare curiously at the corpse, his darting black eyes huge with wonder and trepidation at death, at what had been a man. And like the boy, others also walked up to the sarcophagus, and Kian Teck with them, compelled to witness, to see. All the while the cultivated, courtly priest showered, with practiced casualness, his words, which were in the timeless language of prayer and which sought, not clarity, not to explain the inexplicable, but something else, which might help the living to accept the meaning of death.

While the sun, the true presiding spirit of these proceedings, governs our lives, Kian Teck thought.

And, so that the dead one might pass through, they set his body on fire, using — to speed up the burning — old rubber tyres, pieces of wood, and kerosene oil. A scrawl of thick black smoke rose into the sky, the only unequivocal object on that day of bright light — all the rest, everything, was falsely permanent — but at length, even as Kian Teck watched, that column of smoke failed to rise to any great height. And Kian Teck also gazed into the fire, hunting for some meaning in its flickering light. The dead man! Never to be again! In all of time!

When the afternoon eventually relaxed in the trees, breathing slowly like an animal, Kian Teck and Jay left the cremation, and returned to Kuta Beach.

THE SKY EXPANDED THAT NIGHT, a concavity of stars, with a full moon. Quite idyllic. But for a long time Jay would not speak. And she would only look at Kian Teck sideways, when she thought he wasn't looking. She had been like that since they returned from the cremation ceremony. Perhaps she was just tired, Kian Teck thought, the day's heat so sapping. But when she remained silent as dusk fell, he knew something was wrong. For some reason, she was resentful towards him. He waited. At nightfall, she spoke.

"I want to leave. For a while, as a matter of fact ..." Jay faltered and was silent.

"Well, I was expecting this," he replied, non-commitally.

"I kept putting it off, putting it off. Didn't want to hurt you."

"Don't worry. I'll be all right." No, the world had not fallen apart.

"But today was the limit!" Jay would not let it go. "Really! That awful cremation. I felt *sick*. I don't understand your interest in it. Your morbidity. I was watching your face: you were completely absorbed! No, I shall never understand you, and that's all!"

"I'm sorry. It's just that I felt a compulsion to try to comprehend." Even though he sensed it would be pointless, Kian Teck tried to explain.

"What *is* there to comprehend?"

"Why, everything! Every goddamn thing!" He was surprised himself at his exclamation, and laughed.

"You do see yourself as something special!" Jay retorted, anger now in her voice.

He took the remark — and her tone — to mean that she was "not amused".

"You're just too much of a strain for me," she said.

He turned this statement over slowly in his mind. An echo. Wasn't that what Li Lian had said, the night she left him? Something like that. Yes, there must be something about me then, that makes them react this way. He reflected a moment. On that hot afternoon earlier in the day, the shadow made by the black column of smoke had been yellow, one moment on grey, dry earth, another moment on the green of grass, as the column twisted and turned. One couldn't explain these things because there was no explanation. No, nothing I have done is of any use. I know it. And yet ... He did not say any more, but waited for her to speak.

Above them, the night was limpid, benevolent. It was late. They talked. It all came out. Words fell.

Eventually, she said, "I hope things will work out for you."

He nodded.

"We were simply filling in a gap in our lives. You see that, don't you?"

Part Three

"I know, I know."

When he came off the black hill of the night, Kian Teck took an early flight back to Singapore, the plane silver in the quick of the sun.

4

"Kok Leong's found himself a girl, that's why he's so dreamy," explained Third Aunt, who was wise in these matters.

"But he never mentions her!" Mrs. Chan said, incredulous.

Third Aunt gave an uproarious laugh. The obtuseness of some people!

"Do you *really* think he's got a girl?" Mrs. Chan asked her sister anxiously.

"I'm positive."

"Oh, it will be too good to be true!" Mrs. Chan clasped her hands together tightly, hope filling her fearful eyes.

"But why're you so surprised? It's natural for a man to have a woman." That's how Third Aunt, giving her elder sister a pitying look, saw it. Nature. She was thinking of her own life, with its crowded affairs of the heart, or of the flesh. She thought of the many men in her life, those whom she could remember. Men! She could gobble them all up.

Although Mrs. Chan always regarded her sister as rather hedonistic, and an outrage to her family, nevertheless she knew she could turn to her whenever there was a family problem. When her husband first found work as a toilet attendant, she had sought Third Aunt's counsel. She was worried about the children, about what their neighbours would think.

"Good for him!" Third Aunt had said vigorously. "He's a good man. A strong man," she declared, dismissing her sister's misgivings with a baleful look in her eye, daring Mrs. Chan to be squeamish.

255

Part Three

And now they were discussing Kok Leong's so-called "odd" behaviour. A certain softness had emerged through his normally hard exterior, and there was also, of late, a certain haziness in Kok Leong's manner. When he walked across the hall to his own bedroom, a part of him seemed not to be there.

"All in good time, nature takes its course. There's no going against nature," Third Aunt remarked, mock sententiously.

"You don't know Kok Leong. He's such a strange boy. Sometimes ..." Mrs. Chan shook her head, hesitating, a little repelled by her own candour; after all, he was her own son, "... sometimes, he seems abnormal."

"Nonsense!" rebuked Third Aunt, who did not believe there was such a thing as an "abnormal" person. Stupid, yes. Greedy, yes. And a whole lot of other things. But not abnormal. "It just takes more time for him to come around, that's all. I wonder what sort of a girl he's got? Hee-hee!" she giggled, salaciously.

All the same, Mrs. Chan thought worriedly, it was true. He *was* a strange boy. Even when he had been very small, he had kept to himself, staying away from other children. He never played games with the neighbourhood kids in Sembawang. And they kept away from him, too. But they never trifled with him either, Mrs. Chan remembered. He was never bullied, though he was small built. She recalled one occasion, when Kok Leong was about seven or eight: a bigger boy from the neighbourhood had playfully pinioned his arms behind him and would not let go for a while, even though Kok Leong wriggled and struggled with fury, obviously not enjoying the joke. When the bigger boy eventually released him and moved on to play with the other children, Kok Leong went away but returned with a hefty piece of firewood which he brought down on the boy's head with all the force his tiny arms could muster. The older boy screamed, blood gushing from a bad cut on his scalp. Although Mr. Chan caned Kok Leong afterwards — they had to do this to appease the neighbours — Kok Leong neither flinched nor whimpered throughout the punishment. Rather, he seemed to constrict into himself even more. It was unsettling. And no matter how hard they tried, Mrs. Chan always felt that they had failed to bring him up normally. They simply didn't know how to get through to him.

"Maybe I'll tease him. Coax him to bring her home," Third Aunt ventured.

"Leave h-h-him alone," Mr. Chan interposed. He had been content until now to leave this discussion to the women while he sat at the table reading the afternoon paper. It was his day off.

"You're all too serious," Third Aunt continued.

"Leave h-h-him alone," Mr. Chan appealed again, then turned back to his paper.

"Do you think he'll marry her?" asked Mrs. Chan.

"Hee-hah!" Third Aunt laughed, whooping. "You're really too serious. Who knows how many women he'll have before he's ready to settle down?"

"Kok Leong's not like that at all," his mother protested.

"There's nothing wrong with that. It's normal, healthy. Although I must admit Kok Leong doesn't seem like a womaniser to me. One can never tell, though. 'Still water runs deep', sometimes," Third Aunt nodded her three chins knowingly, happy to show off her knowledge of English proverbs.

Mr. Chan rustled his paper with a deliberate air, to hint at his annoyance. He did not enjoy listening to his son being the butt of feminine gossip.

But the women continued talking, ignoring him in their absorption. This bone was apparently too good for mere gnawing. They couldn't resist worrying it to death.

"How is he getting on with his job?" asked Third Aunt.

"All right, I suppose. He doesn't say much — *you* know him."

Part Three

"Still with the accounts department?"

"Yes."

"He should really take up accountancy. He could attend night classes at the Adult Education Board, get a degree."

Again Mr. Chan flourished his paper, rustling the large, crisp, dry leaves.

"We can never tell him what to do," Mrs. Chan said, helplessly.

"You know what's wrong, don't you? You're all too frightened of him. It's quite ridiculous!" Third Aunt bawled out, stridently.

"What do-do you know?" Mr. Chan demanded.

"Now, now," Mrs. Chan intervened.

"What do-do you know?" the puny little man bristled. "You an-an-and that so-so-called husband of yours. Great way *you've* brought up-up *your* own children!" Unexpectedly, Mr. Chan was in a rare temper.

"That's enough," said Mrs. Chan in a chiding voice, trying to soothe him.

"Don't be so touchy!" Third Aunt continued, undaunted. "*I* never claimed to be a good mother."

"You women have too li-li-little to do," Mr. Chan said heatedly, ignoring his wife's placatory gestures.

"Listen to him! Him, sitting there all afternoon, lost in his newspaper. And *he* says we have too *li-li-* little to do!" Third Aunt protested. One thing about her, she seldom took offence or held a grudge, her great body packed with tons of resilience as well as fat.

"How-how goes it in Jakarta?"

Third Aunt knew very well that her brother-in-law was only playing at being interested. All because he had lost his temper, the poor creature. Men! But she answered his question civilly. "The same. I still take poor suckers from Singapore to the casinos there, to be slaughtered — the damn fools!"

258

A Dance of Moths

But she got her cut both ways: from the gamblers whom she escorted to Jakarta, and from the casino management.

"You are a-a terrible woman," Mr. Chan replied.

"Am I not?" she agreed, smugly, as if she had just been complimented.

"Sinful. And-and evil," he went on, beginning to enjoy the game.

Third Aunt laughed with joy. She loved being skewered, it seemed.

"Really bad, bad!"

She rollicked with laughter.

"Well," Mrs. Chan chipped in, "I suppose some people have money to throw."

"If you mean the gamblers, they don't. Most of them can't really afford it. Yet they're willing to get their fingers badly burnt. There are so many stories I can tell you, but if I do, you'd think I'm a liar. Why, I know of some women — wives, mind you — who've lost so much at the gaming tables that they ..." Third Aunt said meaningfully, leaving out the obvious.

"Tsk! tsk! tsk!" Mrs. Chan clucked, shaking her head like a disapproving hen. "All of them ought to be shut down. Jakarta, Genting. They're such a bad influence, leading people astray. God will punish them." She did not, however, specify which of her gods would do the punishing.

"Starting with this-this bad woman," Mr. Chan said, pointing.

Third Aunt shrieked, "Me? Why? Perhaps I'm the agent of God? Leading all these sinning gamblers to their punishment!"

"Tsk! tsk! tsk! Your *tongue!* " Mrs. Chan scolded, shaking her head again, this time at the blasphemy.

There was a soft click at the door. A moment later, Kok Leong entered.

"Here comes our Romeo," Third Aunt announced heartily.

Mrs. Chan gave her a dark, poisonous glare.

Mr. Chan returned to his newspaper.

"Hello, Third Aunt!" Kok Leong called out with his usual amiability towards this, his favourite aunt.

Part Three

"And how's our Romeo?" Third Aunt asked playfully.

At that moment, Mrs. Chan almost hated her sister.

"Eh?" Kok Leong looked bemused.

"Don't eh? eh? me. Tell me what she's like!" Third Aunt thundered.

"I don't know what you mean," Kok Leong replied, a little taken aback by surprise. Also, he was really not all there, at that moment.

"Oh, you don't? You think your Third Aunt's so easily bluffed?"

As the afternoon progressed, the topic proved too tempting to be resisted, and Third Aunt teased Kok Leong mercilessly. But he chose to remain silent. Mrs. Chan, in her agitation, sought refuge in breaking a pile of long green beans into smaller pieces, and after this chore, she embarked on another, pulling off the tasseled roots of a dish of bean sprouts. Exasperated crackles of the newspaper sounded at intervals from Mr. Chan's direction. But to every one's chagrin, Third Aunt refused to be deflected, staying resolutely on course. Finally, as evening approached, she sailed out of the apartment with a stateliness characteristic of some fat ladies. She would not stay for dinner.

KOK LEONG WENT INTO HIS ROOM, FROWNING, because he still found it difficult to focus himself, to compose his thoughts. It was so simple, and at the same time, so complicated. He sat on his bed, facing a blank wall so that he would not be distracted.

Marry Emily!

At one time, the very thought would have been totally alien. And now, for well over a week, the idea had hummed in his head. It never left him. So much so that he went about in a dreamy haze, trying to grapple with the problem, which he found both momentous and very simple. After all, others did it all the time. He took to scrutinizing married people, examining them minutely, as if they were strange, exotic specimens. There was a certain quality, an aspect, to married people which was absent in singles, although he found it difficult to put into words just exactly what this difference was. All the same, thought Kok Leong, a state of matrimony *does* exist. And he began to look at, and saw, people in a new light. And they were *fascinating!* The more he observed them, the more fascinating they appeared to him: and he wanted to be like them. How he *ached* to be like them.

He tried to imagine what it would be like to be married to Emily, to live in a home of their own, to have children. It was startling, too incredible to be conjured up. But this failure of his imagination did not diminish, in the least, his ardour.

One afternoon after work, while walking past the Toa Payoh Sports Complex, Kok Leong saw some men jogging. He went closer to them and stood by a small tree, watching them jog slowly round the bitumen track. At first, the sight of these men, dressed neatly in white, and toiling around the track in their Bata or Adidas jogging shoes, seemed ridiculous to Kok Leong. There was a preoccupied air about them, pious, an earnest strain on their faces as they ran past, their jaws hinged apart, hungrily sucking in air like a school of fish floundering out of the water, leaving in their wake the scent of Wintergreen. Yet, as Kok Leong watched them finally coming off the track, after about four or five rounds, their skins glistening with sweat, he saw that joy kindled their eyes like flame. He was stirred, whether by commiseration or admiration, he wasn't sure. What were they chasing, and what compelled them, these grimacing men, struggling round the perfect oval? And afterwards, with towels draped around their shoulders, did they return, sated with health, to their homes and families? Kok Leong felt there was something tender about this thought.

A while later, on a delicious cool evening when the moon was in its third quarter and had withdrawn behind a heap of clouds, Kok Leong took Emily out to dinner. She had expressed a desire to visit the Shangri-la Hotel.

"They held last year's Advertising Ball at the Shangri-la Ballroom," Emily had said to him.

Neither of them had been to the ball. Also, neither of them had ever entered this luxury hotel before.

Kok Leong felt exhilarated when they walked through the ornate portals of the hotel. It was the night he had planned to broach the subject of marriage. His heart thumped in his chest. Fit to fly.

The automatic, sliding glass doors swished open silently, admitting them to an interior richly splashed with light, lustre falling through chandeliers from a thousand light bulbs onto the polished marble floors and walls. They toured the foyer and the expensive shops on the ground floor before going into the hotel's Coffee House restaurant. There was little in this glossy temple of ostentation and luxury which excited Kok Leong. While Emily, he quickly noticed, was awed, letting herself be seduced by the surrounding manifestations of wealth.

A Chinese waiter, resplendent in a black suit and dazzling white frilled shirt, came to take their order. Although still young in years, he addressed them with a cultivated gravity, if not an actual haughtiness. Everyone there shared in a conspiracy, Kok Leong thought, which was to intimidate poor people, to discourage and discomfit any would-be interloper, and put him in his proper place.

Through a high wall of clear glass a bright, turquoise swimming pool glimmered between miniature coconut palms in the courtyard garden outside, beyond which the world darkened into shadow.

At length, Emily looked up at the waiter timidly through her thick glasses, and murmured, "French onion soup and Vienna Schnitzel?" Her voice wobbled a bit, uncertain if she'd pronounced this foreign word correctly.

"Anything to drink, miss?" the waiter asked. Supercilious.

She shook her head, like a shy schoolgirl.

Kok Leong ordered fried *mee hoon* and iced lemon tea. When the waiter left with their order, he turned to Emily.

"I've done a lot of thinking ... " he began.

Emily leaned across the table towards him and whispered urgently, "Don't stare! But over there, in that corner behind you, I think that's Mrs. Ong, my boss's wife. Those must be her children. I've never met them, but he keeps their photographs on his desk." She was very excited, her small eyes glinting behind those large spectacles.

To see them, Kok Leong had to turn around. He caught a brief glimpse of a young woman in a smart blue pants suit, and two small boys. He wasn't interested, and turned back to Emily. "For more than a week now ..." he continued.

"I heard they're separated! The girls in the office are gossiping!" She hadn't heard a word he'd spoken.

In the few months since he had come to know her, Emily seemed to have changed. While, in actual fact, she hadn't. It was only that certain traits in her character became more apparent as he got to know her better, and, on her part, as she got used to being with Kok Leong, she showed him things about herself which she would never have done with a stranger.

"Separated, you say?" He thought he might as well use this as a convenient launching pad. "There appears to be a lot of divorces nowadays. I don't think I approve."

"He's in Bali, right now. Maybe it's true, that they're separated!"

"Marriages should be permanent," Kok Leong replied, urgently.

"Bali! Wonder what it's like?"

"What do you think ...?"

"Must be fun to travel."

"... about marriage?"

"Have money!"

"I know it takes time ..."

Part Three

"Lots of money!"

"Lots of time ..."

"I think I will enjoy travelling."

"Something as serious as ..."

"So many places, I've never been to!"

"Marriage. I want to ask you ..."

"So many things, I've never done!"

"What?"

"Stay in a hotel like this. Wonder what it feels like?"

As she mused on this, a look of anxiety crept into her pale face. So she hankers, it seems, thought Kok Leong. And the pathos of Emily struggling so hard to belong, wanting so much to belong, went right through him. He wanted to take her hand, wanted to single out their solidarity, to demonstrate that they, the two of them, were the only sane people in that world of gloss and affectation. But he faltered, sensing that Emily's enthusiasms were turning into envy.

The pots of indoor plants, waxed and shiny, seemed somewhat stupefied, with vivid green lights trained on them, transforming their inherent colour into an unnatural, intenser green. As if they could not leave nature alone, thought Kok Leong, but must tamper with it. Such arrogance! Such sickness!

A group of people, all fashionably dressed, chatting loudly, came to sit at a nearby table. They did not seem to care if strangers could hear what they were saying. Indeed, that might have been their intention.

"That woman looks like Ting Pei!" cried Emily.

"Who?"

"Betty Ting Pei! You know? The Taiwanese actress!" exasperation in her voice.

He had not seen this Betty Ting Pei's films, or if he had, he couldn't remember.

"She *does* look like her!" Emily insisted.

"Maybe it's her."

"Do you think so?" She grew more excited.

He shrugged. At one time, he would have been surprised to discover frivolity in Emily. All the same, he was a little put out. After all, he was almost on the verge of making her a proposal of marriage! How was it, he wondered, that she failed to recognize what was happening to herself? But the last thing Kok Leong wanted to do was to level any criticism at Emily. He was relieved when their dinner arrived.

Emily fidgeted over her food, absorbed by the people at the next table. She lowered her face, if not her eyes, over the bowl of onion soup, her jaws working independently.

Kok Leong's fried *mee hoon* was atrocious. And it cost four times the usual price. What type of fools come here? he wondered.

They ate in silence, Emily watching the other people avidly. Kok Leong thought them too excessively fashionable. Great apes, following the latest fads in dress, in hair style, in shoes and music and thought, if they thought at all. And yet, he pondered indignantly, they dared to wear a superior air, bloated with exaggerated self-importance.

Emily, however, felt more shapeless, if not quite the wrong shape. She could barely conceal her envy, and was wracked by a feeling of worthlessness. This outing, instead of bringing her enjoyment, was having the opposite effect. All this Kok Leong saw. Why was she tormenting herself? He wished for nothing more than to get out of that place. They didn't belong. There was a gulf between them and the other people which Kok Leong had no wish to bridge, while Emily's desire was to be united with her surroundings, to fuse with them, to be engulfed.

In this frame of mind, she could not help but regard Kok Leong's presence as an encumbrance, from which she wished to extricate herself. Though the wish was, of course, unexpressed, Kok Leong was aware that

Part Three

she had stiffened towards him, that she had grown noticeably colder. He did not know how to deal with this. He became annoyed with himself, and then with the world. That night, he did not embark on the subject of marriage any more.

THE FOLLOWING EVENING WAS GREY AND THREATENING, a sky of iron, thronged with clouds through which a feeble light filtered. There was only a vague opalescence showing where the sun should be setting.

Kok Leong was walking home from his bus stop, but then, for some reason, he deviated, maybe blown off course by the strong wind, into the Toa Payoh Sports Complex. It was almost deserted at that hour. He sat on a bench facing the black, bitumen-covered running track, lost in thought. Above him, the swollen rain clouds tossed and churned in turmoil, in disequilibrium, in tune with his mind. And there were the birds, tiny black swallows, questing, in aerial free play, as though turbulence was their element. The sight of the birds made Kok Leong feel restless, and perhaps it was this, or some other strange, mysterious compulsion, which prompted him into action. He was suddenly seized by an urge to run.

He took off his black leather shoes, placed them with his socks under the stone bench, then rose to his feet and began to run.

This activity was so unorthodox for him, he would have faltered had he paused to contemplate it, but was sufficiently self possessed to leave off rationalising, just giving in, instead, to this mysterious compulsion. So he ran on, and soon had gone about half a turn round the track; then the effort first began to show. He found his formal clothes constricting, hindering a fluency which, he felt, was almost realisable. Yet something spurred him on, and he ran headlong, and soon there was less resistance, and greater ease and freedom. He was in solo flight!

It was heady for one who had never soared before, and he rushed and entered the space of air before him as if he were plunging into an ocean, the misty air giving way, parting its sinews of wind. He went on and on, tearing through the dense air. After a time, he felt all ambiguousness, all uncertainty dissolving away. It was an intense sensation of being.

After doing one round, he thought: "Great!" and proceeded to set himself a target. It was completely arbitrary, but once formulated, became an imperative, an unshirkable quest. "Eight rounds! I must complete eight rounds! I must strive to do more than the other joggers. Nothing less!" He jutted out his chin, and set off again; indeed, Kok Leong was ready to run on to the stars.

But by the third round he was tired, and his legs began to hurt, his breath escaping in audible gasps. Still, he felt in good accord with life, with the world. When he had completed his fourth round, the sullen sky trembled, shaking off a fine rain which fell, without direction, blown hither and thither by the wind. The external world was soon blurred, lost in a grey amorphousness in which Kok Leong was marooned. With the rain, the sense of a contracting universe increased until only the hammering in his chest was left. A doubt began to grow. Four more rounds! But he must dispel this doubt, at any cost, or else victory would forever be outside his experience. He ran on, driving himself, and pain annointed him with a certain innocence, lent him courage.

He laboured on until the sixth round, when his pain could not be ignored, nor, it seemed, endured. There was a vise in his chest, his muscles were tearing, his bones groaning. It was difficult to coordinate his limbs, his sinews, they quivered so much, he had so little control over them. But Kok Leong forced himself to be firm, determined to scale this great and terrible mountain, and drove himself as if more than his life depended on it.

"I will, I *must* endure! It is my only purpose!"

Part Three

The rain grew more intense, lashing at him now, and he teetered, clawing the air before him for purchase. There was nothing to sustain him now except a weakening will, when it had been his will that he had wanted to strengthen at the initiation of this mission. Now there was nothing left to summon up, but still he went on, his bared teeth sinking into the bitter air. The track before him seemed to be interminable. One more round to go!

"If I should fall, it would absolve me from this terrible task. Oh, let me fall!"

But he did not fall, and he went on running, transformed, as if his mind were gone. His breath was coming in desperate grunts, but an exquisite sense of ordeal, and of victory, accumulated, and miraculously he finished his course, his head and chest exploding.

LATER, REELING AND DRUNKEN IN THE RAIN, Kok Leong laughed. The next time he saw Emily, there would be no carefulness, no inconspicuous tactfulness. The next time, he would not be put off.

5

In Kampong Java Park, Ong Kian Teck sat watching the day dissolve. The sun had gone. Encroaching darkness broke the sharp outlines of the trees, now soft and blurry with shadow. The distant buildings seemed to hang in the air, dangling, unrelated to earth, as indistinct as dreams. Kian Teck looked at them without joy, without expectation, no longer hungry for distant dreams. He had lingered in the park for well over two hours, but time passed without touching him.

In the past few weeks, the strength had drained out of him. His mood alternated between languor and despair. He could no longer cope with his problems, and there was no solution in sight. When he looked back, everything seemed unreal: his wife, his children, his home. With a pang, he knew his family life could no longer be reconstructed.

He had gone to the park straight from work. Not to jog. Simply to sit, as darkness came down slowly over his head.

Earlier, a young Thai Buddhist monk had walked over to talk to him. He told Kian Teck that he was from Bangkok. But Kian Teck found the conversation uninteresting. The monk only wanted to ask him for directions. Kian Teck scrutinized the close-cropped hair on the monk's scalp; it made his head look like an untidy fruit. He wore saffron robes, with a plain cloth bag slung over a thin shoulder, his clean, bony feet shod in a pair of rubber slippers. He walked with a dragging slod, slod. Afterwards, he gave Kian Teck his engraved name card: The Rev. Sikhon Choonavon. It bore the address of a temple in Upper Paya Lebar Road, and a telephone number.

Kian Teck thought it odd that he had a name card, like a businessman. Somehow, it seemed wrong. A monk should not parade the self, the I, so explicitly. If *he* were a monk, mused Kian Teck, he would like to be nameless, to be dispossessed of his name as well as of all worldly things.

But who was he kidding? When his own life was so unmanageable? And his own helplessness now made so manifest? All he could do was sit and watch the shifting tints of the sky, the contours and textures of the trees as the night came in, and a moon-disc, bone-white, rise, disentangling itself from the lattice-work of trees which festered in deeper shadow. If only he too could follow suit, disentangle himself from the morass into which his life had sunk?

The question was not just rhetorical. The fact was, Kian Teck's financial problems had become crushing. Only that morning, he'd taken time off from work to keep an appointment with one of his bankers, and had endured a very rough session.

As expected, the bank manager had not been satisfied with the arrangement Kian Teck proposed for settling his debt. He rejected it outright and demanded a repayment schedule which Kian Teck couldn't possibly meet. Kian Teck had pleaded with him, but the man, a fat, beefy-faced Englishman, sat scowling behind his massive desk, refusing to budge. He threatened to take legal action unless Kian Teck complied with his repayment terms. The meeting ended without their arriving at any agreement. Kian Teck had stumbled out of the bank a defeated man.

And the same thing had already happened twice that week. On the Monday before, he had endured his first ordeal. On that occasion he had been scolded by the manager of another bank, a thin Chinese wearing horn-rimmed glasses, not much older than Kian Teck. In fact, Kian Teck had known him slightly when they were both students in London. Sitting in Kampong Java Park, Kian Teck's nerves tautened when he recalled the insults hurled at him while he was trapped in the banker's office.

"How could you have been so irresponsible, so reckless? You, a married man with kids! You know next to nothing about the stock market, yet you plunged in like a fool! Didn't you stop to *think?* Gambling way beyond your means? Didn't you think of the consequences? Well, what have you got to say? How do you propose to settle your debt?" All this in a high-pitched, jeering voice, the man clearly enjoying himself.

Smarting from the taunts, Kian Teck had wanted to punch the fellow, or abuse him in return. But he sat there meekly, with no plausible excuse, no obvious solution to offer. Filled with a terrible shame, he was forced to endure a lecture on his own shortcomings. Although no solution had been found, it was a relief to emerge afterwards onto the bright, busy street. Kian Teck felt a spasm of shock to find the world outside unchanged. People sauntered past him, completely oblivious to his predicament, to the ordeal he had just been through. Surely there must be a mark on his face, some tell-tale sign? But no one even *looked* at him; it was as if he were invisible, as if he did not exist.

And still it was far from over. He would have to reckon with the banks again. It was only a question of time. The prospect filled him with dread. He became dejected, tormenting himself by speculating about what would happen, trying to devise stratagems when he knew there were none. And at other times, out of a sense of sheer impotence, he lapsed into fatalism, into a strange lassitude. This was not the same as boredom, a mood for which Kian Teck now had no time. He said to himself, what will be, will be: the credo of hopelessness. What was going to happen would happen, no matter what he did. So, to hell with it! To hell with everything!

Alas, this defiance and anger could only be transient, because the problems, the worries were always present. Sometimes, lying alone at night, he felt he could not breathe. Even the air was suffocating.

There was nothing to do except to carry on. He could only forget his

Part Three

situation when he was occupied, and he was almost gratefully happy when office work was loaded onto him. In fact, he wanted more, as if he could never have enough, working with an avidity bordering on frenzy, on panic. Time was most unbearable when there was nothing to do. After office hours, he found himself growing increasingly restless and frightened. Then he became desperate to find something to occupy himself with, to save him from despondency.

Sitting alone in Kampong Java Park, Kian Teck felt lost and lonely, and suddenly he wanted to meet Old Ho again. He longed to see that once-familiar figure slouched on a stone bench. But although he searched everywhere, Old Ho was nowhere to be found.

As he wandered around the park, Kian Teck met the new park keeper, a thin Malay man in his forties, neat, tidy, and balding, with a gentle air. He was dressed in a smart new uniform: a light yellow shirt tucked into pale brown trousers. On the fourth finger of his left hand he wore a thick gold ring inset with a large opal.

Kian Teck asked whether he knew what had happened to Old Ho, the park keeper's predecessor. Yes, the man said politely, Mr. Ho had left the service. He understood that Mr. Ho was very sick, and could no longer work. Kian Teck heard this with genuine concern. Suddenly, Old Ho meant a great deal to him. He wanted very much to see his old friend. He asked the new park keeper whether he knew where Mr. Ho was staying. The man said he didn't know, but perhaps Kian Teck could enquire from the office.

Kian Teck resolved to seek out his friend. The evanescent evening stirred up feelings of anxiety and loneliness. The full moon was truly white, and as bare as a bone, with a sterile gloss. A rampant flotilla of clouds sailed by.

THE FOLLOWING DAY, at the first opportunity he had, Kian Teck telephoned the Parks and Recreation division of the Public Works Department and asked about Old Ho. It took some while, but they finally gave him Old Ho's last known address. He noted it down, and soon after work went in search of the old man. He learned only that morning that his friend's full name was Ho Yew Hong.

Kian Teck drove down Bukit Timah Road, past the Kandang Kerbau Maternity Hospital, that famous baby factory, and crossed Serangoon Road into Rochor Road, driving alongside the putrid canal, with its waft of stench, on his left. He continued until he reached the junction, then turned right into Queen Street. There was a bus terminal there, the Singapore-Johor Bus Terminal, packed with people queuing for the myriad buses to Johor Bahru.

After a little while he parked his Volks and set out on foot, looking for Tiwary Street, which, he knew, was somewhere in the area bounded by Rochor Road and Queen Street. Eventually, he found the address he wanted in a terraced row of broken-down, old, three-storeyed shop houses in this slummy section of the city. Since there seemed to be no one around, he entered the shadowy doorway.

At once he was enveloped by the distinctive reek of poverty, rancid and musty. The murky air smelt of wood smoke and dampness, of sweat and dust. In the dim, cluttered passageway, the green paint was peeling like flakes of useless, dead skin from the mould-encrusted stone walls. The bare cement floor was grey and dirty. Kian Teck's aesthetic instincts recoiled, and he would have bolted from the place had he not seen an emaciated, old Chinese woman looking at him enquiringly from a doorway. He asked her, in Hokkien, whether a Mr. Ho lived in the building. She pointed up the stairs with a skeletal finger. She did not even mumble a word. Kian Teck nodded his thanks, and, weaving past her, climbed up the narrow, wooden stairs, his weight creaking the old planks. He felt obscene, gross and guilty. He had entered the world of the poor in this

Part Three

decaying house with its attentive silence. The stairs were barely visible, with a single fluorescent tube, begrimed with dirt, hanging in the high ceiling, to shed its ghostly white, cold light onto the dingy quarters. At the first landing, he peered into some small cubicles, but did not come across Old Ho. The people living there all ignored him. Whole families, all as silent as fish. At the next landing, however, he found his friend.

Old Ho's bleary face was vivid, starkly outlined against the dirty white of the pillow case. He looked like a bloated fish, stranded on his narrow bed. Kian Teck approached slowly, stood by the bedside. His friend was asleep, or in a coma, his eyes closed. Bristles of grey hair grew on his upper lip and chin. He looked as if he were in a fever, his brow glistening, his hair plastered down with sweat. He was breathing noisily through snot in his nostrils. His mouth hung open slackly, exposing ruins of stained teeth in a pool of silvery saliva which washed against the shores of his pale, bloodless gums. He exuded a bad smell.

Kian Teck felt a great sadness, looking down at this ravaged, transformed shape of his friend. His breathing was so fitful and spasmodic that Kian Teck feared it might stop at any moment. So defenceless he looked, exposed, like a child, in his stuporous sleep.

A faint convulsion shook Old Ho's body.

Kian Teck made a sound, clearing his throat.

The lids flickered open, and the eyes scoured the dimness. Kian Teck glimpsed a great sun, or a bright chasm, and knew at once that his friend was going to die.

It took several seconds before recognition came.

"Mr. Ong!"

"Hello, my friend!"

And a joyful surprise brightened the sick man's face.

Kian Teck took his limp hand and squeezed it with his own firm grasp. The flesh was warm, almost hot, to the touch. He pressed it again, to transfer the tenderness he felt, unabashed by emotion, but he could not find the words to express his love, his sorrow.

"You came!" said the other, his breath hot and steamy. His words were a distillation of the utter loneliness he had suffered.

"I've only just heard. I contacted your office to get your address. I'm sorry I didn't come earlier," Kian Teck gabbled, wrung with guilt.

"You've come! There's no one ... " Old Ho croaked, sucking in air. The effort was apparent, was ghastly to watch. He could have been scaling a high mountain, so stertorous was his breathing. Tears began to well in his red-rimmed eyes, and a few drops overflowed, rolling down his cheeks.

"How are you?" Kian Teck asked solicitously.

"It's been ... terrible, terrible!"

The tears now fell freely.

Kian Teck groped for his handkerchief and wiped the old man's cheeks. "I'm sorry. Truly sorry. This place is horrible. We must get you to a hospital."

"No use."

"Nonsense! I won't allow it! You need care, you need looking after. I'll arrange for you to be transferred to a hospital."

"Too late," Old Ho panted. "They can do nothing. Nothing."

"You mustn't give up!"

"No use. It's too late. I know."

"Don't say that!"

"I know, I know." And he was wracked by a sudden seizure of coughing. His whole frame shook, his face turned red, his eyeballs almost falling out of their sockets. Afterwards, he worked his throat and brought up some phlegm into his mouth. He was desperate to spit it out and indicated, with a heavy, limp hand, the dirty tin spittoon lying on the floor under the bed. Kian Teck bent down and raised it up close to Old Ho's mouth. He spat out globs of yellowish, sticky sputum. When he had finished, he

Part Three

flopped back onto his pillow; a couple of strands of mucus dangled from his lower lip, clear as dew. Kian Teck put the dirty spittoon back, under the bed. He wiped his hands on his trousers.

"Ah, it's hot!" Old Ho groaned. "So hot!"

Old Ho pointed to a lidless wooden box placed on its side beside the bed; its top served as a bedside table. On it was an old, red metal thermos flask with part of the paintwork gone, showing rusty patches, a red plastic tea cup, a bottle half-filled with a viscous, greenish-coloured medicine, a few clear plastic packets with medicinal tablets in them, a yellow enamel spoon, a plain tin plate, a pair of reading glasses, a large bunch of keys, a pencil, a ball-point pen, a glass jar with some white sugar in it, a tin can containing rancid condensed milk, and an old newspaper. Inside the box was a shabby pair of canvas shoes, a pile of old Chinese film magazines, some clothes and a rather dirty green towel. Kian Teck brought out the towel. Next to the box he noticed a worn, cardboard suitcase. Beside that was a small, black iron trunk. Kian Teck guessed that all of Old Ho's worldly belongings were stuffed into these receptacles. A life time's collection, moth-eaten, gathering dust and mould, all contained within three small boxes.

"I'll be right back," he told Old Ho. He walked to the circular, concrete stairwell at the back of the house, but there was no one about. So he went down the wooden staircase to the landing below. In the first room, a tiny cubicle, a small, sinewy Chinese woman of about forty, with a blank, white face, was bent over an ancient treadle sewing machine. Her eyes were downcast, screwed tight in concentration. At her feet lay a cardboard box filled with odd pieces of fabric — cotton, silk and flannel —spilling over onto the worn, green linoleum-covered floor. Kian Teck asked her where the bathroom was. Downstairs, at the back of the house, she said, scarcely moving her eyes from her sewing.

So he made his way to the ground floor and walked through a narrow doorway, almost tripping on the threshold in the dark, into the shabby back courtyard. Although this cramped space opened up to the sky, it had an air of desolation. Stacks of old newspapers, crates of empty soft-drink bottles, two ancient, rusting bicycles and a dented zinc bucket were all piled higgledy-piggledy against the walls. He weaved through them towards the back, to the small bathroom. The concrete walls were damp and green with lichen. There was a cement trough half-filled with water, into which a rusty faucet dripped. Plop! Plop! Plop! Later, he discovered that it could not be turned off properly. Using a large, empty Milo tin perched on the rim of the trough, he scooped up some water and soaked the towel, then wrung it, leaving it damp. When he left the bathroom, the water continued to drip. Plop! Plop! Plop! The world was leaking.

He climbed up the stairs again. When he got to Old Ho, his eyes were half-closed. He is half gone, on the very verge, Kian Teck thought.

"I'm going to clean you up," Kian Teck told the old man, almost whispering.

Old Ho lay speechless, but his eyelids fluttered, like frail wings beating the air, to fly.

Kian Teck wiped his friend's face with the wet towel, and unbuttoned Old Ho's dirty white shirt and cleaned his neck and chest. He then untied the loose pajama pants and sponged the large, flabby belly. When he had completed this, he turned the sick man over onto his side and sponged his back. His ministrations done, he dressed his friend in fresh clothes from the box. By now the towel was filthy, smelling of stale sweat.

Old Ho seemed to revive after this. His eyes were wide open. His breathing seemed easier.

"Water," he asked, huskily.

Kian Teck poured out some tepid boiled water from the flask into the plastic cup, raised Old Ho, and lifted the cup to his lips. Old Ho slurped greedily, spilling some water down his chin in his haste. Afterwards, he sank back onto the bed.

"Thank you," he muttered.

"Are you better? Are you more comfortable?"

"Yes, thank you."

"Is there anything I can get you?"

Old Ho shook his head.

"Are you sure?"

"Yes."

"It's no trouble, you know."

"I'm all right. I'm really grateful."

"Nonsense! I've done nothing."

"Your coming here means more than I can tell you."

"I would've come earlier, if I'd known."

"You don't know what it means, to lie here, with no one to turn to, no one to talk to. Abandoned to die like this," Old Ho muttered gruffly, trying hard not to whinge.

"Don't talk like that," replied Kian Teck vehemently.

"It's true." Old Ho's soft, husky voice was resigned, not bitter.

"Doesn't anybody look after you?"

"The people here. They come and see me, sometimes. They bring me food and hot drinks. But I can't eat any more."

"What about your own family? Your daughter?"

"I haven't seen her in over a month."

"Perhaps she doesn't know about your condition?" Kian Teck offered. "Perhaps no one has told her?"

"I don't know," replied Old Ho, vaguely.

"Would you like me to get in touch with her?"

"No, I don't want her to see me die. Only you. Will you be with me now and then? I haven't long to go," he pleaded, gazing up into Kian Teck's eyes.

Kian Teck felt both touched and repulsed. "Of course I will. All the same, we must let your daughter know. You must give me her address before I go."

Old Ho looked away, stared at the ceiling. "I know you may be shocked, may think bad of me, but actually I'm not very keen to see my daughter. I know she's my own flesh and blood, but that doesn't mean very much to me. What I say may sound terrible, but I must speak the truth, I must speak simply. There's no time left."

Kian Teck was at a loss as to what to say. Such things lay beyond his experiences.

Then Old Ho turned again to his friend. "I never dreamed I would end up like this. Never dreamed my life would be such a long pain. Ah!" he cried out in anguish, giving way at last to terror, to self pity. "What have I done to deserve this?" But he quickly recovered himself, and sniggered, "Everyone asks that, don't they? What they've done to deserve all this?"

Then he started coughing again, a recrudescence of phlegm rattling moistly in his chest. Kian Teck fetched the spittoon. Old Ho's brow was clammy with sweat, and when he lay back, looking moribund, his nostrils were dilated for air. His big, bulging eyes tried to look out of the small window, where the tremor of far-off traffic floated in like some weird music. Ah, how the world goes on!

"I'm afraid," the old man whimpered. "At first, I used to wonder *why*, when I realized I was going to die. Lying here, sick and wretched, hour after hour, day after day, and not able to do a thing. Can't even get up to shit. Just lie here, useless as a doll. It's so exasperating, so humiliating, you've no idea. For a long time, I rejected the thought, unable to believe that it was happening to me! My life makes no sense at all, but I'm afraid to let go! I know my life has been a failure, but *why* must I die like this, without dignity? Why must I die shaking and crying like a coward?"

"I'll stay with you. Don't be afraid," Kian Teck said. Himself so bereft of comfort, he didn't know what else to say, how else to comfort Old Ho.

Part Three

After a while, Old Ho muttered, "I'm sorry."

"Don't be sorry. You've suffered a lot. You said you're a failure. Well, I'll tell you something. I'm a failure too. You see, my wife and children have left me. I've been playing around, a grown man like me, as if I had no responsibility towards anyone! And now I've lost my family — the ones who mean the most to me. I've also squandered everything, gambled recklessly. Now, I'm in debt, serious debt, and I don't know what to do."

Old Ho opened his eyes and studied Kian Teck.

"I don't know what to do," Kian Teck continued, gazing at the wall behind Old Ho, almost speaking to himself. "I've destroyed everything. Don't know why. So you see, I'm very foolish, *and* I'm a failure. But, you know, there're a lot of people like us. Like you and me. If only I have the grace to understand, then perhaps I can learn. Perhaps what I want to say is that we all share a common fate, all of humanity." Kian Teck did not know what made him choose to confess to his friend, who was engrossed enough in dying.

Old Ho cleared some more phlegm, rattling it in his throat. Then, after swallowing this, he breathed out a long-drawn-out sigh and said, "But that's no consolation! If only this were all a dream, a nightmare from which I would wake up! But this is *real*. I'm *dying*. A failure. And there are no second chances any more!"

By now the exertion was telling on Old Ho, whose eyes flickered shut as he sank back into sleep, then resurfaced for a moment, opening his eyes, struggling to keep awake, then sank back again. Deep into his own country.

Before he sank too deep, Kian Teck asked him for his daughter's address, so that he could get in touch with her. After some persuasion, the old man told him.

Her name was Emily. He gave an address in Upper Serangoon. She worked in an advertising agency in town.

And when it connected, Kian Teck was genuinely shocked. He exclaimed, "I know her! She's my secretary!"

But Old Ho barely heard him. Later, Kian Teck told his friend that he would return the next day, but the sick man was out of reach, in his black sleep.

Outside, in the crowded neighbourhood, everyone was preoccupied with his own prodigious, incomprehensible ceremonies. A world teeming with life. The image of Old Ho stricken in his cubicle grew all but lost in the jostling, tumultuous, indifferent crowd.

Kian Teck saw a young Chinese woman kicking a brown mongrel dog, her curses pursuing the poor beast down the narrow street. He passed a group of old men squatting on the five-foot-way to play a game of Chinese chess, while from the coffee shop next door, a rediffusion set blared out a serial from a Cantonese melodrama. A few doors away in a tiny cubicle partitioned off from the main shop, a thin Indian in a clean white *dhoti* sat watch over his wares, his blood-red mouth chewing betel nut. He sold cigarettes, cheroots, sweets, Social Welfare lottery tickets, condoms, playing cards and cheap plastic toys. Further on, by the side of the road, a trishaw-rider was sleeping, his body curled on the seat of his vehicle; his mouth was open like a cavern to receive the night, his legs covered with an old blue towelling blanket. An old hunch-backed Chinese woman pulled a wooden cart stacked with a pile of old newspapers and two *gunny* sacks filled with empty bottles and tin cans; the iron castors squeaked from the load. Yes, life goes on.

LATER THAT SAME NIGHT, while pissing in the toilet of a restaurant, Kian Teck read the following graffiti pencilled on a wall:

Part Three

> "To do is to be — Aristotle.
> To be is to do — Voltaire.
> Do be do be do — Frank Sinatra."

Kian Teck laughed till tears streamed down his eyes. It was so apt! Brilliant!

And there was another:

> "Life is a shit sandwich.
> The more bread you have,
> The less shit you eat."

The restaurant was called Jack's Place. It was situated on Killiney Road, just off Orchard Road. He had arranged to meet Peter Low there. He had the vague thought that perhaps Peter could lend him some money to help relieve the pressure from the banks. But the prospect of approaching his friend shamed and tormented him. However, there was no one else he could turn to.

So earlier that night at Jack's Place, while Peter Low was eating his dinner, Kian Teck had hesitantly broached the subject. He himself had no appetite, his stomach decidedly queasy, so had chosen not to order anything.

"The meat here is really quite good," Peter said, slicing vigorously into the airflown New Zealand pepper steak. The bloody juices sizzled on the hot iron platter. "Sure you don't want to eat? It's good value for money. That's why I come here."

"How's your luck on the stock market?" Kian Teck asked.

"I'm staying out of it," replied Peter, his mouth full of pepper steak. He masticated for a while, then added, "Now's not the time. South Vietnam's going to fall. A matter of weeks, for sure."

"I did badly. Took a real hammering, as a matter of fact."

"I see. You didn't pull out in time," said Peter matter-of-factly, still chewing. Then he raised his glass of wine and slurped appreciatively.

"I'm afraid not," replied Kian Teck.

Peter glanced at his crestfallen companion over the glass of red wine, and remarked, "A bit rough, this wine."

"I'm in real trouble, Peter. I'm going to be sued."

Peter shook his head sadly, munching a mouthful of red meat.

"I wonder if you can help me?"

Peter finished chewing the bolus of meat, swallowed it, and then asked, casually, "Me? Help? How?"

"Well, I thought you might lend me some money."

Peter raised the glass of red wine to his lips. He drank it with a slight moue of distaste. "I would if I could, old chap. But my liquidity isn't too good."

"I really don't know what to do."

"I'm not that loaded, you know, my friend."

"Never mind ..."

"Can't you raise it somewhere else?"

Kian Teck shook his head.

"Have you tried a bank?"

Kian Teck laughed ruefully. "All the banks are pressing me. They're after my skin."

"Give them some security."

"I've none."

"Come! Come!" Peter protested, disbelieving. To him, this was tantamount to admitting that one was a leper, or worse.

"It's true."

"Too bad!"

"Anyway, thanks ..."

"What about your family? Can't they chip in?"

Kian Teck shook his head. "No. That's out of the question."

"What about Li Lian's family? Your in-laws."

"We've separated."

"Oh, yes, I heard. I forgot. Sorry."

"It's OK."

"So you're still making out with that Yankee bird?" Peter was back in his lecherous rôle. "You sly bastard, you?"

"That's finished."

"Nice piece," Peter said, licking his fat lips and the tips of his lascivious moustache. "She still around?"

"No, I think she's somewhere in Australia by now."

"Pity. Wouldn't mind making a play for her myself. Seeing you've finished with her, of course."

"It wasn't quite like that." Kian Teck was annoyed.

"Come on! You mean you were *seriously* involved? Thought you were. You were always the serious type."

Kian Teck thought about it. Had he been seriously involved with Jay? He wasn't sure. If he denied it, it meant ... what? That he was a shallow prick?

"No, I guess I wasn't seriously involved," he finally admitted, honestly.

Peter laughed. He seemed reassured, relieved. And it seemed to revive his spirits. No, not revive — quite the wrong word. His spirits hadn't been low to start with. He was *never* low, old Peter Low. At least that was what he would have you believe, Kian Teck thought.

"Sorry I can't lend you anything," Peter said, returning to the earlier topic. "Against my principles. I believe that when money comes between friends, that's the end of the friendship," he wound up sententiously.

"It's OK."

But Peter wouldn't let it go. "You always gave the appearance of managing your life pretty well. At least that's what I thought. A good family man. Don't fuck around much. A little standoffish, you always were. As if you were somebody special. Now, *look* at you."

"Yeah," Kian Teck replied, laconically.

"I used to think — who does he think he is? As it turned out, you're really a bloody fool after all!"

Kian Teck stared at Peter's moustache, trying to keep his rage under control.

"Well, neither a borrower nor a lender be, that's my motto," continued Peter, complacently.

"Look, if you can't lend me money, it's OK. But spare me your fucking aphorisms, OK? I don't have to stomach your aphorisms!"

"Sure! Sure! *Relax!* Don't get so touchy," Peter said with a smile. It didn't reach his eyes, though he was pleased at having upset Kian Teck.

Soon after that Kian Teck left the table and went to the toilet.

> "The more bread you have,
> The less shit you eat."

When he returned to their table, he told Peter that he had to go. Peter tried to retain him, but without too much enthusiasm. It was simply for form, for appearance's sake.

FOR THE REMAINDER OF THAT NIGHT, Kian Teck wandered alone from one noisy bar to another, not knowing what it was he was searching for. He thought about the past, about Peter and Shamsuddin and Gopal Nair and their student days in London. Ready to conquer the world, they were. And now? Incipient failure. At least, for himself. The others seemed to be doing well. What had gone wrong for him? He didn't know. What did it matter?

Part Three

He remembered the profound anguish of Old Ho, thrashing about in death like a fish caught in a net, when struggle was in vain. But, was it in vain? The struggle? The struggle was *everything!*

Eventually Kian Teck felt tired, and after eating a plate of *kambing* soup at Newton, went home with no more desire beyond the simple wish for sleep.

THE FOLLOWING MORNING, A SATURDAY, Kian Teck set forth for work, driving his yellow Volks. The light was rich, sparkling; the morning seemed swollen, full, in bloom. And there was so much to do that he had little time to think of his problems. There was his work at the office; he had to talk to his secretary, Emily, about her father; he had to visit his family at his mother-in-law's; he had to find a doctor for Old Ho. But for the moment, there was the panorama of the sea as he crossed Fullerton Bridge, the ships afloat on the serene blue of the harbour. The morning light shone clear through his problems and tasks and responsibilities, and for a while they seemed to dissolve. Yes, light illuminates, shows up our silly dreams. That is how nature confers hope and sanity on a beleaguered and foolish mankind.

When he got to the office, Emily Ho greeted him from behind her desk.

"Good morning, Mr. Ong." Emily was her usual prim, polite self.

" 'Morning, Emily," he said, looking at her as he had never done before. She followed him into his room, placed his appointment book before him, and laid out the day's schedule. It wasn't the proper time to talk to her about her father. As he raised queries, gave instructions, they eased into the old, familiar relationship, of boss and secretary. They related to each other only in this rigid, formal, social context, with its prescribed rules and forms and limitations. She was simply Emily Ho, his secretary of three years' standing. He had never thought of her as anything else. Now he tried to place her in a new rôle — as Old Ho's daughter. But there was not much opportunity, with so much work to attend to. Emily returned to her desk outside, and he plunged into his work with relief, the familiar routine reassuring. It wasn't until noon that the pace began to ease off, and he could think about talking to Emily.

Alone in his office, he swivelled the high-backed chair around and looked out of the huge clear glass window. The whole world was flooded with light: everything mercilessly exposed. Suddenly, something like a fever ran in waves through his hot blood, his temples throbbed, and he could feel his heart pulsing, a trapped bird struggling to get out of, or into, the sun — he knew not which. The memory of Old Ho lying bathed in sweat in his acrid-smelling bed, returned to haunt him. In this heat, Old Ho would be delirious.

Kian Teck turned away from the window, took a few sips from the cup of tepid black coffee, feeling the minute grains on his tongue. With a brusque movement, he activated the intercom.

"Emily, please come in for a minute?"

"Yes, sir."

Emily came in and closed the door. She stood a few paces in front of his desk.

"Please sit down," he motioned her to a chair. "There's something personal I would like to discuss with you."

A look of bewilderment crossed her face, but she did as he asked, sitting down demurely in one of the chairs facing him.

"Emily, is your father's name Ho Yew Hong?"

She gave a slight nod, barely perceptible, sitting erect, still as a statue.

"I'm sorry to tell you this, but your father's very ill."

"You know my father?" she murmured, after a moment of surprised silence.

"Yes, he and I are friends."

"How?" Emily was clearly extremely astonished.

"We met each other by chance. I didn't know until last night that he was your father. He's dying, Emily." Kian Teck was blunt, but after what Old Ho had confided, he didn't see any need for the usual preamble with Emily.

"He's been sick a long time," was all she said.

"I'm afraid his condition is really bad now. I don't think he'll last long."

"Did my father send you to tell me this?" Emily raised her eyes to Kian Teck's. There was a hint of anger in them.

"As a matter of fact, no. I'm doing this on my own accord. I think you should go and see him. It might ease his suffering. You *will* see him, won't you?"

Kian Teck studied her face, lit by the sunlight coming in through the window. It bore no trace of anguish; only a certain sternness, which seemed to grow with every moment, as, her brow slightly furrowed, she slowly composed a reply.

"We've not seen each other for a long while. In fact, we seldom see each other. My father and I are not close."

"All the same, at this moment ..." Kian Teck's voice trailed off. Again, he lacked the experience to cope with such a situation.

"You might think me heartless," Emily said firmly, " but the truth is, I'm not very fond of my father. And neither is he fond of me."

"I'm sure you must be wrong, I mean, about your father's feelings." Even to his own ears this sounded like a meaningless platitude — but what else could he say?

"No, I'm not," Emily's voice was harsh, inflexible. "He's always been a selfish man who only thought of himself. He never showed me any affection, any tenderness, even when I was a child. Don't think I'm trying to blame him now, but I can't pretend that there is any deep feeling between us." This came out in a rush, the words tumbling over each other as Emily's bitterness mounted,

"But your father's dying! Can't you forgive and forget? He's your father!" Kian Teck was very agitated, unable to believe that *anyone* could feel this way.

"Being my father doesn't change anything. He's not a good man," replied Emily, her expression stony.

"But he's a man!" Kian Teck protested, driven by an impulse of loyalty. "He's a man, and I'm not going to say that he's good, or he's bad. Who's to judge?" his voice rose, impassioned.

"Certainly not an outsider!" Emily replied emphatically, her face suddenly flushing, an ugly, mottled red. She paused, composing herself again, waiting for this unfamiliar rush of blood to ebb. "I don't mean to be rude, but no outsider can understand what I went through as a child. My father never loved me. Only *I* know that."

"Couldn't you be wrong?" Kian Teck asked her gently, pitying the ugly, unloved child she must have been.

She looked up at him and smiled, because of his foolishness. "No, I don't think I'm wrong. I'm the one who has lived through it all."

"All right. I won't argue with you. But the point is, your father is dying. He's suffering a great deal, and you can ease his suffering by going to see him. Surely that isn't too much to ask?"

She smiled again, implying, "You're so wrong!" But she only said, "My seeing him won't ease his suffering."

"Have you no *feelings?*" he began hotly, and stopped short. "I'm sorry. I have no right to speak to you like this."

Emily's formal stiffness, her emotional reservation, suddenly melted. She rose abruptly from her chair and walked away stiffly till she was facing the wall to the right of Kian Teck's desk, standing only about a foot from the wall. He could no longer see her face, but he could hear her

Part Three

impassioned whisper: "I don't want to see him die, I don't want to see a man die!"

Kian Teck was moved. He got up and walked towards her. Emily stood as still as a stick, and as brittle, close to the wall. He laid one hand on her shoulder. He wanted to comfort this awkward, strange, high strung, and, he had to admit, rather unattractive young woman.

"Are you all right?" he asked.

The brittle stick suddenly softened, turned into a slender branch in a storm. Emily shook with sobs, and his hand felt the quivering, the tremors. "I don't want to see him die," she said, gulping down her sobs.

"It's all right, it's all right. I understand."

"Do you?" she asked, still sobbing, her voice muffled.

He withdrew his hand. "Yes, I understand."

You only say that, Kian Teck told himself. But do you, *do* you?

Emily gazed earnestly at him through moist eyes. She fished out a handkerchief from somewhere, it seemed to come from the waistband of her skirt, and blew her nose. It was a really tiny handkerchief, about the size of her palm, white, and so thin it was almost transparent.

Eventually, Emily rolled the handkerchief into a ball, squeezing it tightly in her hand. The tendons of her pale, bony fingers stood out, taut with tension. She smothered her sobs and, in a moment, a torrent of words tumbled out like water gushing through a burst pipe. She talked about her father; about how he had neglected her as a child; and how he had never showed her any affection, never uttered any endearments, and never bought her any toys. Unlike other girls, Emily said, she had never owned a doll, nor pretty dresses. She remembered how he would come home after work, change his clothes, then go out again, returning only late at night. And sometimes, not at all. She used to lie awake at night and wait for the sound of his return.

She told Kian Teck that her parents quarrelled all the time. Her mother, "a weak and vain woman," Emily described her, would burst into tears after a quarrel, slam the door of her bedroom, and lock herself in. And the small flat would be filled with a deadly silence. Occasionally, her mother would wear pretty clothes, put on her high-heeled shoes, and go out with Emily's father. Then Emily would be left all alone in the small flat. And after her mother died, her father did not change his ways. He still went out every night. She had to take care of herself. In the mornings, she would make her own breakfast, then go to school, where she would eat lunch at the school tuck shop. When she came home, she had to wash the clothes, both hers and her father's, clean the flat, cook her own dinner, and then go to lie alone in her bed. She was a lonely child. No friends or relatives ever visited them. Sometimes, she said, she had felt as if she were all alone in the world, abandoned, and no one cared at all.

Kian Teck was both appalled and fascinated by her story. He felt as if all the foibles and stupidity, pain and terror of humanity were being bared to him.

After pouring her heart out to "Mr. Ong", Emily felt that a subtle bond had been created between them. So she felt sufficiently bold to ask for his help. "I'll see my father, if you will accompany me." Her voice quavered, sounding a bit breathless. Kian Teck thought it was grief.

And he felt obligated; he could not refuse. So they arranged to meet that evening.

IMMEDIATELY AFTER LEAVING THE OFFICE, Kian Teck drove east towards Katong. Soon, he arrived at the old house and parked his car in the gravelled driveway. He saw his mother-in-law seated on a large woven-cane chair under a mango tree in the garden. Kian Teck went up to her.

He was glad to see her. Since his separation from Li Lian, he and his mother-in-law had grown closer. There was no deliberate conspiracy, but there was this unwillingness on the part of the old lady to acknowledge any estrangement between her daughter and her son-in-law. In fact, she had tried "to talk sense" into Li Lian, but could not prevail against what she regarded as her daughter's stubbornness.

"You're a foolish girl!" she had scolded her daughter. "Think of your Second Grand Uncle! Now, you know he had three wives, and children from all of them. But did Second Grand Aunt leave her husband? No! And what about Ah Chim?" Ah Chim was Li Lian's mother's sister-in-law. It appeared that Ah Chek, Ah Chim's husband, not only kept a second wife, but had installed a girl from the Gay World Cabaret in a flat on Clemenceau Avenue. And Ah Chim never did such a foolish thing as to leave her husband. And so on. And so on. All the family skeletons unlocked as an object lesson for Li Lian. Enough bones to litter a football field! "You modern girls!" Li Lian's mother had chided, shaking her head in disapproval.

The old lady smiled at Kian Teck's approach.

"Mama, are you well?" Kian Teck asked, in Hokkien, standing squarely in front of her.

"Oh, well enough."

"How's your back?"

In the large wicker chair with its ornate, flaring wings, and with her small hands clasped around the carved top of her malacca cane walking stick, she sat, as poised as the old dowager of Katong. Which she was.

"Not bad at all, in this heat. It's only the cold that gives me trouble," she said. But she wasn't one given to complaining. She never whined. A great bird, Kian Teck thought, not with disrespect, but with genuine affection.

"How're the children? Are they naughty? Do they get on your nerves?"

"They're fine. They don't get on my nerves at all. In fact, they're good for an old has-been like me. Good company. But it's not right. You all should be together."

"Yes, Mama. I know."

"When is this nonsense going to stop? It's not good for the boys. Not natural."

"I know, Mama."

"Both of you should have more sense. Look at you! You're not looking too good. You've lost weight. There are dark circles under your eyes. Why you let your health run down like this?"

"But I'm all right," Kian Teck protested.

"All right, my foot! That's what you say. All right, all right! But I don't believe you," the old lady sniffed, tossing her head disapprovingly.

Kian Teck laughed. The air, as usual in that garden, was redolent with the fragrance of crushed, ripe fruit, heavy with fecundity; the afternoon quiescent under the old fruit trees. Only insects made a fuss in the still heat. Flies, mosquitoes and small gnats hovered around an over-ripe, deep yellow papaya, which had fallen and lay broken on the ground, its soft, red flesh and tiny, glistening black seeds exposed. Apart from the insects, worms and birds had also got at it. The mango tree beneath which his mother-in-law sat was in flower — the buds in sprays of hard little yellow knobs. It would bear fruit again — for the second time that year! The sugar cane bush by the back fence had tall tassels of dry, feathery flowers. Irrepressible nature!

"Here come the children," the old lady announced happily.

The boys ran up to Kian Teck and he gathered both of them into his arms, all three of them laughing like lunatics. But when they eventually pulled apart, Kian Teck saw looks of reproach in his children's eyes. Guan Hock, who had grown taller, had a certain appealing fixity in his gaze; there was a hidden knowledge in his eyes, of something already inaccessible to his father. Kian Teck felt immeasurably sad.

Part Three

"Go into the house. Go to your wife," the old lady urged.

So he walked away from the garden of old trees.

Looking out of a window in the large, dim front hall of the old house, Li Lian watched the whole scene, from the time Kian Teck stepped across the gravelled driveway towards her mother, to the moment with their children. In the brooding shadow of the interior, remembrances stirred and renewed themselves within her, and she had no strength, or will, to suppress them. Time, after all, is motion, is shift and change. The hardness of stone can be worn to a handful of sand. And didn't they say, time heals all wounds? Not that she felt any specific tenderness towards that lanky man, his body so wiry and yet so soft, now walking towards the house, his face with that perpetual look of childish bewilderment, with that glint in his eye, who was so heedless and so scrupulous at the same time, wild and yet uncertain, the man who had brought her so much joy and so much pain. No, it was not exactly tenderness she felt, but a feeling of amiability, perhaps even of warmth, as she waited, with slightly bated breath (so slight, it was hardly noticeable, even to herself) as he came nearer. And when he finally walked in, swinging open the wire-meshed, insect-screened door, she noticed at once that his face was worn and hollow.

"Hi!" he said.

"Hello!"

"The kids look great."

"Yes."

"And how are you?"

"Fine. You?"

"Great!" he boasted, his voice light.

He's always like this, she thought, not with anger, nor with annoyance, but ... she knew not what. And then decided — it *was* with annoyance, "Yes! He's always been a transparent liar, he. Yes! He does it to make me feel sorry for him, to make me feel protective towards him. He does it!

He does it! And they have the *nerve* to say we women are coy and coquettish! Christ!" But Li Lian kept her expression impassive.

"*You're* looking great," he added.

"What's wrong?" she asked, bluntly.

"Nothing. Nothing's wrong," he answered, shamming, putting on that baby face.

"You look terrible."

"Do I?" he grinned like an idiot.

"What's wrong?"

He didn't answer. This time, he did not put on his baby face.

"I'm still your wife. Tell me — what's wrong?"

He didn't reply to her question. Instead, he turned vaguely towards the window, finally saying only, "God! It's bright out there. Look! Just look at the kids!"

They could see the children outside, running from tree to tree in play, and the old woman, still seated motionless beneath the mango tree, in the laudanum shade, out of the afternoon sun.

Li Lian turned again to her husband. "It's just like him, to digress," she thought, "weaving and twisting like a hooked fish." Irritation and compassion; both churned within her.

Then, "What's the matter?" she asked gently.

"Everything's a mess. I don't know where to begin," he replied in a strained voice, as if the words clotted in his throat. He did not look at her, but out of the window. He was not looking at the garden either, nor at his children at play, nor at anything in particular. Just gazing into space. "A mess," he went on, "and I'm too exhausted to sort out the wreckage. I'm spent."

"Is there any way I can help?" Li Lian asked. Suddenly shy, self-conscious, she raised one hand to brush away an imaginary stray strand of hair from her forehead.

It was a gesture of hers he had known. All at once, Kian Teck realized how much he loved her. He had to wait a long while before he could speak again. This time, it was about something else.

"An old friend of mine is dying. Dying most miserably. I've been to see him. I guess it must've affected me."

"Who is it?"

As his wife, Li Lian presumed it was someone she also knew. He understood this, and corrected himself.

"No, I suppose he's not really an old friend. You don't know him. He's someone I got to know some time last year. The park keeper at Kampong Java Park." He paused a moment, and realizing that Li Lian was a little bit puzzled, continued, "I got to know him on my outings to the park. That time when I used to jog. I guess I can't really explain our friendship at all. It's most strange. We have absolutely *nothing* in common. We happened to speak to each other a few times, just casual chit-chat, you know? And then, for some reason, I became quite attached to him. No, that's not true, not strictly true. But I got to know him. I took him out once, I remember now. We met quite by chance one evening at the Esplanade. I was strolling along when I saw him sitting by himself on a bench, a figure of dejection, a fat and sick man, desolate and lonely. I felt sorry for him. We talked for a while, and suddenly — I really don't know *what* got into me! — I invited him to join me. It must have been a sudden whim. I don't remember the exact circumstances. Anyway, we ate at the Satay Club, and then I brought him along to the Pebble Bar at the Hotel Singapura — of all places! Poor Old Ho, he was so out of place. Afterwards, we went somewhere else. While we were there he talked about himself, about his fears, his sickness, his loneliness. He talked about his past, when he was young man. It was very real, very interesting, another man laying bare his life for me to see. He told me he had a grown-up daughter who was more or less estranged from him. And the funny thing is — in fact, his daughter is my secretary, Emily. I only found that out last night. It was quite a shock. Funny thing, life! Stranger than fiction."

He stared at the gauzy whiteness of the sky through the window, saying nothing for a moment, his attention caught by a long row of black ants scurrying across the window sill. A safari of earnest coolies. Yes, work goes on. And life. And dying. After several moments of silence, he continued: "And now he's dying. Alone and wretched, in a rented cubicle. He's suffering terribly, and there's nothing I can do to help. Nothing at all!"

This sentiment was too simple, could so easily be shammed, Li Lian thought, still a little on guard, suspicious. But when she looked at him more closely, it was quite plain to her that her husband's despair and sorrow were real enough, and deeply felt. His words and gestures were free of any hint of insincerity, of frivolity. He seemed engrossed, and at the same time easily distracted, his eyes darting here, there, his attention flickering like the elusive reflections of a fire on a wall. She believed he was distinctly chastened. But she was also aware that emotion threatened to overwhelm *her*, and that she had to be quick to check its expression before it was too late. As a result, what she said came out not as solicitude, but preserved their formal distance. "These things happen," Li Lian remarked in a very matter-of-fact tone.

While Kian Teck merely glanced gloomily at the liquid shadows under the trees. A giant, old casuarina towered above the rest, as if making an extra effort to reach the sky, its fine leaves immersed in sunlight, transformed, charged into pale green fire.

"Suffering's a part of life," Li Lian continued, and was immediately unhappy over her choice of words, which seemed a cliché. Sometimes it's difficult to say *anything* right, she reflected frustratedly. Out of fear of saying anything trite, she now chose to remain silent.

"I'm in serious trouble," Kian Teck suddenly announced.

"What is it?"

"I'm afraid it's not a very nice story." He paused, uncertain how to tell her. *What* to tell her.

She looked at him, and waited.

"I'm in serious financial trouble. I lost a lot of money playing the stock market, and I can't pay my debts. The banks are after me," Kian Teck finally blurted out, opting for honesty.

Li Lian felt sympathy for him, as well as anger. The latter emotion was stronger, at the moment. After all, he was supposed to be a husband and a father. He had responsibilities. Also, she was instinctively angry because it just wasn't in her nature to sanction or condone wastage and gambling and suchlike madness. He had no right! So she kept silent, offering no consolation.

"I've been so damn stupid! There's just no excuse!" Kian Teck exclaimed.

She tended to agree with him. A sensible, prudent woman, Li Lian could not understand that kind of foolishness. Moreover, she wasn't given to self-deprecation, so she did not relish listening to her husband's self-recriminations either. Fortunately, he did not go on and on. Did not indulge in any histrionic self-flagellation. Finally, having described the circumstances baldly, he seemed to be at a loss for words.

And so they lapsed into silence, standing there in the deepening, expectant shadow of the old house, while outside, whiteness still clung to the sky, and the air beneath the trees hung heavy and soporific with the scent of ripened fruit, and only the insects were industrious.

And then he said, "Sometimes, I feel that I can't carry on any more. I wish I could end it all."

"Don't talk like that!" she scolded, with considerable force.

"I'm so useless, so ashamed. But I had to bring myself to tell you this."

"I'm glad you did," she said calmly. "We all make mistakes. What's done is done. How much do you owe?"

He told her. If she was shocked, she did not show it. And without any hint of reproach in her tone, she said: "We have to sell the apartment. And whatever else is necessary."

In spite of himself, he stared at her earnestly, and with awe. He had never considered that himself. "But it's our home! It's all we have!" he cried out.

"It doesn't matter. We can start anew."

"No, we *can't* sell the apartment," he said, but, belying his own words, his heart fluttered like a caged bird suddenly let loose. There was a way to freedom after all!

"Sell it. And the furniture. Raise whatever you need to settle the debts. You can move in here. I'll speak to Mama," Li Lian continued prosaically.

"After all that's happened, you still want me?" Kian Teck couldn't take all this in, so unexpected the relief. And joy.

And she nodded her head, her eyes downcast and demure, suddenly as shy as a schoolgirl.

"Do you love me?" he asked, his voice choked with emotion.

She looked up at him, and into his eyes.

"I love you," she whispered.

And with a rush, they flew into each other's arms.

6

Chan Kok Leong stood facing the rain from the verandah of a shop house in New Bridge Road. He was alone, driven to a corner of the evening. The air, the blurred houses across the street, everything was enshrouded by the rain. It seemed to Kok Leong to even inundate his viscera, the pervasive drumming of the rain drops penetrating his mind. For a long time he stood there, without stirring, gazing at this world of shrunken dimensions, nursing a feeling of frustration.

For the past two weeks he had tried to find an opportunity to propose to Emily, but each time she had given him the slip. Then she told him that her father was very ill. He was near death. This effectively restrained him from broaching the subject. He wanted to believe her, but he was also dubious. Nonetheless, he did not make any further approach. He waited, and nothing happened.

Incipient darkness touched the air. The passing traffic swished by, their headlights raking the falling trajectories of rain which billowed momentarily under the street lamps, transformed into showers of glass. His thoughts and feelings also scattered into tiny splinters, and his hours were blown like the fine rain, in gusts of quickening tempo, in flurries, disrupting the normal rhythm of his living.

Kok Leong had never imagined it would be like this. After all, love was supposed to bring joy — lovers holding hands, gazing into each other's eyes, strolling under the moon and all that. Yes, he had experienced that too. There were the nights when he and Emily had sat on the sand along the reclaimed beach out at Katong, under the trembling light of a moon, with the living sea in front of them, the sea sighing and sighing, and they, talking of this and that. There was such a glow, such an intensity then. What had happened? When he thought about it, he felt a mingling of sadness and nostalgia. He had no idea what had happened, only that he was unable to regain that sense of joy, of glowing, of wonder.

The rain fell steadily. What if it didn't stop and went on falling through the night? Well, what of it? He had nothing to do. He might just as well stand there as be somewhere else. And it was difficult to conjure up another location, the rainy world having no definable edge. Still, he wished he could be rid of this feeling. How had it come about?

With Emily, he had experienced moments of the sharpest, purest joy. Being with her, was, for Kok Leong, a way of escaping from the sordidness of the life around him, the meanness of human suffering. Sometimes they saw each other in the office, their eyes meeting, and Kok Leong felt that they shared a mutual recognition which set them apart from the rest of the world. Or he would wait for the moment when, breaking for lunch, they came out into the street, the light streaming down on them; and when he saw her face, honest, plain, simple, he would feel a surge of tenderness. In her presence, things fell into place. The world was beautiful.

And to Kok Leong, it seemed to be no exaggeration to say that Emily was fond of him. As far as he knew, she never went out with anybody else. Only with him.

That was at the beginning. Now things had changed. And he did not know why.

It seemed that the more he tried to win Emily, the more elusive she became. Just when he thought he had caught a glimpse of happiness, a shimmer of colour, it faded from his sight, like a fish flashing gold in a pond, triggered by the sun, and then sliding away, vanishing in the weed-

Part Three

entangled shadows. Yes, lately, Emily had been full of evasions. And the way she chose was not that of silence.

In fact, the amazing, most bewildering thing was that Emily had suddenly become very talkative. It was quite unlike her. She now talked endlessly, and about all sorts of things, jumping from subject to subject, and Kok Leong had great difficulty in keeping track of what she was saying. Yes, Emily was quite unlike her former self, and thinking about this gave Kok Leong misgivings which he did not understand.

That very afternoon, after work, he had walked her to the bus stop. He had offered to ride with her as far as she lived, but she had turned him down.

"I've nothing else to do," he declared.

"*I* have something to do," she said, mysteriously.

He knew he should not ask, but he did so anyway. "What is it you've got to do?"

"I've got to visit my father at the hospital. He's very sick, as I've told you," she replied, with an ironic smile which he found quite unnerving. Her facial expression did not match her words. He had, naturally, expected sorrow, or anxiety — not this enigmatic smile.

"I'm sorry," he muttered in some confusion. "Is there anything I can do to help?"

"No, there's nothing you can do," Emily replied, brusquely.

He fell silent, suddenly becoming conscious of the other people in the bus queue. He looked at their faces, tired, care-worn, creased by the day's deadly routine, and already bearing the imprint of the next day's chores. The roar of the heavy traffic epitomized the cacophony of their lives, the impatient, snarling anger thundering into the rhythm of their hours, grinding their very bones.

"Look!" Emily suddenly cried, pointing. "That girl on the opposite side of the road, coming out of Shenton House, do you like her dress?"

He was taken aback. He did not know what to say.

"I think I saw one like it at the Holiday Inn Metro. But I don't think a brown handbag goes with a blue dress," she observed, still staring at the girl across the road.

He waited a decent interval, and then asked, "When will I see you again? We haven't gone out together for a whole week." He was still resolute in his quest.

"I don't know," she answered vaguely, not looking at him. "I think I'm going to be quite busy," she said with a sigh, and then, à propos of nothing, asked, "Do you know my boss, Mr. Ong?"

"I've seen him in the office," Kok Leong replied, wondering at the way her mind darted from topic to topic.

"Have you ever spoken to him?" she asked, anxiously.

"*He* has never spoken to me," Kok Leong replied wryly.

"Actually, he's very nice," Emily said. There was a fervent animation in her voice. "A very kind person. He's doing so much for my father. He got a doctor to see my father the other day, and then arranged for the hospital and everything. Do you know he's a friend of my father's? Did I tell you?"

Kok Leong shook his head. He was really at a loss by now.

"I was surprised, myself. Fancy him knowing my father! A good friend, too! My father likes him, I can tell," she chattered on.

"Can't I come with you to the hospital? I won't go inside. I can wait outside the ward."

"No, I don't want you to come. Besides, you don't know my father." She was firm.

"I'm not doing it for him. I just want to be with you," he said, but the words came out in a whisper when he saw a thin and gaunt old Chinese man looking at him. The old man's eyes were watery and

Part Three

hazy, and Kok Leong could not really be sure if he was looking at him directly. Still, it made him self-conscious.

"Such a long time the bus is taking. What a nuisance!" Emily exclaimed in irritation.

Kok Leong became even more confused. Simple-hearted, he could not cope with the sophistry of her words. He felt subdued and numb. The continuing noise of the traffic prevented him from regaining a sense of equanimity. So he was actually relieved when the bus finally came and took Emily away.

When his bus arrived a few minutes later, he went directly home and shut himself up in his room. Alone, he was determined to probe the significance of Emily's words, to weigh every nuance, every inflection. If only words were like grains of fine gold to be held in the hand, to be scrutinized and assayed, he thought. Whereas words are as insubstantial as shadows, can slip through any sieve, impossible to grasp.

Had Emily cooled towards him? Was she rejecting him? Certainly, there were skillful evasions in what she said, evasions that he felt were carefully contrived. Or was it just his fevered imagination, seeing things that he himself had conjured up with his excitable and volatile nature? He turned these thoughts over and over in his mind, but came to no conclusion. The effort made his nerves all tangled up, like seaweed caught in a fierce storm, knotted and untidy. He felt could not breathe, and left the confines of his room to walk in the town.

THE RAIN CONTINUED TO FALL, as though out of a dream, in lush streams, quivering like shoals of tiny fish, working through his thoughts, and then leaving part of themselves behind, like a subversion. There was an odour of damp air mingling with the rich, strong smell of Chinese medicine — dried herbs and roots, spirits and tinctures — for the shop house in front of which he was standing was a Chinese medicine shop. These smells were not alien to him; they stalked him from the past. Brews and potions, they had all been administered to his sister, Siew Wan. Whenever someone recommended yet another Chinese herbal medicine to his mother, it was tried on poor Siew Wan, and she gulped them all down with mute acquiescence, while on each occasion Mrs. Chan watched with fervent hope, waiting, always, for the miracle. But the miracle never materialized. Remembering this on that rainy evening, Kok Leong felt that these smells were the vapours of futility, rising like a toxin in the air, and it made him think of getting away. He must escape.

But where to go? He had no clear idea. Only that he should move on.

Quite at random, then, he turned left and walked along the covered verandah of the shop houses. At first he simply walked and walked, mechanically, not thinking about anything in particular. Indeed, moving with complete aimlessness, he was consciously trying to avoid both thought and feeling. After a while, he felt as though he were floating, his feet not touching the ground, his mind and senses enveloped in an abstract vapour. And then, all at once, a transformation occurred, and he saw everything in front of his eyes in a vivid, vital light. He seemed to have acquired a new, an almost bizarre power of observation and concentration, although he had made no special effort. There was no apparent reason for this transformation. It simply happened.

All of a sudden, everything appeared startlingly real and definite, as if scales were peeled away from his eyes. It was as if he had been blind before, and now he saw the world in all its wild purity, clear and authentic: a mildewed, iron rain-pipe running down the squat, concrete pillar of a house; moss and green algae glistening on the sides of the deep monsoon drain; an array of shoes arranged in tiers on display in a glass-fronted shop; old, pitted, aluminum pots and sooty iron woks sitting over clay stoves in a restaurant, the fire curling, furling its tongues; the pale, silvery

Part Three

sheen of a large carp hanging from a thick wire hook; a slab of roast pork with its light brown crust of skin; the shiny glaze of the china bowls and plates; an obese old man, sated after his dinner, diligently digging his teeth with a toothpick, watched intently by a dog whose emaciated belly heaved like a bellows, its long tongue dripping saliva, its eyes agog. And then, from the display window of a photographer's saloon, framed, coloured portraits directed their stilted smiles at him — brides and grooms, gowned scholars on convocation day, family groups, toddlers on all fours and smartly turned-out soldiers on the occasion of their investiture — all the memorable occasions which human beings like to preserve for history, for posterity. As he stared at each in turn, they became etched in his mind, superimposed on all the previous images. But what did it all mean? That there had to be a meaning and significance in this revelation, he did not doubt, but it was something he could find no explanation for. The clarity of detail was so uncanny that everything seemed like a crazy phantasmagoria, belonging to some nightmare rather than reality.

In front of another restaurant he saw the carcass of a steamed chicken hanging by its neck from a steel hook, its skin a pale, creamy-yellow, greasy, goose-pimpled, its flesh cold and white. Piled in an enamel basin were boiled grey gizzards and livers and hearts, and the long white ribbons of chicken intestines, while next to it stood a blue porcelain bowl of clotted, reddish-black chicken blood. Kok Leong was filled with a sudden nausea. The food man eats can be so repulsive! But our sensibilities are blunted, otherwise we would starve. Indeed, far from seeming revolting, these bits and pieces of dead animals and fish and crustacea titillate the gourmet's palate.

Kok Leong walked away, thinking — it's only a hallucination, that's all. Just as when Siew Wan cried out at night, shattering sleep, splintering dream, he used to think, "It's a hallucination, a momentary interruption, no more than that." And when the crying stopped, he would think, "There!

It's over. And now the world can go on as before." In this way, Kok Leong, like everyone else, had learnt to become impervious to life's many unpleasantnesses. But then, life's not always that bad. There are moments when plants burst into flower, the trees bring forth their fruit, the night sky glows with the moon rising.

Suddenly, a deep shifting of the earth. It seemed as if his feet were no longer on firm ground: it dropped away, and he was being plunged into an abyss.

"Fuck your mother's stinking cunt!"* a man yelled at him hoarsely, in Cantonese.

And the brute's cohorts laughed raucously.

Kok Leong was startled. He stood paralysed. The rough voice addressed him again. "Who the fuck are you staring** at?"

Kok Leong realized that he had been gazing blankly into a coffee shop, and, unwittingly, straight at a gang of about half-a-dozen young toughs sitting there. They must have thought that he was staring at them.

"Maybe we ought to bash his fucking head in?" suggested one of the young men. They were all speaking in Cantonese.

"*Weh!* Are you dumb, you son of a whore?" another yelled at Kok Leong, then spat a thick glob of sputum at him, missing him by just so much.

Kok Leong felt paroxysms of anger and fear. It was incredible! Unreal! It was outrageous!

"Fuck your old woman! You still won't answer? I'll count up to three," warned the first man, who was obviously the leader.

Kok Leong made some fumbling, frantic mental calculations, and when he finally opened his mouth to speak, his words came out as a feeble protest: "I wasn't staring! I wasn't staring at you." He made a conscious effort to prevent a squeakiness from entering his voice. He tried desperately not to show his consternation.

---

*"*Tiu lay loh moh ke chow fah hai* " in Cantonese, or, more usual in Singapore, the Hokkien "*Kah ni nah boh chow chee bai.*" A commonly-used form of insult and swearing.
** Staring: in gang warfare a stare is tantamount to a dare — to fight.

Part Three

"I say you're a bloody liar!"
"Let's kick his teeth in!"
"Kick his balls!"
"He's got no balls. See how he shakes!"
"He's a rotten coward!"

Kok Leong did indeed quake and shiver, in spite of himself. His lack of control was sickening to him. To be thus reduced to an object of ridicule by a bunch of brainless bullies! This was unbearable!

And still the verbal abuses came hurtling at him, turning his blood cold. A cruel game played by a mob who derived pleasure from their collective, fatuous, onanistic violence.

Kok Leong stood silently through the heckling and threats, petrified by horror and a clear sense of his own impotence. He had hardly a moment for reflection, but he did look about him for help. There were only a few indistinct faces, suddenly distancing themselves. There was an old Chinese man sitting alone at a table next to the thugs, with his lean elbows on the white marble table top, his back erect, his face carefully calm, his eyes studiously intent on the cup of tea before him: and when he lifted up the brew to his thin lips, he affected a punctiliousness to prove that nothing extraordinary was happening in the coffee shop. His cultivated lack of curiosity betrayed his alarm, his terror. And the others in that coffee shop were the same, anxious only to save their own skins, as terrified as Kok Leong of the gang's potential violence.

The thugs continued to bait Kok Leong, indulging in their puerile, cruel game. He said nothing. The only effective weapon against verbal abuse, he thought, was silence, was disdain, was to withdraw into dignity. "But what have I done to deserve this? Why pick on *me*?" he wondered frantically. "There's no such thing as justice!" In other words, the classical, typical reaction of all victims.

Kok Leong took hold of a moment, turned his face away from the oafs, and savoured looking out at the rain which seemed everlasting, but he was quickly, rudely brought back to the present.

One of the toughs got up, grating his chair noisily, and announced: "I'm going to teach this bastard a lesson!"

And he came, his broad arms hanging by his sides like a gorilla, and still Kok Leong felt it was all unreal, a bad dream — when everything else indicated that only the now, the present, was real. He knew also that he needed new initiatives urgently. Fight or flight, this was the moment. He must act! Must! And failed.

He took in a deep breath in that explosive silence, his stomach wobbling, his heart thumping furiously. The man had already advanced right up to him, face to face. Kok Leong could feel the man's hot breath hissing from his nostrils, and he saw the raised hand just before it flashed. He felt a stinging pain as the hard slap landed on his cheek, and, still in a state of shock, felt the back of the hand on his other cheek as the man swung another vicious slap at him.

He heard the thugs all laughing raucously, gleefully. He felt a sense of dislocation, as if reality had clicked out of joint. It was still unbelievable, impossible! He had been struck by another man, and he was doing nothing about it! Locked within the space of an instant were inchoate emotions — a crashing sense of injustice, of anger, fear, cowardice, and, above all, of surprise. In the midst of this confusion another member of the gang swaggered up to him, a shorter and smaller man, who, without warning, kicked Kok Leong in the shin. Ringing laughter swelled all around him.

The first man who had struck him, the simian, advised: "Say you're sorry and we'll let you go."

"Yes," said the small man. "And also say out loud, 'My mother is a whore!'" The others guffawed even louder.

Kok Leong would not do it. He would neither surrender nor resist.

"Say it, you son-of-a-bitch!" the small one yelled.

And when Kok Leong maintained a defiant silence, the small man punched him hard in the mouth. He felt the soft tissue of his mouth tear within, and tasted his own warm, salty blood. Then the other thug also hit him.

Again they demanded that he apologize, but Kok Leong remained silent, adamant. He thought, "If I don't have the means to fight back, at least I have the will to defy them. I must defy. *Must!*"

His stubbornness and his silence stirred their fury and they punched and kicked him, again and again.

Finally, although Kok Leong did not yield, they tired of the game and let him go.

He limped away, gasping, through the night rain. The physical punishment was over, but Kok Leong knew he would never recover. Never! Never! The wounds suppurated in his psyche, in his spirit more than in his flesh. He did not feel the rain falling on him. He was intent, rehearsing his kill.

7

Ong Kian Teck and his wife sat happily under the old mango tree in the garden in the late afternoon while their children tumbled in the grass. A small brown grasshopper sprang away, disappearing into the thickets by the fence. A tiny yellow ladybird with black spots on its wings climbed up a tree trunk. The sun shot patterns through the leaves, numberless, swimming on Li Lian's skin, and yet, when Kian Teck touched her hand, it was cool. She turned to him and smiled, searching his eyes. He returned her smile. Smile for smile. Sitting comfortably on a canvas chair, he inhaled the smell of fertile abundance, the scent of ripe fruit, easing himself deep into the largesse, and deeper into the penetrable, numinous afternoon.

There was a certain changelessness about life, he thought, as if time had reversed its flow and he was returned to where he had started from: where he ought rightly to have been, if only he had not been such a damned fool! Anyway, here he was, with a new start. Providence had been kind to him. He turned again to look at his wife, for the umpteenth time. He had been forgiven. Yes, fate had been good to him. Touch wood! And he reached out, unsuperstitious he, to touch the tree trunk with a forefinger. Best not to take chances. Old warrior has learnt.

He sucked in the rich air in a long draught, gratefully. The recent past, the bad times, seemed invented, a myth, its memory already hazy; he had to force himself to think about it. After all, he had reformed, and it would not do to pretend that it had all never really happened. That would

Part Three

be foolish, wanton. He did have to learn a lesson, and always to remind himself of it, even if (metaphorically) he had to pinch himself to recall it all. Still, if truth be told, it had become hazy, misted over by the present, fortunately mundane, world. Now he desired nothing more than this. And it was not so much the events, the incidents, not so much other people, but *himself* (the persona of the past, that is) who seemed a myth.

He closed his eyes, the better to see, to assess, to assay. There was also a sense of transience, an inherent ephemeral quality about things, about life, which, perhaps, was responsible for haunting him with a feeling of a vague, of a disquieting, directionlessness. In himself. In life. Maybe all this, the present sense of peace, of happiness, would simply fade away? He did not want that to happen. He wanted to hold it all close to his heart, but feared, or suspected, that he might enfold only air — again, metaphorically speaking. So he stretched out a hand and sought one of Li Lian's, and thus clasped, he felt he was taking a better hold on happiness.

But into that liquid green peace, that idyll, fell a shadow. He had a sense of trespassing, as if his yesteryear self had left a spoor on the green grass. Maybe it was simply his guilty conscience? — that accursed thing? He should be mature enough, modern enough, to dismiss these medieval ghosts. All that was needed now was a dose of cynicism, and they would — pouf! — Vanish! After all, it was only a shadow, nothing more. Yet it was there, that was the point.

Though it hadn't really been too difficult, the soul-baring. The impulse, the urge, in fact the *need*, was so urgent. It just spilled out, out of the flood gates. And what Li Lian was not told, she guessed at, wifely, wisely, both perspicacious and gracious. But for a time afterwards, and almost perversely, Kian Teck kept on searching for some lingering sign of disapproval, for the slightest hint of unforgivingness in his wife — and found none. And still he thought, perhaps this was partly because she had it so well hidden? But she never watched him, not even in secret moments, not in the distilled silences. And in time his sense of relief, of release, grew; so that they could sit there like that, husband and wife, in natural informality, at ease, that afternoon, in the lovely living light in the garden.

"Are you all right?" she asked.

"Yes, I'm fine." He pressed her hand gently, glanced round behind her to where the children were at play, lolloping in the gold. Then looked at her. She smiled at the grass.

Yes, order, harmony, domesticity! Kian Teck was quite happy, and more than willing, to leave the depths, which, he knew, existed — but now somewhere far away from this small tropical garden of old fruit trees and sprouting shrubs. Depths. Profundities. Which might have tempted and tugged had he been inexperienced — but their exertions, attractions, were no longer strongly felt. Indeed, Kian Teck thought he could very well do without them. Now that he knew better.

He recalled that afternoon when he had first come to live in this old rambling household, standing there on the weather-mottled stone steps, facing the garden, facing the world, and a new life, with circumspection and doubt. It was at the hour before sunset, which helped, for a wind moved and the leaves softly stirred, dripping with light, all languid and dreamy. Such a world wasn't really too difficult to enter. And his wife beside him. Sharing. And his children.

Still, the house, so filled with other souls, was new and strange. The old dowager, her servants, her lodgers, to whom he had to nod and smile, to acknowledge at every odd corner and nook of the house, when their own life in their former apartment had been so private and self-contained. Just themselves. Now, save for the occasional moment, it was no longer possible to be alone with his family. Even at night, lying in bed with Li Lian, he could sense the proximity of others, and husband and wife seldom spoke in the quiet darkness, and if they did so, did it in whispers. When they made love, they went to some lengths not to make any sound, Kian Teck holding back, easing into her gently, delicately, trying not to pump too hard. There was in this a certain delicious tension, a sweet suspension, an unhurriedness, a slow rise and flow that they had learnt to enjoy. But even with all their care, sometimes the bedsprings would creak, the sound carrying (it seemed to them!) at least a mile, and Li Lian would not be able to stifle her giggling. He would shush and shush her, unsuccessfully, and then he too would join in. They were like children playing a secret, naughty game, and with children's true innocence, in their own Eden.

And afterwards, tamed by passion, he would lie awake and listen to the night, and in the late stillness he could almost hear his own thoughts ticking.

There was a subtle change in the relationship between Kian Teck and his wife, whether due to natural reasons, or to the fact that they were now living in a different milieu, in the presence of others, he wasn't quite sure. Nevertheless, Kian Teck and Li Lian were sensitive to the fact that they now lived in the midst of other people, and this made them more demonstrative towards each other — rather an opposite effect to what one would have expected under the circumstances. They seemed to be driven closer together, and, on occasion, could be seen holding hands, fingers interlaced, as they strolled in the garden.

They were especially aware of the four lodgers, who were not part of the family. Not that the lodgers were distinctly inquisitive; on the contrary, the old boys really went about their own businesses, most of the time discreetly, so much so that Kian Teck in fact knew very little about them. They were all either bachelors or widowers. Mr. Tan was the small, grave man, often withdrawn, often talking to himself; Mr. Chin was the tall, courtly gentleman, with graceful hands and neat, even natty, clothes; Mr. Goh was fat and paunchy, always drowsing under a tree or in one of the large, sumptuous chairs in the sitting room, and subject to fits of joviality,

A Dance of Moths

and Mr. Leong, silver-haired, lean, handsome, eyes still luminous and black, was often melancholic, sighing and then lapsing into silences, into the blurred mirror of his memories. That was about all that Kian Teck knew about them.

Of their lives, their families, ties and allegiances, hopes and despairs, he knew little. Maybe it was their opaqueness, maybe it was his lack of intuition, his own shortcomings, that stood in the way of a greater knowledge, a greater understanding? There is so much one does not understand about other people, Kian Teck often lamented to himself.

Such as his mother. Who came to call one Friday evening. After the polite exchanges of greetings with Li Lian's mother, after the tea, the patting of the grandchildren's heads, the word or two with her daughter-in-law, Mrs. Ong found herself alone with her son. Something in the air made both mother and son shy with each other. She watched her son thoughtfully. Looking for something. Whether she found it or no, she did not let on, but only said: "You should've come home."

"It's all right, Ma. Li Lian's mother is very kind and considerate; it's more than I deserve."

"That's not the point! You should've come home to your *own* family!" she protested.

He knew he had committed an indiscretion, had contravened Chinese custom which ordains that sons should always return home.

"You have enough burdens, Ma," he explained, trying to soften the hurt.

"You think I'm not used to burdens? You think I'm not capable of caring for my *own* son?"

"I didn't mean that," Kian Teck protested, ruefully.

Her own son. A part of her. Issue of her being. Though, in the present light, it seemed incredible. She looked at him closely, saw weakness and failure. She felt ashamed.

Part Three

"I'm all right, really," Kian Teck reassured her.

"Hunh!" the old lady made a dismissive sound through her taut, dry mouth. She then wet her lips before proceeding, "All right, you say? Well, just take a *good* look at yourself, at your situation!" The accusatory remark came out, in spite of herself.

Kian Teck tried to pacify her, but without much hope of success.

Afterwards, he took a last glance at this thin, grey, dry woman who was his mother, as she stood by the garden gate for an instant, having said her good-byes, but with her eyes averted from him.

"It's not your fault," Li Lian had consoled later, when he told her about it.

"I'm not so sure."

"I know you feel sorry for your mother. But I wouldn't worry any more about it."

"Actually, I'm only sorry because *she* is sorry," he said.

"Let it pass!" Li Lian insisted.

Then it passed. He would survive, it seemed. Pretty intact, too, with a dawning sense of growing to belong to the surroundings, of becoming like the old fruit trees with their lush scent pervading the garden. It simply took time, that's all.

So now he sat under the mango tree with his wife, as the afternoon grew late, facing again the blessed shapes and colours of the fruit, greens, reddish-yellows, smouldering like rich jewels in the mellow, molten gold, with such profusions of green leaves, such abundant light that it portended deliverance, a feeling that the life ahead would be a good one. Somehow his wife must have shared this feeling, for they both got on to a discussion about their future.

What about the future? In one's sanest moments, one just *lives*. And any contemplation of the future would be either oversimplified, or over-complicated.

But from their green sanctum, the future seemed to them to be good, like the light — a patch of which had fallen over them with the shift of sun — or like the leaves, or the fruit, or an amalgam of everything there: rich and promising. Of course they did not ignore their present problems, and considered how best to solve them, calculating that if they should manage to pay back such and such a sum each month, they should be rid of all debts in four, maybe five years. Then they could put aside so much each month, to save for the children's education, and for their own old age. They were being prudent and practical. So they sat under the old tree, planning and plotting, very much carried away, transported by their own dreams, and forgetting that fate, that what lies in store for them, is ineluctable.

THE MORNING AFTER CHAN KOK LEONG WAS ASSAULTED, he woke up with vivid memories of a dream. He recalled entering into a shiny whiteness, a whole continent composed of whiteness, it was like a total state of mind, with elements as untouchable as thoughts, in which he moved with such bliss, such rapture.

Now THIS!

His head wooden, groggy. And the pains starting to crystallize again. Kok Leong cursed his frail flesh. If only he could tear strips of it away, strips, down to the barest, hard bone. If only he could inhabit that white dream again.

Instead of which, he had to continue living his old life. And face all the other things.

But how? How?

From where he lay, sunk in his bed, it didn't seem possible. To resume. To cope. Indeed, he felt it might never be possible again. From a sense of powerlessness, as much as an unwillingness.

Never, ever again!

He didn't much care. On the contrary, it was disgusting, his former acquiescence. He felt so weighted down by his body, when what he needed was lightness and airy essence, to fly and fly, up the tiers of clouds, and up.

Perhaps because of this thought, he rose from his bed — and was immediately wracked with aches and pains in a dozen places. He touched the sore spots here and there, to survey the damage, and found that he was bruised; but intact, alas. He would have liked to dissolve, and his body, or soul, to leak out: like a dawn breaking marvelously, like a wind tumbling in a carefree rush into the trees, the rain drops dripping down, down.

Down.

But the structure, the solidity of his existence could not be dismantled. He didn't know how to disengage himself from himself.

He managed to totter across the room, feeling as if he bore all his years, his days and his seconds, to the opposite wall where the mirror suddenly beckoned. And leaning against the wall, he peered into it, drawn to it not from vanity, but from a true curiosity, as if he could discover something there. But what the mirror revealed was only a pallid face, more submerged than afloat, just a suggestion of blurry whiteness without undertones, the quick sequences of a fish. His features were pushed askew by a large bruise on one side of his mouth, which had swollen and broken into a deep purple. He looked again more closely, and was not impressed by what he saw. So bland! It hardly seemed something that time had fashioned, the flood of time lapping and lapping against, and eating away, eroding, and still it was here, this pasty-coloured, uninteresting face. And what it revealed did not appear to be very serviceable, much less strong. But he was not dismayed. There were the eyes. Something unappeased about them, where fire flickered. He examined his face again, and after a while, sensed he was on the edge. If he fell, it was difficult to say whether it would be into the past, or the future.

Then he frowned. He thought he had peered too lingeringly at the mirror, or at himself, and withdrew.

Later, Kok Leong walked through the sitting room. The family noticed his appearance and were startled into a momentary silence. But on he marched, ignoring their stares and unasked questions, heading for the balcony, for the brittle, morning light.

There!

But his mother, roused and maternal, followed him. "What happened to you?"

He would not answer. Nor look at her. Only at the light.

"Your face! Let me have a look!"

"No!"

"You're all smashed up! What happened? Did you have a fight? Were you robbed?"

It was difficult to concentrate on the light, with all this jabbering going on. If only he could will her away, chuck her, words and all, over the balcony.

"Are you badly hurt? Are you all right?"

He nodded. A rock battered against the insides of his skull.

"Won't you tell me what happened, Leong?" Mrs. Chan pleaded, wringing her hands. "If someone did this to you, you must tell the police or they might do it again. I hear this sort of thing happens all the time. Third Aunt was just telling me the other day, how dangerous it is to walk about in Hong Kong and Jakarta. And now, Singapore also. What is the world coming to?" she asked, of no one, and everyone, and all her gods, scrupulous as always in sharing out her prayers, and, in this instance, her blame. She sighed, looking up at the heavens, which, that morning, were bright and empty. Truly, sometimes it was enough to make one lose faith. Or to have more faith. Anyway, it was safer to pray harder.

She turned to her son again. "You must go to the hospital."

Part Three

"Leave me *alone!* " he snarled, still staring straight ahead, at the light.

"At least see a doctor or a *sinseh*." For one moment Kok Leong looked at her. She saw the look in his eyes, and decided she could not penetrate any further. She shook her head in defeat and returned to the flat.

Kok Leong turned back to survey the light, mesmerised. He knew at that moment he could do anything, and better too than all the other people below, now in their houses and offices and factories, with their always important lives. Hah!

Though he himself had also participated once. All those bloody meaningless small things. No more! For him now, the one quest was to unmake the slow hours, and rush, rush into the light.

The light!

WHITE OF NOON. Lunch break.

Chan Kok Leong felt marooned in the light, engulfed by the sun after his lunch at a coffee shop.

Then he saw the mad woman. There she stood, railing obscene curses at the Asia Insurance Building in a horrible, screechy voice, punctuating her curses by beating a lamp post with a battered, furled black umbrella. Kok Leong froze, fascinated. He had seen her many times before, but today she mesmerised him.

She was a small, thin, white-faced, intense Chinese woman in her sixties, dressed in a severe, blue-topped, black-trousered, *samfoo*. Local legend had it that her only son had committed suicide about twenty years ago by leaping off the top of this building. In the 'fifties, the Asia Insurance Building, at the top end of Shenton Way on Finlayson Green, had been the tallest structure in Singapore, rising eighteen storeys above the concrete pavement. The suicide had occurred almost two decades ago, but the woman had never got over the loss of her son, and daily, rain or shine, she would come and hurl her abuses at the Asia Insurance Building.

Such devotion! Such anger!

There she was, not seeing, not hearing, just hitting the iron lamp post with fury, metamorphosed by madness into electrifying life, her passion, unlike other people's, not so easily manageable, not so easily quenched. Kok Leong was intensely moved.

Ordinarily, people recoil from the insane. On being confronted face to face with a mad person, most people feel a deep embarrassment and fear. They cannot accept anyone who does not seem to behave according to the same social dictates and conventions which govern their lives. And they do not understand, or refuse to understand, anyone who is no longer governed by precept or reason. They have this preference for limits, are terrified of the extraordinary. And terror leads to repulsion, repulsion to anger, and anger to repression.

So the passersby either pretended to ignore the mad woman, or else stood around and sniggered. Such a bizarre creature, who shunned the rules of the game they themselves played. After a while, they would walk away, and put her out of their minds.

After a while, Kok Leong too walked away, haunted. Prompted by the mad woman's obscene salvos, he walked along the streets, but he was actually tunneling deeper into himself, or into the dark, despite all the light around him. He arrived, eventually, at the place where he worked, coming off the whiteness of the afternoon into the dead hours, into a medium pervaded, drugged by the ceaseless commentary of typewriters, the tidiness of their clacking in sharp contrast to the reckless heckling of the mad woman. While she had been inspired and driven, the typists' clacking symbolized the small, formal, cautious acts of existence. Suddenly, normalcy had become far more strange.

And Kok Leong could no longer commit himself to the riskless afternoon. He already felt a burgeoning initiation into madness. And

Part Three

the moment was not far off. He would not shirk from it.

Emily was not in the office. Her father had died, he was told, that morning. He had wanted to see her so that he might know, once and for all. Twice he had asked her to marry him, but she would not even look directly at him. She did not, however, say no. She did not say yes. She only perpetuated the game. But he was growing convinced that beneath her evasions, she was really rejecting him. Perhaps there was someone else? Reflecting on this, his feelings hardened. If he caught her out, he would ... emulate the mad woman! Transmute his passion into the wildest force!

Meanwhile, suspicion gnawed at him.

And time was too long.

AT THE FUNERAL, ONG KIAN TECK FELT THE SUN ON HIM, from a sky so perfectly clear it seemed both real and imaginary.

Time stood still, flooded by the chants of the Taoist priest, droning on and on in the afternoon heat, words completely unintelligible to Kian Teck, the utterances of sound, mystical and objective, flowing over the now defenceless corpse in its massive wooden coffin. Poor Old Ho. He would, Kian Teck thought, have shared my trust, which was not in words, but in silence. For this was final. When there should be no more words.

But the chanting continued, mesmeric, the priest himself, Kian Teck suspected, being affected the most by his own vocal constructions, punctuated by the tinkling of a tiny brass bell held daintily between his fingers. He was a fat and greasy Chinese man wearing flowing white robes and a tall papier mâché hat.

In a moment of distraction, Kian Teck looked about him. They were at the Chinese Cemetery in Lim Chu Kang. He noticed the tops of some trees, the leaves almost combustible in the light. Green grass grew tall between the grave stones. He saw another group of mourners massed around another freshly-dug grave. There were certainly more people in that party than at Old Ho's, which consisted only of Emily and himself, and the priest, of course, and a couple of grave diggers in their rough clothes of a faded blue cotton, with their skins burnt a rich mahogany. Li Lian had not come. She respected that his grief was personal, and should be allowed to be worked out in privacy. However, she did ask him whether he wished her to attend. He had said no.

And death itself turned out to be such a mundane occasion. Kian Teck had to help Emily with the funeral arrangements. She had absolutely no experience in dealing with these matters, and no notion of what to do. It therefore fell on Kian Teck to attend to the formalities of applying for the death certificate, the permit for the funeral, obtaining a burial plot and engaging the services of the priest. He was surprised when Emily asked for a Taoist ceremony. It had never crossed his mind that Old Ho adhered to any religion. But there you are! You think you know a man, and then ... However, one cannot be expected to know everything about a person, not even one's most intimate soulmate, nor even oneself. Did he really know himself? Kian Teck wondered. The soul, of course, is often so elusive that its presence cannot be believed in with any clear conviction. It is so difficult to substantiate. Kian Teck looked down at the gaping hole in the ground, at the raw, yellow, cut earth, and looked and looked, as if looking might lead him on to fresh discovery. But failed to see what he was looking for. It was only a plain, ordinary hole after all, the sides still glistening wet, still smelling of freshness. So he failed again. As he had failed before.

While the priest persisted with his long drawn out chant, as though the act of prayer might succeed, might save, when the mourner himself had failed. Kian Teck had his doubts, though. Doubting everything, that was his problem. Faith always beyond his grasp. It was exasperating. And the sun allowed no prospect of relief, but continued to burn.

He stole a glance at Emily, who stood on the opposite side of the grave. He thought she looked solemn and timid, yet sensed in her a determination to be daring, which only served to make her expression insolent. A strange creature. Not once had he seen her cry, not even on this occasion. A dry being, with no hint of sap. What's inside her? So seemingly tranquil, so unafflicted. And he felt a bit guilty, judging her. And so harshly. For all he knew, (and he knew so pathetically little — it had been proved time and time again) she might be suffering secretly, internally, and not be eager to show it. His own eagerness to judge her now shamed him.

Presently, and mercifully, the priest stopped his chanting, and in the ensuing, conspicuous silence, time flowed again. Even flooded Kian Teck's soul. But time was not air, alas, which could have inflated, and uplifted.

With a gesture to the waiting grave diggers the priest proclaimed that another stage of the rites could now proceed. He looked at the two mourners, probably expecting to find them subdued and reverent, witnesses to the formidable task which only *he* could perform, the necessary rites which lie beyond the capabilities of lay people. After the living words, it was time for the burial. The two faces, though, were discrepant. But this did not disconcert the priest who was, after all, a professional; he, who derived his authority from the mysterious.

So the two grave diggers slowly lowered the heavy coffin, creaking and scraping into the ground, with the aid of thick, brown jute cords slung over two strong wooden poles. Then coarse lumps of earth were shovelled on top of the coffin, which lay solid and anomalous in its hole. It's so difficult, Kian Teck thought, to believe that Old Ho could really achieve a final synthesis with the earth. But earth was thrown in, knocking thunderously on the wood, and the sound in some way seemed to be all the final dues there were for Old Ho. The coffin was soon completely covered, out of sight. During those moments, Kian Teck tried to reconstruct a memory, an image, of his friend, and failed. And all the falling of earth, and the prayers of the priest, and the tinkling of the tiny bell, did not redeem the sense of loss. The grave was soon filled, with unseemly haste, it seemed, and, at the same time, not hastily enough. And all that time Kian Teck could scarcely control his longing to look, but did not manage to preserve anything. It was all but over. The sun blazed down.

Then a bird flew into focus. A big, brown, solitary eagle whose feathers shone in the light. It glided slowly round and round and round above the grave, thrice, riding on air, its wide wings outstretched, and then it drifted away. But it gave the blessing, the affirmation, which Kian Teck had not been able to find all through that late afternoon, and which it achieved so subtly. Not with its material shape, but with something else, which conveyed that life has continuity, that Old Ho was dead, and it was all right, and that Kian Teck must accept that he himself was also intended to die when his time came. The bird vanished into the deepening blue.

Later, when they were leaving the cemetery, a wind came and bowed the heads of grass.

IT WAS A NIGHT OF STILLNESS. There was no wind out in Katong Park, although the sea was not far away. The place was deserted. At about eight o'clock Chan Kok Leong stood on a grassy patch overshadowed by a towering casuarina. A full moon floated above as if in a trance, hazed over by a thin veil of clouds so that its flimsy light lent the night an ambiance of dreaminess and driftingness. It could cast a spell, dupe a person into actions which would not even be contemplated in the full light of day — a night that extolled ambition and kindled fantasies.

So Kok Leong stood, like one possessed. He had been standing there for at least an hour, waiting for Emily. They had arranged to meet at eight o'clock, and he had wanted to be early.

Part Three

When Emily arrived, she saw Kok Leong's face from a distance, a whiteness, moon-fraught, like a ghost. Emily was not normally a coward, but for a moment, she was frightened. There was a certain wildness, an eeriness, about that solitary figure in the park. But, after the slightest hesitation, she continued walking. She knew there was no way of avoiding this confrontation.

"I'm late," she said.

"No. I'm early."

"It's very quiet here."

He said nothing. Only looked at her.

Chit chat, Emily realized at once, would not break the tension between them. She might as well precipitate the matter. Get it over with. So she went straight to the point.

"What do you want to talk to me about?" she asked bluntly. Meaning, what is it you want of me?

Kok Leong sensed a certain guile, a shrewdness in her manner, and an indifference towards him which was new. For him it was proof that there was another man.

"I want you to marry me!" he exclaimed. There was no time for the usual preliminaries.

Not, "I want to marry you!", Emily thought. Such nerve! "No," she said, abruptly.

"Why not?" Kok Leong demanded.

"Because I don't want to," she replied in a forthright manner.

"I love you!" he protested, desperately.

" But *I* don't love *you*."

Actually, Emily got a bit carried away, and ignored the look in his eyes, experiencing a delicious purification, enjoying this new candour, more, this new power. She was surprised and pleased that she could assemble her feelings and thoughts with such lucidity and straightforwardness.

For a while, there was silence.

While Kok Leong's ardour grew in the face of this resistance. Although not at all hopeful, he pressed on: "Won't you change your mind?"

"I don't love you. That cannot be changed." She had not yet learned how to soften a blow; she did not know how to reject a suitor.

"Please!" he pleaded.

She remained unmoved. But thought she ought not now to feel exultant. Which was what she really felt. There's always a kick, however vicarious, in turning down someone. It's great for the ego.

"Please," he repeated, obstinately.

Emily would not look at him now. Only shook her head, stubbornly.

Another silence. The stars ticked in the sky, embodiments of the indifference of the cosmos.

"Is it because I have no money? Or that I'm a nobody?" he asked, self-flagellating.

"Now you're being idiotic!"

"I know I'm just a nobody."

"I think we should simply stop talking right now. It's not going to get us anywhere."

"You mean everything to me!"

"I'm sorry!"

Still, another silence. A long one this time. Emily thought she could hear the faint music of the sea, and wanted to run away.

Suddenly, Kok Leong looked sharply at her. "Is there another man?" he demanded.

"It's none of your business!" she exclaimed, staring at him, startled.

"*Is* there another man?" Kok Leong demanded again.

"You have no right to ask!"

"I have!"

"You surely don't think that just because we're friends, that you own me?"

Part Three

"I must know!" He had raised his voice. It bounded into the darkness. Even the black trees shivered.

"*Is* there another man?" he asked once more. For the third time.

"Yes! Yes! *Yes!* if you must know. Now I must go!" Emily's lie was spontaneous, unpremeditated. She didn't want to think about it, and turned to leave.

But Kok Leong caught hold of her hand. Gripped it in a vise. "Who is it?" he thundered.

She tried to pull away, but could not.

"Who is it? *Who* is it?"

She tugged and tugged, trying to jerk her hand out of his grasp, but could not free herself. She looked about for help. There was nobody in sight.

"Let me go!" she screamed. She kicked at his shin. But he was not going to let her go. She saw that.

"Who? *Who?*" Kok Leong thundered again.

"Mr. Ong! My boss!" Emily shouted out loud. She lied again without knowing why. But it issued from deep within, from under the scars.

Then Kok Leong released her. She ran away from him without once looking back, her feet light as a ghost's over the still grass. But she needn't have worried.

Kok Leong did not chase after her. He stood where he was, even as the night wore on. Once, way past midnight, he looked up at the stars. They were burning so frantically, those ornaments of the cosmos, and he raised up his hands as if to pluck them out, to extinguish them from the sky.

ONE EVENING AFTER WORK, ONG KIAN TECK sat ensconced in the comfortable canvas chair in the garden, having tea with his family. He was thoroughly involved. These were moments when, settling back in the chair, relaxing into the give of it, he had the feeling of being infinitely privileged. A large butterfly descended from the upper branches of the old mango tree and fluttered its velvety blue and deep black wings around them. It was the hour when the night begins to unfold, offering its sequences of petals, like some flower, the clouds in the sky massed constructions of pinks and purples; and Kian Teck caught his wife giving him a transfixed look of love, such a glow, that he felt absolved of everything evil, everything wrong in the world, and more particularly, in his life.

He pursed his lips and blew her a kiss. Her face broke into a mischievous smile. Her face, so beautiful in the flecked shadows under the tree. Then she turned to speak to their child. Guan Hock had come to ask his mother something. It was going to be his tenth birthday on the coming Friday, and there was to be a party that afternoon. Kian Teck looked at his eldest son. Of late there was a faint but fine air of independence about him. Growing up. And Kian Teck could not suppress a spasm of parental joy. His own son! From his seed. But no replica of him. An original. Unique. One day, soon, he would be a man. Knowing what life was, Kian Teck silently prayed that the way would be easier for his son, on his own uncommon, common journey.

Guan Hock raised his voice a little, in some small show of protest against his mother who was evidently denying him something, his bright pupils flecking defiant fire but still looking at his mother to see if he were behaving properly in her eyes.

So Kian Teck knew happiness. To have his own children near him, to have a rich and still perfecting relationship with his wife, and their spoken love, was happiness indeed, was to feel really at home. He now regarded this old house as his true home, his true location in life, even though they were living with other people. It was more of a home than all the other places they had lived in before, including the apartment which they had

Part Three

owned. Yes, this garden was the only place there was, this arboreal green, where he felt so happy that he didn't care about anything else. This was enough, this was living, and there was no more right or wrong, good or evil, only — being.

A silence fell as the sun went down, a silence softly broken by the distant sounds of cars on the main road, heading towards the city. But night-town no longer beckoned to Kian Teck. He was no longer restless to join the frantic, sweltering throngs. Singapore, a tireless, kinetic city, always on the move, but for Kian Teck, there was nothing much to recommend about energetic, night-time Singapore any more. He and Li Lian seldom went out at night, except to see an occasional good film, or else he would bring the whole family out to eat at a favoured restaurant, or at a special hawker stall. On the whole, they were content to stay in the rather ramshackle old house, while the children did their homework or watched the odd TV programme — now rationed — and he and Li Lian sat and read. Later, Li Lian would tell the children bedtime stories and put them to sleep, after they'd kissed him goodnight. And the nights were good.

It really seemed to Kian Teck that he had found domestic bliss, contentment, and love at last. He felt a completeness he had never possessed before. He was content to live out his days devoting himself to his wife and children, and, in the span of family life, to find meaning. And there was still so much to be experienced, to be savoured. An endlessness of experiencing!

In this state of equilibrium, Kian Teck thought that he had finally arrived. He didn't know that there would always be a new beginning awaiting him.

THE FOLLOWING FRIDAY MORNING, Kian Teck drove his little yellow Volkswagen to work, whistling to himself behind the steering wheel. Starry-eyed so early in the morning. But then, that early morning was tinged with wonder and magic. It was Guan Hock's tenth birthday. Kian Teck had given his son a present, which the boy had unwrapped eagerly, his youthful eyes expectant, excited. His son's happiness pierced Kian Teck through and through. The younger boy, Guan Hoe, had also been given a present, as a token, and was equally delighted.

Everyone was looking forward to the party that had been planned for the afternoon. Several of his son's friends and their parents were coming. There would be cakes and sweets, aerated waters, sausages and sandwiches, a treasure hunt, and lots of fun and games for the children. No doubt the parents would enjoy themselves just as much as the younger ones!

He drove on to the city. It was early. There was no need to rush. It was a beautiful morning. Time enough to savour the scenery. And the world. When he reached the sea front, there was the sea, its blue dream melting into serenity, and the sky a pure, consoling azure. Kian Teck was more content that morning than at any other time in his life. He felt a new self, and breathed in the moment, drawing in not only air, but worlds, the cosmos, unto himself; and he was choked with this discovery of life, with this fullness.

So he continued his journey towards the city, to those bastions of finite stone and steel, brick and mortar. And then he went to his office, with a certain setness, acquiescence, obeisance, and was soon swallowed up by the familiar routine. Still, it was all right. He had learnt to accept.

At noon, he decided to go for a stroll in the city, and perhaps to eat an early lunch at one of the hawker stalls by the river.

He walked towards the lift, and waited. When it arrived, he stepped lightly inside, and to his destiny.

Another man, one of the office workers, entered the lift with him. The automatic doors hissed together, the leaves closing tight, like blades. There was a brief silence, and then things happened very quickly. Kian

Part Three

Teck saw the man coming at him with a knife, but it was already too late. Irrationally, in that split second all he noticed was that it was a red Swiss knife — the man's face was a blur, just someone, he registered nebulously, who worked for the firm. He felt the jolt, the shock, as the knife plunged into him once, and after that, again and again. As he fell, Kian Teck tried desperately to hold on to, and never to relinquish, life. But he fell, and life rushed out of him.

CHAN KOK LEONG FELT VERY COMPOSED. He had finally reached the top landing of the Asia Insurance Building. It had not been at all difficult to get there. He simply rode up in the lift, opened a few doors and there he was, on the flat roof. No one stopped him. No one paid him any attention.

The sun blazed down on his head. It was at its zenith. He felt dizzy. From the sun, from the height, from the deed.

He looked about him. All around was sky and air. He moved right up to the verge and looked down from that exalted height. He was tingling all over.

Kok Leong had not climbed up that height to escape. That was never his intention. Instead, he had come from an overwhelming need to consummate. Everything! Everything!

He looked around him. The bright light held everything in a stillness and clarity. The white of the sky, the limpid blue of the sea below, the toy-like ships, the distant islands, the topography of the city, the traffic, the people like ants on the streets — each object appeared to him in its most vivid form, each line the cleanest, each dot exact, everything oh so clear! So clear! As if he were seeing the world for the first time! Though he had meant it to be the last. What was revealed to him at that moment was so defined, so illuminated, it seemed that he had been suddenly blessed with faith, given to him for the only time in his life. But that moment was brittle. Beatitude did not last. The contamination of shed blood became all pervasive. So that Kok Leong was blinded by it. Suddenly, all he could see was red.

He drew in a deep breath and moved to the very edge. Now he no longer saw the structure of the world but only the air, which he knew was designed for him. He had to crash through the last frontier, to reach the luminous air which solicited and enticed him. It would, must, open for him!

Must!

So Kok Leong leapt, to achieve the final union.

Glossary of unfamiliar words
(the number after each entry refers to the page on which it first occurs)

A

Ang-moh kwee (or "kui") 88

lit. "red-haired devil". Not used derogatorily nowadays, a commonly-used Chinese mode of referring to Europeans. (see also "European".)

Azan 65

the muezzin's call to prayer (see also "Muezzin".)

B

banana leaf 118

Large banana fronds are cut into 18-inch long sheets, and used as disposable plates. Originally a South Indian practice, eating off banana leaves is still done in curry shops throughout Singapore and Malaysia.

Bat kut teh 10

A clear chinese soup made with pork spare ribs and a seasoned with herds.

bedak sejuk 164

a powder, in pellet or cake form, made from rice flour and scented lotions. Considered to be cooling, (bedak = powder, sejuk = cold) as well as to keep the user's face untanned, it is mixed into a paste with water and smoothed over the skin. Traditionally used by all Straits born Chinese women, it has now been overtaken by western cosmetics.

betel nut 281

a nut from the areca palm, this is sliced, mixed with a little lime (i.e. calcium carbonate) and chewed (like tobacco) in a wrapped up betel leaf. The resulting juice is a bright red, which permanently stains the user's lips and mouth

bomoh 30

Malay witch doctor

bumboat 33

small cargo boats used for transporting goods from larger vessels in the Outer Roads to the wharves of Singapore.

Brands Essence of chicken 110

Originally made in Britain, these tiny bottles of concentrated chicken essence are very popular among the overseas Chinese (as well as other Singaporeans and Malaysians) who regard "Brand's Essence" as a universal cure all, elixir, etc. It is probably no longer even heard of in its country of origin.

briyani (Mutton briyani) 58

Briyani is a South Indian Muslim rice dish, cooked with saffron and ghee and several aromatic spices. It is usually served with curried mutton or chicken, as well as a curried dhall-and-mutton gravy and an appetizer of pickled cucumbers, chilies and onions.

burong chamar 3

There are no gulls in Malaysian/ Singaporean waters, but this bird, a white sea swallow belonging to the Tern family (Sterna sumatrana), does, from a distance, resemble a gull.

C

casuarina 61

a tall, pine-like tree which is actually not a pine at all, but a deciduous tree – of the genus Casuarina – native to Australia and Southeast Asia. It has tiny greyish-green scale leaves on slender jointed branches, which give it a feathery appearance.

charcoal 10

hunks of wood which are smoked till they become black and brittle, like coal. Used all over Asia for cooking.

charpoy 26

a bed formed by woven rope stretched across a wooden frame. Traditionally used by Sikhs and other Punjabis, it is still slept upon by night watchmen in Singapore and Malaysia

chempedak 164

a large, irregularly cylindrical fruit (belonging to the same genus - Artocarpus *- as the breadfruit and jack fruit), of which only the pulpy flesh surrounding each seed is eaten. Like the infamous durian, the chempedak has a very strong smell, rather sweet, and not at all unpleasing to most Singaporeans/Malaysians.*

chiku 164

a brown, smooth, egg-shaped soft-skinned fruit, (rather like a Kiwi fruit in size and appearance) with a honey sweet, soft, light brown flesh and a few flat black oval seeds.

chucok sanggul 164

a long hairpin, usually with an ornate design at its outer end, used to secure the sanggul *or chignon. Nowadays, used mainly by older Straits Born Chinese women*

Collyer Quay

Singapore's sea front, on which most of the larger companies have their offices

D

Dirty China Kwee 77

Used derogatorily by non-Chinese, it means "dirty Chinese devil".

E

Esplanade 3

Also known as "Queen Elizabeth's Walk" this is a promenade (beside the sea, very close to the city centre) popular with Singaporeans.

European 47

In Singapore/Malaysia (and probably in most of Asia) anyone of so-called Caucasian heritage is referred to as a "European".

F

Five-foot-way 26

In the early architecture of Singapore (in fact, mandated by Raffles himself) all buildings in the town area were fronted by a continuous, five-foot-wide covered walk way, recessed into the front of the ground floor so that it is sheltered by the second storey (of the shop or shop house).

Finlayson Green 320

Far from being a green, this is a short road between Raffles Quay and Collyer Quay in downtown Singapore.

firewood 256

thick chunks of wood (like the split logs of temperate countries) cut from a larger tree trunk, used in Southeast Asia not for heating but for cooking.

fish balls 145

see also "tung hoon".

These are small, translucent, bite-sized balls made of fresh fish flakes. When cooked they turn white, and are often used as an accompaniment to noodle dishes.

Glossary

Four-digit runner 125

hirelings of illegal big-time lottery (the "four-digit" lottery) operators, who collect bets from gamblers

G

gamelan 228

a type of orchestra found in Southeast Asia, (mainly in Indonesia) with string, woodwind, and a wide range of percussion instruments.

Gay World cabaret 292

see "Great World"

Great World 177

an amusement park (like a permanent fun fair) with Ferris wheels, dogem cars, ghost trains, as well as makeshift wooden dance floors on stilts, where patrons can choose girls with whom to dance the joget (a Malay dance in which partners do not touch), covered restaurants, and something known locally as a "cabaret", which is actually a dance hall where women dance for hire. Together with the New World and the Gay World, these parks were very popular entertainment spots (for the whole family) until about the 'Sixties.

gunny sack 281

a sack made of roughly-woven jute, about 4 ft long by 2 ft wide, used in Asia for carrying everything from cloth or charcoal, to onions.

H

"Happiness" ("Kong Hee " or "kiong hee ") 13

a frequently-used Chinese toast, especially on festive occasions like the New Year, birthdays, weddings, etc.

HDB 8

Initials of Singapore's Housing Development Board, which builds low-cost government-subsidized housing (mainly in blocks of apartments), in housing estates all over the island, for either rental or sale.

I

Identity card 233

a laminated credit-card sized card, giving particulars, such as the address, of a citizen (or permanent resident), to be carried by its owner at all times in Singapore and Malaysia.   This practice dates from the post-War Communist Emergency in what was then Malaya, of which Singapore was a part until 1965.

Istana 44

literally "palace" in Malay, in Singapore this is the President's residence.

J

jamban man 217
(see also "night soil carrier")

"jamban" means lavatory in Malay. Before modern sanitation was introduced throughout Singapore, most homes had outside squatting toilets, with an oval bucket for the human waste positioned under a hole, and a door-flap at the back through which the used bucket was removed daily in exchange for a clean one. The jamban man (or "toti man") walked from house to house each morning, carrying the buckets, one on each end of a pole slung across his shoulder. He always wore black shorts and a black shirt, and his social status was considered akin to that of the pariahs in India.

K

kai lan 140

a leafy green vegetable, very popular for its tasty and crisp stalks. A frequent accompaniment to Chinese meals in Southeast Asia.

kambing goreng 58

fried lamb (or goat). In Malay, kambing=goat; goreng fried.

Kandang Kerbau 273

The largest maternity hospital in Southeast Asia, achieving, at one time just after the War, the record for delivering the most babies per minute in the world. Kandang Kerbau, the area in which the hospital is built, was once a buffalo pen, hence the name (kandang = enclosure; kerbau = buffalo).

kati 15

the measure of weight used commonly throughout Malaysia, and, until fairly recently, Singapore as well. It is equivalent to about 600 grammes, i.e. a little more than a pound.

kelongs 60

wooden structures made from long rows of bakau *(mangrove tree) poles stuck deep into the sea bed, rising high above the water level at low tide. Nets for trapping fish are strung around the kelong poles.*

ketapang 210

The Singapore or sea almond (terminalia catappa)*, this tree is native to sandy coasts. It has a succession of tiers of horizontally-spreading branches, so forms a useful shade tree. The very large and green leaves turn a brick red autumnal colour before falling off.*

ketupat 10

small square packets of woven coconut fronds, in which rice is steamed till it forms an almost solid cake. The packets are sliced open and the steamed rice (ketupat) usually served as an accompaniment to satay *and various other Malay dishes.*

kaya 211

a jam made from eggs, sugar and coconut milk, usually coloured green with the juice of pandan leaves

L

laksa 62

thick white rice noodles cooked in a strongly spiced coconut-milk curry, with prawns, fish and other seafood as ingredients.

losman 229

a guest house

M

Majulah Singapura 47

The national anthem of Singapore, the words mean "Let Singapore advance."

makan 118

lit. "food" (Malay)

malacca cane 292

a rich brown cane from the stem of the palm tree Calamus scipionum, *used for walking sticks etc. (from* Malacca *in Malaysia)*

mee (prawn mee) 26

"mee" is a yellow-coloured wheat noodle. It is cooked in a variety of ways, of which prawn mee is one.

Glossary

mee hoon 117

Also called "bee hoon", these are thin white noodles made from rice flour.

merbok 211

a small dove, known as the Zebra Dove (Geopelia striata), this bird mustn't be confused with the merbah *or "bul bul". About 9 inches long, brown and faintly barred all over with black, the merbok does not coo like other doves but calls with a melodious chuckling warble.*

Milo 27

a chocolatey malt drink, tasting rather like a cross between Horlicks and Ovaltine. It is sold (in the form of granules, to which hot water is added to make the drink) in large green tins.

minum 118

lit. "drink" (Malay)

monsoon drain 19

deep, and often wide storm drains, which line most roads in Singapore and Malaysia. Designed to prevent flooding, they carry away surplus rain water, especially during the monsoons when rainfall is torrential.

Muezzin 65

The Muslim caller to prayers. He stands at the very top of a mosque's minaret, five times each day, to sing out the call to worship.

murtabaks 58

a South Indian Muslim dish, this is a wheat flour pancake stuffed with spicy minced lamb, onions, potatoes, chilies etc.

mutton briyani 58

(see also "briyani")
a briyani dish accompanied by curried lamb or mutton

N

Nanyang Siang Pau 211

One of two Chinese-medium newspapers in Singapore (the other being the Sin Chew Jit Poh *) which were published until 1982, when they merged. The merger resulted in a morning Chinese daily called the* Lianhe Zaobao *and an evening paper, the* Lianhe Wanbao.

night soil carrier 217

see "jamban man"

nonya kueh 164

"Nonya" is a term of address for women, especially Straits Born Chinese women, in Singapore and Malaysia. "Kueh" means cake, in Malay, and nonya kueh, *a specialty of the Peranakans, consists of a variety of tiny, delicious, and very colourful cakes made from rice flour, coconut milk, and other typically Malaysian ingredients, such as sago and gula malacca (a brown palm sugar).*

P

Padang 11

lit. field (Malay), in Singapore the Padang *is a large grassy oval, like the* Maidans *of British India, situated right in front of City Hall and the Supreme Court, facing the sea. Cricket and football matches are played on the Padang, which is also used regularly for celebrtion such as National Day.*

padi 65

Rice (plant) in Malay. Cooked rice is referred to as "nasi".

parang 250

lit. a short sword or knife (Malay); a machete.

pencuri 77

lit. thief (Malay). Pronounced "pernchoori".

peons 145

an office boy, messenger, etc., this term, although of Spanish origin, dates from British India where it referred to the Indian office messengers.

Peranakan (Straits Chinese) 44

Also referred to as "Baba Chinese", the Peranakan Chinese are Chinese who came to live in Malaya (as it was known then) several centuries ago. They differ from other Chinese, who came mainly after the British, in speaking a Malay patois and (until fairly recently), in their clothing, hairstyle and customs, which resemble that of the Malays — although they did not convert to Islam.

prahu 228

pronounced "perahoo" and usually spelt "perahu", this Malay word means boat, and sometimes, ship.

pre-War 66

This term is used extensively to refer to the period just prior to the Second World War, and specifically to the period before the Japanese Occupation of Singapore and Malaya.

Puteh 248

lit. white (Malay), the yellow and white cockerel was called "Puteh" for its colouring.

R

rain tree 46

a tall, large and spreading tree of the mimosa family, the rain tree is planted all over India, Sri Lanka and Southeast Asia, often alongside roads or surrounding padangs, for its beauty and shade. It has small, inconspicuous pink and white flowers which look like powder puffs. Sometimes called the "four o'clock tree" because its leaves, like those of its tiny relative, mimosa pudica, close when the dew (or rain) falls on them.

rambutans 164

found mainly in Southeast Asia, this is a small egg-shaped fruit, red or yellow, with a hairy skin. The flesh surrounding the hard seed is a crisp, translucent white, and usually very sweet and tasty. It resembles a lychee.

rattan 62

(see also "rottan")

a climbing palm of the genus Calamus, growing mainly in Southeast Asia, with long, thin, jointed stems. The thicker rattans are used extensively for making furniture.

rediffusion 281

this is a continuous radio broadcast (in the various languages of Singapore) of pre-recorded programmes, relayed from a central receiver. A redifussion set, consisting of a small square wooden box fixed high up on the wall, was (it isn't so popular now) a regular feature in most shops and restaurants, and often in homes as well, where it would usually be left tuned on all day.

rojak 62

lit. salad (Malay), there are two varieties of rojak, the Indian and the Chinese. Kian Teck was probably referring to the Indian rojak, which is a salad of fresh crisp vegetables, diced fried bean curd and sliced boiled eggs, the whole bathed in a peanut-and-chili gravy.

Glossary

rottan 220

*not to be confused with **rattan** (although the word's derivation is the same), the rottan is a cane or knotted rope used for flogging convicted criminals.*

rupiahs 246

The main monetary unit of Indonesia.

S

samfoo 27

one of the traditional forms of Chinese female attire, the samfoo consists of a fitted blouse worn over loose pyjamas, secured at the waist with a drawer string.

sampans 33

a small (usually wooden) boat, originally Chinese (from the Chinese san-ban), with oars, used mainly in the Far East.

Sanggul (or songgol) 164

The chignon, a sanggul is the top notch of Malay/Indonesian and Peranakan women, worn in a variety of designs and secured with hair pins, i.e. the chuchok sanggul.

sarong kebaya 164

Clothing worn by Malay, Indonesian and Peranakan women, the sarong kebaya is a fitted, usually transparent and highly embroidered long blouse (kebaya) worn over a tightly-wrapped batik sarong.

satay 9

grilled kebabs of highly spiced meat, skewered on short, sharpened lengths of the woody spine of coconut fronds. Usually dipped into a spicy peanut gravy and eaten with ketupats and cucumber salads.

Selamat pagi 241

lit. "Good morning" in Malay/Indonesian

serein 118

a fine rain falling in tropical climates from a cloudless sky.

Shanghai tailoring 125

The tailors of old Shanghai were noted (in much the same way as the Saville Row tailors) for their fine sewing; in Southeast Asia "Shanghai tailoring" is synonymous with sartorial excellence.

shellac 111

a lac resin (secreted by the lac insect, Laccifer lacca), melted into thin flakes and used for making varnish for wood. Most wooden furniture in Asia is shellacked.

shop house 66

a house in a terraced row of two- or three-storeyed buildings, with shops on the ground floor and (usually) living quarters above.

sinseh 30

a traditional Chinese doctor, usually specialising in herbal medicine, but also in traditional massage, acupuncture etc.

Straits Chinese (Peranakan) 44

see Peranakan

sup kambing 10

Mutton soup, a South Indian Muslim delicacy, this is a spicy and substantial dish of soup filled with tender chunks of meat. (sup is soup in Malay, while kambing refers to goat or lamb meat)

s/o 220

Indian (esp. Hindu) males have a given name followed by s/o (which means "son of"), then their father's given name. There is no surname as such, so Sundram's (putative) son might be called Jeyasingham s/o Sundram.

T

tembusu 121

A tall, poplar-shaped tree, with small leaves and masses of tiny scented flowers which open at night - once every year - perfuming the air around them. The tembusu has almond-like fruit, very popular with bats

tiffin carriers 49

these are a set of four or five round metal containers which slot into one another, with handles on the side through which a long U-shaped handle slots, holding all together. Traditionally used in India to carry one's "tiffin" or lunch, so that different dishes can be kept separate, the tiffin-carrier is used all over Asia and Southeast Asia. The Chinese version is enamelled.

tikum-tikum 247

a game of chance, popular with children, this consists of a dart board sized numbered disk which is spun around by the tikum vendor. The number it stops at wins the young gambler (who pays a price for his number) a small toy, sweets, or some such inexpensive prize.

touch-me-nots 76

A tiny, creeping plant of the Mimosa *family, with small purply-pink powder-puff-like flowers and green leaves borne in pairs, each with many leaflets. When touched, the leaves close shut like closing doors, hence its botanical name (*Mimosa pudica*).*

Traveller's palm 46

*A tall attractive plant with long green leaves, rather like banana leaves, growing upwards in a fan-like shape from the ground. The stalks curve inwards slightly at the base, so water collects in them when it rains. Called the Traveller's palm because, theoretically, one could drink this water if lost in the jungle. Grown extensively in public parks and gardens in Singapore, this is not a palm but actually belongs to the banana family (*Ravenala*).*

tuck shop 291

a word which probably owes its origin to British colonialism, the tuck shop in Singapore and Malaysia is a canteen attached to a school, where children can buy meals, drinks and snacks at subsidized prices.

tung hoon 145

Also known as "glass noodles" because they are transparent when cooked, tung hoon *is a noodle made from bean flour. It is usually served in a soup, with fish balls.*

U

UOB 169

The United Overseas Bank, one of the larger Chinese banking houses in Singapore.

W

"white eyes" 211

a very small bird, greenish-yellow above and pale grey below, with a ring of white feathers around each eye. The Oriental white-eye ("mata puteh" , lit. white eye in Malay) a favourite song bird, is the only white eye commonly found in Malaysia and Singapore.

Other titles published by Select Books

The Asian house: contemporary houses of Southeast Asia
by Robert Powell. Reprint 1995.

Cities for people: reflections of a Southeast Asian Architect
by William Lim 1990.

Chinese organisations in Southeast Asia: in the 1930's
edited by George Hicks. 1995.

From time to time *(poems)*
by Lin Hsin Hsin. 1991

Focus on environment; implications for S'pore
by Desmond P. Pereira. 1979

The Girl from the coast (a novel)
by Pramoedya Ananta Toer. 1991.

Innovative architecture of Singapore
by Robert Powell. 1989.

Land for housing the poor
edited by Solly Angel. 1983.

Offerings: the ritual art of Bali
by Francine Brinkgreve. 1992

Overseas Chinese remittances in Southeast Asia: 1910-1940
edited by George Hicks. 1993.

A Part of three
by Robert Yeo. 1988

Questioning development in Southeast Asia
edited by Nancy Chng. 1977.

Sunny side up (poems)
by Lin Hsin Hsin. 1994.

Take a word for a walk (poems)
by Lin Hsin Hsin. 1989

Tiger! (a novel)
by Mochtar Lubis. 1991.

Tropical Asian house
by Robert Powell. 1996.

With sweat & abacus: economic roles of Southeast Asian
Chinese on the eve of World War II
edited by George Hicks. 1995.